The Wicked Deeds of
Daniel Mackenzie

The Wicked Deeds of
Daniel Mackenzie

JENNIFER ASHLEY

BERKLEY SENSATION, NEW YORK

THE BERKLEY PUBLISHING GROUP
Published by the Penguin Group
Penguin Group (USA) LLC
375 Hudson Street, New York, New York 10014

USA • Canada • UK • Ireland • Australia • New Zealand • India • South Africa • China

A Penguin Random House Company

THE WICKED DEEDS OF DANIEL MACKENZIE

A Berkley Book / published by arrangement with the author

Berkley Sensation Books are published by The Berkley Publishing Group.
BERKLEY SENSATION® is a registered trademark of Penguin Group (USA) LLC.
The "B" design is a trademark of Penguin Group (USA) LLC.

For information, address: The Berkley Publishing Group,
a division of Penguin Group (USA) LLC,
375 Hudson Street, New York, New York 10014.

ISBN: 978-1-62490-897-2

PRINTED IN THE UNITED STATES OF AMERICA

Cover art by Greg Gulbronson. Hand lettering by Ron Zinn.
Cover design by George Long.
Interior text design by Laura K. Corless.

The Wicked Deeds of Daniel Mackenzie

Chapter 1

He doesn't have the ace.

Daniel Mackenzie held four eights, and he'd backed that fact with large stacks of money.

He faced Mortimer, who was ten years older and had a face like a weasel. Mortimer was pretending he'd just been given an ace from the young woman who dealt the cards at the head of the table, completing his straight. Daniel knew better.

The other gentlemen in the St. James's gaming hell called the Nines had already folded in Fenton Mortimer's favorite game of poker. The entire club now lingered to see the battle of wits between twenty-five-year-old Daniel Mackenzie and Mortimer, a hardened gambler. So much cigar smoke hung in the air that any consumptive who'd dared walk in the door would have fallen dead on the spot.

The game of choice at this hell was whist, but Mortimer had recently introduced the American game of poker, which he'd learned during a yearlong stint in that country. Mortimer was good at it, quickly relieving young Mayfair aristos of thousands of pounds. And still they came to him, eager to learn the game. Eleven gentlemen had started this round, dropping out one by one until only Daniel and Mortimer remained.

Daniel kept his cards facedown on the table so the nosy club fodder wouldn't telegraph his hand to Mortimer. He gathered up more of his paper bills and dropped them in front of his cards. "See you, and raise two hundred."

Mortimer turned a slight shade of green but slid money opposite Daniel's.

"Raise you again," Daniel said. He picked up another pile of notes and laid them on the already substantial stack. "Can you cover?"

"I can." Mortimer didn't dig out any more notes or coin, obviously hoping he wouldn't have to.

"Sure about that?"

Mortimer's eyes narrowed. "What are you saying, Mackenzie? If you'd like to question my honor in a private room, I will be happy to answer."

Daniel refrained from rolling his eyes. "Calm yourself, lad." He lifted a cigar from the holder beside him and sucked smoke into his mouth. "I believe you. What have you got?"

"Show yours first."

Daniel picked up his cards and flipped them over with a nonchalant flick. Four eights, one ace.

The men around him let out a collective groan, the lady dealer smiled at Daniel, and Mortimer went chalk white.

"Bloody hell. I didn't think you had it." Mortimer's own cards fell faceup—a ten, jack, queen, seven, and three.

Daniel raked in his money and winked at the dealer. She really was lovely. "You can write me a vowel for the rest," he said to Mortimer.

Mortimer wet his lips. "Now, Mackenzie . . ."

He couldn't cover. What idiot wagered the last of his cash when he didn't have a winning hand? Mortimer should have taken his loss several rounds ago and walked away.

But no, Mortimer had convinced himself he was expert at the bluffing part of the game, and would fleece the naive young Scotsman who'd walked in here tonight in a kilt.

A hard-faced man standing near the door sent Mortimer a grim look. Daniel guessed that said ruffian had given Mortimer cash for this night's play, or was working for someone who had. The man wasn't pleased Mortimer had just lost it all.

Daniel rose from the table. "Never mind," he said. "Keep what you owe me as a token of appreciation for a night of good play."

Mortimer scowled. "I pay my debts, Mackenzie."

Daniel glanced at the bone-breaker across the room and lowered his voice. "You'll pay more than that if ye don't beat a hasty retreat, I'm thinking. How much do ye owe him?"

Mortimer's eyes went cold. "None of your business."

"I don't wish to see a man have his face removed because I was lucky at cards. What do ye owe him? I'll give ye that back. Ye can owe me."

"Be beholden to a *Mackenzie*?" Mortimer's outrage rang from him.

Well, Daniel had tried. He stuffed his winnings into his pockets and took his greatcoat from the lady dealer. She helped him into it, running her hand suggestively across Daniel's shoulders as she straightened his collar.

Daniel winked at her again. He folded one of the banknotes he'd just won into a thin sliver, and slipped it down the top of her bodice.

"Aye, well." Daniel took his hat from the slender-fingered lady, who gave him an even warmer smile. "Hope you can find tuppence for the ferryman at your funeral, Mortimer. Good night."

He turned to leave and found Mortimer's friends surrounding him.

"Changed my mind," Mortimer said, smiling thinly. "The chaps reminded me I had something worth bargaining with. Say, for the last two thousand."

"Oh aye? What is it? A motorcar?" The only thing worth the trouble these days, in Daniel's opinion.

"Better," Mortimer said. "A lady."

Daniel hid a sigh. "I don't need a courtesan. I can find women on me own."

Easily. Daniel looked at ladies, and they came to him. Part

of his charm, he knew, was his wealth; part was the fact that he belonged to the great Mackenzie family and was nephew to a duke. But Daniel never argued about the ladies' motives; he simply enjoyed.

"She's not a courtesan," Mortimer said. "She's special. You'll see."

An actress, perhaps. She'd give an indifferent performance of a Shakespearean soliloquy, and Daniel would be expected to smile and pronounce her worth every penny.

"Keep your money," Daniel said. "Give me a horse or your best servant in lieu—I'm not particular."

Mortimer's friends didn't move. "But I insist," Mortimer said.

Eleven against one. If Daniel argued, he'd only end up with bruised knuckles. He didn't particularly want to hurt his hands, because he had the fine-tuning of his engine to do, and he needed to be able to hold a spanner.

"Fair enough," Daniel said. "But I assess the goods before I accept it as payment of debt."

Mortimer agreed. He clapped Daniel on the shoulder as he led him out, and Daniel stopped himself shaking off his touch.

Mortimer's friends filed around them in a defensive flank as they made their way to Mortimer's waiting landau. Daniel noted as they pulled away from the Nines that the bone-breaker had slipped out the door behind them and followed.

Mortimer took Daniel through the misty city to a respectable neighborhood north of Oxford Street, stopping on a quiet lane near Portman Square.

The hour was two in the morning, and this street was silent, the houses dark. Behind the windows lay respectable gentlemen who would rise in the early hours and trundle to the City for work.

Daniel descended from the landau and looked up at the dark windows. "She'll be asleep, surely. Leave it for tomorrow."

"Nonsense," Mortimer said. "She sees me anytime I call."

He walked to a black-painted front door and rapped on it with his stick. Above them a light appeared, and a curtain drew back. Mortimer looked up at the window, made an impatient gesture, and rapped on the door again.

The curtain dropped, and the light faded. *Tap, tap, tap,*

went Mortimer's stick. Daniel folded his arms, stopping himself from ripping the stick from Mortimer's hands and breaking it over his knee. "Who lives here?"

"I do," Mortimer said. "I mean, I own the house. At least, my family does. We let it to Madame Bastien and her daughter. For a slight savings in rent, they agreed to entertain me and my friends anytime I asked it."

"Including the middle of the bloody night?"

"Especially the middle of the night."

Mortimer smiled—self-satisfied English prig. The ladies inside had to be courtesans. Mortimer had reduced the rent and obligated them to pay in kind.

Daniel turned back to the landau. "This isn't worth two thousand, Mortimer."

"Patience. You'll see."

The rest of Mortimer's friends had arrived and hemmed them in, blocking the way back to the landau. The bonebreaker was still in attendance, hovering in the shadows a little way down the street.

The door opened. A maid who'd obviously dressed hastily stepped aside and let the stream of gentlemen inside. The drunker lads of the party wanted to pause to see what entertainment she might provide, but Daniel planted himself solidly beside the door, blocking their way to her. They moved past, forgetting about her.

Mortimer led the way to double pocket doors at the end of the hall and pushed them open. Daniel caught a flurry of movement from the room beyond, but by the time Mortimer beckoned Daniel, stillness had taken over.

They entered a dining room. The walls were covered with a blue, gold, and burnt orange striped wallpaper, its many colors bright in the light of a hearth fire. A gas chandelier hung dark above, and a solitary candelabra with three candles rested on the long, empty table. A young woman was just touching a match to the candlewicks.

When the third candle was lit, she blew out the match and straightened up. "So sorry to have kept you waiting, gentlemen," she said in a voice very faintly accented. "I'm afraid my mother is unable to rise. You will have to make do with me."

Whatever Mortimer and the other gentlemen said in response, Daniel didn't hear. He couldn't hear anything. He couldn't see anything either, except the woman who stood poised behind the candelabra, the long match still in her hand, the smile of an angel on her face.

She wasn't beautiful. Daniel had seen faces more beautiful in the Casino in Monte Carlo, at the Moulin Rouge in Paris. He'd known slimmer bodies in dancers, or in the butterflies that glided about the gaming hells in St. James's and Monaco, enticing gentlemen to play.

This young woman had an angular face softened by a mass of dark hair dressed in a pompadour, ringlets trickling down the sides of her face. Her nose was a little too long, her mouth too wide, her shoulders and arms too plump. Her eyes were her best feature, set in exact proportion in her face, dark blue in the glint of candlelight.

They were eyes a man could gaze into all night and wake up to in the morning. He could contemplate her eyes across the breakfast table and then at dinner while he made plans to look into them again all through the night.

She wasn't a courtesan. Courtesans began charming the moment a gentleman walked into a room. They gestured with graceful fingers, implying that those fingers would be equally graceful traveling a man's body. Courtesans drew in, they suggested without words, they used every movement and every expression to beguile.

This woman stood fixed in place, her body language not inviting the gentlemen into the room at all, despite her words and her smile. If her movements were graceful as she turned to toss the match into the fire, it was from nature, not practice.

She wore a plain gown of blue satin that bared her shoulders, but the gown was no less respectable than what a lady in this neighborhood might wear for dinner or a night at the theatre. Her hair in the simple pompadour had no ribbons or jewels to adorn it. The unaffected style hinted that the dark masses might come down at any time over the hands of the lucky gentleman who pulled out the hairpins.

The young woman spread her hands at the now silent men. "If you'll sit, gentlemen, we can begin."

Daniel couldn't move. His feet had grown into the floor, disobedient to his will. They wanted him to stand in that place all night long and gaze upon this woman.

Mortimer leaned to Daniel. "You see? Did I not tell you she'd be worth it?" He cleared his throat. "Daniel Mackenzie, may I introduce Mademoiselle Bastien. Violette is her Christian name, in the French way. Mademoiselle, this is Daniel Mackenzie, son of Lord Cameron Mackenzie and nephew to the Duke of Kilmorgan. You'll give him a fine show, won't you? There's a good girl."

As the man called Daniel Mackenzie came around the table and boldly stepped next to Violet, her breath stopped. Mr. Mackenzie did nothing but look at her and hold out his hand in greeting. And yet, every inch of Violet's flesh tingled at his nearness, every breath threatened to choke her.

Scottish, Violet thought rapidly, taking in his blue and green plaid kilt under the fashionable black suit coat and ivory waistcoat. *Rich*, noting the costly materials and the way in which the coat hugged his broad shoulders. Tailor-made, and not by a cheap or apprentice tailor. A master had designed and sewn those clothes. Mr. Mackenzie was used to the very best.

He topped most of the other gentlemen here by at least a foot, had a hard face, a nose that would be large on any other man, and eyes that made her stop. Violet couldn't decide the color of them in this light—hazel? brown?—but they were arresting. So arresting that she stood staring at him, not taking the hand he held out to her.

"Daniel Mackenzie, at your service, Mademoiselle."

He gave her a light, charming smile, his eyes pulling her in, keeping her where he wanted her.

Definitely danger here.

Old terror stirred, but Violet pushed it down. She couldn't afford to go to pieces right now. She'd come down here to placate Mortimer, letting her mother, who'd nearly had hysterics when Mortimer had started pounding on the door, stay safely upstairs. Violet, who could handle a crowd of several hundred angry men and women shouting for blood, could certainly cope with less than a dozen half-drunk Mayfair gentlemen in the middle of the night.

Mr. Mackenzie was only another of Mortimer's vapid friends. Violet saw the barrier behind Mr. Mackenzie's eyes, though, when she risked a look into them. This man gave up his secrets to very few. He would be difficult to read, which could be a problem.

Mr. Mackenzie waited, his hand out. Violet finally slid hers into his gloved one, making the movement slow and deliberate.

"How do you do," she said formally, her English perfect. She'd discovered long ago that speaking flawless English reinforced the fiction that she was entirely French.

Daniel closed his large hand around hers and raised it to his lips. "Enchanted."

The quick, hot brush of his mouth to the backs of her fingers ignited a spark to rival that on the match she'd tossed away. Violet's nerves tightened like wires, forcing the deep breath she'd been trying not to take.

The little gasp sounded loud to her, but Mortimer's cronies were making plenty of noise as they shed coats and debated where each would sit.

Daniel's gaze fixed on Violet over her hand, challenging, daring. *Show me who you are*, that gaze said.

Violet was supposed to be thinking that about *him*. Whatever the world believed about the talents of Violette Bastien, medium and spiritualist, she knew her true gift was reading people.

Within a few moments of studying a man, Violet could understand what he loved and what he hated, what he wanted with all his heart and what he'd do to get it. She'd learned these lessons painstakingly from Jacobi in the backstreets of Paris, had been his best pupil.

But she couldn't read Mr. Mackenzie. He didn't let anyone behind his barriers, not easily. But when he did . . .

When he did, worlds would unfold.

Violet snatched her hand from him and turned to the others. "Please, gentlemen," she said, striving to maintain the calm note in her voice.

She moved to sit down and found Daniel Mackenzie's hand

on the back of her chair. Violet forced her gaze from him and
seated herself, trying to ignore the warmth of his body at her
side, the fold of open coat that brushed her shoulder. The
breath went out of her again as Daniel eased her chair forward, his strength unnerving.

Shaking, Violet laid her hands flat on the table, trying to
use its cool surface to calm herself. She needed to appear
utterly composed, sugar-sweet, and ready to help.

Inside, she was in turmoil. *I hate this, I hate this. Why the
devil can't they leave us alone?*

She gave the others an appealing look. "Will you gentlemen give me a moment to prepare myself?"

The gentlemen agreed without argument. Many had been
to the house before, most often as Mortimer's guests, but
some had returned alone for private consultations with Violet
and her mother.

Mr. Mackenzie sat down beside Violet and looked her in
the eye. "Prepare yourself for what?"

One of Mortimer's friends, Mr. Ellingham, answered, "To
contact the other side, of course."

Daniel kept his gaze on Violet. "The other side o' what?
The room?"

"The ether," Ellingham said impatiently. "She's a spiritualist, man. Didn't you know? Madame and Mademoiselle Bastien are the most famous spiritualists in London."

Chapter 2

The flash of disappointment in Daniel's eyes stung Violet. Stung her hard. Why she should care what this man she'd never seen before tonight thought of her, she didn't know, but she did.

Plenty of people didn't believe in spiritualism and scoffed at what Violet and her mother did. They didn't believe a trained medium could contact those beyond the veil, to let the dear departed send comforting messages to the survivors.

Just as well, Violet's inner voice drawled. *You don't believe it either.*

Violet knew she'd never felt the cold touch of the otherworld or the trembling ecstasy her mother found in her trances. She'd never seen a ghost or a spirit, and had never had one talk to her, or knock at her, or do any of those other useful things spirits could do.

But she'd become very, very good at pretending she did.

That Mr. Mackenzie didn't believe shouldn't bother her. Jacobi had told her never to argue with an unbeliever, but to ignore him and move on to the next mark.

Violet should close to Mr. Mackenzie and concentrate on

the other gentlemen, to make him feel that he was left out somehow, to make him doubt his own disbelief.

So why didn't Violet turn away with her superior little smile, her amused disdain? Why did she keep wanting to look at him, to explain that she did this for survival, and beg him not to dislike her for it?

Daniel leaned his elbow on the table, stretching the fine cloth of his coat. "The other side, eh? I'd like to see that."

Mortimer said, "You're in for a show then. That's why I said she's worth more than a motorcar or a horse."

A motorcar or a horse? Violet's anger surged. She wished she did have the powers she claimed to, so she could curse Mortimer into living out his life as a rabbit, or at least being a disappointment to any ladies he took to bed. *A horse. God help us.*

The gentlemen finally ceased speaking, quieting to watch her prepare. Violet's preparation was part of the show—when she closed her eyes and drew long breaths to calm herself, her breasts pressed hard into her tight décolletage. Distracted the clients wonderfully.

When she opened her eyes again, however, she found Mr. Mackenzie not distracted in the slightest. Instead of letting his gaze drop to her rising bosom, as the other gentlemen had, Mr. Mackenzie smiled straight into her face.

Never let skeptics make you nervous, Jacobi had said. *Give them a show in spite of their disbelief. Make them doubt their own doubts.*

Violet glanced around the table, trying to ignore Daniel. "All is calm tonight, the veil so thin. Mr. Ellingham, I believe we were very near reaching your father the last time. Shall we try again?"

Before the eager Mr. Ellingham—who was attempting to find out where his now-deceased father had hidden away about ten thousand pounds—could answer, Mortimer broke in.

"Contact someone for Mackenzie. He's my guest tonight. His dear old mum, perhaps." Mortimer's eyes glinted with dislike.

Violet didn't miss Daniel's flash of anger. The flicker was brief and instantly gone, but Violet had seen it. Whatever had happened to Mr. Mackenzie's mother, his anger about it ran deep; the hurt that accompanied it, massive.

"Perhaps that would not be for the best," Violet said quickly.

Mr. Mackenzie's mask dropped into place. "Aye, let me mum rest in peace. Tell you what, why don't you contact me dad, instead?" He sent her a guileless look.

Too transparent. Violet gave him a sweet smile. "If you wish me to contact your father, Mr. Mackenzie, I suggest a telegram, because that gentleman is very much still living."

Mr. Mackenzie stared at her for a heartbeat then burst out laughing. His laugh was deep and true, a man who knew how to laugh for the joy of it. "You were right, Mortimer. She truly has the second sight."

"I don't need second sight to read the newspapers," Violet said. "First sight will do. Your father appears in many pages of the sporting news. Now, if he'd like me to tell him which of his racehorses will do best this year, his lordship is welcome to join us."

Daniel wound down to a chuckle. "I'm starting to like you, Mademoiselle."

Violet let her eyes go wide. "I am pleased to hear it, Mr. Mackenzie. However, if you have come tonight to mock me and my work, I will have to ask you to depart. Or at least wait in the hall."

"Why?" His eyes held an impish twinkle. "Does my mockery disturb th' spirits?"

"Of course not. Those on the other side can be quite forgiving. But *I* find it a bit distracting."

Mr. Mackenzie raised his hands in surrender. "Forgive me, lass. I'll be the model of goodness from now on. Promise."

Violet knew better than to believe him, but she returned her attention to the others. "Shall we see what spirits are close tonight?"

The other men readily agreed. They liked the show.

"Then, as you know, I must ask for silence."

Violet closed her eyes again, and thankfully, the gentlemen quieted down, their guffaws finally dying off.

Violet let her breathing become slow and deep. She rocked

her head forward then let it go all the way back, turning her face to the ceiling. She kept her eyes closed as her breathing grew more rapid, faster, faster.

Soft noises escaped her mouth. Violet moved her head from side to side, making sure she didn't overdo it. Too much gyration looked fake. A little bit was far more frightening, a person in the grip of forces she didn't understand. Violet also knew that a young woman moaning, perspiring, and letting her bosom move with her panting froze gentlemen into place.

A large, warm hand landed on hers, and Mr. Mackenzie said in a quiet voice, "You all right, lass?"

The concern in his words sent a shock through Violet, and her eyes popped open. For a moment, her rapid breaths choked her, and she struggled for air.

No one had ever spoken to her thus—not her mother, not Jacobi. Daniel Mackenzie, a stranger of warmth by her side, touched her in worry and asked after her with a protectiveness never before directed at her.

It nearly broke her. A moment ago, Violet had prided herself on being able to handle a roomful of unruly gentlemen. Now she felt her façade crumbling to reveal the lonely and weary young woman she was—nearly thirty years old, taking care of an ill mother, living by her wits and her skill in hiding her lies.

Violet found it easy to keep a barrier between Mortimer and his ilk, but she recognized that Mr. Mackenzie could rip down any wall she erected with one touch.

She tried to catch her breath, tried to keep her persona in place, but for a moment, she was only a frightened young woman angry at a man for exposing her.

Mr. Ellingham, oblivious, broke the tension. "Damn it, Mackenzie. We'll never get a contact if you interfere with the medium's trance. Everyone knows that."

Daniel kept his gaze on Violet. "You sure you're all right, love?"

Violet moved her hands to the table again, pressing down to stop their trembling. "Yes, I'm fine. Thank you."

"You're an ass, Mackenzie," Mortimer said, his voice tinged with fury. "Now we'll have to start all over again."

"No, we won't," Daniel said, still looking at Violet. "We'll go and leave Mademoiselle Bastien to her sleep."

"The hell we will," Mortimer said, standing up. "We're not leaving this house. Not until we have satisfaction."

Daniel shot Mortimer a look of disgust. He knew damn well why Mortimer didn't want to leave—the ruffian waited outside for him. Mortimer wouldn't make it back home tonight without trouble.

Mortimer met Daniel's gaze with rage and fear mixing in his dark eyes. Why the idiot wouldn't take Daniel's offer of paying off the bone-breaker, Daniel didn't know. Daniel had been sympathetic at first, but watching how Mortimer treated Mademoiselle Violette had wiped away any sympathy. Mortimer would be the loser tonight.

Mortimer went on. "If Mackenzie is too prissy to watch Mademoiselle Violette go into her trance, then let us bring out the talking board."

The other gentlemen eagerly agreed. Before Daniel could voice an objection, Ellingham had sprung from his chair with the energy of his twenty-two years. He seemed to know his way around Mademoiselle Bastien's dining room, because he made for the sideboard, opened one of its lower drawers, and brought out a wooden board and planchette, which he set in the middle of the table.

The wooden board was rectangular, burned with the letters of the English alphabet—*A* through *R* on the first row, *S* through *Z* on the second. Below the letters were the numbers 1 through 9 with a 0 at the end. In the top-left corner was the word *Yes*, in the right, *No*. On the bottom in the middle were the words *Thank You* and *Good-Bye*. A very polite piece of oak.

Daniel hadn't seen a talking board before, but he'd heard about them. The idea was for the medium and her guests to put their fingers on the planchette—a more or less oval piece of polished wood—and ask a question of the spirit. The planchette would then obligingly drag itself to the letters to spell out an answer—which supposed that the spirit was fluent in the language of the questioner and a reasonably good speller.

Daniel had his own idea about how the planchette moved— the questioners moved it themselves, he believed, even if they didn't realize they were doing it. Thoughts fixed in the head stimulated muscles in the arms and fingers, making the person pull the planchette to spell out what they wanted the spirit to say. Amazing what the human brain could convince the body to do.

As soon as Ellingham resumed his seat, eager hands shot to the planchette. Mademoiselle Bastien waited for Daniel to place his fingers on it, before she put hers next to his.

The warmth of her hand touched Daniel through his glove. He liked her fingers, not too delicate, but long and strong. He had a swift image of those fingers unbuttoning his shirt, peeling it from his body, running across his exposed skin . . .

Daniel shifted in his seat, hot and suddenly hard.

"Are you ready, Mr. Mackenzie?" Mademoiselle Bastien asked him. God help him, Daniel hoped he wasn't blushing. "This can be quite daunting for the novice," she went on. Her dark blue eyes held a light that said she was ready for his challenge.

And I'm damned good and ready for hers. "Carry on, lass."

Mademoiselle Violette took another of those bodice-lifting breaths that left him dizzy and said, "Very well. Spirit, do you have a message for anyone here?"

Candlelight brushed the polished wood of the board, the gloved hands of the gentlemen present, and Mademoiselle Violette's bare fingers, so feminine and beautiful amidst the sea of masculinity.

The planchette was only so large, so several of the men, including Mortimer, got left out. Mortimer didn't seem to mind. He sat back and watched, his dark gaze planted on Violette's body, his ratlike face not hiding his lecherous thoughts.

Beneath Daniel's fingers, the planchette wobbled then started to move. Ellingham drew an excited breath.

The planchette stopped, rocked again, and moved in the opposite direction. After a few seconds it changed once more. *Every hand trying to drag it where the gentleman wants it to go.*

Daniel relaxed his fingers, waiting to see what Mademoiselle Violette would do.

She called softly into the darkness, "Spirit, do you have a message for us?"

Any spirit hearing Mademoiselle Violette plead to it in that sensual, contralto voice should spring forward and agree to do whatever she wanted. Daniel moved in his seat, trying to still his rising fantasies. He was as bad as Mortimer.

The planchette trembled, then made a rapid but smooth move to the word *Yes*.

A collective sigh went through the men present. Difficult to believe that a few hours ago, they were hardened gamblers trying to win packets of money at poker.

"To whom is the message directed?" Mademoiselle Violette asked the air.

The planchette fanned back and forth among the letters, seeking. Finally it stopped at the letter *M*.

"Mortimer?" one of the gentlemen asked.

The planchette nearly ripped itself across the board to the word *No*. It then backed away to a neutral area, as though apologizing for its rudeness.

"Will you show us more letters?" Mademoiselle asked.

The rest of the gentlemen leaned forward. Daniel had no doubt that those with *M*'s in their names—including him—silently begged, *Please, please, let it be me.*

The planchette traveled slowly across the letters again and stopped at *C*. It moved on to *K*, then to *E*, *N*, and *Z*.

"Mackenzie!" Ellingham shouted. He jerked his hand from the planchette, and it stopped.

Of course the thing had spelled out *Mackenzie*. Or at least *McKenz*. Daniel shot a glance at Mademoiselle Violette, who studied the board with a serene look.

Little vixen. His estimation of her rose again. She knew bloody well that Daniel knew she was a charlatan, and she was going to play on him every trick she could.

So she thinks.

Violette asked the air in her smooth voice, "Do you have a message for Mr. Mackenzie?"

The planchette said *Yes*.

Mademoiselle Violette was very good, but Daniel was good too. "What message?" he asked.

Ellingham joined them on the planchette again, and it started to move. Around and around it went on the board, back and forth, sliding toward a letter only to slide away before it could stop. Daniel felt Violette's subtle but steady pull, and he subtly but steadily pulled back.

Mademoiselle kept her countenance absolutely still. If the spirit's indecision vexed her, she made no sign.

The planchette at last halted at the letter *F*. Ellingham said excitedly, "Someone should write this down."

A gentleman obligingly drew a small notebook and pencil from his coat pocket and wrote *F*.

The planchette moved again. It stopped at *U*, paused for a time, then slid innocently to the letter *C*. After another pause, it began a rapid journey toward the letter *K*.

Mademoiselle jerked her hand back, and the planchette stopped dead. The room filled with snickers and chortles.

"Well," Violette said, turning to fully face Daniel. "The spirit seems in a mischievous mood tonight."

Her eyes sparkled like candle flames on a frosty night. They looked at each other, neither offering to glance away first. Mademoiselle's cheeks took on a faint flush, but other than that she sat as still as marble.

Damn, but she was beautiful, and defiant too. No simpering miss in her first Season, hoping to snare the wealthy Mr. Mackenzie, one of the most eligible bachelors in Britain. Why the hell young women were taught that pretending to be frail should make men fall madly in love with them, Daniel didn't understand. The frail act made Daniel want to suggest the lady eat robust food and take plenty of exercise until she felt better.

This young woman could walk five miles in a storm, brush off her skirts, and comment offhand that the wind was a bit brisk today. Then in the next breath she'd tell someone like Daniel and all his money to go to the devil.

Mademoiselle Violette's lips parted. The moisture between them beckoned. Daniel wanted to send Mortimer and his irritating cronies out into the cold and have Mademoiselle to himself, to ask her to perform for him alone. No layabouts of the English ton watching, no Mortimer. Just Daniel and this lovely lady, a candlelit room, and time.

"Enough of these parlor games," Mortimer broke in angrily. "I told you, Mademoiselle, Mackenzie came here to see the whole show. So give it to him."

Daniel had to turn away from Violette's beautiful eyes, and for that, Mortimer would pay. "Shut your gob," Daniel said. "She's done enough for tonight, and you still owe me two thousand quid."

Mortimer was halfway out of his chair. "I'm paying for a show, and by God, I want one."

Daniel started up himself, ready to go over the table to him, but Mademoiselle raised her hands, her voice cutting through the impending tempest.

"The spirits are here! *Now!*"

A freezing wind swept through the dining room, extinguishing the candles in one go. The room plunged into darkness. In the middle of the table, where the candles had burned, a pale, luminescent blob began to form and spread.

Before Daniel could sit down, a heavy grip seized him by the arms, and someone very strong dragged him up and out through a door and into a pitch-dark room. The door shut, cutting him off from the wind, Mortimer, and the enchanting Mademoiselle Violette.

Chapter 3

Daniel twisted and swung around, his punch contacting flesh in the dark. A man grunted, then an answering blow landed on Daniel's face before he could spin out of the way.

More blows came down. Daniel fought back. His punches landed on a gut like a brick wall and an iron-tough jaw. Giant fists hit him in return, on his eyes, face, chest. Finally Daniel's punch contacted a solar plexus, and the man grunted again, wheezing bad breath over Daniel's face.

Daniel shoved the man away and steadied himself on his feet. He couldn't see a damn thing, and his first step led him smack into a table on which things clattered and clinked. A heavy thud and hoarse breathing told Daniel where the gentleman had fallen, but there was no telling how long he'd stay down.

The short fight had been brutal, the man deadly strong. Daniel shook out his right fist. So much for not hurting his hands.

Daniel took another step forward, this time connecting with a chair. Good enough. He sat down and stripped the gloves from his stinging hands.

"If I can't finish my motor in time, I'm blaming you," Daniel said, pulling a box of matches from his pocket.

"I only want the money," the man on the floor said between gasps.

"You're the bloke who's been following Mortimer tonight, aren't you? What does he owe you?" Daniel struck a match against his boot, and a spark flared to life.

"Five thousand."

Daniel gave a short laugh. "The idiot. And he owes me two."

"I'll have it out of him. I'll have it out of you. You took all his money."

"No, I won it fair and square. What he owes you is between him and you."

The light from the match showed Daniel a table beside him loaded with trinkets. A hurricane lamp waited in the midst of the clutter, and Daniel lifted its chimney to touch the match to the wick.

The glowing light fell over the hard-faced man who lay stretched out on the floor. He looked less intimidating with his arm over his stomach, his face sickly green.

"I can't go back until I have it," the man said, struggling to breathe. "It'll be my life." He had a London workingman's accent.

"Hired hand, are ye? What's your name?"

"Simon. Matthew Simon."

"Nice and biblical. So it's kill me or go back and be killed, is that it? Brutal times we live in."

"That's the size of it," Mr. Simon said grimly. "Sorry and all that. But don't really see a way around it, sir."

The man did sound regretful. But not apologetic. He had a job to do, and he would use any means to get that job done.

"Tell you what, Mr. Simon, why don't you come and work for me? Right now. You won't need to run back to your master empty-handed. You can stop beating on me for the cash, and I'll pay ye a decent wage."

"Work for you?" Simon gave Daniel a long, suspicious stare. "Doing what?"

Daniel shrugged. "Lifting and carrying, keeping an eye on things, helping me with my engines when I need it. What do ye say? If ye have another go at me, I guarantee, I'll do my best to make sure you crawl home."

Simon's breathing was easier, but he made no move to get off the busily patterned carpet. "No man's ever knocked me down before. I thought I was too big."

"There's a trick to it."

"Ye know about fighting." Simon sounded admiring. "Dirty fighting."

"I was raised by men who fight dirty. Rules are for the polite. How about it, Mr. Simon?"

The man went silent. Daniel could almost hear the gears turning in Simon's head as he went through the possibilities open to him. Finally he heaved a long sigh. "I'm your man."

"Good," Daniel said. "Now, how did ye get into the house? Ye didn't hurt that poor little maid to do it, did ye?"

"Naw, I just scared her a bit."

"Hmm. I think she needs a rise in wages."

From the dining room, Daniel heard excited voices—*Did you see that? Ellingham, it's behind you!*—but in this room all was calm.

Daniel looked thoughtfully at the kerosene lamp amidst the trinkets on the table. He saw by the lamp's light that, as in the next room, a gaslight chandelier hung overhead, unlit, and gas sconces adorned the walls. Yet Mademoiselle Violette and her mother kept kerosene lamps in here and candles in the dining room. For the ambience? Or because the gas had been shut off?

Simon sat up and drew a long breath. "You have a mean punch, Mr. Mackenzie."

"You know who I am then?"

"Everyone knows who *you* are. Me and me mates always have a little flutter on your dad's horses. Sir."

"Wise of you."

Daniel looked around at the wood paneling that covered the room, which was much older than the furnishings. He put the house as built in the last century. In those days, covering the walls with raised panels outlined with molding had been common, and much more tasteful than the garish wallpaper that adorned most people's houses these days.

The paneling was also convenient, because it could hide any number of things. This sitting room was in the front of the house, the dining room behind it. But the dimensions of both rooms did not match the length of the hall that ran from the front door to the back of the house. Daniel, who could keep calculations in his head to the nearest inch, had noted that immediately.

He rose and made his way to the wall that divided the sitting room from the dining room. Not an easy journey, because the room was crammed with potted palms, potted ferns, side tables, sofa tables, rugs on rugs, and bric-a-brac of every size, shape, and color.

A narrow door through which Simon had dragged Daniel, closed now, led to the dining room. Daniel ran his hands over the wall panels next to it.

His fingertips found a catch. Working it, he pried open a panel about five feet high and a foot and a half wide. Behind this lay a shallow niche full of thin ropes and wires attached to gears. Two metal levers a little below Daniel's eye level controlled a couple of the wires, but the rest of the ropes and pulleys ran up into the wall as far as Daniel could see.

"Oh, you clever, clever lass."

"Wha' is it?" Simon asked, still on the floor and not very interested.

"The secret of Mademoiselle Bastien's success."

Simon grunted again, which Daniel took to mean he cared more about his immediate circumstances than unraveling secrets of fraudulent mediums.

Daniel craned to look upward, wishing he had better light. Whoever had set up this rig had taken advantage of the bell system—ropes and wires woven through the house so the lady upstairs could summon a maid from the depths of the servants' hall without bestirring herself too much.

The bellpull systems were sophisticated enough that a specific servant could be hailed from a specific room. Daniel had delved into the paneling in the walls in the house he'd purchased in London to put in pneumatic speaking tubes, so he'd be able to communicate instantly with his staff—whenever he got around to hiring staff.

Daniel closed the panel and made his way back through

the overstuffed parlor to the door to the hall. Simon heaved himself up and followed Daniel, rubbing his bruised face. Daniel took pity on him and told him to rest himself on the hall bench while he explored.

The housemaid was nowhere in sight. Daniel ran lightly up the stairs, which were lit only from a glow from above. He found another kerosene lamp burning in the upstairs hall, set on a table between two doors. Another flight of stairs continued upward, but Daniel was fairly certain he'd find what he sought on this floor.

The first door in the hall opened to a dark and empty room. No furniture, no people, nothing. But that room was over the parlor. The room next to it lay above the dining room where Mademoiselle Bastien held court.

Daniel opened the door of the second room. It too was bare of carpeting, although it contained a few pieces of furniture pushed against the walls. Two kerosene lamps on one table lent their glow to the housemaid, who was kneeling in the middle of the floor. Several floorboards had been lifted away, and the maid was gazing into the opening, her hands on something inside.

So intently was she focused on her task, she never heard Daniel until he walked around her and crouched down in front of her.

The maid lost her hold on a lever with a little cry, and stared at Daniel, her eyes round. Below Daniel heard Ellingham say, "What the devil happened? Where did it go?"

Daniel glanced into the opening. Beneath a series of levers, a square spy hole opened into the dining room ceiling, right through the chandelier—probably one reason the gas was not on. The chandelier swayed a bit from residual motion, but the otherworldly wind and noises had vanished.

"Oh, sir," the maid whispered, face paling. "You ought not be in here."

"Neither should you. Get on up to bed, and leave the theatrics to me."

The maid's mouth popped open. She was about thirty years of age, pretty, with dark hair under a white starched cap, her accent putting her from South London. "To you, sir?"

Daniel gave her his warmest smile. "You must be exhausted, lass, with Mortimer tramping in with his friends in the dead of night. You go up and make sure your mistress is well, and go to bed. I'll take over for you. I know a bit about manipulating machinery."

"But you can't . . . I can't . . ."

"It's all right, love. Your mistress sent me up. Let me give this a whirl."

The maid eyed Daniel in sharp suspicion. "Did she? Where did Miss . . . I mean Mademoiselle Bastien find you?"

"Oh, lying about." Daniel winked. "Her secrets are safe with me."

The housemaid came to a decision. She truly did look exhausted, wanting the relief of sleep. "Well, get a move on. She's needing a bit more down there."

She climbed to her feet, shook out her skirts, and left the room. Daniel noticed that rather than shoes, she wore soft slippers, which made only the faintest of noises on the board floor.

Once the maid had closed the door behind her, Daniel lay flat on his stomach, stripped off his gloves, and looked through the opening to the dining room below.

The room was in darkness now, the gloom relieved only when Mademoiselle lit a single candle in the candelabra. The candle's light fell over the openmouthed faces of the gentlemen and haloed Mademoiselle Violette's pale face and ringlets of dark hair.

She spoke in soothing tones, though she sounded a bit breathless. "Sometimes the spirits go suddenly, just like that. The ether closes, and the connection is lost."

"Not entirely." Ellingham pointed upward at the chandelier, which started to sway again, its facets tinkling.

Violette looked up, the extraordinary attractiveness of her face softened by the lone candle.

Daniel could expose her at that moment, call down to those below that he'd discovered how she'd tricked them all. But he knew he never would. Not because Mortimer was a bully, and not because of Mademoiselle's anger, though she showed plenty of that. And not because of her pleading look, though it was nearly lost under all the anger.

It was her cheekiness. In the middle of the night, Mademoiselle Violette sat alone in a room of gentlemen, which could spell ruin for any other young woman, and played upon them like a master musician played his piano.

These bachelors of London's best families, who cut dead anyone who didn't fit their extremely rigid rules of behavior, sat like tame puppies while Mademoiselle Violette made fools of the lot of them.

She ought to look gleeful and revel in her power. But Mademoiselle only looked worriedly upward, frightened that someone was about to end her show, possibly for good.

The desperation she tried to hide while she looked up through the chandelier—realizing her trusted maid was no longer above her—decided it.

Daniel gently pulled another lever, and a rap sounded deep inside the dining room wall.

"What was that?" one young man gasped.

Daniel pulled the lever again, producing another loud knock. Mademoiselle Violette must have rigged a block of wood or something to bang against a wall or another block, to make a hollow, rapping sound.

The lever operated smoothly, needing the lightest touch. After a little experimentation, Daniel discovered he could control the pacing and volume of the knocks.

"Is it trying to send a message?" Ellingham asked.

Violette took a deep breath and forced her gaze from the chandelier. "It is indeed. Hush now, while I listen."

Daniel wondered how many of the club fodder below knew Morse code. Had they ever operated a telegraph machine? Or were telegrams only what they dictated to lackeys to send for them?

Daniel rapped out . . . *I am the ghost of* . . . No, wait.

Mortimer is an ass.

From the expressions below, none of the gentlemen had so much as seen a telegraph machine. They waited patiently for Mademoiselle to tell them what the sounds meant.

Violette kept her countenance serene. Wonderful woman. "The spirits are unhappy," she said in her whispery contralto. "They wish us to stop. To leave them alone."

Daniel kept knocking in code. *You are lovely, do you know, lass?*

A blush spread over her face. She knew exactly what Daniel was rapping out, which meant she knew Morse code herself. Interesting.

How did a fine lady like you become a confidence trickster?

"Enough!" Violette said abruptly, rising to her feet. "Evil spirits, be gone from this place!"

Daniel left off the knocking and pulled the chandelier again. It swayed and rocked. He tried another lever, which released a cluster of tiny spheres on thin wires. The spheres, painted with phosphorescent paint, swirled and danced like ghost lights. Yet another lever released a groaning sound, probably through bellows or a bag of some kind.

He also found the lever that controlled whatever machine had blown the cold wind—it not only turned on the machine but regulated the speed. Wonderful. Daniel wanted to get his hands on *this* machine, more sophisticated than the other tricks. He'd take it apart and see how it worked.

The wind blew out the candle again. Daniel worked levers until the room below was filled with moaning, the chandelier swaying, ghost lights dancing in the wind. Violette plopped down to her chair, giving up.

Ellingham and the others stared, round-eyed, as the room lost control. When Daniel decided they'd had enough, he slammed all the levers back to their resting places.

The wind died, the ghost lights vanished, the noise stopped, and the chandelier creaked slowly to a halt. The facets gave one last shiver, then went still.

Violette rose, and another match flared to life in her hand. "Well . . ."

Her words were drowned out by thunderous applause. Ellingham got to his feet, face glowing, gloved hands clapping hard. "My word, Mademoiselle, you have a wonderful gift. I've always said so."

"They didn't hurt you, did they, Mademoiselle?" another man with a little more compassion asked. "Are you well?"

"I will be." Violette took out a handkerchief and delicately dabbed at her forehead. Oh, she was a master. "I have some protection from them. But I fear, gentlemen, that I feel a bit faint."

The gentlemen climbed to their feet, suddenly solicitous, assuring her they'd leave her to rest, that they were grateful to her. And when could they come back and bring their friends who needed to see, to believe?

Daniel watched Violette as she handled them all, on her feet, but holding the table as though barely able to stand. She encouraged them to make return visits, but with an appointment, so they might be better able to reach the spirits. Violette apologized for her weak talent—her mother's was much better. Worth it to wait until her mother was well.

The gentlemen fell all over themselves agreeing with her, only Mortimer silent.

Daniel also heard the lads speculating on what had happened to Mackenzie. One said he'd seen Daniel run out of the room, no doubt in a fright when the spirits had started up in earnest. Ah well, everyone knew the Scots were yellow.

Mortimer was the last out of the dining room. He paused at the door. "A fine show, Mademoiselle," he said. "You are to be commended."

Violette inclined her head, managing to look haughty and meek at the same time. "I thank you, sir."

"Hmm." Mortimer kept his hand on the door frame. "Well, I'll be back, Mademoiselle, in the daylight. To speak to you."

"I look forward to the meeting," Violette said.

She didn't. She'd rather eat a toad. But she only wrapped a light shawl about herself as she spoke, her exhaustion not feigned.

Mortimer gazed at her another long moment before he made a bow and said good night. Daniel heard him join the others at the front door, the door close behind them, and their voices on the street. None of them mentioned Simon, so Simon might have ducked away out of sight, or perhaps he'd gone home to nurse his wounds.

Daniel lingered, fascinated by the pulley system. There were more levers he hadn't tried. One sent a deep bell tolling—a person could imagine the specter of Death himself following such a noise. Another . . .

A pair of feet in white leather boots stopped in front of his face. The laces of the boots covered a fine pair of ankles. Better still, from his position, Daniel could glimpse the legs that rose from the boots, gossamer black stockings fitting tightly over shapely calves.

He rolled over onto his back and put his hands behind his head. From this angle, he looked all the way up her straight skirt to the tight bodice that swelled over her bosom. "As grand a setup as I've ever seen," he said. "The pulley system, I mean. What engineer strung this for you? Whoever it was, I want to meet him."

Mademoiselle Bastien's schooled face remained carefully blank. "I did it," she said.

"Did you, now?" Daniel's eyes widened in amazement and he brought his ungloved hands together in a burst of clapping. "Brilliant. I think I'm in love with you."

Chapter 4

Arrogant, impudent . . . Violet and her mother were about to be ruined by this scion of aristocracy, and he was *laughing* at her.

Mr. Mackenzie returned his hands behind his head and lay full-length on Violet's floor, relaxed and confident. What did he intend to do? Expose her? Alert the newspapers? The police? Violet's heart beat hard. She needed to wake up her mother, to pack what they could, to *leave*.

But Mr. Mackenzie remained unmoving, eyes glittering in the lamplight, his handsome face and athletic body the best things that had ever decorated this room.

Violet had no business thinking of that, absolutely no business. Existence was difficult enough. Men believed that women's lives were theirs to dictate, to own. Look what had happened the last time Violet had thought a man sympathetic to her, had trusted him. Absolute disaster.

"You used the bell system," Mr. Mackenzie was saying. "Piggybacked on the pulleys and tubes already available to you. Very wise. Though a bit inconvenient if you want to summon someone to bring you hot water."

"The consultation is over, Mr. Mackenzie," Violet said, keeping her voice brisk and businesslike. "The other gentlemen have gone."

Daniel pushed himself up to a sitting position and crossed his legs. His kilt fell modestly over his knees, but not before Violet caught a glimpse of the strong thighs beneath. Oblivious of her scrutiny, Daniel pulled a cigarette case from his pocket, extracted a black cigarette, and put it between his lips. He shoved the case back into his coat, took out a match, and struck it on the bottom of his boot.

Leisurely, he lit the cigarette, shook out the match, and leaned his head back a little to suck in the smoke. After a few moments, he released the smoke from his mouth, his tongue curling softly as wisps drifted around it.

Violet realized she was staring at him, her gaze fixed on his lips, which pursed around the cigarette again, like a kiss. Many gentlemen liked to smoke, yes, but Daniel made the movements an art—strong fingers loosely holding the cigarette, lips and tongue almost caressing it and the smoke that trickled from his mouth.

"Ye need a bit more than that," he said.

"What?" Violet jerked. Oh, he meant the rigging. She forced herself into the persona of Violette Bastien again. "I beg your pardon, Monsieur?"

Daniel dragged in another long pull of smoke, his mouth closing around the cigarette in a sensual caress. The end of it glowed. "Downstairs," he said, smoke floating out with his words. "If ye had something that released ectoplasm, had it crawl up the walls maybe, you'd have them worshipping at your feet." He smiled, his gaze going pointedly to her high-topped shoes. "I'd be honored if you showed everything to me." The double entendre rolled off his tongue as he ran his gaze the length of her skirt again, back to her face.

Bloody conceited . . . Violet sank down to her heels, wrapping her arms around her knees. "Are you certain it's honor you're after? Or my secrets? Thinking to set up a rival business, are you?"

Mr. Mackenzie laughed out loud—true laughter, no artfulness about it. "Me, a clairvoyant? My friends would laugh me out of London, and my family would tease me senseless. Makes me wonder, though, why you do it? Ye don't look naturally deceptive to me."

"Oh? What does naturally deceptive look like?"

More laughter. The sound had warmth to it, a little growl, deep and rasping. "Much more innocent than you, lass. Like my wee baby sister. She can give you a look from her big gray eyes, blinking under those golden red curls. Meanwhile, she's put three frogs in your bed. She's seven years old, the bonniest lass you ever saw, and the mischief she can get herself—and me—into . . ." Mr. Mackenzie shook his head, his look so fond that it pulled at Violet even as it surprised her.

Then again, Violet recognized a confidence trickster when she saw one. A man like Mackenzie would throw things like infectious laughter and an adorable little sister at her to get under Violet's defenses.

"So why do it?" Daniel asked her again. He sounded genuinely interested, not just flirtatious.

Violet made herself remain businesslike. *Take what a person believes about you and turn it back on him.* "To make a living, of course," she said. "But you're wrong, Mr. Mackenzie. My mother's talent is real."

"Pull the other one, love. You're all theatrics—beautiful theatrics. Your wind machine fascinates me, though. I'm trying to build something like it myself. Where did you get it?"

"I built it myself," she said, feeling a spark of pride. "Purchased the parts in Berlin."

Daniel let out an aggravated breath. "Of course. Bloody Germans. They're going to take over the world one day. All the same." He tucked the cigarette into his mouth, got his feet under him, and in one graceful, sinuous movement, rose to his feet.

He reached a hand down to help her up. Violet studied the sinewy strength of the gloveless hand, virile, tight, powerful, stretching down to her. Daniel expected her to take the offer of help without reluctance, to let him steady and guide her.

Fortunately Violet had learned a long time ago what a lie such an offer could be. But she was not so terrified of him that she would not at least let him help her to her feet. Any metaphor beyond that was useless.

Violet put her hand into his. Mr. Mackenzie's strong fingers closed around hers, the warmth in them palpable.

Daniel didn't guide her upward—he pulled hard, lifting Violet nearly off her feet. Her heels tapped the board floor as they came down. Daniel's hand went to her elbow to steady her, and she found herself pulled against the length of his tall body.

The twinkle in Daniel's dark amber eyes made her shake. "Naturally deceptive also looks like me," he said, his voice low. "From where do you think my wee baby sister learned it?"

He wouldn't let go of her. Daniel had a solid grip on Violet's arm, strong enough that she couldn't tug away and scorn him with a freezing glance. Freezing glances would bounce from him in any case, or else be caught and thawed by him. There wasn't a bit of chill anywhere in Mr. Mackenzie.

He was all heat. And Violet was so cold.

She smelled the smoke on him, whiskey from earlier tonight, and dust from her floor. Daniel held the cigarette loosely, and the smoke curled around Violet as though trying to pull her into an embrace with him.

Daniel's face was hard, but not as hard as that of his father, or at least what Violet had seen of his father in the newspapers. Daniel's dark hair had been cut short, but he'd managed to rumple it so one part of it stuck out in a different direction than the rest. The lamplight burned red highlights in his hair, subtle ones that would show only in strong light and only to someone standing close to him.

Daniel lifted the cigarette. Without releasing Violet, he took another pull then offered the cigarette to her.

Violet eyed the dark stick and its faint glow at the end. She knew that some scandalous women smoked alongside their lovers, but Violet had never formed a taste for it. She found she preferred the warm, herbal scent of pipe smoke in any case, although cigar smoke was what clung to most gentlemen these days.

She imagined Mr. Mackenzie's fancy ladies wouldn't reject an offer to share his smoke. The young debutantes he'd be courting, on the other hand, to put an heir in his nursery, would be shocked and turn up their noses. Or they might giggle at Daniel's audacity.

The thought of those giggling, perfect young debs with their soft fingers and no worries in their spoiled little heads made Violet almost snatch the cigarette from him.

She closed her lips around it. Violet had learned when she practiced on cigars—ghostly smoke appearing in a room while her mother was in her trance never hurt—that if she closed up her throat and didn't let the smoke into her lungs, she could tolerate it.

Daniel watched her, standing so close that she could smell the shaving soap he'd used before he'd ventured out tonight. She also caught the scents of cigar smoke mixed with that of the cigarette, plenty of whiskey, and a woman's heavy perfume. Her heart burned.

Violet exhaled the smoke little by little, while Daniel fixed his gaze on her. As the last of the smoke trickled out, Daniel leaned down and fitted his lips over hers.

The pressure was barely a kiss at all, only a resting of his lips against hers, allowing her to feel his smooth mouth, the bite of warmth, the strength of him.

No hesitant kiss of a man who knew he was being more forward than he ought. Likewise, it wasn't a commanding kiss—it gave more than it demanded.

Daniel eased back, a smile spreading across his face. "Ah, lass, I knew ye'd taste fine."

She could only stare at him. Time for a biting quip, the wit Violet had learned that put a forward gentleman into his place. Time for the half-amused, half-scornful look the Parisian courtesan called Lady Amber had taught her—it stopped men before they got above themselves, Lady Amber had assured her.

But Violet's heart pounded, and she couldn't move. Flashes of white light slapped her eyes, and the flickering lamp across the room didn't help.

"Ye all right, love?" Daniel asked, stooping to look into her face.

The quiet question almost killed her. Violet wanted to wrap her arms around him, to hang on to him until everything, absolutely everything was all right again.

But that way lay danger, and terror so great it immobilized her. Lady Amber had tried to help Violet become right again, but Violet had long ago faced the sad fact that she never could be.

"Yes. Fine." She made herself sound brisk. "The hour is late."

Daniel touched fingers to Violet's chin, the caress so gentle her knees threatened to buckle. Violet thought he'd kiss her again—hoped—but Daniel only took a step back, ground out the cigarette on the bottom of his boot, and said, "Now, show me this wind machine."

Without waiting for her to escort him, Daniel left the room.

Violet had to hurry after him, her heels clicking on the bare floor. He moved fast, his long stride carrying him down the stairs before Violet could catch him.

By the time she reached the ground floor, Daniel was already in the dining room, all the candles lit, he standing in the middle of the room, turning a slow circle. "Your bobbing ghost lights issued from that register," he said, pointing upward. "The icy breeze of death from . . . ah."

He walked unerringly to the wallpapered panel and removed it from the wall. Behind the panel lay the cables that ran the machine, which issued the air through the register below it. Daniel had the machine unhooked and out of its slot in two minutes—it had taken Violet an entire day to put it in.

The device was a fan encased in a metal box, turned by gears hand-cranked by the lever in the room above. Tubes of water circulated around the fan, cooling the air that came out of the machine to a chilly temperature.

Daniel examined the device closely, turning it this way and that. "Oh, what I couldn't do with this." He turned it over again. "You know, if you hook this up to electrics, ye could get more power from it, get the fan to turn faster."

Violet watched his quick eyes take in every facet of the machine, his fingers running over it. "Mind if I take this away with me?" he asked. "Won't keep it long. I'm trying to build something like it—as a part of something even bigger."

His gaze held interest, a focus more intent than Violet had seen in him since he'd entered the house. Gone was the lazy aristocrat, bored by the entertainments of his acquaintances. Gone even was the roué who'd dared her to take the cigarette, who'd kissed her lips with such finesse.

He was alert, interested, and had a razor-sharp intellect. Dangerous.

Daniel held in his hand evidence of Violet's fraud, the fact that she took money from people and pretended she brought forth spirits in return. Mr. Mackenzie could rush out of here and take the device to the police, or worse, a newspaper. The police could arrest and imprison Violet and her mother; the press could stir up a mob to chase them out of the country—again.

Though Daniel's eyes didn't hold the vindictive glee of a man wanting to expose her, he might show the device to his friends. What if Mortimer discovered the secret?

"No," Violet said quickly. "I need it."

"To impress gents like Ellingham? You know, your gift is enough without props. You had them in the palm of your hand, love. You're a master."

"Not really. My mother has the true gift." Violet's mother, Celine, could hold a room—indeed, a concert hall—in thrall with her trances and her conversations with her spirit guide. Violet didn't trust her own talents to keep an audience's attention without effects.

Daniel looked at the device with a kind of hunger Violet had seen men reserve for courtesans. Not an average gentleman, was Daniel Mackenzie.

Daniel looked over the device one last time then replaced it in its niche. He closed the panel, dusted off his hands, and straightened up. Violet found him standing in front of her, very close.

"Mortimer brought me here tonight because he owes me money," he said. "He was banking on me being so impressed by your performance that I'd forgive the debt. He used you. I don't like that."

Violet shrugged. "He is my landlord. He can come into the house whenever he likes."

Daniel frowned. "Don't stand still and resign yourself to him. He's a right bastard, and if I'd had less compassion tonight, I would have let the bone-breaker have him."

"Bone-breaker?" Violet hadn't seen such a person in the dining room, only Mortimer's friends, fair flowers of the English aristocracy.

"A man who works for a man to whom Mortimer owes even more money. Except the bone-breaker now works for me." Daniel leaned forward a little, taking all the space around Violet. He didn't do it deliberately, as though he tried to intimidate her. He merely leaned to her, uninhibited, as though they were great friends. "I don't like you beholden to Mortimer. If he gives you trouble, you tell me, eh, lass? Right away. Promise me?"

Violet opened her mouth to say something like, *Why on earth should I?* But the breath for the words drew in his warmth, the scents of smoke and liquor, and the words melted on her tongue.

Daniel was speaking again before Violet could drag her thoughts together, and she only caught the last words.

"And all this has given me a beautiful idea."

A smile replaced his scowl so quickly that Violet blinked. Mr. Mackenzie's lightning-swift changes of mood were astonishing and a little bit frightening.

The next moment, Violet found her back to the colorful wallpaper, Daniel an inch away from her, his touch on her face. He was shaking his head, his smile vanishing again, his voice low, almost as though he spoke to himself.

"You're the loveliest lass I've seen in a long time."

"Mr. Mac—"

"It's cold here." Daniel's words cut through hers, drowning sounds and thought. "Come home with me, and let me warm you."

Violet had taught herself a hundred retorts for forward gentlemen, but they dissolved under Daniel's heat, and then the touch of his mouth. Daniel kissed her, replacing her breath with his.

Let me warm you.

Upstairs, he'd stunned her with a quiet press of lips. This time he kissed her fully, pushing her back against the wall, his mouth on hers.

Violet couldn't breathe; she couldn't stand. She put her hand to the sideboard next to her to steady herself, and Daniel's strong hands came around her waist.

He parted her lips with his, his body a firm length of heat.

No one should be so strong and vibrant at this hour of the night, no one this overwhelming. Violet's knees were buckling. Only Daniel's arms and the solidity of the sideboard kept her from falling.

Daniel brushed his lips to the corner of her mouth, so softly he made her shake. Then he licked his way inside her mouth again, the taste of him bold, dangerous.

Black spots spun before Violet's eyes. She gasped and found her mouth full of Daniel, tried to break away only to be wedged between the sideboard and wall, blocked by Daniel's body.

Because Daniel was a handsome, virile, funny, intriguing, and sensual man, the situation should have had her melting in surrender. And Violet might have, despite her better judgment, if the panic hadn't come.

Daniel's face vanished, to be replaced with flashes of another—a red-bearded man with a white, mean face, small eyes, and hands that took and hurt. Sixteen-year-old Violet screamed and beat on her attacker. *No, no, please no! Someone help me!*

But no one came. Her fists contacted an unyielding body, a weight she couldn't move. Violet screamed again, terror swallowing her. *This can't be happening! This can't be happening!*

"Lass?" a voice asked from far away. It was a voice Violet wanted to reach, one that meant safety, but waves of panic poured over her and wouldn't let her free.

"Are ye all . . ." the distant voice said, and then it grunted.

Violet's vision half cleared to see Mary, her maid, with the bolster from the parlor sofa in her hands. Violet's attacker backed from her, rubbing his neck.

Her panic returned. She needed something stronger than a pillow to stop him. Violet's hand connected with a heavy vase on the sideboard. Without stopping to think, she lifted it, brought it around, and bashed her attacker on the side of the head.

Violet heard a heavy groan, a "Lass," and Mary's startled cry.

Her vision cleared completely. Violet was standing in the dining room of the London house, a vase in her hand, a round-eyed Mary next to her holding a red velvet bolster.

Mr. Mackenzie, blood on his face, stared at Violet with a stunned expression. He said, "Lass," one more time.

Then he fell over like a tree in a high wind, crashing head-long onto the dining room floor. The vase slipped from Violet's numb fingers and shattered next to him.

Mary dropped to her knees, the bolster rolling away, her hands going to Daniel's cold face and closed eyes.

"He ain't breathing," Mary said frantically. She patted his cheeks.

Violet sank next to Mary, her movements wooden. She stared down at the handsome face of Mr. Mackenzie, his lips pale now, his chest not rising.

Mary hastily unbuttoned his coat then tore open his waist-coat and shirt, pushing aside his undershirt to jam her hands to the space over his heart. Dark hair curled over his chest, his pectorals well defined. "I can't find his heartbeat," Mary said.

Violet's numbness left her with a jolt. She brushed Mary aside, and leaned down to put her ear to Daniel's bare chest, trying to hold her breath and listen.

She heard nothing but the pounding of her own heart. The room whirled around her, undulating as though the machines were running again, the spirits rampaging.

Violet lifted her head. "Mary," she said, barely able to squeeze out the words. "Oh God, I think I've killed him."

Chapter 5

Mary got to her feet in panic. Violet shook Daniel, patted his cheeks, pried open one eye. He never responded, and his skin was growing clammy and cold.

"Mary, quickly, go for the doctor."

"It's too late for that," Mary said, voice filled with fear. "Miss, if you've killed him . . . Oh Lord, he's a rich man, and we're nothing. We'll go to prison. We'll be hanged." Mary's hands fluttered. "What about your poor mum?"

"Stop! Stop, let me think."

But Violet couldn't think. She sat back on her knees, the room still darting and spinning. Mary waited to be commanded, because Violet always knew what to do.

But this was different from deciding how much to charge for the performances or from Violet telling her mother what to wear every day, and where to go and what to do. Violet had done all this since the age of seven, when she'd realized her mother had no idea how to take care of a daughter. Or herself, for that matter.

Violet pressed her fingers to her temples. If she'd killed Daniel Mackenzie, even accidentally—a man from one of the wealthiest families in Britain and nephew to a powerful duke—Violet would be made to pay.

If she claimed she'd struck out in fear, that Daniel had attacked her, Violet would be blamed for putting herself into his power in the first place. If she argued that Mortimer had brought Daniel here, and Daniel had lingered inappropriately, she'd be blamed for taking up such an unladylike profession. After all, she'd allowed gentlemen to enter her house, unchaperoned, at such an hour.

Even if the jury were sympathetic to her, Violet still would be punished for killing him or hurting him, if he recovered. She'd be sent to prison or transported, Mary along with her, and possibly her mother too. Violet had seen firsthand the unevenness of the law and its prejudice against women. A jury of men would look upon Violet and happily condemn her before leaving the courtroom to visit their mistresses on their way home to their wives.

"Help me get him into the cart," Violet said quickly. "And go wake up Mama and pack what you can. We are going."

"Going? But miss—"

"We can't risk staying. Mortimer and his friends will know Mr. Mackenzie came here tonight. Even if we've only hurt him, we can't count on the Mackenzies not bringing the law down on us. No matter what, if we are far away when he's discovered, the better for us."

Far away, in another country, with different names and different personas. If no one connected Daniel and his visit to this house tonight, well and good. If they did connect it, then Violet, her mother, and Mary wouldn't be here to answer awkward questions. Not being here when the investigation was conducted would be best. At least Violet's mother, upstairs in her laudanum slumber, was truly innocent of everything.

Pieces of the vase had blood on them. Violet instructed Mary to put the broken vase into a box, which she would drop over the railing of the boat on the way to France. Mr. Mortimer might rage over the price of it, but that was the least of her worries.

The next hour was one of the most harried of Violet's life. Time seemed first to crawl and then to fly past.

She and Mary arranged Mr. Mackenzie's body on the handcart on which they carried groceries home from the markets. As they buttoned up his clothes again, they discovered a fat wad of money stuffed into his coat pocket.

Mary and Violet looked at each other over it. So much cash, right in their hands.

"Some thief will just take it if we leave it on him," Mary pointed out.

But if constables caught up to them, and Violet had all Mr. Mackenzie's money, her claim of hitting him in her own defense went out the window.

Violet compromised. She peeled several large notes away from the others, and put all the rest back into his pocket. A small amount from such a large stash wouldn't be missed, would it? And Violet would need the money to buy tickets.

Violet changed out of what she called her parlor clothes to an old pair of breeches, over which she put a wide skirt and linen shirt. To finish, she tied a scarf over her hair. Any person who spied her in the dark would see an elderly immigrant woman, perhaps taking foodstuffs home or getting ready to go clean for the day at a middle-class woman's home.

Mr. Mackenzie still lay motionlessly on the cart when Violet went out into the tiny yard behind the house to wheel him away. No moon shone tonight, London so thick with coal smoke in January that no moonlight or starlight could penetrate the gloom. Better for her errand.

She and Mary covered Mr. Mackenzie with sackcloth and then stacked a few bags of coal on top of him. The shapes in the cart Violet pushed would be several small upright lumps, not the horizontal form of a man.

Violet went alone, guiding the cart through the passages to the main street and quickly across to the warren on the other side. She saw a constable down the block of one street, but he was walking the other way and never saw her.

She was thoroughly sick to her stomach by the time she decided she'd laid a false enough trail. Violet doubled back with the cart until she reached a quiet, narrow street east of Portman Square, and the house where she knew a doctor lived. He was a kindhearted man, Violet had come to know, often looking after people in the neighborhood for no charge. If Mr. Mackenzie wasn't truly dead, the doctor would help him. And if Mr. Mackenzie *was* dead, the doctor would make sure he was returned to his family.

Violet waited until the street was free of constables or any late-night strollers. This was a poorer neighborhood, with gaslights fewer and farther between. She crept forward, happy she'd kept the handcart well oiled. In the shadows of the silent house, Violet pulled back the sacks and rolled Mr. Mackenzie from the cart.

As his body landed on the cobblestones, Violet choked back a sob. Daniel had been so warm when he'd kissed her in her upstairs room, so vibrant. He'd looked into her eyes and known her for the fraud she was—a fraud in every way.

He'd seen to the heart of her as no one had before. He'd kissed her, because he'd known Violet wasn't a respectable lady, but at the same time he'd been tender, not demanding.

Tears filled her eyes, and Violet tried to banish them. Crying never helped.

She leaned to Daniel's inert body and kissed his cold lips. "I'm sorry," she whispered. She smoothed his hair. "I'm so sorry."

Wiping her eyes, Violet climbed to her feet, restored the sacks to the cart, and pushed it away, her stomach roiling.

She made her way back to their rented house, taking a roundabout route. Halfway there, she abandoned the cart and changed from her peasant clothes into the plain skirt and shirtwaist she'd brought with her. Violet walked the rest of the way back to the house as herself, a basket over her arm, as though returning from a very late errand.

Back inside, her bewildered mother was out of bed, demanding to know why they had to go. Violet had already sworn Mary to silence about Mr. Mackenzie, knowing her mother would fall to pieces at the truth. Instead Violet invented the story that Mr. Mortimer had come here tonight to make trouble about the rent, and had thrown them out.

Her mother believed her and in a remarkably short time was ready to leave. Celine could move quickly when her fear of bailiffs was roused.

The morning was still dark when Madame and Mademoiselle Bastien and their maid left their London house for Dover, and ceased to exist.

~~~~~~

Daniel opened his eyes, let out a groan of pain, and snapped his eyes shut again.

Some daft idiot had left the curtains to his bedroom open, and the light of morning stabbed directly into his brain. He never opened the curtains until at least noon, often later, depending on how bad was his hangover.

Today's was a pounding monster of one. What the hell had he been drinking?

Time passed. When Daniel made himself peel open his eyes again, the light was not as agonizing, though the headache remained.

He didn't at first recognize the man who turned from the fireplace in Daniel's upstairs bedroom, then he remembered Matthew Simon, bone-breaker and debt collector, who had pounded his fists into Daniel until Daniel had subdued him.

But the blow that had put this dent in Daniel's skull hadn't come from Simon. He remembered all that had happened now, as clearly as the afternoon light pouring through his window.

"Mr. Mackenzie, sir." Simon leaned over the bed and released a sigh of relief, with a breath that made Daniel note he would buy the man a toothbrush and tooth powder. "I thought you were a goner for sure."

"I'm a robust, obnoxiously healthy Scot," Daniel said. He tried to sit up then decided the pillows were the best place for his head. "How did I get here? What happened?"

"A constable was called to a doctor's house in Marylebone—he'd found you near to his doorstep. I was coming to find you after having a little rest at me old mum's place, to take you up on your offer of a job. I asked around about where you lived—everyone knows, so it wasn't hard to find. When I got here, a couple of constables were carrying you inside. I said I was your new man, and I'd take care of you. They didn't know no more about what happened to you than where they found you."

"So she dumped me in the street," Daniel said, putting his

hand to his temple. His skin stung there, and he made a soft noise of pain.

"The doc stitched you up," Simon said. "But I can look after you. My brother, he was a boxer afore he died of it, and I used to look after him regular. They said the doc thought you was dead, though, when he found you. But you were knocked senseless is all. You needed to be warmed up and tended, and a few blows on your chest didn't hurt either."

"So *you* say." Daniel lifted the collar of his nightshirt and observed the fist-sized bruises on his solar plexus. "Why did you feel the need to punch me in the chest? Hitting a man after he's down?"

"I didn't do that. The doctor what found you did, so constables said. See, sometimes the heart forgets to beat, but the man is still alive. I saw it in a boxing match once—the fighter was on the floor, and his trainer slammed his hand to the man's chest. Fighter woke up gasping. It's like the heart needs a little boost."

"Like pushing a motorcar to start it. Well, whether it worked or not, here I am."

"What happened, sir? Did Mortimer and his bullies jump you?"

"No." Daniel tried sitting up again, and this time it worked. He leaned against his headboard and wished that in the clutter of his bedroom, he knew where he'd left his cigarette case. "It had nothing to do with Mortimer. The last thing I remember, Simon, is a beautiful woman swinging a deadly vase at my head. You ever been thumped by a woman for kissing her?"

Simon's mouth twitched. "Aye, sir."

"And what did you do?" Daniel rubbed his head, looking around for a cigar, a decanter of whiskey, anything to blunt the pain.

"Kissed her again."

Daniel laughed. "Aye, well, I didn't get the chance, did I? Help me to my feet, so I can get dressed. I need to go ask a lovely lass why she felt the need to crash an ugly vase into my skull."

An hour, a too-bumpy carriage ride, and half a flask of Mackenzie malt later, Daniel was back at the house near Portman Square where he'd met Violette Bastien.

The front door was partway open. Daniel descended from his carriage in one step and walked inside.

The house smelled cold and empty. A box of cutlery sat on a table in the hall near the staircase, and an empty valise waited forlornly on the steps. Daniel heard footsteps upstairs and voices, angry and male.

He went down the hall and on into the dining room, remembering his first sight of Violette as she stood alone behind the table, a long match in her hand. Candlelight had fallen on a face that had taken his breath away.

Now the room was cold and dark, the drapes shut. Daniel pulled open the curtains, letting in what light filtered through the high houses around them. By that he saw panels ripped from the walls, Violette's devices gone.

Of course. She'd take those and leave mundane things like cutlery and clothing. She could always find new dresses and new spoons, but her devices were unique.

Daniel heaved a sigh, a little surprised at his disappointment. Violette should be just another female to him—she wasn't as physically beautiful as the woman who'd dealt the cards at the gaming hell last night. Daniel had taken lovers in France and Italy with more striking looks than Mademoiselle Violette's. None of those ladies had been anything like Violette, with her hair trickling from her pompadour, her intriguing devices, her cocky rejoinders.

And eyes that held secrets. Violette Bastien—if that was even her name—was a woman who'd lived far more than the debutantes who currently pursued Daniel with determination to land him in matrimony. Even the courtesans he'd known had lived very narrow lives. Mademoiselle Violette fit neither mold.

Find her, something inside Daniel said. *Pluck out those secrets and discover what she's made of.*

But Daniel had no time to go chasing after a woman who'd fooled a group of club fodder with her theatrics and skipped out on the rent. Good for her. He'd only gone to the hell last night to clear his head. Playing cards, thinking in simple numbers and odds, helped him solve more complicated mechanical difficulties. Daniel was finished with the encounter, and he had plenty to do.

But he thought again of the first touch of Violette's lips, how the taste of smoke only enhanced the taste of her. The subsequent kiss in the dining room had awakened a need in him he'd never felt before. Daniel had sensed the beginning of Violette's surrender, her body going pliant and soft.

Then a blow had landed on the back of his neck, followed by Violette looking at Daniel in absolute terror. No mistaking the blind panic—Daniel had frightened her half to death. Hence the blow with the vase.

But why? In the upstairs room he'd read desire in her. Downstairs, fear. What change had one flight of stairs wrought?

He wanted to know, and now she was gone.

"Find them, damn you!" The cry rang down the stairs, echoing Daniel's sentiment, but with much more fury. He recognized the voice and left the dining room to confront its owner.

"Your bird has flown, has she, Mortimer?" Daniel asked.

Fenton Mortimer swung around, greatcoat billowing, from where he'd been haranguing a young constable and a man in a business suit and bowler hat on the stairs.

"What are you doing here, Mackenzie?" Mortimer demanded. "If you have anything to do with this, I'll . . ."

He trailed off, his focus moving to the bruise and cut on Daniel's temple. He decided not to complete the threat. Wise man.

"I'm looking for Mademoiselle Bastien, same as you," Daniel said. "Frighten her off, did you?"

"Madame Bastien and her daughter owe my family two months' rent. Of course they fled. I don't care how fine a show they gave us last night—they're tricksters and thieves, and I will prove it."

"What, you don't believe in the spirit world?" Daniel asked. "And you dragged me here so eagerly."

"Because I thought you'd like the girl and forgive my debt if you had a night with her. What did *you* do to make them flee?"

"Not a damn thing." But then, Daniel thought again of the fear in Violette's eyes. She'd struck him to the ground, and now she was gone.

She'd apparently dragged him down a few streets to lie alone until someone found him. Lucky for Daniel he hadn't been quietly knifed to death, though he'd noticed that the wad of cash he'd won last night had vanished. Had a thief rolled him, or had Violette helped herself from his inert body?

Perhaps everything between him and Violette had been false—the spark of passion, the beginnings of surrender, the fear. All contrived so she could smash wealthy, gullible Daniel over the head, steal his money, and slip away to a softer life in another place.

Violette Bastien had admitted to him that she put on a show for the customer, using her fancy devices. He'd felt sorry for her at the same time he'd admired her ingenuity.

But perhaps she was a confidence trickster all the way down, playing upon Daniel's protectiveness to get what she wanted. And Daniel had walked into it with his eyes open. He was as much of an idiot as Mortimer.

"Let her go," Daniel said. "She'll be miles away by now."

"Let her go?" Mortimer's eyes were red with rage. "She owes me. The bitch is going to pay every penny of my debt to you as well. I'll find her, I'll have her in prison, and I'll squeeze her dry."

Mortimer was a bully, plain and simple. Daniel remembered Simon saying that Mortimer owed money to a very bad man. Mortimer was the kind of person who would turn around and take out his fear and anger on those he thought weaker than he. Violette Bastien might have played Daniel for a fool, but he wished her out of Mortimer's grasp forever.

"How much did she owe you?" Daniel asked.

"Forty pounds. And I want the two thousand I owe you out of her too."

The businessman cleared his throat. He alone of the three men pretended he didn't notice the bruises and abrasions on Daniel's face, although the constable studied them with interest.

"That would be unwise," the suited man said to Mortimer. "The law will help you gain your rent money, but nothing you incurred with another party."

Daniel grinned. "And stating you brought me here last

night so I'd forgive your debt in exchange for her body makes you a procurer, Mortimer. Not the best thing to say in front of a constable and a solicitor."

Mortimer's weasel-like face became even more red. "That is *not* what I meant . . ."

But he *had* meant that—Mortimer simply couldn't control his tongue. Daniel knew as well that Mortimer had come here this morning for more than the rent. A debt of forty pounds to his family wouldn't have him that hot under the collar, not when he owed someone who would employ a bone-breaker five thousand. Mortimer had come to badger Violette, likely to demand she pay him in another way. He'd no doubt summoned the constable and solicitor only after he'd found Violette gone.

Daniel clenched his fists behind his back so he wouldn't haul off and punch Mortimer in the face. "Tell you what," he said, running his gaze along the staircase, to the ceiling, and back to Mortimer. "How much do you think this house is worth?"

Mortimer's eyes narrowed. "Why?"

"I'll buy it from you—or whoever in your family actually owns it. That way Madame Bastien's rent is owed to me, not you. Knock off two thousand from the price, and I'll consider the amount you owe me paid. Knock off another five, and I'll buy your note back from Mr. . . . Who are you in up to your neck with?"

Mortimer flashed an uncomfortable glance at the constable and magistrate. "Sutton," he said, barely audible.

Daniel's day brightened. "You mean *Edward* Sutton? Are you a fool? Or just fond of pain?"

"It's none of your business," Mortimer said angrily. "It has to do with America, and is between Mr. Sutton and myself."

Now even the constable looked amused. No constable would dare march to the house of Edward Sutton in Park Lane and tell him to release poor Mr. Mortimer from his debt, which was likely an illegal one. The solicitor, likewise, was pretending he didn't hear this part of the conversation.

"Figure the price for the house, and then knock off seven thousand from that," Daniel said. "Give me your note of hand to Sutton, and I'll run round and pay it for you."

Mortimer stared in astonishment. "What the devil? Why would you do that?"

"In return, you'll promise to abandon any chase of Mademoiselle Violette and leave her to her fate."

Mortimer bristled. "But she—"

Daniel held up his hand. "I buy the house, I pay off Sutton for you, and in return, you leave Mademoiselle Violette alone. The price of assuaging your pride is this house plus me settling your debt. Take it, or I can tell Sutton about this lovely abode you have. I'll guess he'd take it in lieu. Of course, he wouldn't give you the money to make up the price of it, and your family might have something to say about that. What a right mess. I'm your best bet."

The solicitor cleared his throat again. They did that, solicitors, gave a dry cough that preceded sage advice. They must learn it when they apprenticed—morning lessons featuring precise throat clearing.

"Mr. Mackenzie's offer is good, Mr. Mortimer," the solicitor said. "One that will save you much trouble in the end."

Mortimer's indecision was comical. He so much wanted to lay his hands on the Bastiens to satisfy the bully in him, but likewise he wanted the threat of Edward Sutton out of his life. Would he lord over the weak, or keep the strong from lording over him?

Fear won. Mortimer gave Daniel a nod. "Very well. My solicitor will draw up the agreement. My father will comply. He's been wanting to sell the house for ages."

"Excellent," Daniel said. "Thank you, constable. You can go now. No longer needed, I think."

The constable touched his hat and backed away, happy to be out of it. Daniel pulled a card from his coat and gave it to the suited man. "Make an appointment with my solicitor, and we'll sort this out. Meanwhile, I'm off to pay a call on Mr. Sutton."

"Hum," Mortimer said, eyes glittering in dislike. "Don't play fast and loose with me, Mackenzie."

"I said I'd pay your note, and I will," Daniel said, taking up the hat he'd left on the hall table. "Sutton won't be interested in you once he's been paid, so he won't send more men after you. The one he sent last night works for me now, anyway."

Daniel liked the worry in Mortimer's eyes. Daniel was effectively taking Sutton's place on the bully scale, and Mortimer, in his way of thinking, now had to placate Daniel.

Whatever he liked. Daniel had no more interest in Mortimer. As long as the man stayed away from Violette, all was well.

Daniel left the house and walked back to his hired carriage, whistling.

Daniel's errand to Edward Sutton in his Park Lane house didn't take long. In sharp contrast to the overloaded parlor at Mortimer's house, the study in which Sutton received Daniel was the epitome of plain elegance. In evidence were the clean lines of the new Arts and Crafts style—everything fashioned by artisans, nothing factory made. Priceless paintings from around the world hung on the walls.

Sutton, a thin, spare man with graying hair and eyes that saw too much, was happy to receive five thousand for Mortimer's debt and tear up the note.

"Thank you," Sutton said, his voice as dry as Mortimer's solicitor's. "I dislike Fenton Mortimer and was tired of dealing with him. Serves me right for giving him the money in the first place. And you say you've stolen the man I sent after him?"

Daniel shrugged, pretending he didn't notice the other bone-breakers Sutton had stationed around the room. "I need a man, and I like one who's good with his fists. I lead an adventurous life."

"You will if you entice good servants out from under the noses of men like me." Sutton's cold eyes pinned Daniel. "But I'll surrender him with good grace, since you've paid Mortimer's debt. Some advice, Mr. Mackenzie. Don't be so hasty to do good services for men like Mortimer. They'll come back for more."

"Not in this case," Daniel said. "And as I said, I had my reasons."

"To do with a woman, no doubt," Sutton said, his voice even drier. "I see it in your eyes. An even more foolish motivation, Mr. Mackenzie. But you come from a family of fools. They were formidable until they went soft."

"But they're happy, Mr. Sutton. My uncles are so much easier to live with now that they're family men."

"If you say so. Go after your woman, Mr. Mackenzie. And if you ever need a favor—*not* about a woman—feel free to come to me. I prefer to deal with honorable men."

Daniel agreed to keep it in mind, but he made no promises. Sutton was the kind of man to twist a favor into lifelong servitude. Even Uncle Hart wasn't as cold-blooded as Edward Sutton.

Daniel entered his carriage again, but when the coachman asked where he wanted to go, Daniel had to debate. What now?

If he wanted to find Violette, Daniel had resources at hand. Hart Mackenzie, the Duke of Kilmorgan, had a network to rival that of the best police force in Europe. But Hart, as head of the Mackenzie family, would demand to know why Daniel wanted to find the Bastiens, would want every detail, and wouldn't help until he was satisfied with Daniel's explanation. Or he'd refuse point-blank. Even if Hart did help, his assistance always came with a price. If Sutton was a cunning man, Hart Mackenzie was the very devil. Who knew what he'd ask from Daniel in return?

Then there was Chief Inspector Fellows, another uncle, who was as tenacious in pursuit of his prey as any of the Mackenzies. Fellows could uncover Violette Bastien's whereabouts faster than Hart if he wanted to.

The trouble was, Fellows was a stickler for the law. The Bastiens were frauds, they'd absconded without paying rent after tearing up the house, not to mention Violette swatting Daniel over the head and leaving him in the street. Fellows would find Violette all right, then arrest her and her mother and turn them over to the magistrates.

No, Fellows must be kept clear of Daniel's problems. Daniel's uncle Mac would ask as many questions as Hart, and Cameron, Daniel's father, would as well. Cameron would be livid to learn anyone had hurt Daniel, and not be sympathetic to Mademoiselle Violette's plight.

The only member of the family who could be discretion itself was Ian—Ian never talked to anyone about anything if he could help it.

The trick with Uncle Ian was persuading him to be interested. Once Ian found a puzzle intriguing, nothing and no one could stop him solving it. On the other hand, if Ian decided he had no interest in the problem, it would cease to exist for him, and no amount of persuasion would convince him otherwise.

A risk, but one Daniel would take. He shouted to the coachman to drive him to Belgrave Square.

Chapter 6

The handsome house in which Daniel's uncle Ian, aunt Beth, and their three young children lived belonged to Beth. She'd inherited it in a trust from a woman for whom she'd been a companion, and the trust did not obligate her to hand the deed over to her husband.

Not that Ian cared one way or another—the man had little use for sumptuous houses or piles of money. Uncle Ian could fish for a week in the wilds of Scotland, sleeping on the ground rolled in his kilt. He'd be as content living in a hovel with his wife and wee ones as he was in this monstrosity of elegance.

"Afternoon, Ames," Daniel said to the stolid, middle-aged butler, who had replaced the butler Beth had inherited when she'd finally persuaded the elderly man to retire. "My uncle about?"

"Yes, sir. In the lower study, sir. I believe he's practicing . . . mathematics."

The butler intoned this as though relating that Ian was busy casting magic spells. But then, when Ian went at his maths problems, he might as well be doing magic for all anyone else understood. While Daniel used his love of mathematics to build things and tinker with the real world, Ian descended into a world of theory where only the sharpest minds could follow.

Disturbing Ian while he was working an equation . . . That was tricky.

Fortunately, Daniel had secret weapons at his disposal. He thanked Ames and went, not to the study, but up the stairs to the nursery.

He walked into the sunny room at the top of the house to find three children in the middle of lessons with their rather prudish governess, Miss Barnett. Hart had tried to engage Miss Barnett, one of the most sought-after governesses in England, for his own children, but the lady had preferred the quiet of Ian's house to the constant whirl of Hart's. Hart had gone into one of his ducal furies, but Ian, of course, had won the battle. Ian generally did.

Ian and Beth had three children: Jamie, the oldest, going on nine; Belle, between the ages of seven and eight; and Megan, about to turn six. They each had dark hair highlighted with red and fine blue eyes. They all were spoiled rotten by their father.

Ian was proud that his children had not turned out like him, with his strange focuses and difficulties. His children were normal, he'd boast. Beth argued with him about his definition of *normal*, but Ian was so pleased with his children that he won all those arguments too.

The governess was not happy that Daniel walked in without announcement or permission, but his three cousins were.

"Danny!" Megan hopped from her seat and ran at him, throwing her arms around his legs. "We haven't seen you in ages. Will you take me riding in your motorcar?"

"Me too," Jamie said. "I have to go if Megan does."

"When it's finished." Daniel lifted Megan, reflecting that the youngest of Ian's daughters grew every time he turned around. Beth would have something to say about Daniel taking her children out in the machine he was building, but he'd leave that discussion for later. "Now then, lad and lasses, how about a visit to your father?"

"Mr. Mackenzie," Miss Barnett broke in. "I really cannot have you interrupting lessons. Master Jamie will be entering school soon."

"And then he'll have more lessons than he can take." Daniel winked at Jamie. "Trust me, lad. Live while ye can." He turned his most winsome smile on Miss Barnett, along with the innocent look that had served him well when he'd been Jamie's age. "Surely you could spare them an hour to take tea to their poor papa?"

Miss Barnett's eyes narrowed, the lady not fooled. "*Half* an hour," she said. "And only because it is nearly time for their morning walk. They may give up part of that to visit with their father."

"Hooray!" Jamie wasted no time slapping his book closed and running out of the room.

Megan held on to Daniel as he carried her out, pleased to get away with a little truancy. Belle was the only one who looked unhappy, closing her books and stacking them with reluctance.

"Miss Barnett is right," Belle said as she caught up to them on the landing. "One should keep to a timetable, if one is to learn as much as one can and succeed in school."

"*One* should, should *one*?" Jamie said. "Ye sound like a bloody schoolmarm. I don't need to go off to school anyway. I'm going to be a jockey. Uncle Cameron says I have the gift for riding."

That was true. Daniel's father Cameron had mentioned time and again what a natural seat Jamie had, and that the lad could be a champion rider if he chose. Beth was not terribly delighted with this news, hoping her son would be more interested in pursuits of the mind than the dangerous sport of horse racing.

"Jockeying is not for the faint of heart," Daniel said. "Jockeys get hurt quite a lot, and sometimes can't race anymore after."

"I've fallen off horses lots of times," Jamie said, undaunted. "Big ones. Broke my arm once, remember?" He held up the appendage, which looked perfectly straight and whole now. "Mama was upset, but I'm resilient. Like you, Danny."

Daniel didn't answer. Ingratiating himself with Ian meant ingratiating himself with Beth, so any encouragement of Jamie to dangerous sport was out.

Belle broke in. "That's all very well for you, Jamie. But I have to study hard to go to university, because I'm a girl." Belle was the quiet Mackenzie who preferred reading over all other activity. Her dolls and toys were lined neatly on her shelves and rarely played with. She did ride horses, but only because others made her go out and exercise.

"Ye won't go to university," Jamie scoffed. "You'll get married. All girls do."

"I *won't*. I don't want a husband to tell me what to do all day. I'm going to be a doctor and cure people of dreadful diseases."

"Girls can't be doctors," Jamie said, though he sounded less certain.

"Yes, they can. Women go study in Edinburgh now, and in Switzerland."

"I know, but I bet *those* women are really smart."

Belle gave her brother a look of vast disgust, stuck her nose in the air, and swept past him. Megan hugged Daniel and said, "*I* want to get married when I grow up, and have lots of babies."

Megan liked babies. She was trying to persuade her mother to have more of them. A baby brother, Megan said, would be so much better than an older brother. Older brothers were *bossy*.

"I'm sure you will, pet," Daniel said. "A cute thing like you will have lots of men wanting to be your husband."

Even as he said it, Daniel felt a surge of protectiveness. Megan was a pretty child, and in ten or twelve years, gentlemen would be flocking around her. They had just better be the right ones and treat Megan as though she were a queen, or Daniel would have something to say about it.

Megan kissed Daniel's cheek. "I'll marry *you*, Danny. Aunt Isabella says it's common for cousins to marry."

"Nah," Jamie said. "If you breed horses too close to the bloodline, the foals start being weak or having something wrong with them. Same with people. We need fresh stock."

"Horses aren't the same as people," Megan said, confused.

Daniel bounced her in his arms. "A bit of advice, lass. Never say those words to your uncle Cameron. His horses and his children are all the same to him. Now then, let's be getting on with talking to your da. It's important."

The little procession went down the stairs, Jamie first, Daniel carrying Megan, and Belle bringing up the rear. Belle repeated stoutly that she *would* be a doctor and prove her brother was an idiot.

Daniel tapped on the study door before he opened it, but he knew Ian would have heard them coming. His offspring had not learned the lesson that children should be seen and not heard. Thank God.

Ian pushed aside his papers when the four came through the door, and rose to his feet. The three children cried, "Papa!" as though they hadn't seen him for months instead of the few hours since breakfast.

Megan, Belle, and Jamie ran at him with open arms. Ian swept up the younger two, sat down on his desk chair, and dragged a second chair over for Jamie, who now considered himself too grown up to sit on laps.

Ian Mackenzie, the youngest of the Duke of Kilmorgan's brothers, was a large man with auburn hair and whiskey-colored eyes. Those eyes could either hold keen intelligence or be as blank as a bleak moor, and could shift from one to the other as quickly as Ian could blink.

For now, Ian gazed at his children, meeting their eyes without worry. He connected fully with them, as he did with Beth, though much of the rest of the world was still somewhat remote for him. But Ian saw no reason to embrace the world when he could embrace his family instead.

Only when Ian had kissed his daughters' cheeks, ruffled his son's hair, and listened to them tell him incoherently about their lessons did he lift his head and deign to notice Daniel standing in wait. Ian gave Daniel a nod over the dark heads of his daughters.

"Hello, Uncle Ian." Daniel gave him a fond grin. "I wondered if you could help me find someone. A mother and daughter who disappeared in the night. I don't know their real names, or where they came from, whether they left London by train or coach, or whether they left at all. I need to find them, and I need to find them now. Do ye think you can help me?"

Ian considered the question slowly, as he did everything else, his gaze going remote while he contemplated.

He looked back at Daniel, a sharpness entering his eyes. "Why?"

Daniel shrugged. "I'm intrigued. You'd like the daughter, Ian. She can make machines, and I'd like her help making mine."

Ian watched Daniel in silence again, pinning Daniel with his gaze, something he rarely did with anyone but Beth and his children. Whatever thoughts ran behind those eyes, Ian gave no sign.

Finally Ian looked away then back down at Megan, kissing the top of her head. He glanced back at Daniel, but didn't focus on him again.

"Yes," Ian said.

Chapter 7

"Why do I have to be the countess?" Celine asked, pushing out her lower lip. "I still do not understand why you insisted we leave London, Violet. I'm not well."

"I know, Mama. I'm sorry."

Violet gazed out the window of their small boardinghouse flat, two floors above the street. Flaking plaster, exposed walls, and crooked shutters looked picturesque in this French seaside town, but the reality was cold and damp rooms with wind coming through cracks around the windows.

Though many people wintered in the cities of southern France, good for Violet's trade, they did not come because it was terribly warm. About ten degrees warmer than England, yes, but hardly the tropics. Warmth was found farther south, in Italy and the Greek isles beyond.

"I liked being Madame Bastien," her mother continued. "Madame Bastien was kind and helpful. The countess is such a haughty woman. Cool and distant. And the turban makes my head ache."

"You do not have to wear the turban if you don't want to."

Violet drew her shawl closer about her shoulders and turned from the windows.

Her mother sat in the warmest chair in the house, pulled next to the white porcelain stove. A knitted shawl wrapped her upper body, and she'd laid another over her knees. It was true that Celine easily took sick, and also that she must keep warm and well, because she was the real draw of their show.

"Why do I have to be the countess at all?" Celine asked fretfully. "It is difficult to remember to speak with a Russian accent all the time. They don't come to see me because I'm a countess, or Russian, or whatever you're having me be this time. They come for my gift."

"I know," Violet said.

Her mother was amazing. Her trances were real, Celine having no memory of what went on in most of them. She'd speak in a variety of voices, from the child who was her spirit guide, to men and women from all walks of life and all nationalities. Violet had never been able to decide whether the spirits truly spoke through her mother or whether she was simply an extremely gifted mimic. All in all, people came to see Celine perform, and even the most skeptical left entranced by her.

"Then why the costumes?" Celine asked.

"To attract punters," Violet explained patiently. "They've not heard of us here. Once they're inside the theatre, *then* they understand why you are special, and they'll tell everyone they know. But we have to have a hook to make them come in the first place."

"Jacobi always used to say that," Celine said. "Tiresome man."

"He was right." Whatever Violet thought of Jacobi now, he had understood the importance of showmanship. "You must admit that we did very, very well in London as the Bastiens, the frail mother and her daughter, her guide."

"The guide part is real, you know. I rely on you, dear Violet."

Her mother did. Any thought that Violet would leave her—to travel, to be a wife, to do anything—was met with terror and weeping. Celine needed her Violet. How could she survive otherwise?

But while Celine was a slave to her weak health and her

gift, she could also be keen-minded and strong as an ox when she wanted something.

"I still don't understand why we had to leave London," Celine said again. "We'd have found a way to come up with the rent. We had another performance at the end of the week."

Violet didn't answer. Neither she nor Mary had told Celine what had happened with Daniel Mackenzie, or the true reason they'd fled in the night.

Violet hadn't seen any mention of Mr. Mackenzie in the newspapers here, but the French papers didn't always take much notice of what went on in England. The few English newspapers she'd glimpsed had not screamed out about his death. For the most part, though, Violet was avoiding English newspapers, to preserve the fiction that she and Celine spoke little English. Even here, inside the boardinghouse, they spoke only French.

The story for the stage Violet had wrought was that Celine—now Countess Melikova, a widow—had been forced to flee Russia when her gift for clairvoyance was deemed too dangerous. She'd left the splendor of her late husband's manor house for a peripatetic existence in France, Germany, Italy, and Switzerland, giving readings and séances for coin.

Violet was now Princess Ivanova, the countess's deceased best friend's daughter. Princess Ivanova had left a string of broken hearts behind her from Saint Petersburg to Budapest, and had been forced out of Russia because four men had fought to the death over her. She'd been told never to return. The princess and the countess had agreed to travel and live together, and here they were.

Violet and her mother had used the personas once before, in Italy, where they had worked well—at least, until the winter had turned unusually bitter, sending tourists home. Violet and her mother had moved to a milder climate then and transformed themselves into Romany women.

Violet turned to the window again to avoid her mother's continuing questions about why they'd left London. Violet had relived the dreadful moment in the dining room of the London townhouse again and again—her fear clearing to reveal Daniel giving her a look of confusion before he fell to the floor.

He alone of the gentlemen that night had been kind to her. He'd discovered Violet's secrets, but instead of being outraged and exposing her, he'd laughed and been interested.

And the kisses . . . Violet remembered the smoke on Daniel's breath, the touch of his lips. His gentle kiss in the upstairs room had awakened fires in her—fires, not fear. For the first time in her life, Violet had kissed a man without terror.

Why, why then had she struck him when he'd tried again in the dining room? She wished she could be transported back to that moment, wished she could change her split-second decision. In the new scenario, her hand would never have landed on the vase, and she'd not have swung it, not seen his blood . . .

Violet had left him on a doorstep like unwanted trash. A man, a human being, and Violet had left him alone, ready pickings for any thief.

The kind doctor or a constable must have found him, Violet told herself once again. Found Daniel, found out who he was, sent him home to his family.

Violet's breath caught on a sob. She didn't want him to be dead. She wanted that night back, to slow down with him and get to know him, to hear his warm laughter one more time.

The police would be investigating what had happened. They'd learn that Mr. Mackenzie had been to the house Violet and her mother rented. Violet had been right to flee, or else she, Celine, and Mary might be in a prison cell right now.

As always, Violet had done what she'd had to do. She couldn't take it back, and she had to move on. She and her mother would perform, they'd count the takings, and they'd survive. That was Violet's life.

Her tedious, empty life.

Marseille.

Daniel stared down at the note he received from Ian a few days after he'd sought his uncle's help. The thick sheet of writing paper bore the one word in careful script, nothing more.

"Could you be more specific?" Daniel said to the air.

"Sir?" Simon appeared from the back parlor, which held two-thirds of a motorcar and not much else. He'd been helping

Daniel reseat the pistons. Daniel had wiped his hands and come out to answer the door, finding a delivery boy with the note.

"Never mind," Daniel said to Simon. "My uncle Ian can be so very cryptic. If he says they're in Marseille, they're in Marseille. Fancy a trip to the south of France, Simon?"

Simon looked doubtful. "Never been, sir."

"Your chance to go now. I need to send off some telegrams. Kill a few birds with one stone."

Simon didn't answer, having, in the last few days, come to realize that Daniel talked a mile a minute in several different directions and didn't always expect a reply.

Even as Daniel readied himself to go, looking regretfully at the motorcar before shutting the parlor door, he wondered why he should bother. Violette's volatile reaction to his kisses meant she wanted nothing to do with him. The fact that she or someone in her household had carried him out and left him on the street reinforced that fact.

Then came the memory of Violette in the curve of Daniel's arm, her lips puckering around the black cigarette. He hadn't been able to resist the temptation of her red mouth. She'd tasted of honey, smoke, and desire. One sip of her had made Daniel want more, and more.

In the dining room, Daniel had wanted to kiss her again, then lift her to the table, pull their clothing aside, and lose himself inside her. Something in his heart had craved her, and it craved her still.

Who was Violette Bastien, and where the devil was she?

Marseille, Ian's note said. "Pack me some clean shirts, Simon," Daniel called, folding the note and tucking it into his pocket. "When I get back from the telegraph office, we're off to France."

~~~~~

The concert hall was nearly full. Violet liked to see bodies in every seat, because theatre owners sometimes demanded a larger percentage of the take if they didn't fill the hall. But it wasn't bad tonight. Theirs was a new show, and the bored expatriates and wealthy French of Marseille wanted novelty.

The lights went down and the curtain opened on their

simple tableau. Violet's mother sat on a curved rococo-revival chair, her back straight, the train of her old-fashioned black bombazine gown trickling to the floor. At the last minute, she'd declared she would wear the turban after all, and its shimmering brocade shone against her graying black hair.

Next to Celine was a table holding an empty glass and a pitcher of water, and Violet was walking to the table as the curtain opened. Violet had dressed in a fashionable dove gray gown, covering her face with a sheer black veil that hung to her waist. In addition, she'd donned a blond wig so that wisps of pale hair occasionally curled below the veil. The wig itched a bit, but the fine, fair hair completed the illusion.

In the advertising for the show—and the word of mouth Mary had begun—it was hinted that Violet must keep her face hidden, because one glimpse of her incredible beauty drove even the calmest gentleman insane. Violet was highly aware of the men in the first two rows contorting themselves to try to look under her veil.

The chandeliers above the audience had been dimmed, and gaslights glowed at the edge of the stage, illuminating Violet and her mother. The smell of packed bodies, wool, and perfume rose like a wall in front of them.

Violet poured her mother a glass of water, keeping her movements graceful, then she looked out at the audience and said, "The countess will open the paths to the spirit world. She must use all her concentration to do this, and so you will confine your questions to me. I will listen to your petitions and decide who she has the greatest chance to reach."

Violet scanned the audience as she spoke, dividing them into categories—true believers, watchful skeptics, and those who'd come here to be entertained. As usual, only a few hands went up at first, one or two hopeful, one or two from gentlemen obviously out to catch Violet and her mother in a trick.

Violet nodded at one of the hopefuls, a middle-aged woman in black. Violet held up her hand before the woman had spoken more than a few words. "It is difficult, I know," Violet said, twisting her French to sound as though someone from Saint Petersburg spoke it. "He went too soon, long before his time. In battle, was it?"

The woman nodded, looking surprised. Poor thing. Violet had seen the lady's bleak expression, coupled with the lock of hair in a brooch on her chest next to an insignia denoting an officer in the French army. She'd lost a son in some colonial war, either in Africa or Asia.

"He was so very far away," Violet said. "I am sorry."

The woman's face crumpled, and Violet's heart ached for her. There were those who claimed Violet and her mother played upon the grieving to take their money, and Violet didn't always disagree, but at the same time, she knew that what she and her mother did brought some comfort. This woman, for instance, wanted to make certain her son was all right. He likely had died in much pain, in a distant land, and his mother hadn't been able to hold his hand when he went. Mothers who had lost sons or daughters had the most haunted looks of all.

Not natural, Violet thought with anger. Mothers shouldn't lose their children. She thought about Daniel, and pictured the bleak look in his father's eyes when the news was brought to him.

Violet forced herself to turn from the edge of the stage and continue. "Countess?"

"Yes." Celine lifted a handkerchief to dab away real tears of sympathy. "I will find him."

The hall went quiet. Celine closed her eyes, rested her hands on her lap, and went into her trance.

Violet watched her closely, ready to assist at any sign of illness or faintness. Sometimes her mother could render herself unconscious—once, she'd fallen from her chair and struck her head before Violet could catch her, and had bled profusely.

"The veil," her mother murmured, her breath coming rapidly. "It is parting. I see light, I see . . . ah."

Celine trailed off. When she spoke again, her voice took on a high-pitched, childlike tone—her spirit guide, Adelaide, a Parisian child of ten. "Do not worry, Madame. I will find him. He is here, and so lonely."

The mother's cry rang out from the audience. The young woman sitting next to her—a stranger from the way she'd kept herself as distant as the seats allowed—now patted the woman's arm comfortingly.

Celine spoke again. This time, her voice was deep, the Russian accent gone, her French flawless, but provincial. From the coast, in a town not far from here, Violet guessed.

"*Maman*, are you there?"

The woman sprang to her feet, handkerchief clutched to her breast. "Jules? Jules, is it you?"

Celine remained silent until Violet turned and said to Celine in her halting accent, "She wishes to know whether this is her son."

"*Maman*," came the answer in relief, spoken through Celine's mouth. "I am here, *Maman*. Do not cry, I beg of you."

"You are all right? She said you were lonely."

Violet conveyed the question, and Celine answered. "Lonely for you, *Maman*. I am worried for you, now that you are alone."

"I am fine. Really, my darling. I have my friends, and they care for me. But what about you? I can't bear thinking of you, lying alone . . ."

"The form in the grave is but clay. I have left it far behind and crossed over. Papa is here, and little . . . little . . ."

"Brigitte? Brigitte is with you?"

The hope in the woman's voice broke Violet's heart. Celine, she knew, would firmly believe she spoke to the dead soldier called Jules, but Celine was also using the trick—whether consciously or not—of getting the client to supply information they didn't have.

"Yes, Brigitte is here. She misses you."

"And I miss her. Tell her that her *maman* misses her so much. And you, Jules. But you are happy, that is good. One day we will all be together."

Statements like this always worried Violet, but the woman looked healthy and possibly was too staunch a Catholic to contemplate suicide. She also looked very relieved to learn that her family was all together in the afterlife. If they were taking care of one another, she wouldn't have to worry about them.

"I must go, *Maman*. The veil is thin. You have my love . . . my love." The voice drifted away, and the childlike voice returned. "He has gone."

The woman sat down, tears on her face. The young woman next to her, less of a stranger now, put her arm around the woman's shoulders.

The crowd was more eager now to petition Celine to contact those dear to them. Violet sifted through the requests, granting one to a man who needed to apologize to his sister, another to a scared-looking young woman who asked her mother whether she should stay with her stepfather who beat her. The first man's sister accepted the apology with gracefulness. The second woman's mother, when contacted, agreed that the stepfather had always been a brute, and the young woman was not obligated to live with him.

The audience grew more excited, happier with every person able to speak to their loved ones and learn answers.

They needed this, Violet had realized long ago. Religious leaders or social rules could not let some people find comfort or relieve guilt, and so they came to Violet's mother, who gave them what they sought. Celine congratulated herself on her gift, and Violet had long ago decided to go along with it. Violet might not believe, but her mother did, and so did all these people. If Celine could relieve their pain, who was Violet to stand in the way?

Remain detached, Jacobi had always said. *You are the messenger, the conduit, not their mentor or friend.*

Well, Jacobi had known all about detachment, hadn't he?

Violet shivered. She gave the signal for Mary to let down the rigging high above the stage, which they'd set into place beforehand. Violet always prepared little phosphorus-coated balls to dance on strings above her mother or above the seats if the proceedings lagged a bit. She didn't need to as much tonight, but the tangible evidence of the "veil" never ceased to delight.

As Mary let down the cascade of balls on their wires, heads swiveled upward, people pointed, and some even applauded. The questions had died down, but now a new voice broke through, in English, but with the accent of the Highland Scots.

"So, tell me, Mademoiselle," the man said, his words tinged with a hint of laughter. "Do ye believe in ghosts?"

Chapter 8

Daniel Mackenzie stood on the floor just below the stage, upright, whole, and definitely not dead.

His gaze pinned Violet into place, and though he didn't smile, the twinkle in his dark amber eyes held impudence. He wore a suit similar to the one he'd had on the night she'd met him—black coat, ivory waistcoat, Mackenzie plaid kilt. His hair was neatly combed, his face newly shaved, his gloves in place. Violet couldn't help thinking he'd looked better disheveled, with his hair sticking out and his strong hands uncovered.

Violet realized several frozen heartbeats of silence had gone by, and the audience, Daniel, and her mother awaited her answer.

Her returning breath nearly choked her. "When the veil parts," she said hoarsely, remembering at the last moment to speak French with a Russian accent, "all manner of things may come through."

The audience murmured their agreement. Daniel regarded Violet with eyes full of mischief, the sparkle in them rivaling the brightest of the glowing balls above them.

"Ye don't say. I couldn't ask a question of me dear old mum, could I? Gone these twenty-four years or so?"

Violet kept staring at him. What was he doing? Daniel had gone hard with anger when Mortimer had suggested she contact his mother in front of the gentlemen in the London house. What was he up to now?

She needed to turn away from him and move on to the next petitioner. But her tongue cleaved to the roof of her mouth, and she couldn't make her feet move.

The audience started applauding, taking up a chant of "*Oui, oui.*" Over this, Celine, in the voice of the child Adelaide, interrupted. "She is here, Monsieur. She has been waiting for you."

Daniel's back was to the audience, and he didn't hide his amusement when he flicked his gaze to Violet's mother. "Is she, now? That's interesting."

Celine's voice changed pitch again, sounding more contralto, with rich, velvet tones. "I am so sorry, my son," she said in perfect English. "I did not know my own mind. I never meant to hurt you."

Daniel's smile didn't waver. "That's all right, Mum. Don't you worry about it, now."

Celine breathed a soft sigh. "Thank you."

The audience sighed with her.

Daniel winked up at Violet, then he patted the edge of the stage, turned from it, and strolled away, his kilt moving over his backside. Violet watched him as he made his way to an empty chair in the rear of the theatre, speaking congenially to the others in the row until he settled into his seat.

He wasn't going to leave. He would sit there for the entire show.

And then what? Denounce her? Tell the audience that the countess and princess were confidence tricksters, newly come from London?

Daniel folded his arms, watching Violet, his grin in place. Her mother's contact with *his* mother had not impressed him one whit. Violet forced herself to turn away, but her body was shaking, and she could barely stammer an answer to the next person.

Daniel remained in the back row as the performance went on—they were contracted for the full two hours. At any moment, Violet expected Daniel to stand up and declare the whole night to be nothing but flummery, that the audience should demand their money back and never trust Violet and those like her again. He'd tell them what Violet had done to him in London, and that he'd come here with magistrates to cart her off to prison.

But Daniel only watched as Violet talked to petitioners until her throat was dry, her ability to evaluate them evaporating. Fortunately Celine, who noticed nothing wrong, went on speaking to the spirits and conveying what the loved ones wanted to hear.

Violet was exhausted by the time Celine finally drooped back in her chair, her hands falling limp at her sides. "I can do no more," Celine said in a tired whisper.

The gaslights on the stage flared up once, hissed, and went out. Mary was good at cues.

The audience burst into wild applause. There were cries of thanks, shouts for an encore. Violet signaled for Mary to pull the curtain closed, hiding her mother. Then Violet stepped out in front of the red velvet, her legs shaking.

She immediately looked to the back right of the house, where Daniel had been sitting. But that row was mostly empty, Daniel gone. Maybe he'd been a ghost after all, come to stir her guilty conscience.

The audience started to quiet, waiting expectantly. Violet raised her hands and launched into her rehearsed speech. "Please, the countess has given all she has. She is spent for the night, but she will reappear here on Saturday, after she has rested and meditated. If you wish a private consultation, you must write to the address on the card her maid will hand to you as you leave. I thank you for coming, and the countess thanks you." Violet jerked around to look through the crack in the curtain, as though someone had called her. "What . . .?" She whirled to face the audience again, her veils trembling. "The countess. Please, you must go. I must . . ."

Violet broke off and scurried back through the curtains. The stage behind them was empty, Mary having long since escorted Celine away.

Violet paused to catch her breath as the fold of velvet dropped closed behind her. Dizzy and dry mouthed, she caught up the half-full pitcher of water, thrust her annoying veils aside, and drank a long draught.

Mr. Mackenzie was alive, and here, unless Violet, in her overwrought state, had dreamed him. Perhaps she'd played so long at spirits that she'd started to believe she truly could see the dead.

Tommyrot. He was alive.

How the devil had he found her? Violet had bought train and boat tickets under a false name, had taken the rooms to let here under still another name, neither of which were Bastien or their personas of the countess and princess. At the boarding-house, she and her mother were plain Madame and Mademoiselle Perrault, from Rouen, with a maid. Mary kept her own first name, pronouncing it *Marie*, but no one paid much attention to maids, many of whom were called Marie, regardless.

How did Daniel discover that Violette Bastien and Princess Ivanova were one and the same? Daniel had not seen Celine at the London house, and Violet was always careful to never have their likenesses printed anywhere. Concealing herself behind her black tulle veil had obviously made no difference.

Had Daniel truly come here to have them arrested? Or perhaps to blackmail Violet for his silence? He could not have come to Marseille for any benevolent reason—for that he'd have stayed in England and left her in peace.

Violet wanted to rush to the dressing room, grab her mother and Mary, and run again. Somewhere, *anywhere.* Maybe to Russia in truth, a place they'd never been.

She made herself swallow a little more water and calmly walk to the theatre manager's office to secure the takings. She'd learned to collect the money right away, after one unscrupulous manager had disappeared with all the cash one night. Violet counted the money, gave the manager his cut, then stashed their share inside her corset and hurried down the hall to the dressing room at its end.

Celine was there in a soft armchair, truly exhausted. She rubbed her bare forehead. "I should not have worn the turban. The blasted thing is so heavy."

Her South London accent crept into her English for a moment before she heaved another sigh and reverted to cultured French. "Please, may we go home, Violet? I have such a headache."

"Of course, Mama. You and Mary go in the carriage. I'll change my clothes and walk home. It's not far, and it's still early." And if Daniel lingered with constables to arrest Violet for assaulting him, her mother might have a chance to get away.

"You are so good to me." Those words came often out of Celine's mouth, in her weary tone, but Violet knew she meant them.

Violet gave Mary the takings to lock away at the boardinghouse. She wasn't fool enough to walk down the street, even in this fairly safe part of town, with thousands of francs inside her bodice. And if constables were coming, her mother would have the money.

But no one waited to pounce on them outside the stage door. Violet made sure Celine and Mary were safely away in the hired carriage, with no one following them, before she returned to the quiet dressing room, breathing a little more easily. She changed out of her costume, packed their things, including the turban, into a valise, and slipped out the stage door again.

Violet walked down the narrow lane behind the theatre toward the main street, her head down. She now wore a workingwoman's garb of plain skirt, shirtwaist, and coat, with a flat hat pinned over her simple knot of hair. She might be a typist or a telegraph worker hurrying home after a long, tiring day.

Before she reached the street, a hand landed on her shoulder, and Daniel Mackenzie pulled her back into the shadows of the passage.

*

Daniel had never seen a woman look so terrified. Violette Bastien stared up at Daniel with dark blue eyes wide with fear. Wariness lurked behind the fear, like that of an animal who has been repeatedly kicked.

Daniel softened his grip on her shoulder. "Easy, lass. I'm not going to hurt you."

"Then what the devil are you doing here?" Gone was the French with the Russian tinge, gone was the French itself, even the faintest accent she'd had in London. She sounded English through and through, and not well-bred English. London, south of the river, if he were to guess.

"Ah, Mr. Mackenzie," Daniel said in a mocking tone. "How good to see you again. And that you're unhurt after I whacked you over the head with my finest vase." He rubbed his temple. "What was the damned thing made of, eh? Granite?"

"I'm sorry," Violette said stiffly. "I never meant to hurt you." They stood in deep shadows, but her pupils were pinpricks of shock. "You frightened me."

"That was obvious. I remember you not minding me kissing you in your upstairs room. Not so downstairs. Or did you change your mind when your maid hit me with that sandbag of a bolster?"

"I never meant to hurt you." The words softened as she repeated them. Violette lifted her hand as though to touch the still-closing wound on Daniel's temple, but she stopped herself. "I swear to you."

"It's all right; ye only stunned me senseless. I've had ladies slap me before, but never with such vigor."

Violette took a step back, letting out a heavy breath, some of the paralytic fear leaving her. "Well, you had no business kissing me like that. I'm not a doxy."

"You're right, lass. No business at all." Daniel moved to her again. "But we were alone, it was night, and finding a woman who understood engineering excited me. It was your genius with the machines that did it. I tried to behave well, but once I'd seen your wind machine, I couldn't resist stealing another kiss from you."

The frozen terror eased further from her eyes at this speech, Daniel was glad to see, but the wariness remained. "You were after more than kisses, Mr. Mackenzie."

"Aye, I don't deny that." Daniel ran his gaze over Violette's body, not well hidden under the formfitting coat and cotton blouse. She still took his breath away.

Finding her, the triumph of it, beat through him. He wanted

to catch her in his arms, push her back against the dirty bricks of the theatre, and find his relief with her.

"You are a beautiful woman," he said, making himself stay in place. "Says so on your poster, doesn't it? *A beauty that drives sane men to madness, gentle men to duels.* That's brilliant, is that. I bet the punters come flocking."

Violette gave him a sharp look. "You are mocking me, Mr. Mackenzie."

"I am indeed." Daniel stepped beside her and held out his arm in his tailored coat. "Let me escort you home, Mademoiselle Bastien, if that is your name. Even if it isn't your name, I'm pleased to escort you anyway. There might be ruffians about."

"This is a respectable part of town." Violette's chin came up. "The only ruffian in it is you."

Daniel burst out laughing. "A shot to the heart, but accurate, lass. Dead accurate. Still, even respectable gentlemen might lose their minds when they come face-to-face with the stunning beauty of Princess Ivanova."

Daniel kept his arm out, expecting her at any moment to turn and run, or at least look about for something else to hit him with before she went. Then he'd have to follow her, because damned if he'd let the woman he'd tracked halfway across the Continent slip from his grasp again. He'd found her, and he was keeping her.

Daniel hid his jolt of glee when she slid her fingers under the crook of his arm. "Very well. But only because it is darker out here than I thought."

Got her, Daniel's mind sang as they turned together out to the main street.

Ian's direction of *Marseille* had brought Daniel here, and almost immediately he'd seen the advertisement that the clairvoyant Countess Melikova and her assistant, Princess Ivanova, the deadly beauty, would speak to an audience at a concert hall.

Walking in late to the performance, Daniel had beheld on the stage a middle-aged woman in black with a gold brocade turban, and the upright form of Violette, wearing a long black veil that concealed her face and hair. But he'd known she was Violette. He'd recognize that enticing body and sensual voice anywhere, didn't matter how much she hid her face or what accent she put on.

"The bit of hair you let us glimpse behind the veil was blond." Daniel touched a dark curl that fell over Violet's cheek. "Clever. If smitten gentlemen waited for you at the back door, they'd strain their eyes for a woman with flaxen hair. Only I was on the lookout for the real Violette Bastien." He winked at her. "Except that Mademoiselle Bastien doesn't exist either, does she? Is the *Violette* real? Or were you christened with another name?"

"It's Violet," she said in a firm voice.

"No surname?"

"It was a long time ago."

"Hmm." Daniel drew her a little closer. They walked slowly down the street like any courting couple, avoiding carriages with clopping horses and the little steaming piles that the clopping horses left behind.

Plenty of people strolled about—friends arm in arm, couples, businessmen walking from clubs back home to their families. None paid any attention to Daniel and Violet, except for a glance at Daniel's Mackenzie plaid kilt. Daniel was the exotic creature on the street at the moment, not Violet.

"I commend you and your mother on your performance," he said. "Well done. The phosphor-luminescent balls were a nice touch."

Violet shrugged. "People expect to see tangible evidence of the ether."

"No machines tonight?"

"My mother doesn't need them as much as I do. I don't have her gift."

"Gift," Daniel repeated, remembering the performance. "Aye, she has quite a good one. She's masterful at telling people what they wish to hear."

"Do not be so quick to dismiss her, please. She is always spot-on, and not only using what I tell her. What about what your own mother said to you through her? My mother was right, wasn't she? And I told her nothing. I didn't know you would be here—I thought you were . . ." Violet faltered, her fingers tightening on his arm.

"Deceased?" Daniel supplied. "Departed? Shuffled off this mortal coil?"

"Yes."

Daniel heard the catch in her voice, and he took heart. "Poor lass. No wonder you ran from England."

Violet loosened her grip again. "But my mother was right, wasn't she? About your mother?"

Daniel shrugged. "Near enough."

"Well, there you are, then."

Daniel couldn't stop his laughter. "Violet, sweet love, the gossip about my family and my crazy mum is common knowledge. Everyone who hears my name knows my mother tried to off me with a knife when I was a tiny babe, before my dad threw me out of the way and stopped her. Then Lady Elizabeth Mackenzie was dead. Did she kill herself, or did her husband, Lord Cameron, do it? People have speculated for years. Now, if your mum had given the correct answer to that riddle, *then* I would have been impressed. Only my dad knows the truth."

"You're saying my mother's a fraud," Violet said stiffly.

"A very good one. So are you, love. The best ones always get away with it."

Violet gave him a haughty look. "We have been questioned before. Put through rigorous tests by other mediums, not to mention scientists and priests. We've passed every time."

"As I said, the best ones always get away with it." Daniel put his warm hand over hers. "Now, did you bring your machinery with you? And would you let me have a look at it? I was interrupted before I could examine it to my heart's content last time, by being nearly done in."

"That's why you've come to Marseille, is it? For my machines?"

He enjoyed the dry skepticism in her voice. "Certainly. That, and I like Marseille. So much history—you know it was once a Greek colony? Then the Romans obligingly left us plenty of ruins to wander through, and there's the Château d'If, where Dumas imprisoned poor Monte Cristo. One of my favorite novels as a boy was the *Count*. Have you been out to see the prison close to? It's chilling."

Violet stopped, skirts swinging. A man in a bowler hat pushed past them, growling a little. "Stop playing with me, Mr. Mackenzie. You came here to find me so you could drag me to the magistrates."

Daniel made a show of looking around them. "Do you see me dragging you anywhere? We're walking calmly through a reasonably thin crowd, and I'm escorting you home."

"And once you get me there, and your hands on my machines—*then* you will send for the magistrates. You think me a fraud, an imposter. And I assaulted you . . ."

"Your crimes, they keep increasing, don't they? If I'd wanted the magistrates on you, lass, I'd have contacted my uncle the police inspector, who would have contacted his colleagues in the French police, who would have had you and your mum arrested and locked away long before I arrived. Then I would have strolled in, rifled through your gadgets, and taken what I wanted."

Violet's widening eyes started to fill with fear again. "Then I don't understand. If you didn't find me to arrest me, why did you come?"

"To see you again." *To feast my eyes on you.* Daniel tucked the lock of hair on her cheek behind her ear. His gloved hands didn't let him contact her skin directly, but the heat of her came through the thin leather. "To look at you." *To dream about having you.* "And to ask you why the devil you hit me over the head."

"I told you. You frightened me."

"There's much more to it than that, I wager. You're not a lass who frightens easily. You stood up to Mortimer and his mates and were disgusted by the lot of them. Me, the one gent that night who would never have harmed you, you looked at in terror before you reached out for the nearest weapon. I'm going to find out why." Daniel traced her cheek one more time then pulled her back into walking. "You might as well trust me."

"I don't trust anyone."

"That's obvious. But you're going to learn to trust *me*."

Daniel felt Violet's trembling, and he also felt her draw herself up, trying to master herself. "You are arrogant," she said.

"That's true, but is that the best you can do? I've been called far worse than that."

"All right, then you are an insufferable, full-of-yourself, aristocratic prig."

She kept her eyes straight ahead, a flush on her cheek making him want to kiss it. He settled for laughing again. "Not bad. But still not the best you can do. You, Mademoiselle, are a deceitful, cunning minx and a very talented liar. I heard you pinpoint every person's greatest desires in that concert hall. You made them tell you everything you needed to know."

Her flush deepened. "It's part of the show."

"It's a rare skill, and one you exploit to amazing lengths. I'd love to know how you do it."

Violet glanced up at him, the wariness back in her eyes. She might be deceitful, but she wasn't sly. She was deceitful out of necessity, not enjoyment.

Daniel wanted to find out all about her, and not only because he was curious. Since the age of fifteen and his first tumble with a lass, Daniel hadn't been short of female company. Women were his for the taking, whenever he reached out his hand. His uncle Mac laughed that Daniel was carrying on the Mackenzie family tradition. Women wanted the Mackenzie men—that was easy. In matters of the heart, however, the Mackenzies fought long and hard battles.

So Daniel was beginning to understand. Violet was different from his previous lovers, and not only because she was a few years older than Daniel or any more or less respectable than his usual sort of woman. Violet Bastien—or whatever her name was—was different because she was Violet.

Since he'd seen her standing in the dining room of her London house, girding herself to face Mortimer and his friends, Daniel had wanted her. Even now, he wanted to carry her off to his hotel, peel back her plain and sensible clothes, and discover the lush woman beneath. He wanted her in his bed, to scent her ready for him, to taste her skin and mouth, to feel her around him.

Daniel craved her, and he would have her before he left France.

The boardinghouse they reached was clean, neatly painted,

and respectable. Lights glowed in the upstairs rooms as well as in the downstairs parlors. "Thank you," Violet said, stopping. "I'll go in alone."

"Right you are." Daniel released her and tipped his hat. "Good night, Miss Bastien. I'll keep calling you that until I learn another name."

Violet gave him a nod, her face softening. "Good night, Mr. Mackenzie. I truly am glad you are well."

"Glad because I won't come down upon you with the full extent of the law? You're lucky I've got so much kindness in my heart."

Violet's glare returned with his teasing. "I *am* glad, for your sake. But you may think what you like. Good night."

She spun away and made for the door to the boardinghouse, her head high. Her skirts swayed enticingly across her hips, her upright stride a joy to watch.

Violet didn't look back at Daniel as she opened the door to the boardinghouse with a little jerk and walked inside.

She was good. She was very, very good. Daniel smiled at the closed door, tipped his hat again, and walked on down the street as though satisfied.

When he came to a narrow passage between houses on the opposite side of the street, he stepped into the shadows, drew out a cigarette, lit it, fixed his gaze on the boardinghouse, and waited.

Ten minutes, he gave her. Enough time for Daniel to make it to a main thoroughfare and hire a carriage to take him to his hotel.

After ten minutes had gone by, Daniel dropped the spent cigarette and ground it out under his boot heel. At the same time, Violet walked out of the boardinghouse again. She looked up and down the street, scanning every shadow, before she started walking back the way they'd come.

Clever lass.

Too bad for her that Daniel knew this city so well. As a boy, he'd managed more than once to follow his father to the Riviera, despite Cameron's efforts to leave his son behind. Daniel had learned how to coerce others to get him to the Continent, and when he was a little older, to buy his own

tickets and come himself. He'd spent many an evening sur-
reptitiously following his father around Marseille, hurt
because his dad would rather take up with fancy women than
sightsee with his son. Therefore, Daniel knew exactly how to
weave through the streets to reach the main avenue before
Violet did. Again, he ducked into a doorway and waited.

She turned onto the street, walking briskly, determination
in her stride. When Violet reached the doorway where Daniel
hid, he stepped out in front of her.

"Now then, Mademoiselle," he said, grinning at her. "How
about we walk to where you really live?"

Chapter 9

He'd drive her mad. Violet's heart thudded as she stared at Daniel, with his captivating smile, his warm eyes, and his uncanny ability to predict her every move.

Never let anyone know all about you, Jacobi had stressed. *A person who knows your secrets has a powerful hold over you. If you never let yourself be known, you will always be free.*

Daniel was so tall. He stood, unmoving, not about to let her walk around him. Or he might, then catch her with his strong arm and pull her back again.

Violet wet her dry lips. "Why must you know? Surely it makes no difference whether I stay in this boardinghouse or that boardinghouse . . ."

"It makes a difference to you," Daniel said. "Your key will work only in the right door, for one. And you'd keep all your things in one place, wouldn't you? Unless you have a network of rooms all over the city. That is handy, I admit. I often keep several places at once for stashing things."

She tried to put on a lofty look. "Why do you care, Mr. Mackenzie?"

"Because you do. And because I want you to get home

safe. Now, come on." He held out his arm. "If we debate in the street, that nice policeman over there will come and tell us to move on, or maybe arrest us for breaking the peace. And the police would be sticklers about finding out your name, your nationality, where you come from, why you're here. Safer to walk home with me, isn't it?"

Daniel held out his arm, so polite, so gentlemanly, but behind the courteous gesture was a man of ruthless intent. He wanted to know all about her, and by God, he was going to find out.

Violet made a noise of exasperation, turned from his extended hand, and started striding back the way she'd come.

Daniel easily fell into step with her, strong fingers coming around her arm. "So, did you bring it with you?" he asked.

"Bring what?"

"The wind machine. I want to borrow it."

He was too close to her. Violet easily smelled the scents that clung to him—smoke, the remnants of whiskey, the musk of himself under his wool coat. The scents made her remember how he'd leaned to her in the upstairs room in London, how he'd tasted her mouth, how he'd stunned her with the brief, warm press of lips.

"Borrow it why?" she managed to ask.

"Because I'm working on something, and I want to see if it will help me. Or give me a clue as to what would. If you don't want to let the thing out of your hands, you can come with it."

"Come with it where?"

"Little town about twenty miles from here, down the coast. Have a friend who will let me use his workshop. How about it? Tomorrow?"

The man was maddening. Violet was curious now as to *what* he was building, and how he just happened to have a friend with a workshop twenty miles down the coast from where Violet was staying. Did he know that the workings of engines and devices fascinated her? How exactly to entice her?

Not being able to read him was a terrible disadvantage. When Daniel spoke of machinery, his eyes lost their predatory look, and his focus changed. That he was interested in her wind machine was plain. And he was right that she didn't want to let it out of her sight, because it had been expensive to build, and she'd tinkered with it until it did exactly what she wanted.

"I can't," Violet said flatly as she strode along. She tried to set a swift pace so he'd grow bored and go away, but Daniel walked along beside her without even breathing hard. "I signed a contract with the concert hall. I have performances to do."

"Not tomorrow, you don't. I heard you tell the audience Saturday. Tomorrow is Tuesday. Plenty of time."

"My mother needs me for her private consultations. The machine is handy then."

Daniel shrugged, walking close enough to her that she felt the movement. "Make all the consultations for later in the week. I'm right that you handle all the appointments, aren't I? She'd welcome the rest, I'd wager."

"Blast you." Violet clenched both hands now. She wanted to go with him, to see what he was building, to find out what on earth he needed her wind machine for.

But how gullible was she? If Violet went somewhere with this man alone, he could take her anywhere, do anything to her, and Violet could do nothing about it. She was as helpless with him as she'd been with Mortimer.

"Blast me all you want," Daniel said. "But bring the wind machine. This will be interesting."

He was so easy, so casual. As though Violet could throw everything to the wind and run off with him, instead of stay in the boardinghouse looking after her mother, doing the accounts, paying the bills, setting appointments. Her life was real life. Daniel's was . . . a fantasy.

The eager girl in her, the one who'd been interested in life in all its variety, longed to go with him. The woman Violet had become advised caution.

"So it's arranged," Daniel said, meeting her gaze. "I'll call for you tomorrow—with a cab this time, and tickets for the train. I'm not walking all the way to my friend's workshop."

"I haven't said I'd go."

"But you want to." Daniel's grin told her he knew he was

right. "You're curious. Think on it tonight, and I'll call on you tomorrow. Either way, I want to borrow your device. Better you come with me to make sure I don't damage it. Or I might take a liking to it and decide to keep it."

Violet stopped abruptly, this time in front of the boarding-house where she and her mother truly stayed. She hoped Daniel had no intention of following her in. Her landlady had a strict *no gentlemen* policy—fine with Violet—and she couldn't risk them all being turned out.

"Must you always have everything your own way, Mr. Mackenzie?"

"Aye, I think so. For a long time I was an only child, and you know how spoiled they get to be."

Violet ignored the glint of humor in his eyes. She was an only child herself, but she'd never had the chance to be spoiled. "You said you had a 'wee baby sister.'"

"Aye, and a little brother even more wee. Best thing that ever happened to an only child, Dad marrying again and having more children." Daniel shook his head. "The trouble those two can get into and blame on *me* is beautiful to behold. I'll introduce you sometime. They'd like you."

The offhand way he spoke about Violet interacting with his family—his wealthy, powerful, untouchable family—unnerved her. Such people had nothing to do with young women like Violet.

Violet hadn't known much about Daniel before he'd turned up at her house in London, but since then she'd made it a point to find out as much about him and his family as she could. The Mackenzies were well known not only for their money and standing, but for the scandals they'd engendered. Not one of the four Mackenzie brothers had managed to marry without some kind of scandal, and the two older brothers—one of whom was Daniel's father—had taken some of the most notorious courtesans in England as their lovers. One of the younger brothers, Mac, had become a painter, living the most open life in Paris. He'd even taken his young wife among the artists and their models, before she'd left him. The youngest brother was said to be insane, though he too was now married and had children.

Daniel was gaining his own notoriety. He'd taken a degree in Edinburgh so quickly that everyone remarked on it, and had traveled extensively through Germany and France in the years since, meeting inventors and eccentric scientists.

Not that he wasn't decadent as well. Daniel usually had a woman with him, from all reports—never the same one twice—and the three-day-long crushes he hosted in whatever house in whatever city he happened to be living in were not for the faint of heart.

Daniel had plenty of money—his mother's family had put a fortune in trust for their daughter, which Cameron had been unable to touch, and Daniel had inherited it. He'd always had a generous allowance, but came into the full money of the trust when he'd finished university.

As far as Violet was able to make out, Daniel was a man who lived as he pleased, did what he wanted, then moved on to his next interest, next town, next woman. The likelihood of Violet meeting his pampered little sister and brother was so small she didn't bother to answer the suggestion.

But she made her decision. "Very well, Mr. Mackenzie. Call tomorrow morning at ten o'clock, and I will place my device in your hands. I will require a receipt. And its replacement if damaged."

Daniel's eyes warmed with his smile. "That's more like it. I'll be here."

Violet gave him a nod and tried to step away, but Daniel's strong hand closed around her elbow, keeping her in place.

"Good night, lass. Sleep well." Instead of letting her go, he kept hold of her and brushed his thumb lightly over her lower lip.

The warmth in the touch made her shake. Violet had always held herself rigid, because she had to. Any bending or breaking would be disastrous for her.

Now Daniel stood close and merely touched her, fingertips sending a trickle of fire through every nerve. If Violet leaned into his tall body, she'd just fit under his chin. His large arms would come around her, pulling her close, keeping her safe.

The image of him holding her was so palpable that when Daniel removed his touch from her face, Violet was startled to find herself standing a foot away from him. So much empty space between them . . .

She cleared her throat. "I truly am pleased you're all right."

Daniel's amusement vanished to be replaced by something dark and dangerous. "You know, lass, I think that's the sincerest thing you've said all night."

Violet pulled back, uncertain how to respond. She swallowed, trying to keep her voice steady. "Well, good night, Mr. Mackenzie."

His gaze held her as solidly as an iron chain. "Good night, lass." Even though he wasn't touching her, Violet couldn't move until he released her.

As he had at the other boardinghouse, Daniel stepped back and tipped his hat, then stood still, waiting for her to go inside. This time he didn't smile, but watched her with his unnerving scrutiny.

Violet finally made herself turn away and walk the few steps to the house. Her hand trembled on the door latch, and she found the door locked.

A maid answered her knock immediately and let her in. The foyer was bone cold, but Violet was still hot from Daniel's touch.

She went up the stairs, clutching the wooden railing for balance. Once inside her bedroom, in their little suite of rooms, Violet moved to the front window and lifted the curtain to look out.

Daniel was still there, scanning the windows, waiting to make sure she'd gone into the right boardinghouse this time. He saw Violet, broke into his smile, and gave her a lazy salute. Violet lifted her hand in farewell, then forced herself to let go of the curtain, cutting off Daniel from her sight.

~

Daniel arrived at precisely ten the next morning to be ushered into a dreary parlor on the ground floor. He'd had to talk swiftly to be admitted at all, but finally the landlady agreed that Violet could speak to him in the parlor, if they kept the door open, and he departed right away.

Two middle-aged ladies fled through a far door as he was

let into the parlor from the hall—probably nothing masculine had walked into this room in a decade. He heard whispers and giggles from behind the cracked-open door, which he pretended to ignore.

This parlor was not as crowded with keepsakes as the sitting room at the Mortimer house in London had been, but there were enough tables draped with cloth and covered with trinkets that would make brushing past them a disaster. Daniel navigated the safest path he could to a side chair under a gaslight, where he sat, pulling his kilt modestly over his knees. The giggling intensified. Likely the ladies had never seen a man in a skirt before.

Violet walked into the parlor, thanking the severe-looking landlady who had come with her to it. Giving the far door a hard look, Violet moved to Daniel, who had sprung to his feet.

"You are punctual," she said.

"One of my many skills," Daniel said, trying not to be obvious about feasting his eyes on her. "Punctuality."

Violet didn't look as refreshed from a night's sleep as she might. Her eyes were red-rimmed, though her hair was pulled neatly into her pompadour, her shirtwaist buttoned to her chin, her skirt holding nary a wrinkle. Even with her slightly haggard look, her skin was flawlessly smooth, and her eyes— those dark blue eyes that could reach a man's soul—fixed on him and wouldn't let him go.

Violet held out a wooden box about two feet wide and one high, with heavy hinges and a sturdy clasp. "Take good care of it. It cost me a bit."

"Oh, I will, lass." Daniel took the box, unfastened the clasp, and peeked inside. The machine didn't look like much—a metal casing, fan blades showing through a cage, and a few wires.

Violet gave the box an anxious glance as Daniel closed it, as though she'd handed a stranger her only child. "What will you do with it?"

"See if it will enhance an engine idea I have. I don't have the engine here, but my friend down the coast has something close, and a vehicle for testing it. He's letting me loose on it with my theories today, trusting man."

"What kind of vehicle?" Violet asked, interested. "Is it a motorcar?"

The excitement in the question changed her. For a moment Violet the careful woman vanished, as did the Violet who used blunt rejoinders to keep those who might hurt her at bay. Daniel liked this Violet, curious and interested.

"Not a motorcar. I haven't finished building mine. When I do . . . that will be a fine day."

"What, then?"

Violet's eagerness was unmistakable, as was the wistfulness with which she looked at the box. Daniel caught her hand in a sudden, hard grip.

"Come with me, lass, and see."

Again the hesitation, the little frown, the quick look upward, to where her rooms lay. "My mother . . ."

"She can do without you one day, can't she? With all these ladies here to look after her?"

"Well . . ."

Daniel tightened his grip. She needed this, and he needed it. A day spent in Violet's company, with the opportunity to peel away her layers and find out all about her, was not to be lost.

"I'm not letting you say no," Daniel said. He gave her what he hoped was his most promising smile. "Come on with me, and I'll give you a day out you'll never forget."

⁓

Madness, absolute madness. Violet's thoughts flipped one over the other as she sent word up to Mary that she was going out, possibly all morning and on into the afternoon.

The next thing Violet knew, Daniel was leading her out of the house, past the interested ladies who'd stuck their heads out of the next room to watch them go. He took her out into the street and pushed her up into his tall, hired carriage.

The coach took them to the nearest train station, and not many minutes later, they were boarding a train, for which Daniel had already bought two tickets. *Two*, the presumptuous man.

The train glided out of the city, steam pumping, bells clanging. Violet and her mother and Mary had arrived in Marseille at night, traveling through most of the southern part of France in the dark. Violet had seen nothing of the countryside. Now she trained her gaze out the window to high hills, swaths of empty fields, and cliffs tumbling to the sea, which was gray under scattered clouds. The winter wind was brisk, but the private train compartment was toasty warm, with coal boxes for their feet and oil lamps to chase away any darkness.

Of course it was a private compartment. Daniel, lounging back on the seat opposite her, seemed surprised when Violet mentioned it. When he traveled in England and Scotland, Daniel said, he often used his ducal uncle's entire private car attached to the back of whatever train he wanted to take.

He said it casually, not boasting. In the next breath Daniel explained that when he didn't take his uncle's private coach, he rode rough by himself or with his friends in second class. But he'd thought Violet would appreciate the soft seats of first class today.

The statement brought home how different Daniel's existence was from hers. Violet regarded riding second class as a luxury up from third, while Daniel obviously thought nothing of making a train wait while a separate car was attached for himself and his family. Violet and her mother had often hunkered in crowded stations waiting for privileges to be given to wealthy men like Daniel.

Daniel leaned back into the corner of his seat and swung his long legs up on the cushions, resting his hands behind his head as the train swayed on. He said, with a wink, that he didn't sit next to her, because it was bad etiquette, as they weren't related. Besides, she needed somewhere to put her machine.

The box rested next to Violet, she not wanting to put it on the rack above. The mechanisms could be delicate.

The journey to the small town near the coast took about an hour. They emerged from the train to the sound of seagulls and the smell of fish and brisk sea air. The wind was cold but not nearly as dank and bone-chilling as in London.

Daniel, speaking French with a strange mixture of Parisian slang and coastal dialect, hired a cart. He explained to its

owner that he wanted to drive the cart himself, and reinforced
his request with a large handful of francs.

The man laughed with Daniel, slapped the horse on the rump,
and said in a dialect so thick Violet barely understood him, "Tell
Dupuis, that old bastard, that I said he owes me money."

Daniel grinned, helped Violet onto the front seat with him,
and touched the reins to the horse.

"Sorry it's not a better conveyance," Daniel said as the cart
jerked from the middle of the village up a steep hill. There
was no other seat but the driver's, and Violet was squeezed
tightly against Daniel's side. "The ducal coaches all seemed
to be out."

"It's perfectly adequate." Violet pulled her coat closer
about her, but it was Daniel who kept her warm.

"You're a sweetheart, you are. The females of my acquaintance, with the exception of my resilient aunts, would be
shrieking in dismay. Pierces your eardrums, those shrieks.
My aunt Eleanor, on the other hand, would tell them to buck
up and enjoy the fact that they didn't have to walk."

"Isn't your aunt Eleanor a duchess?"

"Aye, she is now. And she was an earl's daughter, but she
grew up without a penny, and learned how to fend for herself.
You'd like her. You'd like my stepmum too. She's as resilient
as they come."

"Your stepmother was a lady-in-waiting to the queen of
England," Violet said in a rather bewildered voice.

"What do ye think made her resilient? The queen, she
doesn't believe in heat in her drafty Scottish castle, and she's
a hearty woman. Very hearty. Her frail look and any worry
about her health is a nice façade. She can ride around the
countryside in her little cart all day long and then stay up all
night demanding to be read to. Marrying Dad was a relief to
poor Ainsley. Putting up with him is easy in comparison."

Violet had never met anyone who talked about a queen
behaving like a real person. A few of her mother's clients had
believed they were queens, or had been queens centuries ago,
or claimed they knew the deceased Prince Albert. None of
them had ever mentioned driving around in pony carts or
skimping on coal in the palace.

Daniel, son of a lofty lord and nephew to a duke, drove the rattling cart and old horse with competence. "Not much longer," he said after a time. He clucked to the horse. "Come on, old fellow, you can make it. Then a nice long rest for the afternoon, eh? Better than dragging a cart up and down a cobbled street all day." The horse flicked his ears back to Daniel, seeming to like his voice.

Their destiny turned out to be an old farm in the hills away from the sea. This one looked ancient. Three wings of a two-story house surrounded a pitted courtyard, the house's doors and windows facing the courtyard rather than outward to the land. Plaster crumbled around the walls' wooden half-timbering, revealing worn bricks beneath. A barn and storage rooms took up the entire lower floor; the living quarters for the farmer and his family looked to be on the upper floors.

The farm, however, was long gone. The fields around them were overgrown, though farther away, on the next farm, neat plowed rows, bare with winter, lay ready for spring planting. The courtyard was littered with coils of metal and pieces of wood, and the only animal in the barn was one large draft horse.

Two men were carrying what looked like a giant basket out of the courtyard as Daniel pulled up. One of the men broke away from the basket and came to take the horse's reins as Daniel jumped down. The man was large, with a hard face and a nose that had been broken more than once.

Daniel reached back and handed Violet out of the cart. "Lass, ye remember Simon? Who followed Mortimer to your house with every intention of beating five thousand guineas out of him? Or maybe you never saw Simon that night. He works for me now. Carry on, Simon. I'll take care of the cart."

While Violet stood aside and Simon returned to help the other man carry the basket, Daniel deftly unhitched the cart. He left it braked on one side of the courtyard, and led the horse past Violet to the stall next to the draft horse. He talked to the cart horse all the way, little endearments in his broad Scots as he gave the old animal a brief brushing down and made sure it had hay and water.

What kind of a man, with all the trappings of wealth, who

could live the softest possible life, took the time to comfort a working cart horse?

Daniel seemed to think nothing of it. He emerged from the stall, took Violet's box from the cart as he passed it, then led her out to follow Simon.

At the top of a hill was a flat, fallow field, which had been hidden from view by the wide house. In the middle of this field bobbed a giant bubble of red and yellow, half on its side, a buoy in a sea of dark earth. The bubble was being held down by four men, straining against ropes. Mr. Simon and the other man carried the basket toward it.

Violet stopped in her tracks. "Mr. Mackenzie, what on earth . . . ?"

"Monsieur Dupuis is lending us his balloon," Daniel said. "For my experiments with your wind machine."

Violet stared at the balloon, which was coming to life, men holding the ropes as though they fought to contain a wild stallion. "You're going up in *that*? Now? With my machine?"

"Aye. Ye see, it's my theory that hot air is a much safer and more useful method of keeping a balloon afloat than hydrogen gas. At the present time, though, if you want to use hot air, you fill up your balloon on the ground, and that's all you have. You either have to tether the balloon for your ascent, or go wherever the wind blows you. *But,* I'm thinking that if I have an efficient heat source I can take on board, I can manipulate the balloon, not just float where it wants me to go. Understand?"

Violet blinked. "Not really."

"If I can fix a good engine above the basket after the balloon is inflated, I can replace the hot air while I'm flying, and give the balloon a boost when I need it. I came up with the engine design, but never had a good way to shoot the heated air into the envelope while aloft—I don't want it to burn up the blasted silk when I'm two hundred feet off the ground. When I saw your machine, with its efficiency of pumping out a great blast of air, I thought, *bloody marvelous.*"

Violet strove to follow his speech without looking too bewildered. "And you brought your engine with you?"

"No, but Dupuis let me tinker with one of his to make a similar one, and now I'm going to enhance it with your machine.

My idea is to make hot air balloons dirigible—steerable—but smaller and lighter than the airships people are working on now. I'm thinking of making single-man crafts anyone can afford. You want to go across the downs and visit your friend in the next town? Hop aboard your own little dirigible and float there in comfort."

"In good weather," Violet said, looking up at the relatively clear sky.

Daniel shrugged. "Well, if it's pouring down rain, you want to stay home by the fire anyway."

Violet, who rarely had the luxury of staying home by the fire, gave him a skeptical look. "Won't the machinery be too heavy for the balloon?"

"That's what I mean to find out. Don't worry—I've done a few test runs at my dad's in Berkshire, and I've figured the ratio of weight to balloon size. That's why I came to Dupuis. He's a dedicated balloonist, experiments with several different kinds of them. He's interested to see whether I can take a machine-driven balloon aloft."

Violet followed as Daniel walked eagerly toward the waiting balloon, which was generally upright now. She watched his kilt move with his long stride, his broad back strong as he went swiftly up the hill.

He baffled her. Daniel Mackenzie, from one of the wealthiest families in Britain, rubbed down old horses, tinkered with machines, and said offhand that he traveled around Europe in second-class train compartments with the hoi polloi. He was equally comfortable speaking jumbled French dialects to French villagers or discussing the Queen of England's private household. Every time Violet thought she had the measure of him, Daniel turned into something else.

They reached the basket. It was a large one, with room for several people. Mr. Simon and the man who must be Monsieur Dupuis had attached a net of ropes from the balloon to the now tethered basket. As the balloon rose from its reclining position, the bulbous top full now, the basket strained to rise with it. The tied lines kept it down. A platform had been fastened above the basket, suspended up inside the balloon's envelope, and a large metal box with coils rising from it rested on the platform.

"Nice day for it," Dupuis said to Daniel in French. "Is this it?"

Daniel climbed into the basket and lifted Violet's wind machine out of its box. "We'll give this a try." He looked down at Violet. "Well, come on up, lass. I'll need your help. And a spanner."

Daniel was not the sort of man to shut a woman out of male activity, it seemed, especially when things turned interesting. Simon boosted her into the basket, and not long after, Violet was working with Daniel, her gloves off, helping him integrate her wind machine with his engine.

"It's useless without a generator," Violet pointed out as Daniel started connecting wires and tubes from her wind machine to his engine on the platform. "It won't run."

"But I have fuel, which will both keep the burner alight and turn the wind machine's fan—for as long as the fuel lasts, of course."

Daniel finished whatever he was doing, then fitted a crankshaft into a slot on the side of the engine. He advised Violet to step to the other side of the basket, then he gave the crankshaft a sharp heave.

The engine coughed once and died into silence. Daniel cranked again, and again, grunting with the effort. He stopped to drop his coat to the bottom of the basket, rolling up his shirtsleeves, then went back to the machine, his shirt stretching over muscled shoulders as he worked. Violet saw that a black design of an oriental-looking dragon had been inked over his right forearm at some time in his life. Her gaze went to the tattoo and stayed there.

Daniel kept cranking. Finally, sparks went off, a grinding like gears sounded, and the basket vibrated.

"Cast it off!" Daniel shouted to the men below.

Violet grabbed the basket's lip. "I believe it's time for me to disembark."

Daniel laughed. "Too late."

Violet's eyes rounded. She looked down at Simon and the men, who'd started releasing the ropes tethering the basket. "I'm not going up in this thing! Let me off."

The basket shuddered again and rose straight into the air.

"No choice now," Daniel said, his grin in place. "You're coming with me."

Violet protested, but the men dropped the last of the lines, and the balloon climbed into the sky, taking Violet right along with it.

Chapter 10

Violet grabbed the nearest rope, her heart in her throat as Daniel gave the engine one last crank.

"Don't worry," he said over the motor's splutter. "I've done this before."

The balloon gave a hard jerk and rose higher. Violet yelped and dared to look down. Simon, Dupuis, the rest of the men, the house, and the spread of the old farm had already receded. Violet calculated they must be about fifty feet from the ground when a gust of wind caught them and shoved them rapidly east.

Daniel cupped his hands around his mouth and called behind them. "Looks like we're heading to the valley. Meet us!"

Violet clamped her hands around the ropes, her hat tugging against its pins, her coat and skirts billowing. She caught her breath, then amazement struck her.

"We're flying!" she shouted.

"I hope so, love. Better than the opposite."

The land grew smaller, the heavens, wider. The silence of it, except for the gurgle of Daniel's engine, opened up and swallowed them.

Violet had lived in cities so long she'd grown used to constant noise—the rumble of carriages and wagons, the clopping of horses, shouts of men, high-pitched yells of boys, vendors calling on every market street, steam engines and train whistles in the railroad yards.

The balloon lifted Violet above it all. She saw a train, miles away, on the line that had brought her and Daniel to the village, chugging noiselessly into the station. From up here, it made no noise at all.

Daniel was still working. Gazing up inside the balloon, he gave the engine a few twists with a spanner and pulled down on a cord. The balloon kept climbing, but their sideways thrust became smoother.

That is, until another gust nearly tipped the basket on its side. Violet gave a little scream and shifted her grip from ropes to the basket itself.

"Come over here with me," Daniel called. "We need to balance against the drift."

Violet stared at him in fear. "You are completely mad, do you know that?"

"Get over here, lass. Or we'll tip."

Violet made her fingers loosen from the basket's side, and she half climbed, half scrambled to where Daniel stood. With her weight and his on one side, the basket righted itself and glided smoothly again, now heading a bit north as well as east.

Daniel's arm came around her waist. "We have sandbags to counterweight as well," he said. "But this is much more enjoyable."

Violet sucked in a breath, torn between exhilaration and terror. "You are the most bloody incorrigible madman I've ever had the misfortune to meet!"

"I have no doubt." Daniel held her close against him, his grin infectious. "Do ye know, when you're this angry, you speak in your own accent. London, is it? A bit south?"

"Now you are a dialectician as well as a horseman, inventor, and balloonist?"

"No, I'm friends with a bloke from Southwark. You're not French at all. You're one of the bloody English, aren't you?"

"My father's family is French," Violet said. "Came to England from a village outside Paris. My father was . . ." She trailed off, not sure what to say. She had no idea what her father had been, and only a vague idea *who* he'd been.

"I like that you have difficulty lying to me," Daniel said, his hand warm on her back. "Ye do it so easily to others."

"I don't lie."

"Not outright, but you deceive. Amounts to the same thing in the end. Me, now, I'm never anything but honest."

"You are, are you?"

"Look around." Daniel gestured with a broad hand. "Did I not promise you a day out to remember?"

Violet looked, and the last of her fear loosened and flew away. They were higher now, higher than the tallest building she'd ever seen, higher than any hill she'd climbed. The French countryside spread out before them, sharp hills studded with dark evergreens marching northward, snow on the highest peaks.

Behind them was the Mediterranean, vast and dappled blue gray under the sunshine, white gray cliffs of the coast tumbling to the sea. Waves of white foam formed neat lines as they marched toward the cliffs and narrow strips of shingle.

"It's breathtaking. I've never seen . . ."

"Only fools of aeronauts get to see the world like this." Daniel's arm tightened around Violet's waist, his breath in her ear. "I wanted to show it to you."

"Why?" The wind dragged Violet's question away.

"Why would I want to show you this? Because it's breathtaking, like you said."

"No, I mean . . . why me?"

"You mean because you hit me over the head with a vase?" Daniel's smile was as warm as his body. He should be freezing without his coat, but his shirt was damp with sweat, and the heat of him cut the wind. "It's because I've never met a woman with such beautiful eyes as yours."

His gaze, so close, trapped her. Daniel's eyes were the color of dark whiskey, with sparkles of gold in them like the depths of a fire. He had a hard face for so young a man, and a haunted look he kept buried under many layers. A woman would only see it if she recognized pain, and only if she bothered to look closely enough.

But no woman in Daniel's arms would be studying him to discover his pain. She'd be trembling, her heart thudding, her legs weakening as she wondered whether he'd kiss her, and if she'd be lost if he did.

Violet felt the hard of the spanner still in Daniel's hand against her lower back as he pressed her up to him and removed the space between them. He took his time, his gaze flicking to her mouth, before he gently touched her lips with a gentle kiss.

Slow, satin smooth, warm. The light kiss held nothing of the swift desire Daniel had shown in the dining room in London. Nor was it like the sensual kiss he'd given her when they'd shared the cigarette in the room above.

This kiss was careful, tender. Daniel eased his lips across hers, brushing, touching, the tiny contact sending more fire through Violet than his burner sent upward to keep them aloft.

He closed his mouth over her lower lip, suckling a little. The pain was tiny, erotic.

Time slowed and stopped. Nothing existed but Daniel holding Violet, his lips playing with hers, the flicker of his tongue into her mouth. Then came the taste of him, wild and heady, like the best young wine.

Wind sliced across the basket, bringing with it the chill of winter, but in Daniel's arms there was nothing but warmth. Violet was flying high above the world, joined to Daniel in the quiet but fierce kiss, safe in his embrace. As in the upstairs room when he'd tasted the smoke on her tongue, Violet experienced a jolt of heat, sweet excitement, and no panic.

Daniel's gloveless hands were strong on her back, the spanner stiff against her spine. Violet's breasts tightened in a pleasant way behind her corset, and the heat between her legs was a new sensation. Desire had always been closed off from her—something only the lucky felt.

Daniel eased his lips from hers, but he didn't step away. Still holding her against the length of him, he glanced to either side of her, taking his time.

"What are you doing?" she asked shakily.

"Looking for something you might hit me with. Wait a moment." Daniel had her right arm pinned to her by the way he held her, and he now laced his free hand through her left, binding it fast. "There."

"I don't want to hit you." Violet sounded choked.

"You certainly did then."

"You frightened me. Sometimes I go into . . . I don't always know what I'm doing or why. Just a flash, and then it's gone."

With his eyes so close to hers, she knew Daniel saw the lie—that Violet knew exactly why she'd panicked but didn't want to explain.

"Someone made you afraid, didn't they?" Daniel asked, his look too shrewd. "Someone not me."

Violet couldn't answer. At times—when she heard a particular timbre in a man's voice, or when someone caught hold of her with a certain pressure—the images came to her and swept away all reason. When Daniel had pinned her to the wall, Violet had struck out as she had all those years ago. Only at sixteen, she'd not been strong enough to fight.

"You never have to be afraid of me," Daniel said. The teasing note in his voice, the smiles, had gone.

Violet shook her head and tried to laugh. "I'd never be afraid of you, Daniel Mackenzie."

"I'm serious, lass." His deep baritone rumbled. "I never will hurt you. I want you—I wager you can't mistake that. But I'm not one to take what isn't freely given."

I want you. Violet felt his hardness through the wool of his kilt, a man aroused. Gone were the bustles and crinolines of previous decades—free and easy skirts let a woman feel a man's wanting against her, even through layers of clothing.

They were in a balloon, a hundred and more feet above the earth, winter wind knifing past them, and Daniel wanted her. He had to be mad.

And yet . . . if it could be only Daniel and herself, floating forever, the troubles of the world left on the rocky slopes below them, Violet could find happiness. The basket pushed at her feet as the balloon lifted her away from the petty worries of her life.

Up here, she could enter a world of true sweetness, if only for a little while. This was her magical barge, and Daniel was the magician who could banish all the monsters.

For answer, Violet rose on her tiptoes and kissed his lips.

The spanner fell with a clatter to the bottom of the basket, Daniel's strong hand splaying across her buttocks to lift her to him. His kiss turned harder, masterful. His mouth opened hers, tongue sweeping in to take. Violet met him halfway, her heart beating wildly.

His arms were hard, his shirt a thin layer over solid muscle. Violet let her hands play over him as he kissed her, running her touch up his arms and down the firm length of his back.

Daniel's strength took her breath away, and yet at the same time, he poured strength into her. Her magician was working his magic, taking away all pain, all sorrows.

When Daniel pulled back from the kiss, cold slapped at her. "Oh, you tempt me, Vi," Daniel said, a warm glow in his eyes. "You tempt me much. I'm sorry I told Dupuis and Simon to chase us."

Violet glanced down, the ground so far away it was heart-stopping. A man on a large horse—the draft horse she'd seen in the barn—trotted along a road that cut through the valley below them. Much farther behind was a man driving a cart. The horseman looked up and waved, and Daniel waved back.

"It is only a kiss," Violet said. Her voice still didn't work right. She who could master five languages and various accents in each one now could barely pronounce scratchy words in English.

"*Only* a kiss?" Daniel's arms tightened around her. "Grind me to powder beneath your heel, why don't you?" His hand on her buttocks lifted her again, the touch intimate and yet freeing. "Let me—"

He broke off and looked up. *Let me . . . Let me what? Have my wicked way with you?* Violet leaned closer to him, caring for nothing but the words on his lips, his lips themselves, the radiant heat of his body. *I need you, Daniel. And I'm scared.*

Daniel released her suddenly as the balloon swayed hard. The basket shoved upward, a strong gust sending it rocking. Violet shouted, her yell carried away on the wind, as Daniel grabbed ropes, pulling hard until the basket stopped its sickening spin.

He thrust the ropes at her. "Hang on to these. Now we see if my hot-air personal dirigible is truly dirigible."

"Now we see?" Violet stared at him as she grasped the lines. "You said you'd done this before."

"Flown a balloon before, yes. Never tried to steer one with this system. Now, when I tell you *right*, you pull the rope in your right hand, *left*, the one in your left. Can you do that?"

"I think I can remember right from left," Violet answered shakily and started to wrap the ropes around her hands.

Daniel grabbed her. "No. You *hold* them. If one jerks wild, I don't need it pulling you out of the basket at worst, tearing off your fingers at best."

Violet's eyes widened, and she unwrapped the ropes. Daniel retrieved the crankshaft, stuck it into his engine, and wound it again. A larger flame jumped from the top of the open box, the basket tipped, and Violet let out another yelp.

Daniel laughed. "I like that you like to scream. Left, now. *Left!*"

Violet yanked the rope as Daniel continued to crank, the flame spurting. The basket righted from its horrible listing, and the balloon rose higher still.

Wind buffeted them. Violet watched Daniel's body move as he worked, and wondered why he wanted to go so high. It was freezing now, the wind dry but icy.

Violet glanced ahead of them, and suddenly understood why he wanted the height. Rocks and cliffs rushed at them, the trees on them looking so close she might be able to reach out and touch them. She sucked in a breath.

"Higher!" she shouted. "We need to go higher!"

"What the bloody hell do ye think I'm doing? Pull the right rope! *Right!*"

"I'm pulling it!" Violet yanked on it with all her strength.

Daniel kept pumping the fire. The rocks rushed at them. At any moment they'd hit, the basket would splinter, and she and Daniel would tumble down. Would they land on rocks, arms around each other, hurting but surviving? Or be plunged to their deaths?

Violet didn't want to plunge to her death just yet. She wanted to be pulled back into Daniel's embrace, to feel his desire for her and taste it on his lips.

At one time in her life, Violet would have welcomed death. But not today. Not when she'd finally found this *aliveness*.

Daniel kept cranking. Violet's wind machine blew the hot air up into the balloon's silken envelope. The basket soared upward, over the cliffs. The crags at the top of the little peak seemed to reach up to grab for them, but then the balloon was clear. After a minute of soaring inches above trees on the other side of the ridge, the land fell away to the next valley, and the balloon floated gently above it.

Daniel stopped the crankshaft and straightened up, stretching his arms high. He whooped. "Well done, lass!"

Laughing, he caught Violet in his arms, lifting her from her feet and kissing her. His face was cold now, cheeks ruddy, hair mussed by the wind. Violet, still holding the ropes, kissed him back.

Daniel's gaze was all for her as he lowered her to her feet and gently took the ropes from her. "Thank ye, love. We make a good team."

"Yes." The word came out a croak, Violet unable to think of anything else to say.

Daniel turned around to look at the world, and spread his arms, the ropes moving with him. "Never been this high before." He whooped again, and Violet laughed.

The land opened out before them, a long river valley dotted with farms and small villages. Patches of snow clung to the shadows of trees and rocks on the slopes of the ridge they'd just crossed. Far below, smoke rose from the scattered farmhouses, and one or two people moved about on the remote roads.

No one in the wide world knew where Violet was at this moment. Though she'd told Mary she was accompanying Mr. Mackenzie to a village outside Marseille, Violet had not known Daniel would take her aboard this wonderful machine and off into spaces unknown. No one but Daniel knew where she was now—they'd even left Monsieur Dupuis and Simon behind in the last valley.

Violet was truly alone, floating on air, with only a man who was nearly a stranger to keep her aloft. Daniel had isolated her from everyone she knew, taken her far from the help of anyone. Violet should be terrified, brought to her knees in one of her attacks of panicked hysteria.

But she could feel no fear. She watched Daniel as he dropped the ropes, held the side of the basket, and looked around, enraptured. The world was beautiful, Violet was alone with the man who'd shown her its beauty, and her heart was light. This must be what happiness felt like.

When Daniel turned and looked at her, Violet wished the moment could be suspended in time. She never wanted to forget *how* he was looking at her. Not in lechery, not demanding anything from her. He studied her as though he liked looking at Violet, for herself, as though nothing in the world mattered to him but her and this moment.

I could love you, Daniel Mackenzie.

In this place of contentedness and freedom, the warmth of the words took form, and wouldn't leave her.

Daniel turned away, scanning the horizon again. "We should find a place to set down."

"I don't want to." Violet spoke before she could stop herself.

Daniel glanced at her again, his smile returning. "I don't either. But those clouds are thickening, and a balloon is not a good place to be in a rainstorm. Or possibly a snowstorm, this far from the coast."

True, now that the Mediterranean's breezes had been left behind, the wind had a wintry bite.

"Over there, I'm thinking." Daniel pointed to a flat space of land covered with bare black fields, plowed furrows making dark crisscrosses in the ground.

"How do we land?" Violet looked up at the balloon, which was stretched full. "Do you know where we are?"

Daniel shrugged. "Somewhere in France. When we bring this thing down, I plan to ask."

How wonderful to go where the wind blew, to not worry about where you were or where you were going. Daniel moved through life expecting it to get out of his way, while Violet frantically scrambled to survive.

Daniel started working with ropes again, and turned knobs

on his engine. The fire in the machine died down, and the balloon slowly, regretfully, began to descend.

"Hmm," Daniel said.

"What?" Violet was at his side again. "What do you mean, *hmm*?"

Daniel gave her a dark look. "Better hold on to something."

Violet clutched the side of the basket, her heart hammering. "Why?"

A gust of wind caught them. The balloon rocketed sideways, at the same time the basket rapidly slid toward the earth.

Daniel pulled down hard on a rope, and high above them, a hole opened in the silk to let out the air. He yanked on the steering ropes some more, then finally let go of everything and slammed his arms around Violet from behind, grabbing the basket on either side of her. He shielded her with his body as the plowed field rushed at them, the balloon deflating.

A corner of the basket scraped the ground. The balloon bounced upward, wind grabbing it again. Violet squealed in alarm but hung on. Daniel around her, strong and solid, gave her the false illusion that she was safe.

The basket scraped the ground again, then it tipped halfway over, the bulb of balloon still upright on the wind. Daniel's hands around Violet whitened with his grip. He was cursing, and she heard screams coming from her own throat, both in elation and absolute terror.

The balloon dragged the basket across the field, pulling up stubble of last autumn's late harvest. Birds exploded from the furrows, rabbits dove away from them. A fox lifted its head and stared as they skittered by.

It would stop, Violet reasoned. The balloon would deflate, the basket would tip over with a thump, and she and Daniel would spill out into the mud. Comical but not deadly.

The basket reached the edge of the field, the balloon still pulling it. They went up over gorse and rocks that lined the field, and suddenly the world plummeted out from under them.

The half-deflated balloon sailed out over a river gorge, the river itself sparkling merrily at the bottom. The sides of the cliffs, pockmarked with snow, reached up to them.

Daniel's curses changed to one long yell, Violet's joining

his. The balloon swept them across the narrow gulf and up the other side of the gorge, straight toward a line of evergreens. Daniel shoved Violet to the bottom of the basket and landed on top of her, curving his body over hers.

The basket broke through the saplings at the edge of the gorge, smacked into the boles of slightly thicker trees, and spun around once. A noise like a great wind shook the branches as the silk of the balloon caught, ripped, and snagged fast. The basket rocked, banged once more into the smooth side of a tree, and stopped.

Chapter 11

Daniel lifted his head. Violet lay very still beneath him. Her eyes were closed, and she had a bruise on her face.

The world had stopped spinning, and now wind moved them gently, the only sounds rustling branches and flapping silk. Daniel's engine was dead, silent, and so was the wind machine.

"Are ye all right, love?" Daniel brushed tangled hair from Violet's face, heart beating swiftly in alarm.

If he'd hurt her . . . If his arrogance had led to broken bones or worse, he'd never forgive himself. He could have left Violet alone, borrowed the wind machine and not insisted she come with him, but no. Daniel had wanted to show off to this breathtaking woman. He'd wanted Violet to throw her arms around him and exclaim how wonderful he was to be able to pilot a balloon.

"Violet. Lass, wake up."

Violet blinked her beautiful blue eyes open. "Are we down?"

Daniel let out a breath of relief. "We've stopped. Are ye hurt?"

"I don't think so."

Violet sat up, resting her back against the basket, and

shakily pushed her hair from her face. Daniel ran his hands up her arms, squeezing a little, checking for broken bones. She let him, understanding what he was doing, though she watched him warily from behind thick lashes.

Daniel swallowed the need that had been maddening him and concentrated on making sure Violet was whole. She didn't flinch until he ran his hands up under the warmth of her skirt, his touch skimming from ankles to knees.

"I said I was fine," she said, jerking away.

Daniel withdrew, difficult when his fingers had brushed the soft heat of her thighs. "Need to check every bone. I broke my tailbone once, falling off a horse."

"My tailbone appears to be unsevered," she said primly.

The quiet words, contrasted with their wild ride over the gorge, made Daniel laugh. "I think I'm unsevered too. How about we find out where we are?" He put his hands on the lip of the basket and pulled himself upright. "Oh."

Violet was up beside him in a hurry. "Oh," she echoed. "My."

The basket hung about twenty feet from the ground, nestled in the branches of two close-growing trees. The basket swayed the slightest bit, but it was stuck fast. The silk envelope, deflated, draped over trees, hung from branches, and dripped in tatters to the ground.

"Dupuis will not be happy with me, I think," Daniel said. "Never mind. I'll give him the cost of the balloon plus a little extra. He can make a better one."

"He'll understand if he's such a great friend of yours," Violet said.

Daniel gave her a look of surprise. "Not a great friend. I only met him a few days ago."

Now she stared. "I thought you came to Marseille to meet him and try out your idea on the balloon."

"No, I came in search of you, as I said. Meeting Dupuis was of secondary importance—I telegraphed friends here and asked them if they could point me in the direction of a fellow balloonist. Marseille is a good-sized city. I knew someone would know someone, and I'd heard of Dupuis by reputation."

Violet's lips were parted as she listened, uncertainty in her eyes. Daniel touched her cheek. When they were finished here—and safely on the ground—he'd explain a few things. He'd convince her he'd come to France for *her*. He could have stayed in England to try his experiments—he knew plenty of mad aeronauts there. He hadn't thrown a few belongings into a valise and jumped onto the first train to Dover because he fancied the Mediterranean air. He'd make her see that.

First, though . . .

"I'll climb down," Daniel said. "And find a way to extract you. Won't be long."

He made sure his gloves were on tightly over his hands before he grasped the nearest branch and started to pull himself out of the basket.

The basket listed alarmingly, his weight and Violet's together the only thing keeping it level. If Daniel climbed out, the basket would tip over, and Violet would fall.

"We both go at the same time," Violet said. "I can climb a tree." She looked at the branches around her and then down through them to the ground.

"We might not have to." Daniel cupped his hands around his mouth. "Oi! Up here!"

Voices gathered below, answering shouts in French. Then followed a long debate, to which Daniel contributed, about the best way to get the crazy foreigners out of their love nest in the tree.

Daniel ended up untying the counterweights and gathering up ropes, still attached to the harness that held the basket to the balloon.

"I'll lower you down a bit," he said to Violet. "They have ladders, but they won't reach this high."

Violet looked at him in alarm. "If I go out, everything will unbalance, and you'll fall."

Daniel wound a rope around her waist and under her arms. "I'll be directly behind you, sweetheart. Trust me now."

"You're a madman," she said. But Daniel saw exhilaration in her eyes behind the fear.

"Ready?" Daniel knotted the rope tightly and grabbed hold of it where it fastened to the balloon. He wrapped his other arm around Violet and lifted her to the lip of the basket. "One, two, *three* . . ."

Violet let out a cry as the basket tipped, but Daniel had climbed into the branches above her, holding fast to the tree and to her rope at the same.

The basket went all the way over, sending down counter-weights, the engine, and Violet's wind machine, as well as extra ropes and Daniel's coat. Everything crashed down through the branches, extracting a yell from their rescuers. Above them Daniel and Violet clung to the tree.

"Go on, love," Daniel said. "It's all right."

Slowly, slowly Violet picked her way down. A woodsman of burly peasant stock climbed a homemade ladder to meet her, catching Violet around her waist and carrying her down with him. Not until Violet's feet touched solid earth did Daniel relax in relief.

He climbed quickly down behind her, the branches burning his hands through the gloves, cold wind cutting him. By the time he reached the ground, the men had unwound the rope from Violet, and she was shivering.

Daniel caught up his greatcoat, which had landed on a pile of fallen branches, pushed away the last of the rope, and wrapped the coat around her.

"You all right?" he asked.

"Fine. Perfect." Violet was breathless, but he read no pain in her eyes.

Daniel turned to the men who'd rescued them. Farmers, woodcutters, hunters with shotguns. "Thank you all," he said in his mixed-dialect French. "Are we near a village? Is there somewhere my wife can rest?"

He felt Violet start slightly at the word *wife*, but they were deep in the countryside, and the locals might behave better if they thought Daniel and Violet man and wife and not a man and his fancy lady. In Paris or even Marseille, it might not matter, but villagers could be sticklers for propriety. Violet would never pass as Daniel's sister, mostly because Daniel would never be able to treat her like one. No, the fiction of man and wife was best.

One of the hunters said he'd lead Violet to the village and his brother's coaching inn there, where she could rest and eat and stay the night if necessary. Daniel gave Violet a smile and squeezed her hand.

"You go on. I'll salvage what I can and join you."

"Yes. Of course." Violet, bless her, didn't argue, but turned and walked away with the hunter and another man.

They were deferential to her, Daniel was happy to see, and he knew they had swallowed the story that she and Daniel were married. Or at least were willing to go along with it. They also recognized from Daniel's clothing and the fact that he'd arrived by balloon, that Daniel was a wealthy man. He doubted they'd have a qualm about taking his money for food and drink and a night's rest.

Daniel looked up at the basket still dangling from the tree. "Right." He brought his hands together. "Let's see what we can take."

The men who walked Violet to the village were respectful if taciturn. The village was not far—down the hill through the woods and then out past a farmer's field. The track they followed turned into a muddy road that led between a cluster of farmhouses, a shop or two, a church on a little rise in the middle of the houses, and an inn. Large parts of the old walls that had protected the town in wild medieval times still stood, integrated now into the walls of houses or barns.

The last time Violet had stayed in a village like this— stranded when they'd been traveling in a torrential rain— Celine had begun having visions. The innkeeper's wife had not liked this, declaring that Violet, her mother, and Mary were Romany witches and not welcome.

The innkeeper's wife and other villagers had escorted the three of them to the edge of town and shut the gates, letting them suffer the weather. Violet had always been sure they'd been lucky not to have been beaten before being driven out.

I am so sorry, my dear, Celine had said as they'd trudged through the mud and the pouring rain. *I could not help what I saw. Terrible things happened in that house.* The inhabitants of the house obviously had not wanted to be reminded of those terrible things.

How different to walk into an inn and have the innkeeper's wife welcome Violet with a smile, telling her she'd make up the best bedroom while Violet waited by the fire in the parlor. The innkeeper brought Violet warm wine, and prepared a cup for Daniel to await his arrival.

Daniel had charmed these people before they'd even met him.

Violet pulled Daniel's coat closer around her shoulders as she drank the thick wine. The room was not yet warm enough for her to remove the coat, and besides, she didn't want to. The wool had captured Daniel's warmth and the scent of him. Violet closed her eyes and breathed it in, the wonder of this marvelous day still with her.

Daniel came in a half hour later. She saw him through the window, approaching the inn surrounded by the farmers and woodcutters. Daniel was swapping jokes with them—a few of them off-color, Violet could hear—all laughing like old friends. They entered the inn together, the men happy to stop for a jug of wine.

Daniel strode into the parlor, followed soon after by the innkeeper's wife bearing a tray loaded with full platters and crocks. The odor of hot food made Violet's stomach growl in longing.

"Thank you kindly," Daniel said in French as he stripped off his gloves. "Flying is hungry work. Mmm, are those roasted potatoes I smell? In garlic and cream? My favorite."

He took the heavy tray from the innkeeper's wife and set it on the table for her, keeping up a conversation with her as he helped her lay out the food. Violet watched mutely from her place on the sofa. When the table was laden with steaming dishes, Daniel walked the innkeeper's wife to the door, carrying the tray for her, onto which he tossed a few coins before handing the tray back to her and thanking her profusely. The woman was blushing and smiling as she ducked out and closed the door.

Daniel turned back, rubbing his hands. "I'm starving," he announced in his big voice. "Ate far too early for my good this morning. Aren't you joining me?"

Violet would have to lay aside his coat to join him and eat. She hated to give it up, as though she'd be giving up a part of him.

But the food called to her. Violet rose and hung Daniel's coat on a hook on the wall, running her hands over it until the last possible minute. Daniel didn't notice, still standing over the table and admiring the food.

Daniel waited until Violet sat down at the table before he took the seat closest to hers and started dishing out the food. He filled a plate with sausages, potatoes, greens, and sauce, and added cheese and bread before he laid the plate in front of her. "Grub smells good."

"You've landed on your feet," Violet said. She took up the bread and spread soft cheese on it as Daniel loaded a plate for himself. "I imagine you always do."

"Not always." Daniel shoveled creamy potatoes into his mouth and washed them down with the rough-tasting red wine. "When you laid me out with that vase, I landed on my back."

Violet looked up at him, stricken. "I will apologize forever for that. It was horrible when I thought I'd hurt you so much."

Daniel's eyes glinted with good humor. "Stop. I was teasing you. Mackenzies are hard-headed. Difficult to kill. I imagine I'll tease you about it for a long time to come."

Implying they'd be friends for a long time to come. Friends who kissed, flew in balloons together, and shared dinners at out-of-the-way country inns.

Violet had never had such a friendship, especially not with a man. And she'd never desired a man before, but she couldn't cease thinking about the kisses he'd given her. She thought again of how Daniel had cupped his hands around her backside in the balloon, pulling her hard up into him. The experience of wanting was entirely new, entirely strange, and left her confused.

"Do you think the balloon can be repaired?" she asked, switching to a safe topic.

Daniel returned to his food. "No. And if I'm right, the woodsmen and farmers will make themselves feel better about me destroying their trees by cutting up the silk and selling it or turning it into new clothes. Come summer in this place, everyone will be wearing yellow and scarlet."

"You don't seem bothered."

He shrugged. "As I said, I'll give Dupuis the price of it. His next balloon will be even better."

Violet licked cream from her spoon. "It's the mark of a rich man to be able to give up things so easily. You let it go and buy something new, no worry at all."

Another shrug. "They're only things. Besides, these people will save the cost and labor of new cloth. If ye've noticed, the innkeeper's given us the very best in the house, which means they don't have much overall."

Careless kindness and generosity flowed from Daniel so easily. He was a man who gave and thought nothing of it.

A gust of wind hit the window, banging a shutter into it. The wind was followed by rain, icy fine, with snowflakes mixed with it. The sunshine outside had gone.

"You were right about the weather changing," Violet said. "I'm glad we came down before this." She shivered, feeling winter cold permeate the room, in spite of the fire. "Quite a squall."

"Ye've seen nothing of squalls until it's the snow whirling around Kilmorgan Castle in a wild white blizzard. But Kilmorgan's a fine place in the height of summer, when the light never really goes away. 'Tis beautiful. You'll like it."

Violet stopped, her fork halfway to her mouth. Daniel went on scraping the last of his sauce from his plate, not noticing her hesitation.

Again he was implying they would be friends for a while. That he'd show her this place with the lofty title of Kilmorgan Castle, in the summer when light lingered into night.

"You shouldn't make promises you can't keep," she said lightly.

Daniel looked up at her, his smile rich and hot. "Oh, sweetheart, I always keep my promises."

The innkeeper's wife entered again before Violet could think of a reply. The woman started piling empty dishes onto the tray, taking their compliments on the food in stride. "Just a bit of home cooking," she said. "Now, we've fixed the bedroom upstairs for you. The day is short, the storm is upon us. You'll not be flying anywhere tonight." She chuckled. "To be sure, when Jean ran in to tell me a man and his lady wife had been flying high and were now stuck in a tree, I thought he was having fancies. But you're foreign. What you get up to is beyond me." She shook her head at them, more amused than dismayed.

Here was another difference between Violet's life and Daniel's. People were instantly kind to Daniel, as though his charm were contagious. Violet had not forgotten the cruelty of the villagers who'd forced her and her ill mother out onto the road and into the tempest. These people seemed kind and caring, but Violet knew that if she'd arrived alone, without Daniel with his charm and wealth, they would have regarded her with deep suspicion.

"Thank you," Daniel told the innkeeper's wife. "I confess, it would be better to rest our weary bones here than to try to make our way back to the coast tonight, even if my man could reach us with a cart. Which he can't. He'll have been cut off by the gorge—I'm sure Simon and Dupuis sensibly returned home. We'll spend the night here and return in the morning."

Spend the night. Violet ceased to breathe. To rest in a warm, soft bed, tucked away with Daniel, hidden from the world . . .

"I can't." Violet jumped to her feet, speaking rapidly in English. "My mother won't know where I am. She'll worry herself frantic."

Daniel lifted his hand. "No matter, my love. We'll send a message." He switched on his smile as he spoke again in French. "Do you have a telegraph office nearby, Madame?"

"There's a train station in a village three miles from here. They have a telegraph."

Violet felt obligated to put forth one more argument. "If there is a train three miles from here, then we can go back. Three miles is an easy journey, even in a storm."

The innkeeper's wife chuckled again. "City folk. It's not the Gare du Nord, Madame. Train stops twice a day, once each way, and you've already missed both."

"Ah, well, that decides it," Daniel said, not worried.

"That decides it," Violet echoed. She was going to spend the night here, as Daniel's wife, no matter what.

The innkeeper's wife took them upstairs to the first floor,

and unlocked a room that was about ten feet square. An enormous bed, which took up most of the room, rose under the beams, a bright fire danced on a hearth, and a tray laden with hot coffee and cups lay on a table near the fire.

"I've brought you out a nightgown, Madame," the innkeeper's wife said, shaking out a long, slightly yellowed cotton gown. "I'll help you undress, same as a lady's maid. And my husband will do for you, Monsieur."

"I don't need much doing," Daniel said. "You get comfortable, Vi. I'll take care of the message to your mum. She doesn't need to worry about us."

He kept up the verisimilitude well. No stammering, no embarrassment, no forgetting parts of the fiction he was weaving. But at the same time, he was giving Violet time to change out of her clothes without him near in this tiny room.

Daniel departed on his errand, the innkeeper's wife agreeing that mothers worried—she worried every day about her son off working in Aix-en-Provence instead of helping them tend the inn.

"Not that we have much to do here," she went on. "City folk come out seeking country air in the summer, and sometimes the shooting parties get this far, but in spring, with the planting, and city folk keeping to their theatres and operas, not many come out to see us."

And the inn was a bit away from the railway, Violet finished silently, and those with money took the fast trains from Paris to the coast. Not much call for a coaching inn these days. Daniel had been right that these people could use extra money.

Still chattering, the innkeeper's wife unbuttoned and unlaced Violet's dress and petticoats, helped her out of her corset, and slid the warmed and pressed nightgown over her head. Violet hadn't been waited on in such a very long time . . . or had she ever been, like this? As though she were a true lady, married to someone like Daniel.

Daniel returned in little over half an hour. By then it was fully dark, and he came noisily into the bedroom, bringing with him a wave of cold and the smell of wood smoke.

Violet had curled up on the soft chair before the fire after the innkeeper's wife had gone, and remained there, too tired to rise. She'd wrapped a borrowed dressing gown and a blanket from the bed around her, her feet pulled up under them. "You walked three miles there and back awfully fast," she said to Daniel. "The coffee is still warm, I think."

"I met a boy from the next village halfway along, and he carried the message back for me. He was expecting me. Gossip must be spread by carrier pigeon between these villages."

He came to pour himself a cup of the coffee, which put him close to Violet. His coat still held the cold of outside, but the wool of his kilt smelled warm. The heat of him slid through Violet's blanket and made her draw herself closer.

"The innkeeper's wife brought a nightshirt for you," Violet said, clutching her cup. "It's laid out on the bed."

Daniel shucked his coat and hung it on a hook, caught up the nightshirt, and sat down in the other chair, resting the nightshirt on his lap. "Kind of her."

"They're being very kind, I've noticed." Violet kept to English, knowing anything overheard in French would be all over this village and the next by the following morning, presumably by carrier pigeon. "They like you, and perhaps sense your aristocratic connections."

Daniel grinned. "They sense my jingling pockets. Remember this country's history—these folks' great-great-grandparents rose up and threw the French aristocrats out on their bums a hundred years ago. Forty years ago, they sent the last emperor rushing for the safety of England. They're not awed by my proximity to a title. If they like me, it's because they know the benefit of a paying guest."

Violet wasn't so certain. Daniel did carry a certain weight of authority she noticed aristocrats had in any country, the knowledge that lesser beings would get out of the way for them. It wasn't an arrogance with Daniel—he just *knew*.

Daniel took a last sip of coffee and set down his cup. "Now then, the night is cold, the villagers go to bed with the sun, and I'm beat. Why don't you get into the bed and cover up while I slip into my sleeping togs? I'm not modest, but you might be."

The thought of Daniel peeling off his clothes while she lay

in bed made Violet nearly swallow her tongue. He would be too near as he slid off his waistcoat and the shirt she'd earlier seen dampened with sweat against his well-honed arms. He'd bare all his skin, which would likely be as liquid tanned as his face and arms.

Violet masked her sharp intake of breath by fumbling her way out of the chair and clattering down her coffee cup. She kept the blanket around her until she reached the bed, then she tossed it on top before climbing the steps to the high bed. She found the covers warmed with wrapped bricks that had been slid to the bottom of the bed.

"Where will you sleep?" Violet asked Daniel. She settled under the quilts, trying not to look his way. "There isn't a sofa, and the floor looks hard. There aren't many covers up here to spare either."

Daniel laughed. "I'm sleeping in that bed with you, lass. I'm exhausted, and the floor, as you say, is far too hard. I'm an aristocrat, remember? I like things soft."

Chapter 12

Violet peered over the top of the covers in alarm. Daniel was just settling the nightshirt across his broad shoulders, the garment too small for him. It bared his forearms and the flowing tattoo, then fell to just above his knees. His legs were as tight and strong as the rest of him, his bare toes pressing the board floor.

"That bed's big enough to float a battleship," he said, not bothering to hide his near nudity. "We'd never find each other if we wanted to."

He didn't give her time to argue. Daniel climbed up the other side of the bed and slid under the covers while Violet stared at him, the quilt clutched to her chest.

Daniel laughed at her as he lay down. "Go to sleep, Vi. You'll need your rest for tomorrow."

He punched the pillow into shape, then flopped the covers over him, a man settling down for a winter's nap. The rush-light on the other side of the room, which hadn't emitted much glow in the first place, burned out with a sharp smell. The only light now was from the fire, which was licking at fragrant wood to warm the small room.

Violet lay down again, remaining on her side, facing him. Daniel reposed on his back, one arm behind his head, the other holding the covers to his chest. He closed his eyes, the lines of his face brushed with firelight.

She watched him awhile longer but he never moved. Confusing. Daniel had brought her here, posed as her husband, and insisted they share the bed, but now drifted to sleep as though they were trusted friends. Casual, comfortable, in the same way he shortened her name. No drama, no fear. Just Daniel's warmth between Violet and the rest of the world.

She liked it. Violet had never felt safe and protected, not since she'd learned the truth of life.

Up here in their aerie, in this bed of cozy warmth, Daniel belonged to her. For a little while, Violet could pretend she was Daniel's, that he loved and cherished her, that today was only a small part of a long life of happiness. Tomorrow, they would return to reality, but for tonight, he was hers, and she his.

A fine dream. One Violet would hold tightly to herself against the hour she'd have to let it go.

⁕

If Daniel got through the night with his sanity intact, it would be an astonishing thing. To have the most beautiful woman on earth *in his bed*, three feet away from him, and not touch her, was going to kill him.

The courtesans at the very expensive houses Daniel visited to keep his needs at bay would laugh if they knew he kept an arm's length between himself and Violet. He'd set up the tale that they were man and wife not only to keep the villagers from treating Violet poorly, but also so that no one in this house would think it odd if they heard him easing his passion with her.

But when he'd seen her look at him worriedly over the covers, he remembered her profound terror when she'd struck out at him in the London house. Daniel had scared her senseless. Not for anything he'd done, he'd come to understand, but because Violet had been hurt by someone else. She'd reacted to Daniel because he'd put her in mind of that incident.

Daniel wished he knew what had happened, and who'd dared to frighten and touch her. He'd coax the story out of her when she was ready, and then Daniel would visit that gentleman and explain a few things.

For now he lay quietly next to Violet, scenting her, feeling her warmth, and did nothing. His cock was so hard he could lift the covers with it. He wanted to squeeze himself and relieve the pressure, but he knew that if Violet woke to Daniel stroking himself off beside her, she'd be as terrified as she'd been in London, and likely even more disgusted. Plenty of weapons for her to use on him in this room.

Besides, he didn't want to hurt her. He liked the way Violet had looked at him today, as though everything he did pleased her. He wanted to spin that out as long as he could.

She'd been amazing up in the balloon. Violet had been afraid, but also excited. He remembered how she'd screamed and then laughed when the balloon did something unexpected, how she'd called him the most bloody incorrigible madman she'd ever had the misfortune to meet. But she'd followed Daniel's orders to the letter, no arguing, no falling in a weeping fit, no demands that Daniel take her to safety immediately. She was no wilting violet, his Violet.

Daniel couldn't stop his chuckle, which shook the bed.

"Are you all right?" Violet rose beside him like a goddess, her dark hair tumbling, her blue eyes picking up the fire's glow. Her nightgown gaped a little at her neck, showing him the softness of woman inside.

Daniel wanted to push her back down into the bed, bury himself in her, and never come out.

"No," he said, shoving the covers away. "No, I'm not." Daniel scrambled out of bed, feet missing the steps, so he thumped to the floor. "I need another walk. To settle my . . ." He trailed off as he grabbed his kilt and coat, heading for the door. "Go to sleep. I'll be back."

Daniel shut the door on her bewildered expression, dressed in the hall, and pulled on his boots on the stairs. He walked on down and out of the inn into wind and freezing rain, but it was a long time before his cock went down again.

Violet woke to sunshine, a fine winter day, and Daniel draped over her.

He was asleep, one large leg shoved between hers, Violet spooned back against his chest. He held her securely with one arm, his breath in her hair steady and even.

Violet didn't move. If she woke him, Daniel might yank himself away, leave the bed again, perhaps go for another walk. Violet had fallen asleep long before he'd returned.

If he stayed curled around her, she could keep pretending Daniel was hers. The memory needed to last her a long time.

A door slammed somewhere below. Daniel moved behind her, his breath quickening. Violet braced herself for him to roll away and leave her cold, but he didn't. She turned her head the slightest bit, and found his amber gaze fixed on her.

Daniel's eyes were the strangest shade of hazel brown, touched with a golden hue, like the depths of strong whiskey. His rumpled hair was dark, burned with bits of red where the sunlight through the shutters touched it. His face had a hardness that would increase with age, and given the number of times he smiled, lines would soon brush the corners of his eyes. He was a strong man, virile, young, beautiful.

Daniel slid his hand from her waist to the open neck of her nightgown. Buttons held the garment closed in front, and Daniel slowly, without much movement, slid the buttons open.

One, two, three . . . He glided his hand inside the nightgown until he reached the warmth of her breast.

Daniel closed his eyes as he cupped Violet's breast in his work-worn palm. Her breath came faster, which pushed her breast right into his hand.

He was gentle, so gentle. No pinching, squeezing, hurting. Daniel caressed her breast with soft pressure, lifting the weight of it, smoothing his thumb over the areola.

He turned his face to hers and kissed her lips. It was a half kiss, landing on the side of her mouth, but the warmth in it, and the desire, were obvious. A point between Violet's legs burned.

Daniel very slowly rolled her onto her back, his body now

half covering hers. The weight of him was like the finest, warmest pillow, not trapping her but pressing her down into the layers of quilts that cushioned the hard mattress. He drew the placket of her nightdress apart, eyes flicking down to admire the breasts he caressed.

The next kiss he gave her was like breath itself. Then Daniel licked inside her mouth, slow, tender, sensual.

Violet's lips opened under his, the slow kiss becoming thorough, loving. Daniel braced himself with one hand on the mattress, while the other smoothed her breast, closing her nipple between his fingers. Their mouths came together again as they tasted each other, learning, a tender moment of discovery.

A heavy rap on the door was followed by the door banging open and the innkeeper's wife striding in with another full tray. "Good morning, Madame and Monsieur. A little *petit-déjeuner* for you. Nice and warm after the storm."

Daniel casually rolled away from Violet and sat up, moving the quilt to cover her open nightgown. "Madame, you are too kind."

Violet remained in place, her heart hammering at her sudden sense of loss. She felt Daniel's heat dissipate from around her and knew she'd never be warm again.

Simon and Monsieur Dupuis arrived in a large cart by midmorning. Daniel left Violet to ready herself while he led the two men and some villagers back to the woods to wrest the basket from the trees and load it onto the cart.

The morning was fine and crisp, the sunshine bright, but that couldn't make up for the fact that Daniel had to leave his warm nest with Violet and return to everyday life.

He'd been right that the villagers had already made off with every bit of silk from the balloon. Daniel promised Dupuis more than the price of it, and Dupuis was satisfied. Daniel always paid his debts.

Dupuis was much more interested in Daniel's experiments with his onboard combustion engine and the wind machine. Dupuis offered to take the wind machine in trade for the ruined envelope, but Daniel said no. The machine belonged to Violet.

The wind machine was relatively undamaged, though whether it still worked would have to be seen. Daniel wrapped it up and stowed it in the wooden box Simon had brought, then rode back with them and the basket on the cart to the inn.

Violet looked surprised that Daniel had returned for her. He caught her sitting at the table in their bedroom, counting out coins for a third-class ticket on the local train and inquiring from the innkeeper's wife what time it left the station.

Lord, what had people done to her? When Daniel made Violet his permanent lover, she'd understand that she would be treated better than the false Princess Ivanova ever could have been. Violet would have every luxury, and she'd have them for as long as she could put up with Daniel, and even beyond that.

Daniel steered Violet firmly downstairs to the cart and helped her onto the back of it, taking his place beside her. He said nothing about Violet's assumption he'd leave her to find her own way back to town, and Violet offered no explanation.

The drive would be long—twenty miles they'd flown in the balloon from point to point, but traveling back on the road would take much time. They had to go a long way south, Dupuis said, before finding a bridge that crossed the gorge.

Daniel loved how comfortable he felt with Violet. They held hands and dangled their feet off the back of the cart, the large basket cushioning their backs, as Simon drove them onward. Violet pointed out things she'd seen from the air, marveling on how fine it had been to have the same view as birds.

"Next time, the flight will be a little more controlled," Daniel said. "Yesterday's experiment gave me more ideas for a steering mechanism. I'll take you up in Scotland, at Kilmorgan estate—there's no place so beautiful as northern Scotland. In the summer, I mean. I wasn't joking about the snowstorms."

Violet gave him a startled look, again surprised at any indication he'd want to be with her in the future.

Daniel started to grow angry. Violet wasn't afraid of him anymore, but she still didn't trust him either. Daniel had the feeling that winning Violet's trust would be one of the most difficult things he ever did.

To calm himself, Daniel switched the conversation to the motorcar he was building, one he determined would break land-speed records for years to come. He liked how Violet's eyes lighted with interest when he talked about mass-to-speed ratios and pumps to cool the powerful engine. Another point in her favor—the debutantes currently pursuing Daniel with matrimonial intent would stare at him with unconcealed boredom whenever he mentioned the words *crankshaft* or *straight four*. Violet not only understood what he meant, but asked questions that sparked more ideas.

They reached Dupuis' farm by late afternoon. Violet and even Simon looked tired, but to Daniel the drive ended far too soon. Dupuis offered them a bed for the night, but Violet was adamant she return to Marseille and her mother. Daniel thanked Dupuis, accepted the basket of dinner Dupuis' housekeeper fixed for them, and drove Violet and Simon back to the train station.

Simon joined Violet and Daniel in the first-class train compartment, all three eating hungrily of the crusty bread, cheese, meat, and wine Dupuis had given them. Then Violet, worn out from their adventures, fell asleep against Daniel's shoulder.

Simon snored on the seat opposite, but Daniel was wide awake. He looked down at Violet's dark hair snaking across his coat, her flushed cheek, her dusky red lips parted in sleep. Her hand, limp, rested on the seat, very near Daniel's thigh.

Yes, she could stay with him as long as she wanted. He'd take care of her. Daniel didn't like casual, brief affairs, having seen his father carry out too many of those. Lord Cameron had taken a string of mistresses in rapid succession throughout Daniel's childhood—his women would come into Daniel's life and then vanish, often before Daniel had time to learn their names.

Daniel came to understand, as he grew older, that Cameron had been vastly lonely. He'd used the affairs to try to fill the hollow place Daniel's mother had brutally carved into him. Cameron hadn't trusted women, so he'd pushed them away before he could form any sort of attachment to them.

What Daniel had learned from his father's actions was that short affairs led to emptiness and impermanence. He'd made a vow long ago not to let that be his life. What he had with Violet he wanted to last a long, long time.

For now, having the soft weight of Violet's head on his shoulder was fine. She was giving him the tiniest touch of trust, lying here with him, surrendering to sleep.

Daniel hated to wake her as the train slid into Marseille, but Violet blinked as they came to a halt. She looked a bit embarrassed to have fallen asleep on him, but otherwise made no fuss.

They disembarked, and Daniel hired a cab to take them the short way to Violet's boardinghouse.

He told Simon and the cab to wait while he walked Violet to her door, the box with her machine under his arm. Night had fallen, and with it came cold. Lights warmed the windows of the boardinghouse, but the street was dark.

It seemed wrong to say good-bye to her at the front door of the prim house and leave her. Daniel should be taking Violet to his hotel, moving them to a sumptuous suite, keeping her there with him. He wanted again to stretch his body alongside hers and slide his hand into her nightdress as he'd done this morning. He remembered the satin-silk of her skin, the warm weight of her breast, the firm point of her nipple rising against the brush of his fingers. Daniel would ease her with his touch then teach her what other magic they could find together.

But slowly. Violet was skittish. He had to woo her.

"Good night, then," Daniel said to her. He took Violet's hand in a friendly handshake then remained holding it, not letting go. "I'd say that was a fine day out."

Violet made no move to withdraw her hand. "One day changed to two. My mother will scold."

"Tell her you were with a reckless man, but he took care of you just fine." *And I'll take care of you longer, if you'll let me.*

"She won't believe me. Or you. Good night, Mr. Mackenzie." Violet leaned forward and kissed him on the cheek.

A friendly kiss, or it should have been. Her lips lingered on his skin, and Daniel turned his head in the dark to lightly kiss her mouth.

Her lips were warm despite the cold, and soft, sweet. Daniel wanted to take the kiss deeper, to taste her again.

He drew back as someone passed along the street, and Violet slipped her hand from his. "Good night," she said.

"Wait. Your wind machine." Daniel took the box from under his arm, and leaned down and kissed her cheek. "Good night."

Violet took the box. "Good night."

Daniel grinned, not moving. "Good night."

Violet shifted the box to one hand, braced it against her hip, and reached for the door handle. "Good night."

Daniel stepped down from the doorstep to the street. "Good night."

She smiled over her shoulder. "Good night."

Violet opened the door, and Daniel tipped his hat. "Sleep well."

"And you."

"Good night, then."

"Good night."

Simon was watching with interest, leaning on the cab's back wheel and smoking a cigarette. He grinned as Daniel turned around one last time and waved to Violet.

"Good night," Daniel called.

"Good night," Violet returned and finally disappeared inside.

Daniel heaved a sigh, dragged a cigarette from his pocket, and accepted Simon's offer of a light. The driver looked down at them impatiently, but Daniel leaned on the coach wheel beside Simon and waited.

Simon guffawed. "If you hurry home and go to sleep, sir, you can see her again in the morning."

"Cheek," Daniel said, drawing in smoke. "Am I that bloody obvious?"

"You look as my youngest brother did when he was first wooing his woman. Didn't like to take his eyes off her for nothing."

"No?" Daniel gazed up at the window in which he'd seen Violet before. "What happened to him then?"

"Married her. And they lived happily ever after. Well, as happily as they can in a small flat with four children and a dog."

"Sounds idyllic."

"They think so. There's the light you're watching for."

A curtain went back in the upper window, a faint glow of a kerosene lamp behind it. Violet's silhouette appeared, she looking down into the street. Daniel raised his hand, and Violet returned the wave, hers graceful.

She didn't turn from the window. Violet watched Daniel, and Daniel watched her.

"Is this going to go on all night?" Simon asked. "If so, I'll step to a wine shop. I don't much understand the pubs in this country, but I'm learning to like the jug wine."

"Get into the damned coach," Daniel said. He knew he was making a complete fool of himself, but he couldn't stop.

He took off his hat, blew Violet a dramatic kiss, jumped onto the step of the coach, and told the driver to go. Simon tossed down his cigarette and flung himself inside through the other door as the carriage pulled away.

Daniel remained on the step, waving with his hat as the coach rumbled down the street. Violet shook her head and let the curtain fall, but Daniel knew she was laughing at him. He clung to the side of the carriage all the way around the corner and into the next street.

If Daniel was going to make a fool of himself, he might as well do it all the way.

~~~~~

Violet had no idea why, the next day, she put on the best dress she owned and made a fuss over her hair. Daniel wouldn't come. Their adventure was over, finished.

Not that Violet was finished with it. She'd lain awake most of the night, reliving the memory of Daniel lying behind her in the bed, his arm around her. She felt again the moment he'd rolled her over and parted her nightdress, then kissed her with such caring thoroughness. She remembered every touch, every heartbeat, every breath.

Violet dozed off as morning came, and she awoke to a tray of croissants, coffee, and a bite of cheese, but no Daniel. She donned a peach-colored broadcloth dress, the fabric so fine it felt like satin. The bodice had lace and braid appliqué, the sleeves modestly puffed, the skirt graceful. She couldn't help but picture a warm look of approval in Daniel's eyes when he saw her in it.

But he didn't come at midmorning, nor at luncheon. As the afternoon wore on, Violet made herself stop pacing, sit down, and have tea.

Outside, the short winter afternoon was ending. Celine finally came out of her bedroom, where she'd been resting all day.

"Ah, Violet, darling, there you are." She was dressed in her black bombazine, the brocade turban in her hand. "It's almost time for our appointment. I'm glad to see you've dressed well for it. We're going to be late."

Chapter 13

"Appointment?" Violet's hand jerked, and the tea in her cup nearly landed on her lovely peach skirt. "What appointment?"

Celine stared at her. "You've forgotten? You never forget appointments. But I see now why Mary had to rouse me. *She* didn't forget. Monsieur Lanier, a banker, very rich. We're going to his house to give his wife a bit of table-turning, remember? He's not a believer, and neither is his mother, but Monsieur Lanier indulges his wife. At least, that's what Mary says. She learned everything about him while you were gallivanting in the country, leaving your poor mother all alone in a strange city."

"Oh," Violet said. "That banker." Monsieur Lanier had sent a letter to the concert hall, which Mary had collected the morning Daniel had whisked Violet away. Mary trotted every day to the concert hall for their mail, which was the address on the cards she gave out to the audience. They never told anyone where they truly lived.

Monsieur Lanier had asked for a private consultation in his letter, offering to pay well for it. Violet would have dealt with answering the letter and setting the appointment, but Daniel had arrived, and she'd gone.

"You agreed to go to his home?" Violet asked. "You know we should set up the consultation at a place of our choosing, especially if unbelievers attend."

"Don't be silly. Mary says the Laniers have a comfortable house, and it is easier to turn unbelievers if they see incontrovertible evidence of the truth in their very own homes. Besides, Mary says their cook makes excellent cakes, and the house has good heating." For someone so attached to the spiritual, Celine loved her bodily comforts.

Violet sighed and quickly drained her teacup. "Blast. This means I have to wear those dratted veils."

Celine gave her a triumphant smile. "If I have to wear the turban, you have to wear the veils. The next place we go, we'll be Romany again and dress in easy skirts and scarves. Much more manageable."

Monsieur Lanier had offered to send his private coach, but Violet negated that idea, much to Celine's disappointment. They must go by hired coach, Violet said. That way, they could leave the boardinghouse as the respectable widow and her daughter and change into their personas on the way. Violet wanted no connection between the stage shows and the two ladies at the boardinghouse. Saved trouble all around.

Monsieur Lanier and his wife and mother lived on a fashionable street of elegant town houses, each with tall windows hung with thick drapes. Lights shone behind the draperies, making the houses look cozy and warm inside. The hired coach stopped at the doorstep of Monsieur Lanier's house precisely at eight, and Violet and Celine were ushered inside. Mary took their wraps and followed one of the housemaids down the back stairs to wait until they were ready to leave. All as usual.

The younger Madame Lanier—a thirtyish woman with blond hair and large brown eyes—wished to contact her deceased mother, whom she'd much loved. Her husband, who was a little older than his wife, made it clear, as they took seats around the dining room table, that he thought this all nonsense. But his little Coralie had to have her notions.

The older Madame Lanier said nothing, but she obviously thought little Coralie a complete fool and nowhere near good enough for her son.

Celine took her place at the head of the table, and Violet, garbed in her peach gown and the dark veils, stood a little behind her left shoulder. Violet would be on hand to bring Celine anything she needed, to catch her if her trance made her faint, or to provide special effects when necessary. Celine didn't like the special effects, but sometimes they made a difference when a client hesitated to believe Celine could contact the spirit world. When Violet used the effects, they always got paid.

"Do you have something of your mother's prepared for me, Madame?" Celine smiled kindly at the shy young Coralie. Coralie nodded and dropped a locket into Violet's gloved hands. Violet passed the locket to Celine, who took it between both hands and closed her eyes. "The connection, it is quite strong," she said in her Russian-accented French. "She gave this to you."

The elder Madame Lanier snorted. "There's no magic in knowing that. Who else would a mother leave her locket to?"

Celine ignored her. She had a gift for focusing only on the believers and entering into their world. Everyone else ceased to exist for her.

"She is near," Celine said. "I feel her. She misses you."

"And I miss her," Coralie said in a near whisper. "Can you tell her? Please?"

The poor woman was starved for love. Violet watched the family from under her veils, seeing contempt from old Madame Lanier and bare tolerance from the husband.

Violet knew exactly what Coralie felt. Spending the day and night and another day with Daniel had been like being given a taste of a feast she hadn't been invited to partake of. The trouble was, the taste made Violet crave the feast all the more.

"You may tell her yourself," Celine said to Coralie. "Let us turn the lights low and see if the spirits will let us through."

Violet moved to the wall and turned down the gas to the chandelier. Once the room had dimmed, Violet lit the candles in the silver candelabra they'd brought with them. While Madame Lanier went on about how ridiculous it all was— *How are we to see whether they trick us in the dark?*—Celine closed her eyes, joined hands with Coralie, and sent out her supplication to the spirits.

Violet sat down at the table this time, pulling on gloves as she took a place between her mother and the older Madame Lanier. She had few tricks to employ when she couldn't set up a house or theatre beforehand, but she had already pressed her bare palm, coated with phosphor-luminescent paint, onto a wall when she busied herself turning out the lights. Behind Celine, a handprint began to glow in the dark.

Coralie gasped, then gasped again when a loud rap broke the stillness.

"Ah," Celine said, her eyes closed, hands rigid. "Are you there?"

One loud rap indicated *Yes.*

"She's here," Coralie said excitedly. "*Maman?*"

"Of course she isn't here," Madame Lanier said. "The girl in the veils is knocking on the table."

Violet took her gloved hands from her lap and laid them on the table just as the spirit gave a decided double rap. She always enjoyed employing her tricks right in front of the most skeptical. Misdirection was the key. *Make them doubt their own doubts.*

"Two knocks mean *no*," Celine said. "Are you still there, Spirit?"

One hard knock. Violet lifted her foot carefully from the small pedal she'd dropped on the soft carpet under the table. It connected with a little drum with a speaking tube attached, which she'd found at a market in Paris. The contraption made a considerable noise but was small enough to tuck into the box with her matches and extra candles, or slip into her pocket in a pinch.

"Can you open the veil?" Celine asked the air. "Let me through? We are looking for Madame Saint-Vincent. Seraphine Louise Saint-Vincent."

Coralie gasped again. "How did you know her name? I never said."

Celine knew because Mary had gathered every bit of information on the client she could beforehand. Violet usually helped her, but Mary was an expert. Few noticed a maid running an errand on the street, and servants were happy to stop and pass the time in gossip. Mary was open and friendly with women, coy and cheeky with the men, and fluent in several languages.

"*She* knows," Celine said. "I shall try to find my guide now. Hush. I need quiet."

While Celine sat still, preparing for her trance, Violet's thoughts wandered.

Daniel had not come today. And why should he? Violet had no business putting on her best dress and waiting for him like a love-struck schoolgirl. Daniel didn't owe her a call. He had things to do, people to see, engines to invent. He might have gone back to visit Monsieur Dupuis, to talk about the balloon adventure, or about propulsion and internal combustion, things of that nature.

Or Daniel was busy being a wealthy man-about-town. This was the south of France in the winter season, and Daniel must know people in the highest circles. He might even now be drinking wine with a count, smoking with a duke, dancing with a duchess. Or planning to move on to Nice and Cannes, or Monte Carlo, where the lovely young butterflies in the Casino would touch their fingers to his arm, and smile at him, and entice . . .

Violet's heart stung, and her foot slipped. A loud knock burst through just as Celine began speaking as Adelaide, the Parisian girl.

"Oh," Celine shrieked in her little-girl voice. "She is here!" In the pause, Violet gently moved the drum and pedal back under her skirts.

Celine's voice changed again, taking on a lower note and a scratchy tone. "Coralie, my love, is that you?"

"Yes!" Coralie's eyes swam with tears. "Yes, *Maman*, I'm here."

"Are you well, *petite*?"

"I think so, *Maman*. I had that awful cold, but it's been gone weeks now."

"But are you happy, child?" the voice of Madame Saint-Vincent went on. "It is a different thing. Your husband, he means well, but perhaps he is not as attentive as he ought to be."

Coralie shot a look at her husband, whose brows drew down. Monsieur Lanier was a well-fed man, not quite fat, with soft hands and an expensive suit. If he kept eating his cook's fine cakes, he would become portly later in life, not having the height to carry weight well. He had all his hair, though, thick waves of it slicked with pomade. He pomaded his chestnut brown moustache as well.

"Oh no," Coralie said nervously. "He is . . . a very good husband."

"I never liked him," said Celine as Madame Saint-Vincent. "Perhaps he will grow kinder when his goat of a mother is no longer there to command him."

"Oh . . ." Coralie's cheeks went red as she flashed a glance at her outraged mother-in-law.

Celine went on, still in the scratchy voice. "If his mother is here, tell her I am watching her. I will know if she is not kind to you, and I will take steps."

"No, no, *Maman*. No need. Madame Lanier is quite kind to me."

"Ha!" The sound rang through the room. "The lie becomes you, my darling. You are so angelic, little Coralie. But beware. Treachery surrounds you." The table shook and shook hard. "I will look out for you, but you must beware."

"Stop!" The elder Madame Lanier sprang from her chair, her face dark with anger. She pointed at Celine. "This woman is a liar and a fraud. And *that one . . ."* She swung her rigid finger to Violet. "She has a device under the table that is making noises and moving it."

"Madame, I assure you, no." Violet didn't need a device to move the table. Bracing her legs against it and rocking it sufficed.

Madame Lanier jerked up the tablecloth and peered beneath. Violet, with the drum safely beneath her skirts under the chair, didn't move.

"You," Madame Lanier snapped at Violet. "Stand up. Turn out your pockets. I want to see what you have in there."

An empty bottle that had contained the phosphor-luminescent paint was all Violet had in her pocket. The glowing hand was fading behind her mother—she or Mary would wipe the wall clean before they went.

"You had better do as she says," Monsieur Lanier said to Violet in a stentorian voice.

Before Violet could decide whether to risk showing the empty, unlabeled bottle, her mother's voice rose to a shriek. "No. *No! Adelaide . . . help me!*"

Celine clutched her throat, her eyes widening at some fear only she could see. She writhed in the chair, her breathing hoarse, spittle flecking her lips. She continued to wail, the sound rolling around the high-ceilinged room, then she began striking at unseen attackers.

Violet rushed to her side. "Please, fetch help! The countess is in danger!"

Monsieur Lanier and his mother remained rooted in place, staring in shock at the display. Coralie leapt to her feet and yanked a bellpull, then rushed to Celine, trying to catch her flailing hands. As several footmen, two maids, and Mary tumbled in, Violet retrieved her pedal and drum and concealed them in her box.

Mary produced smelling salts, which calmed Celine. Coralie hovered, wanting to help, but Madame Lanier held out her hand, her anger making the curls of her carefully coiffed gray hair tremble.

"Come away, Coralie. These are tricksters and frauds, and they are not getting a penny of my money."

Oh, damn and blast. Violet ground her teeth. They *needed* that fee.

Coralie showed some backbone at last. She refused to leave, gave orders to the servants, and oversaw getting Celine into a hired conveyance she sent a footman to fetch.

Madame Lanier loudly announced her intention to retire, ignored by everyone but her son, and marched upstairs as Celine was bundled out the door. Celine, surrounded by servants and breathless with gratitude for them taking care of her, entered the coach. While the attention was around her, Violet stepped back into the dining room, wiped the remains of phosphorus paint from the walls, and stuffed the handkerchief into her pocket. She'd already shoved the box of their accoutrements and the candelabra at Mary.

Violet reached the foyer again to see the hired coach pulling away from the door, Mary looking anxiously out the window. Violet rushed out, but the coach kept moving, its lights growing smaller in the darkness. *Bloody . . .*

A touch on her arm made her jump. Monsieur Lanier stood next to her, a look of apology on his face. Violet remembered, in her agitation, to remain in her persona. "But where have they gone?" she asked, her Russian accent heightened.

"I told your coachman to drive on. I would like to speak with you, Mademoiselle le Princess."

What about? Violet hesitantly followed him into a parlor, which was opposite the dining room. Monsieur Lanier kept the door open, and stood looking at Violet without asking her to sit down. She watched him nervously, noting the distance between herself and the door, and the obstacles she'd have to navigate to reach it—a sturdy armchair, a tall table with square legs filled with knickknacks, a little desk.

"Mademoiselle, I must ask you to remove those veils."

"Oh no, Monsieur." Violet needed no hesitation over that. The veils both provided a fiction and anonymity. She could run about the city in her ordinary clothes and have no one connect her to their show. "I cannot. It is forbidden me."

Monsieur Lanier's lips relaxed from their stern line. "Nonsense, you are a guest in my house. You may trust me."

He moved quickly for a sedentary man. Before Violet could evade him, he deftly caught and threw back the veils.

Violet swung away and made for the door, but Monsieur Lanier got ahead of her, cutting her off and closing the door before Violet could reach it.

"Really, Monsieur, I must go."

"In a moment. Don't worry, I will not be summoning the police. I had a wager with myself—either you covered your face because you truly were a dangerous beauty, or you were so ugly you feared you'd drive your audiences away." He gave her an admiring look. "I am pleased to see that the beauty is true."

"You are too kind, Monsieur," Violet said, pretending shyness. She ducked her head—he'd seen her, nothing she could do, but she didn't need him memorizing her features.

"I also wanted to apologize for my mother's behavior,"

Monsieur Lanier said, sounding businesslike now. This banker would not fall to the ground and worship a deadly beautiful princess. "My mother is elderly and sometimes forgets her manners. She said she will not pay you, but please accept this for your trouble."

He held up a roll of banknotes. The bundle was pleasantly thick, but Violet, who could count notes faster than a bookmaker at a racetrack, knew it was still only about one-quarter their usual fee.

Monsieur Lanier pressed the money into Violet's hand, closing her fingers around it. He kept his hand wrapped around hers, and clamped the other about her wrist.

"And perhaps you may do me the honor . . ." He smiled into her face. "My wife is of a sickly disposition. Not often at home to me, if you know what I mean."

Violet's mouth went dry, her heart jumping in the beginnings of panic. "Monsieur, I must go tend to the countess. She needs me."

"Why? She has plenty of servants. You're a *princess*, aren't you?" He said the word with a knowing sneer. "Not the sort of woman who waits on other women. The countess is a good actress, and she will be quite well when you reach her."

"Truly, I must go." Violet tried to pull away, but his grip was powerful.

Monsieur Lanier grabbed her other wrist. He pushed her against a wall—the wallpaper a pleasant cornflower blue with sprigs of white roses on it. The shape and size of the little climbing roses fixed in Violet's mind, the loops of the vines becoming a mesmerizing pattern.

Monsieur Lanier released one of Violet's wrists so he could squeeze her breast, hard. Violet tried to scream, but her throat closed up in dryness.

She struggled—*how dare he?*—and kicked with her high-heeled boot. Monsieur Lanier blocked her kick with surprising deftness, and he curved over her, his breath wine scented, his eyes glittering.

"Now, you stay still and give me what I want, and your fee will be considerably higher. Be a good princess . . ."

He said more, but his words were lost as Violet's fear came.

Stay still, girl. The voice drifted from the past. *You have me so randy, it won't take long.*

Violet could hear nothing more, but she could feel, sensations tearing her back to the moment twelve years ago. *Rough hands inside her bodice, pantalets yanked down, cold fingers between her thighs. She tried to fight, but the hands were too strong, his fingers over her throat pushed her into the wall . . .*

"Be quiet, damn you. I said, be *quiet!*"

The voice saying the words was in the present, immediate and insistent. Violet swam back to awareness to hear a high-pitched keening coming from her own throat. She was still dressed, on her feet, her head against the wall with its cornflower blue wallpaper and too many white roses.

A slap sounded. Violet felt the sting on her face, heard her keening turn to hiccups.

Monsieur Lanier shook her, her head banging into the wall. "Stop it. What is the matter with you?"

Violet found her strength, and fought. Monsieur Lanier slapped her again, then grabbed her swinging fists as he shouted, "Help me! She's gone mad!"

Violet barely registered the Lanier servants hurrying into the parlor. Her veils were down again, concealing her face, but she continued to flail against Monsieur Lanier.

Strong hands seized her, and she found herself stumbling into the hall then the foyer. The front door was open, cold air cascading into the house. A shove on her back, and Violet staggered out into the street. Her coat landed on the cobbles next to her, and the door slammed firmly behind her.

Violet's self-preservation made her snatch up her coat and take a few hurrying steps down the street. She stopped a few houses along and hung on to railings in front of it to catch her breath.

She was all right. She was on her feet, her heart was beating, her clothes were whole, and her gloved hands kept her upright by holding the cold railing. She was all right.

Violet realized she'd thrust the wad of money Monsieur Lanier had given her into her skirt pocket. Something inside her had made her not let it go. *At least we salvaged that from this disaster.*

The coach taking her mother home had long gone, but Violet didn't worry too much. Violet, Mary, and her mother had a rule—if something went wrong at a sitting or presentation, they were to escape on their own and meet at a designated spot. No waiting for one another, because they had a better chance of slipping away into the streets on their own.

Violet had instructed that for their Marseille sojourn they'd meet back at the boardinghouse, unless that had been compromised. But it hadn't, thanks to Violet insisting on not using Monsieur Lanier's private conveyance. They'd have a warm place to sleep tonight. *Small mercies.*

Violet thrust her shaking arms into her coat sleeves. She wanted to run, run, back to her tiny room to curl around herself and weep. Instead, she dragged in a breath and started down the street, moving at a brisk walk.

When she judged herself far enough from the Lanier house, she ducked into a darker passage and jerked off the veils, which she stuffed into her coat pocket. They were so gauzy they rolled up almost into nothing. Violet smoothed her hair and settled her coat, ready to be the young woman walking home from work again.

But before she could take a step, her heart began pounding sickeningly fast, and bile rose in her throat. Reaction.

Violet feared she'd have to stop and heave up her small dinner against the wall. She hugged her arms over her chest, willing herself to breathe normally, but sobs came regardless, the small sounds of them loud in the darkness.

Think of Daniel.

The thought sailed into her head as though one of her mother's spirits had spoken it to her. *Think of Daniel.*

The comforting weight of him as he'd kissed her in the high bed, the way the wind had tugged his hair as he'd frantically tried to steer the balloon. Daniel's shirt sticking to his damp torso, the black tattoo that curled around his tanned arm. Violet thought of the comfort of his hand in hers as they rode away from the village in the cart, then his ridiculous romantic farce of clinging to the side of his carriage and waving at her after he'd said good night last night.

Violet's knot of terror began to loosen. Yesterday morning

in the inn, as she'd eaten a brioche with fresh butter, she'd watched Daniel shave himself. He'd lathered his face with the soap and brush the innkeeper had brought him then carefully scraped at his cheeks, watching himself in the small, dark mirror above the washstand.

So cozy and intimate they'd been, Daniel shaving without embarrassment while Violet breakfasted a few feet away. The bed behind them had been rumpled from their sleep, as though they'd been husband and wife in truth.

Violet's fear faded still more. She drew a long, cleansing breath and moved out from the passage, fancying she could still hear Daniel's laughter.

No, she *did* hear it. This was a fashionable part of town, the street she emerged into lined with restaurants and cafés. A knot of young men and women stood near the entrance of one of the restaurants, either coming out or going in, Violet couldn't say.

Daniel was with them. He wore a greatcoat and high silk hat like the others, but his kilt set him apart, as did his broad frame and his deep, booming laughter.

The men with Daniel were in their twenties or early thirties, she judged, his friends and cronies. The ladies who accompanied them glittered. They wore frocks of blue, green, gold, silver, the bodices daringly cut, delicate skin protected from the cold with furs. Diamonds sparkled on bosoms and hair, cheeks were rouged, hair crowned with feathers. Long gloves hid slim arms but showed off bejeweled bracelets.

These were not the shy, young debutantes of society; they were courtesans.

As Violet watched, the red-haired lady next to Daniel wound her fingers around his arm and ran her other hand up his back to his shoulder. Daniel turned to laugh down at her, the smile on his face full of warmth.

Violet's heart squeezed so hard she had to put her fist to her chest. She ducked back into the shadows, but Daniel never turned, never saw her.

Not for you, a voice inside her head said. *Not for you.*

Violet watched numbly as the group turned from the restaurant and sought waiting coaches. Daniel helped the red-haired woman up into his carriage with the same gallantry he'd used to assist Violet. He removed his hat as he stepped into the coach with the woman, followed by another gentleman and lady.

The other men and women swarmed into the rest of the carriages, but Violet scarcely noted them. Her gaze was all for Daniel, his broad arm that rested against the window, the flash of his face as he threw back his head and laughed at something.

The carriages jerked forward, moving off in the direction of theatres and cabarets.

Violet remained in place until they'd rumbled well away. She tried to force herself to stand upright, to leave the shelter of the passage to continue her way home.

She ended up against the dirty wall, half doubled over, her fists balled into her stomach. Sobs wracked her body, and tears streamed down her face.

Violet cried as her heart broke, the warmth of her night with Daniel dissolving before the heat in his eyes as he'd smiled at the courtesan.

*

Daniel was happy to see Richard Mason, an old university mate with a brilliant mind, but Daniel hated watching the man waste that brilliant mind on drink and sexual diversions.

The women Richard had brought for Daniel and his other friends were charming but they had nothing in their eyes. Before meeting Violet, Daniel would have happily dallied the night away with one or two of them, wallowing in a warm bed and all kinds of debauchery. Why not? Bodily pleasures must be sated or they distracted him too much. At least, that was his excuse.

But now Daniel had met Violet.

The looks the ladies gave him contained too much avarice. Daniel was rich, and they wanted him to move some of his money from his pocket to theirs.

He'd seen such sentiment all too often in the women his father used to bring home, and he wasn't much interested tonight. Nor was Daniel interested in sating himself while remaining detached. Not appealing. Not after Violet.

He'd tried to call on her earlier this evening, but the prim landlady had informed him Violet and her mother had gone out. No, she didn't know where, and it was their business, wasn't it? Daniel had thanked her and departed.

In Richard's carriage on their way to a cabaret, Daniel feigned exhaustion from his long balloon flight, mention of which brought boredom to the ladies' eyes. Daniel contrasted this with the glowing excitement in Violet's as they'd soared across the countryside.

When Daniel said he'd return alone to his hotel, Richard expressed genuine sorrow to lose Daniel's company tonight. Daniel silently vowed to spend more time with the man. Richard needed true friends.

Daniel said good night to them in front of the cabaret, slipping a thick wad of banknotes into the hand of the red-haired courtesan to ease the sting of his leaving her. Her disappointment lessened considerably.

Richard and his ladies would be surprised to learn that after they entered the cabaret, Daniel left the glittering hotels, restaurants, theatres, and illicit casinos of the city to walk to a more frumpy side of town, replete with boardinghouses and shops for the poor but respectable.

More surprised to watch him stop across the street from one particular boardinghouse, step into the shadows of a closed shop's doorway, and look up at the soft glow of a window opposite.

Daniel waited there until he saw the glow go out, then he kissed his fingertips toward the window and walked away.

Back on the glittering side of town, he entered his hotel room, truly tired now. Every lamp had been lit in the parlor of his suite, in anticipation of Daniel's return, including the multiarmed gas chandelier and a host of wall sconces.

All these provided bright illumination for the figure of the girl child lying fast asleep on the scrolled French sofa, she curled up around herself, her red gold curls tumbling over her cheeks.

Chapter 14

Daniel stifled his dismay at the sight of the little girl. He lifted a throw from the armchair and draped it carefully over her. With any luck she'd continue sleeping.

The girl's eyes popped open, gray and full of mischief that matched her mother's—both the color and the mischief. She squealed in delight and sat up straight. "Danny!" she shouted in a voice that would wake half the hotel. "I waited for you!"

Daniel retrieved the throw from the floor and wrapped it around her again. "I see that, mite. What are you doing here? If you've run away from home again, your mum's going to scold both of us something bad."

"I didn't run away." Gavina Mackenzie smoothed her hair in a very grown-up gesture. "Only down the stairs. We're staying in your hotel. Isn't that grand, Danny?"

"Staying here? Who is?"

"All of us. Mum and Dad. And me. Stuart is with Aunt Eleanor, because he's too little to travel all this way." Gavina looked very pleased with herself that she at seven was more grown up than her four-and-a-half-year-old baby brother. "Mummy said we should stay here and surprise you."

Daniel pressed his hands to his chest. "Consider me surprised."

And a bit annoyed. Daniel loved his family, but the collective lot of them could never mind their own bloody business. Obviously Daniel's stepmother Ainsley had dragged out of Ian where Daniel had gone and decided to rush off to France to find out what he was up to.

A tap at the door was followed by Ainsley Mackenzie herself. She was dressed for evening in a gray silk trimmed with maroon lace, her shoulders bare over small puffed sleeves. Tiny diamonds sparkled in her hair and at her throat—Richard's courtesans in contrast had coated themselves with the things.

Ainsley had fair hair, which she'd dressed in the latest fashion, but somehow Ainsley never looked overdone or artificial. The spirit of her shone through, and Daniel regarded her fondly. She was the woman who'd rescued his father.

"Hello, Danny. I saw you come in." Ainsley enclosed him in a lemon-scented hug. "Gavina wanted to wait in here for you. I forbade her, but I see she managed to get here anyway."

"Without a key," Daniel said. "What have you been teaching her, Stepmama?" In addition to her womanly charms, Ainsley was also an excellent picklock.

"The maid let me in," Gavina said. "I said I was your sister and gave her a coin."

She was learning young. Daniel leaned down and lifted Gavina into his arms. She was growing tall and strong.

"You haven't answered the question, either of you," Daniel growled. "Why are you here, Stepmama, and not in London helping Aunt Isabella run the Season? Or preparing to go to Berkshire for the training?" Ainsley and Daniel's father moved to Berkshire every year so Cameron could prepare his horses for the racing season. The entire Mackenzie family would descend upon them there later in the spring, as per tradition.

Ainsley gave Daniel a little frown. "I was worried about you, Danny. I heard you were done over by louts and left in the gutter. But you never said a word." Ainsley touched Daniel's cheek where the bruises were still fading, covered by new ones from the rough balloon landing. "What happened to you?"

"Nothing interesting. Uncle Ian peached on me, did he?"

"Ian?" Ainsley's eyes widened. "You don't believe I could pry anything from *Ian Mackenzie* he didn't want me to know, do you? No, I pried it out of Beth. She's worried about you as well."

"And she told you I'd gone to Marseille," Daniel said guardedly, while Gavina watched from the safety of Daniel's arms. It was midnight, and the girl didn't look tired at all.

"Beth didn't know why," Ainsley said. "Are you in another scrape?"

Daniel couldn't help his laugh. "I haven't been in a scrape since university. I gave them up. My friend Richard Mason is here, and I've been spending some hours with him." Not a lie.

"Ah yes, the young man you're worried is wasting away in debauchery. I have no doubt you'll set him straight. You're good at that sort of thing. I did hear you went off ballooning and wrecked the thing. Don't look so surprised. Word travels, especially among the English abroad." Ainsley gave him a knowing smile. "*And* I heard a young lady was with you when you crashed. I see she is not with you now. She must have decided being in your company was too fraught with danger."

"Something like that."

"Probably for the best." Ainsley reached for Gavina, and her daughter readily wrapped arms around her. "If a lady cannot keep up with a gentleman she chooses to pursue, she has no business pursuing him. I ought to know. That's how I ended up with your father."

Ainsley had proved she definitely could keep up with Cameron, much to Cameron's surprise. The man who'd shut love out of his life had not been able to shut out Ainsley.

"It's lucky you're here," Ainsley went on. "My friend Leonie is having a grand ball at her house tomorrow evening. We're attending, and she would love to see you there."

Daniel stifled a groan. Leonie was the Comtesse de Chenault, who'd become Ainsley's friend when Ainsley worked for Queen Victoria. She was wealthy, influential, and had a large house outside of Marseille to which the fashionable flocked. "I can guess what for. It's bad enough Aunt Eleanor and Aunt Isabella are thrusting debutantes at me right and left, but I thought you had more heart. Don't tell me you're joining their schemes to get me shackled."

Ainsley blinked in innocence. "I said nothing about debutantes. Did you hear the word *debutante* come out of my mouth?"

"But that is who attends grand balls given by comtesses, isn't it? Debutantes, pushed forward by their mamas with an enthusiasm that's chilling to see. Why this rush to marry me off? Eleanor's two boys and Dad stand between me and the ducal throne, and they're all healthy, thank God."

"We aren't thinking about heirs," Ainsley said, looking indignant. "We want you to be happy, Danny. To be settled."

"To me, *happy* and *settled* are not the same thing. Give me a bit more life first, and tell Isabella and Eleanor to stop throwing insipid eighteen-year-olds at me."

"Eighteen?" Gavina broke in. "That's *old*. You should get married, Danny, and have babies so I can play with them."

Ainsley gave her daughter an admonishing look and went on, "You know I am the last woman in the world to tell you not to follow your heart. But how do you know you'll not find a young lady to steal that heart if you never let yourself go near them? You have to try, you know. Will you at least come with us to the ball?"

She met his gaze, something hopeful in her gray eyes. Though Ainsley didn't condone Eleanor and Isabella coercing Daniel to every soiree, ball, supper party, and boating party rife with eligible young misses, Daniel knew she shared his aunts' wishes to see him wed. She wanted Daniel to have a happy marriage and children of his own. To begin right, to erase the fact that Daniel's growing up had been hard on him.

This was important to her, and Ainsley was important to Daniel. She'd made their broken family whole again.

"Aye, very well," Daniel said, resigned. "I'll go."

"Thank you." Ainsley pulled Daniel into another hug, her arms still full of Gavina, who at last was starting to look a *little* weary. "Good night, Danny. We'll see you at breakfast."

She and Gavina departed, both looking happy, and Daniel closed the door behind them.

He sighed as he stripped off his coat and cravat. He'd told Simon not to wait up for him, so he had the rooms to himself now, as long as Gavina didn't sneak back in. No saying she wouldn't pretend to fall asleep in bed and then be right back down here.

Daniel poured himself a large measure of whiskey and wandered into his bedroom, his thoughts mixed.

He'd go to the bloody grand ball and be civil. He wouldn't marry any of the girls the comtesse shoved at him, but he could be polite.

Daniel knew the ball would not introduce him to a wife, because when he thought about breezing into a home filled with his inventions, dogs, and small children, it was Violet Daniel saw, with startling clarity, lifting her head to give Daniel a welcoming and loving smile.

～～～

"Miss," Mary said, coming into Violet's darkened room where she lay in bed. "Ain't ye going to get up, miss?"

"Why?" Violet asked, listless.

She'd been here dozing on and off throughout the afternoon. Her terror at the hands of Lanier, followed by the emotional jolt of seeing Daniel with a lover, had given her another sleepless night. This morning Violet had lapsed into a stupor that was not quite sleep, leaving her groggy and unwilling to rise.

"Your mum's worried about you," Mary said. "And we have another job tonight."

Violet sank further into the pillows, giving in to lethargy. "Why?" she repeated.

"Monsieur Lanier stiffed us most of the fee, didn't he? Your mum is so tired after last night, and we need coin, you know we do."

Violet lay still, while sorrow and exhaustion spilled over her. "What job?"

"Fortune-teller for a fashionable party."

Violet let out a long sigh. That meant Violet dressing up as a Romany and sitting at a table for hours, telling giggling young women they'd marry tall, handsome men and have many prosperous children. Violet had a knack for palm reading, so any call for a traditional fortune-teller was down to her.

Celine didn't believe in fortune-telling, in any case. She considered palm reading, card reading, or crystal gazing the height of nonsense. *The spirits communicate directly through me—when they wish to,* she'd say. *I can't call them with cards or by looking at the lines on someone's hand. They scoff at that.*

However, Celine was not averse to Violet earning some coin by her skill. As attached to the spirit world as she was, Celine did have a practical side.

"I can't," Violet said, barely able to utter the words. "Mary, I just can't. I'm so tired."

"But we need the money, miss."

"I think we should leave here," Violet murmured wearily. "Go somewhere we've never been before." Somewhere Daniel and his fashionable friends were not likely to follow. "Canada, perhaps. I've heard Montreal is a fine city. We can speak French there."

Mary shook her head. "You know Madame will never travel that far over the sea." She came to the bed, straightening and smoothing Violet's covers. "And our contract at the theatre is until the end of the month. We have to live here at least until then." Mary, dark haired, plain faced, kind, and practical, always said what needed to be said.

"I know, blast it."

Violet closed her eyes. She saw again the French countryside unrolling before her under the balloon, heard the sound of wind in the ropes and the hiss of Daniel's machine, smelled the scent of the sky, and felt the warmth of Daniel beside her.

Life and its petty troubles flowed away behind her. Aloft over the world, she could be Violet, not the fake Princess Ivanova, or Mademoiselle Bastien, or any of the other personas she'd invented in her life.

Up in the balloon, Violet had been no one but herself, someone she hadn't been in a long, long time. Whatever else he'd done, Daniel had given that to her.

"When we're finished with the contract, we can go," Mary was saying. She patted Violet's knee through the blanket.

"Someplace nice. Maybe a spa town in Germany. Those are always pretty."

Violet opened her eyes, the sanctuary of her vision fleeing. "Thank you for trying to comfort me, Mary. Tell Mama I'll do the job."

If Violet could rise from her bed. The images of the balloon flight vanished, and she again felt the horror of Monsieur Lanier's hands on her, the sting of his slap on her cheek. Then the kick to the gut when she'd seen Daniel climb into the coach with the courtesan, he smiling at her the same way he'd smiled at Violet.

No other man in her life had made Violet feel completely valued for herself alone. She'd sworn that Daniel had seen through her, all the way to the shivering pieces of her soul. And he hadn't turned away in disgust, hadn't treated her like the whore Monsieur Lanier assumed her to be.

Daniel had treated her like a friend.

"Miss?" Mary asked, worry in her voice.

Violet opened her eyes again and sighed. "I'll do it," she said in a dull voice. "Fetch my costume and help me dress."

Daniel spent his day with Richard Mason. While Daniel breakfasted with his family in their suite, Simon had brought a message from Richard, who'd pitifully begged Daniel to come see him.

Daniel found Richard in elegant rooms at another hotel, in bed, feverish, hungover, and despondent. Richard expected Daniel to settle in for the day, reading newspapers and lamenting on the state of the world, sharing whiskey until Richard felt better.

Daniel was impatient with tending him today, wanting a chance to return to Violet. His time with her hadn't been nearly long enough yet. He needed more of her.

But Richard was in a bad way, and so unhappy that Daniel stayed. Daniel suspected something else was wrong with the man besides a hangover and too much debauchery. Richard didn't say, but he was tired and moody, and the edge had gone from his razor-keen mind. Daniel realized what was the matter

before he departed later in the afternoon—Richard was syph-
ilitic.

"You need to tell the woman you were with last night,"
Daniel said, stubbing out his last cigar and rising to leave.

Richard looked at him in surprise. "Tell her what?"

"About your affliction. Only fair she knows."

"What?" Richard stared, flushing.

"And get treatment. Doctors are brilliant nowadays.
There's a man in Munich, Doktor Schauman. He's intelligent
and will actually heal you, not give you a quack cure. Tell him
I sent you."

Richard remained openmouthed, color deepening through
his skin. "He treated you?"

"No." Daniel had been wise enough to avoid the affliction.
"He's a friend. He's working on cures for many dreadful diseases, including this one. Just trust me, lad. Go. And when
ye've done and can speak like the reasonable human being ye
once were, look me up."

"Right." Richard sank back into his chair, his eyes too
bright. Sad waste of a man. "Thank you, Danny. You're a
friend. Not a word of this to anyone?"

"Of course not." Daniel took his hat and coat from a servant who looked relieved Daniel had talked some sense into
his master, and departed.

He walked back to his hotel deep in thought. Cameron, he
realized, had worried that Daniel would turn out like Richard.
Dissipated, ill, broken at a young age. Daniel had given his
father plenty of reason to worry—he'd been more interested
in cards, ladies, and drink than studies, and had more than
once run away from school to pursue decadent pleasures.

But Daniel had been reacting to Cameron's habit of sending him off to his uncles or tutors while Cameron disappeared
with his women. Daniel had always supposed his father was
pushing him away, not wanting the bother of his son.

Daniel understood more charitably now that Cameron had
feared himself to be a bad father, that Daniel might turn out
just like him if they spent too much time together. Cameron
had been a womanizer and a drinker, devoted to nothing but
his own pleasure. The only things that had saved Cam from

being completely dissipated were his love for his horses, which he cared for meticulously, and his son, whom he loved but didn't know how to.

Poor Dad. I gave him hell, didn't I?

When Daniel reached the hotel, he stopped at his father's suite. A servant let him in, and Cameron turned from the fireplace, where he'd been enjoying a cigar.

"Good, Daniel, I've been meaning to ask you—"

Cameron broke off in surprise when Daniel put his arms around his father and pulled the larger man into a hard embrace.

"You did your best, Dad," Daniel said. "Even if I was an ungrateful little monster."

Cameron returned the embrace somewhat bemusedly, then drew back. His Mackenzie-golden eyes fixed on his son, smoke from his cigar curling around them both. "Daniel, what the hell are you talking about?"

"Gratitude from an ungrateful child. Take it. You did well."

"You must be drunk."

"Maybe a little. Sat with a sick friend nursing a whiskey decanter. Too much time on my hands makes me think."

"I see that."

The edge Richard had lost was still honed on Cameron. Cameron had married in scandal, lost his first wife in a tragedy that only increased the scandal, then muddled along trying to raise a son on his own. Finding Ainsley had given him a chance to try again.

"What were you meaning to ask me?" Daniel asked.

"About a horse. It doesn't matter now. Ye've broken my train of thought."

"Sorry. Ran into it with one of mine."

"Ainsley told me she talked you into going to this do of the comtesse's," Cameron said. "Some advice—keep your wits about you around the debs. One remark on the weather and they'll run back to their fathers and say you proposed. Some of them are desperate for husbands."

"Poor things if that's true. I like the way Ian's Belle thinks—that a woman can be something on her own without marriage."

Cameron made a noise of disparagement. "When she's out of the schoolroom and a handsome young man winks at her, she might change her mind."

Daniel grinned. "That will be Gavina soon enough."

Cameron gave him a dark look. "Don't remind me." His expression softened. "Doesn't seem fair, does it, that I was so hard on you, but I spoil her and Stu rotten?"

They'd almost lost Gavina once. Daniel recalled the cold winter night when hope had been dust in his mouth, when he'd thought he'd have to watch his parents be broken by the loss of their beloved baby daughter. Tragedy had been averted, but the fear had left its mark.

"Don't be so hard on yourself," Daniel said, patting his father's shoulder. "You're only human. And don't worry, I won't let Gavina become too much of a brat." He drew a breath and let Cameron go. "Now, I'd better get a move on and dress for this ball, or Ainsley will never let us hear the last of it."

The rambling manor house of Comtesse de Chenault, which reposed on a hill overlooking the lights of Marseille, was overheated and overfull. Violet had been sitting at her table in a corner of the drawing room for an hour now, telling fortunes to the comtesse's eager guests.

She'd dressed in a voluminous skirt, loose blouse, and tightly laced black bodice, with a scarf over her head and a long necklace of coins clinking on her bosom. A worn pack of cards lay next to her on the scarf-draped table, and a crystal sphere she'd found in a junk shop in Liverpool sat upright on a stand. She was the very picture of a Romany from the stage and penny novels, which was the point. Everyone would see what they expected to see.

Violet had held up well so far, pulling on her persona like a well-worn pair of gloves, handing out fortunes with smooth aplomb. But then she looked up to see Daniel walk by in the hall, and misery crashed down on her.

Violet couldn't look away from him. As unhappy as she was, she needed the sight of him, to hear the sound of his voice.

Daniel paused outside the drawing room door. He was speaking to, and laughing with, a blond woman in a gray satin ball gown and a giant of a man who wore a kilt of the same plaid as Daniel's. The man's casual stance echoed Daniel's, and when they both turned to greet someone new, their movements were identical.

Father and son. Violet's heart squeezed with a strange yearning. She wanted to know his father, to talk with him and his stepmother, to learn the way they saw Daniel.

"Tell our fortune, miss?"

Three young ladies arrived to block her view of Daniel. She'd watched these three, in their blue, green, and yellow silk gowns, move around the rooms with haughty aplomb. Clearly they were the leaders of their set—or at least they considered themselves to be.

Two were English and one French—the French girl being the comtesse's daughter. All three wore ball gowns with bits of puffy sleeves, tiny waists, and narrow but flowing skirts. Hair was dressed in loose curls on the tops of their heads, glittering gems tastefully interwoven into the coiffures. The French miss and one of her English friends were dark, the second young English lady, Lady Victoria Garfield, daughter of a marquis, the lightest blond.

The dark-haired English girl sat down. "Me first."

She dropped a coin into the bowl on the table, then tugged off her glove and laid her hand flat, palm up. She'd done this before.

Violet kept her movements elegant, her voice dusky with a hint of accent. She'd let Mary brush her face and hands with dark theatrical powder to stain her complexion, and the faintest touch of kohl under her eyes made her irises look darker.

Violet lifted the girl's hand in her own and brushed a finger across the lines on her palms. She didn't have to make up things to please people—every line on the palm meant something, as did the number of lines, the way they crossed and where, and where they were broken. She'd learned reading from a Romany woman, who had the uncanny knack of being right about everything. Violet could only imitate—whether her fortunes came true or not, she never knew.

After studying the young woman's hand for a time, tracing the lines this way and that, Violet said, "You will be well loved. Your path might take you far from home, but your love will endure."

"Oh." The girl's cheeks grew pink. "I've never been told that before. But you might be right about my path taking me far from home. My beau is an officer."

"This line is long," Violet said, gliding her finger along it. "It means that your love will not be broken, no matter what, no matter how wide your travels."

The young woman smiled happily and shot a glance across the room, where a man in uniform was engaged in loud conversation with a knot of men. Violet, while quietly setting up her table earlier, had heard him confess to a friend that he was madly in love with the dark-haired young woman but worried she wouldn't follow him into army life.

Looking into the young woman's eyes now, coupled with what Violet had overheard her telling *her* friends, Violet knew the girl would follow her soldier to the ends of the earth.

"You should tell him your choice," Violet said, keeping the mysterious note in her voice. "He needs to know."

"I will. Yes, I will." The young woman's eyes glowed. "Thank you."

"Now me." Lady Victoria slid herself into the seat, forcing her pleased friend out of it. "I want to know if I have a handsome husband in my future too." Her look turned sly. "Someone Scottish, perhaps?"

The French girl giggled. "She wishes you to tell her she will marry the Scottish man Daniel Mackenzie. She is, as the English say, *gone* on him."

Violet's mouth went dry. Lady Victoria smiled a knowing smile, waiting for Violet to tell her what she wanted to hear. Violet had only to touch the girl's palm and say that yes, her husband would be tall, handsome, and Scottish. Lady Victoria would go away feeling smug and leave Violet alone.

But another glimpse of Daniel made Violet's heart pound. He was in the hall again, speaking to the hostess. Being gallant and charming, no doubt, excelling at it. He could charm paint off the walls.

Violet's anger surged. She traced the lines on Lady Victoria's palm with a light finger. "I can tell you only what I see."

Lady Victoria leaned forward, eager, and in the background, Daniel laughed, the sound warm and smooth.

"You will not find love where you assume," Violet said, trying to shut out the laughter. "It might take you a long while to find love at all, and you might have to go far. You might think it hard, but from this hardship will come strength."

Lady Victoria's blond brows slammed together, and she snatched her hand away. "I don't like that fortune."

Violet shrugged, trying to look indifferent. "That is your destiny." She truly had seen that in the girl's palm—the lines read exactly as the Romany woman had taught her. "What we like or do not like is not of interest to Fate."

Lady Victoria got huffily to her feet. "It's all nonsense anyway. Fortune-telling is lies. I'll wager you're not even a real Gypsy."

Violet drew herself up with all the dignity of her Romany teacher. "I was born in a field in eastern Romania. My mother was Romany. My father . . . who knows? That is my lineage."

Lady Victoria had a mean light in her eyes that her dark-haired English friend didn't notice, but the comtesse's daughter did. As Lady Victoria strode away, the comtesse's daughter dropped two coins into Violet's bowl and thanked her. Lady Victoria hadn't bothered to leave a tip.

When they'd gone, Violet balled her fists in her lap and drew long breaths. She heard Daniel laugh again. She both wanted to push the sound away and grab it and wrap it around her.

No one approached the corner for a moment, so Violet took the opportunity to close her eyes and try to compose herself. There was no use being upset. The world wouldn't change for Violet because she had one nice day out in a balloon.

The soft young ladies who were now clustered together like a clump of butterflies were the sort of ladies Daniel would marry, and that was the way of it. The titled classes intermarried, striving to keep money and property circulating amongst themselves. A business arrangement. The debutantes might believe this man or that in love with them, but what the gentleman usually saw was a deb's dowry or title, or perhaps the influence of her family.

When a debutante followed her heart with a man not of her privileged world, scandal and ruin ensued. Likewise, when a highborn gentleman married below his class, that wife was never truly welcome in the family. She could be ridiculed and shunned. And a stern father could banish a son who didn't marry to his pleasure.

Violet had seen such things time and again while doing performances in the big houses. Theirs was a closed world. Transgressors were harshly dealt with.

But witnessing Daniel in this setting, especially when she saw the comtesse stop him and introduce the three girls to him, made Violet want to be sick.

If she could get through this night, she'd do her best to come to her senses, return to being Princess Ivanova until the end of the month, and then decide where she and her mother should go. Violet would have the memory of two lovely days to savor, and then they'd be gone, lost in the mists of might-have-been.

She opened her eyes as two eager young men approached her, and smiled at them, forcing herself into her role again.

～◦～

"We've practically known each other forever, do you not think?" Lady Victoria Garfield said over the orchestra as Daniel whirled her in the waltz. "We have so many mutual acquaintances, people I've known and you've known for all our lives, even if this is the first time of us meeting."

Daniel had hoped that spinning Lady Vic around fast enough would stop her talking, but it wasn't to be. This young lady could chatter over a barrage of artillery fire.

He should feel sorry for her, really. The comtesse had told Ainsley that Lady Victoria hadn't taken in her first two Seasons, so her mother had sent her to France to try her luck. Seeing the rather mad ruthlessness in Lady Vic's eyes, Daniel couldn't blame the English aristos for fleeing the other way. In a few years, Lady Vic would be a redoubtable matron, commanding her husband with the firm hand of a determined sergeant major.

A man needs to see a little warmth in a smile, Daniel wanted to advise her. *Not an obvious calculation of what she hopes to gain for herself.*

Contrasting Lady Vic's predatory stalking to Violet's open-eyed excitement was unfair to poor little Lady Vic, but Daniel couldn't help himself.

How long could he stay before his departure wouldn't be considered rude? He didn't want to embarrass Ainsley, but he needed to go. He'd make his way back down to town, knock on the door of a boardinghouse, and take Violet out anywhere she wanted to go—a restaurant, a cabaret, a theatre. Hell, they could walk down to the strand and watch street performers; he wasn't bothered.

"And the comtesse brought in the most marvelous fortune-teller," Lady Vic was saying. She squeezed Daniel's shoulder. "Do you want to guess what she said? About me? And maybe about you?"

Daniel's scattered thoughts roared together. "Fortune-teller, you say?"

"Yes, a Gypsy lady. Very proud of herself, she is. But guess what she said about me."

"That you'll travel far and marry a handsome man?" Daniel said distractedly.

"How did you know? Not only a handsome man, but a handsome *Scottish* man."

Could the dear girl be any less subtle? "Where is this fortune-teller?"

"In the drawing room." Lady Victoria's smile widened. When the waltz ended, she latched her fingers tightly on to Daniel's arm and all but dragged him out of the ballroom to the drawing room.

The fortune-teller had skin the color of milk-laden tea, wore a voluminous blouse held in place with a black corset-like bodice, and had covered her head in a closely tied red scarf. Gold rings decorated her slim fingers, and a necklace of coins clinked around her neck.

Her eyes were the same dark blue as when she'd first looked up at Daniel in the house in London, her hands the same gentle ones that had lit the candles.

Violet saw Daniel, took in Lady Vic hanging on his arm, and didn't miss a beat. She smiled the dark, mysterious smile of a Romany woman, and gestured to the chairs. "Would you like to know your future?" she asked. Her voice was dusky, low. "For but a coin in my bowl, I can reveal all."

Chapter 15

Daniel's eyes sparkled with mirth, but he kept his face straight. Lady Victoria plopped herself into a chair and tugged Daniel into another.

He was here, where Violet could reach out and touch him. In spite of Lady Victoria's presence, Violet saw only Daniel, the chatter of the debutante like the buzz of an annoying insect.

"He wants to know all about his future," Lady Victoria said. "Especially in regard to his *married* future."

The sparkle in Daniel's eyes turned mischievous. "Aye, tell me something that will put my poor old dad's mind at ease."

Violet noted that his accent had become different, less Highland and more working-class Glaswegian. She was good at accents, and Daniel, it seemed, was too.

Violet pushed her bowl toward him. "You must gift me with silver first."

"How about gold?" Daniel reached into his pocket and dropped a gold sovereign to the top of the lesser coins in the bowl. "That way you'll give me a very *guid* fortune."

"That is English money, my lord," Violet said. "This is France."

"A bank will change it for you. And I'm not a lord. Never will be. Just plain Mr. Mackenzie is me."

He tugged off his glove and laid his hand, palm up, on the table. No soft dandy was Daniel. As Violet had seen on their adventure, he had no qualms about stripping off his gloves and working with his hands. His palms and fingers bore plenty of calluses. Violet recalled how his blunt fingertips had felt when he'd caressed her in the bed, touching her with such gentleness.

Violet rested her finger on the pad below Daniel's forefinger. Bare skin to bare skin. She could hardly breathe. Even this contact, so small, made her blood run hot.

She couldn't do this. If she continued touching him, she'd make a complete fool of herself. And possibly she might not care.

Violet let out her breath and lifted her hand from Daniel's. She pulled the heavy crystal in its stand between them, and Daniel leaned forward, interested.

"What do you do with this?" He touched the sphere. "Test frequencies?"

"For such a deep fortune, I must look into the crystal," Violet said. "But I must warn you, it does not always tell you what you wish to hear."

"I'm willing to risk it."

Still Daniel didn't smile, but the wickedness in his eyes made Violet want to laugh. He was doing it again, putting Violet into his full focus, making her forget he trained that focus on anyone else.

"You'll like it," Lady Victoria said. "You'll see." Gone was the girl's conviction that Violet was a fake. And if she clung to Daniel's arm any harder, he was in danger of her peeling off his skin right through his coat.

Violet moved her hands over the crystal as she'd been taught, making her movements languid. She peered into the depth of the clear quartz, frowning a little as though she saw something besides the heart of the stone. "Hmm."

She looked a while longer, making her expression so troubled that Lady Victoria leaned forward worriedly. "Good heavens, what is it?"

Violet gave a dramatic shiver. She made a sign against evil to the crystal, then sat up and rested her hands on the table.

"I'm afraid it is not good, Mr. Mackenzie."

Daniel's brows went up. "No? Shall I buy my da a mourning suit? Give my stepma a lock of me hair for a mourning brooch?"

"No, indeed." The thought, even though he was playacting, made Violet grow cold. She'd thought him dead in London, and that had upset her, but things were different now. Now she knew Daniel. He'd carved his way into her life, and losing him would be hard, too hard.

"What then?" Daniel asked in genuine curiosity.

Violet looked into the crystal again and shook her head. "I see poverty, I'm afraid, Mr. Mackenzie. Bone deep. You shivering in tiny rooms, a fire barely going. There's a man—you owe him money. He's beaten you and left you alone. But . . . ah . . . here is a woman. Your helpmeet, I think, though she is dressed in rags. Yes, she holds you, she weeps over you. You try to comfort her, but know you cannot. She is very pretty, this wife. Or once was. Her hair is blond . . ." Violet trailed off, moving her hand over the crystal as though trying to wave away the mists inside.

Lady Victoria had gone pale. "That's not a true vision. Mr. Mackenzie is ever so rich, and so is his father."

"Lost," Violet said, making her voice dramatically low. "Everything lost. And his father casting him out."

"Aye." Daniel sat back, shaking his head, the Glaswegian accent growing with every word. "It could come true. My gambling habit most like. I can't get a bit of coin between me fingers I don't want to toss on a horse or a turn of cards. I thought if I married a rich lady, it might help. But if your vision is real . . ."

Lady Victoria made a pained noise and let go of Daniel's arm. "Of course it isn't real. She's a fake. I said so."

Daniel looked bewildered. "No, ye said she was the real thing. But she's likely right. I'd run through me poor wife's fortune like it was wa'er."

"Honestly." Lady Victoria rose to her feet, and Daniel, ever the gentleman, rose with her. Lady Victoria glared at Violet. "You ought to be ashamed of yourself. You don't know anything. Excuse me, Mr. Mackenzie, I must attend my hostess."

She glided away, head high, but her feet moved quickly. Daniel saved his laughter until she'd gone out the door and into the bright hall.

"You're a wicked, mischievous minx, you are," Daniel said, sitting down again. His smile was the warmest thing Violet had felt all night. "What am I to do with you?"

She kept up her Romany persona. "I must speak what I see."

Daniel chuckled. "Do you know what I see?"

Violet dropped the Romany accent and spoke in haughty, blue-blooded English tones. "I cannot imagine, Mr. Mackenzie."

Daniel slid the crystal on its stand toward him and peered into it with an expression so like that of the woman who'd taught Violet, she couldn't stop her laughter.

"I see a young woman wrapped in crimson scarves, meeting with a young man. He seems to be wearing a kilt, he does. And they're . . . on a terrace. Interesting. When the clock strikes the half hour."

Violet's voice was tight. "You can see that far ahead, can you?"

Daniel took a watch from his pocket, opened it, and nodded. "The half hour. Eighteen minutes from now. Let's see if the fortune comes true, shall we?"

He slid the watch back into his waistcoat, winked, rose, and strolled away, leaving Violet alone and breathless.

Daniel watched Violet step out of the house to the terrace on the half hour exactly, and something tight eased in him. She'd bundled up in a big shawl over her costume, smart girl. The wind was icy.

Daniel blessed his good fortune. He hadn't thought she'd come.

He'd had to waltz with a few more debutantes before he could break away. He'd excused himself to smoke, and he'd heard the comtesse praise his good manners to Ainsley as he walked away.

Daniel had quickly passed the room set aside for gentlemen with cigars and whiskey, and emerged onto the terrace. Because it was frigidly cold, he was the only one of the party who'd dared the out-of-doors. He'd lit a cigar for verisimilitude and sucked its smoke while waiting.

Daniel said nothing as Violet scanned the terrace then turned her steps toward him. Closer and closer, the moonlight in the clear sky touching her face and the red of her kerchief. She'd put something on her face to make her skin darker, but Violet's eyes were just as blue behind the outline of kohl.

"I think you lost me a potential wife in there," Daniel said lightly when he reached her. "Who's going to help me in me old age now?"

Violet raised a brow. "Are you disparaging my ability to predict the future? The husband I saw for Lady Victoria was English, thin, and balding, with nothing to say but *yes, dear*, a hundred times a day."

Daniel burst out laughing. "I think you've hit on it. She'll be happy as a lark." He held his cigar out of the way and slid his arm around her waist. "Hell, Violet, you are ten times the woman of any here. Why do you do this?"

Violet looked up at him, she utterly confident, strong, and unflinching, this wonderful lady. "To make a living, of course."

"You don't need to, not like this. Putting up with insipid lords and ladies begging you to tell them that their perfect little lives will go on being perfect. Stop doing it, Vi. They don't deserve you. Promise me no more fortune-telling."

Violet didn't look impressed. "The comtesse has paid me a rather large fee. Plus I have all my tips."

"Why do you need the money so badly? What did you do with the wad you stole from me? Spend it at the horse races?"

Now Violet blinked. She flushed behind her makeup. "I did take a little of the money you had in your pocket. About a hundred pounds in all, enough to get us away from England and settled here. I planned to pay you back, or your family, once I'd saved enough. And Mr. Mortimer his rent."

Daniel laughed again. "You're precious, lass. So, you had

me unconscious on your floor with about two thousand quid on me, and you peeled off a hundred and left the rest?"

"I'd have picked a nicer boardinghouse if I'd taken more."

"You're mad, you are. Why not take the lot?"

Violet shrugged, looking troubled. "I'd hurt you—I didn't know whether I'd killed you. It would look bad for me if I had robbed you too, and I thought your family should have the money."

"My family. Oh, God, you really believe that, don't you? My family doesn't give a horse's balls about the money. Doesn't matter—some light-fingered thief took the rest when I was a-lying out in the dark. You should have waited until I came to. I would have handed it over, anything to get you away from Mortimer. How the devil did I get to where the constable found me anyway?"

The troubled look turned to one of pain, and shame. "A handcart. I dressed like a peasant and hid you under a few sacks of coal."

Daniel whooped. He tossed down his cigar, dragged Violet against him, and whirled her around. And around.

"Vi, I think I love you. A cart? Sacks of coal? Oh, that is priceless."

"No, it isn't. It's horrible."

Around again. Wind tugged at Violet's scarf, her body warm against Daniel in the cold. "No other woman in the world would think about carrying my body through the streets under sacks of coal and dumping it—and then leaving a great thick roll of banknotes for a street person to steal. Or maybe the constable took them. They don't earn much, poor lads."

Violet braced herself on his arms as she gazed at him. "You can't tell me you're *glad* I did what I did."

"Mightily impressed. Even the most resilient women of my acquaintance would be fainting on the floor, or running about on the street screaming for help. You could have gone for a policeman and told him I'd tried to ravish you."

"But you hadn't." The desperation in her eyes hadn't lessened. "You hadn't done anything. And would a policeman have believed me? You're a wealthy man, and I'm . . . who I am."

"Probably they wouldn't. You did the right thing, running away before you were arrested. *Your* bad luck I'm related to the most obsessive man in the universe. Uncle Ian thought tracking down a woman with no name and no address, who disappeared into the night, an entertaining problem. Only Ian Mackenzie could have figured it out." Daniel stopped spinning, lowering Violet in his arms. "My *good* luck."

"And then you took me ballooning."

"Aye, and it was grand." Daniel touched the curve of her cheek.

Violet's lips still curved a little with the laughter they'd been sharing. Daniel leaned to her and kissed the half smile.

Lips warmed where the air was cold. Daniel slid his hand under her scarf, finding the heavy softness of her hair.

His heartbeat quickened as he opened her lips, taking the kiss to a deeper place. Violet's breath touched his cheek, and her hands flattened to his chest. Daniel pressed his thumb to the corner of her mouth, licking behind her lip.

The wind pushed at them, air from the sea and the land mixing to become a cold flow. Daniel wrapped his arms all the way around her, turning with her into the shadows. The terrace's stone balustrade touched his legs, cold through wool.

He ran his hands up Violet's back, feeling her body bend into his. Her lips parted, her eyes soft and half closing. Her cheeks showed pink beneath the dark powder, which rubbed off on his glove.

Violet's kiss was smooth—gentle warmth. Daniel darted his tongue inside her mouth and tasted a bite of tea laced with honey. He licked again, wanting more.

"Vi."

Violet's hands curled on his chest as she looked up at him. Daniel read desire in the depths of her eyes, and uncertainty. His own heart was beating faster, pumping plenty of blood through his body.

"We need to get away from here," Daniel said. Somewhere, anywhere they could be alone.

Hope left her face. "I can't. We need the money. I can't leave the post."

"Don't worry, lass. I'll retrieve your tips, and I'll square it with the comtesse. She's a friend of my stepmum's. She'll pay your fee."

"I already have the tips." Violet patted a pocket of her skirt, which jingled. "I never leave the bowl unattended. Habit."

"Smart lady. If you have the goods, then let us be off, my lovely."

She didn't move. "Your mother and father will grow angry with you. With me."

Daniel shrugged. "They're used to me. I'm five-and-twenty, and not dependent on them for my living. I come and go as I please. Always have." He leaned to her again. "Come away with me, Violet."

"Come away where?" she sounded desperate.

"All the way to Marseille."

Not to his hotel, though. Gavina was no doubt curled up in Daniel's bed, waiting for her brother to come home and tell her all about the ball. She'd been most put out she'd had to stay behind with her nanny tonight.

Not Violet's boardinghouse. Daniel would not get her turned out for having a dalliance there. Not Richard's rooms— Richard would either be entertaining ladies again, or resting. Hopefully resting.

That left Daniel's other retreat. Not in the nicest part of town, but it had the benefit of peace and quiet.

Daniel took her hand. "Come on, then."

He started walking her toward the end of the terrace, but she pulled him to a stop. "Where are you going? The doors are behind us."

"I'm not escorting you back through the house and out, for all the world to see. Besides, love, we're adventurers. We don't need anything as common as doors."

He was glad to see Violet smile again, her breath steaming. "You're an eccentric, Mr. Mackenzie."

Daniel took off his greatcoat, which he'd donned to come outside, and wrapped it around her. "Over we go."

He placed his backside on the stone balustrade—chilly

through his kilt—grabbed Violet around the waist, and slid over with her to the ground a few feet below. The house was built on a slope, the terrace and ballroom nearly level with the ground in the back. Daniel had scouted this when he'd come out to the terrace to plan his escape.

Violet let out a cry but stifled it as they landed in a rose garden, the roses pruned back for January. Mud squished under Daniel's boots as he caught Violet and set her on her feet. He took her hand again, and they ran together to the cluster of carriages that waited near the house.

Daniel found the coachman who'd driven him here with his father and Ainsley. The man looked up from keeping warm with a flask and conversation with his fellow coachmen.

"Twice your fee tonight if you take me and my lady back to town," Daniel said. "And return for my dad and stepmum without a word."

The coachman didn't need to ponder. He slapped the stopper onto his whiskey flask and went to the coach, opening the door for them. Daniel handed Violet in, the coachman climbed to his perch, started the horses, maneuvered them out of the crush.

Violet brushed the velvet of the padded seat to hide that her fingers were shaking. The cushions were soft, and the interior of the coach had been kept warm with tin boxes of glowing coal.

How wonderful it must be to ride about in vehicles like this all the time. Daniel didn't even seem to notice the luxury around him.

Daniel sat right next to her, giving her his smile as he covered her hand with his. The heat inside his coat warmed her magnificently.

He knew as well as she did what they'd do this night. Everything that had gone before—the walk home from the theatre, the day out in the balloon, the innocent night at the inn, the teasing over her fortune-telling—had been leading to this. Violet, in Daniel's bed, tonight.

She couldn't stop shaking. Violet wanted it to happen, obviously, or she would have come up with any excuse to go back into the house and continue telling her inane fortunes to insipid debs. Instead, she'd let him talk her into running away with him.

Daniel looked as calm as a sleeping cat, but then, he took ladies back to his hotel with him all the time. Last night it had been ladies with diamonds in their hair and rouge on their cheeks. Violet had dark face powder on her cheeks and her necklace was made of fake coins. She started to laugh, and the laugh was a bit hysterical.

Daniel's smile broadened. He leaned to her and kissed her lips.

The kiss was warm, brief. Daniel tugged the red scarf from Violet's head and ran his fingers over her loose braid.

His touch was sure, knowing. He knew how to love a lady, and tonight, he would love Violet.

And after?

Violet refused to think about after. Getting through tonight would be enough. Desire wound through her, heating her even in the cold winter night. But she was terrified.

The coach ride was not long, the comtesse's house lying only a few miles from Marseille itself. When they reached the edge of town, Daniel tapped on the roof and gave directions to the coachman.

When the coach stopped a short time after that, Violet looked around in surprise. The street on which they'd halted was blowing with litter and smelled of horse dung. A wine house, lit and full of noise, overflowed with patrons, and streetwalkers, female and male, strolled along, looking for marks.

A man like Daniel should stay in the best hotel in the heart of the fashionable area. Surely his glittering ladies would insist upon it. Even Violet's boardinghouse was in a far more respectable neighborhood than this.

Daniel climbed up to give the coachman his promised fee, then he took Violet's elbow and steered her down the street toward the corner.

"Where the devil are we?" she asked.

"The dregs," Daniel said cheerfully. "I've set up a hideaway here, where I can be undisturbed. You wouldn't believe the distractions one has in the fancy hotels. Needy friends, little sisters . . ."

This was an older part of town, with narrow streets, plaster crumbling from bricks, and arched passages connecting lanes with even smaller lanes. Daniel took her through one of these arched passages, the wind cutting in the small tunnel.

They emerged into a courtyard. Shuttered windows broke the walls around them. A rickety wooden staircase ran up to a narrow gallery with doors and windows in it, all sheltered by a tiled roof.

Daniel pulled her up the stairs to the gallery and led her to a door at the end. He produced a thick key from his pocket, unlocked the door, and let Violet inside.

To cold and clutter. Daniel touched a match to an oil lamp, then another, lighting the small room with a warm glow.

As the light increased, Violet saw that the furniture in the room was fine, whole, and new. The clutter came from boxes, machine parts, papers, and books. Every available surface was covered with sketches of machines, list of equations, and open notebooks filled with scrawled writing. Books lay everywhere, some stacks put together to be resting places for the bits of machinery.

A narrow bed stood in the corner. It had a solid wooden bedstead, but the mattress was covered with more books, sketches, and maps.

A wide, cushioned window seat was the only place in the room not covered with things. The window's shutters had been closed against the night, making the window seat a cozy nook.

Violet picked up a sketch from the table. "What is all this for?"

"A motorcar," Daniel said.

Violet studied the drawing. A low-slung vehicle, looking a bit like a phaeton, had been rendered in great detail. Four wheels hugged the ground, coach lights hung alongside the doors, and the seats looked as luxurious as that of the coach they'd just ridden in. Variations on this vehicle occupied other drawings.

"That's only the chassis," Daniel said. "What I'm trying to do is build a more efficient engine, not just a more powerful one. Daimler's are very good, of course, but he's more interested in industrial machinery—motorcars are more of a sideline for him. His engines will propel his horseless carriages at about fifteen or twenty miles per hour on a flat surface—provided there's no mud. I want to make my engine ten times as powerful, and design the carriage to be able to run even on bad roads. I want more gears to give power on hills or hard terrain, and wheels better than carriage wheels with a strip of rubber on them. I'm trying pneumatic tires—with air between the wheel and the rubber." He moved another sheet. "I'm working on a motorbike as well, something more innovative than just putting a motor on a bicycle. Kind of like a cross between a bicycle and a car."

Violet studied the drawings with interest. "I thought you were a balloonist."

He shrugged. "My career as an aeronaut is a passing hobby. My real concern is designing engines to make vehicles go where I want at my command. Needs much work, as you saw, firsthand. Here's the motorbike."

Daniel came next to her to push papers out of the way. The drawing he pulled out showed different angles of what looked like a bicycle with large tires and a large box for the engine where the pedals should be.

"Haven't got the design quite right, yet. The engine box can't be too big, or the rider won't be able to keep the thing upright. But not too small, or there won't be enough power to make it faster than a regular bicycle. But bicycles can run across fields and through mud where even horses have difficulty."

Daniel's animation as he spoke about his designs made him different from the Daniel she'd observed with his friends on the street or at tonight's ball. Both places he'd been full of lazy smiles and cultured charm, speaking with the same ease to courtesans as he did the comtesse.

Now his gaze held intensity, his focus all for the inventions he loved. His body hummed with his excitement, the heat of him next to her cutting through the cold in the room.

Violet liked him best like this, his hair rumpled, his eyes warm as he focused on his passions. Daniel was letting Violet into his world. The energy he exuded as he talked her through the drawings rendered every gentleman she'd met at the ball tonight languid and dull.

Then he stopped. "Damn, listen to me." Daniel dropped the drawings to the table. "I bring a beautiful woman back to my rooms, and I talk about engines."

"I like engines." Violet did. Everything about the balloon and these motorcars and motor-bicycle fascinated her.

"I know you do. That's why I adore you, lass. Hang on a minute."

Daniel made a path to the fireplace in the corner, shoveled a bit of coal into it, and lit it with a few matches. After a moment, fire began to flicker around the coals, on their way to bringing warmth to the room.

"Better." Daniel wiped his hands on a rag that was already stained with coal dust and tossed it down. "I'll show you what I've done on the bike and the motorcar when we get back to London. For now . . ."

He peeled the greatcoat from her shoulders and ran his hands up Violet's arms. In spite of him forsaking his gloves when they'd entered, his hands were already warm, dragging heat into her skin.

Violet still shook, her heart alternately squeezing in cold pulses or pounding hot.

She wanted this. She wasn't a shrinking virgin, was she? Daniel was amazing, handsome, funny, kind. He'd brought her here to be his lover for the night, in this place of his heart, tucked away where no one would find them.

Why not take what he offered, even if only once?

But she sensed the terror lurking inside her, coiled like a waiting snake.

Daniel wasn't the monster. Violet's past was.

Daniel continued to caress her, his hands coming up to clasp her shoulders. His first kiss would be gentle, she already knew that. And then he'd touch her and slowly open her.

The slowness might kill her. Too much time for the fear to take over, to dictate what happened.

Violet could think of only one thing to do. She shoved his hands from her shoulders, slammed her arms around him, closed her fingers in his hair, and yanked him down to frantically kiss his lips.

Chapter 16

The force of Violet's kiss, the small pain of her tug on Daniel's hair, made everything go foggy for him. Her mouth was hard on his, her tongue scraping inside him. Daniel opened his lips for her and tasted her desperation.

Violet's hands scrabbled to open his frock coat, his waistcoat. She pulled on the buttons of Daniel's shirt until a few ripped away, then she grabbed the waistband of his kilt.

Daniel broke the kiss and caught her seeking hands as one snaked down to cup him through the plaid wool. Violet's eyes held need, but also fear, the same fear she'd shown in London the moment before she'd reached for the deadly vase.

"Love," Daniel said. "Slow down a little. Let me savor you."

"I can't." Violet yanked her hands out of his grip and seized his shoulders, dragging him against her. "I can't go slowly. I can't." She kissed his lips, his chin, the rough stubble of whiskers. "Please, Daniel."

Daniel gently but firmly held her back. Violet looked up at him with wild blue eyes in a face pale behind the dark powder.

"Lass, I'm hungry for you too. Believe me, I am. But I'm not going to fall on ye and devour you. Much as I'd like to. I want to get to know you." His grip softened, and he drew one finger across her cheek. "I want to know all of you, Vi, my sweet South London Sassenach."

"I can't." Violet grabbed his shirt, jerking it apart, the remaining buttons tinkling to the floor. "I need to do this. *I* need to."

"Violet." Daniel's voice went stern. He seized her wrists to still her wild clawing. "Stop this."

"I can't. Why should a man be able to rip into a woman . . ." She trailed off as the fear welled up, spilling tears from her eyes. "I can't." Her sobs came up, heaves that shook her chest. "I can't. It's not fair."

"Vi."

Violet jerked out of his grasp, spun away, and ended up sitting on the window seat. She clasped her arms over her belly and rocked back and forth.

"I can't have you," she said. "I can't . . . have . . . *you*."

The room undulated under Violet's feet, the window seat like a rock in a rushing tide. Her breath was coming too fast, but she could find no air. Violet heard the sobs in her throat and knew she was going to pieces, but she couldn't stop it.

The scent of whiskey brushed her nose, and something cool and metallic touched her lips. Burning liquid poured into her mouth.

Violet gasped, started to cough, then swallowed hard. The whiskey slid down like a river of fire. The next gasp let in air, and Violet could breathe again.

Daniel sat down next to her on the window seat, his hard thigh against hers. He kept the flask at her mouth, waiting until she drank a little more before he took the flask away.

Violet coughed again, pressing her fingers to her wet lips. She had no idea where her handkerchief had got to.

Daniel's strong arm wrapped around her shoulders, his warm hand rubbed her arm. "There now," he said, voice low and soothing. "It's all right."

Jacobi used to hold her thus, when she was ten years old and scared. He'd given her comfort—and then he'd taken it all away. After that, Violet had never known comfort again.

Until now. Daniel was strength beside her, his warmth touching where she was so cold.

"Someone hurt you, didn't they, love?" he said, his voice a soothing rumble. "I asked you that before. I'm thinking someone pushed you against a wall and forced you. They must have done."

Violet nodded. She didn't wonder how Daniel knew. He was good at reading people, almost as good as Violet was.

"You're going to tell me all about it," Daniel said. No question, no asking her.

"I can't." Shame, misery, and pure rage clogged Violet's heart, stopping her words.

"I want to know, sweetheart," he said. "I want to know what we're fighting."

What *we're* fighting. As though she and Daniel were in this together.

She'd never told anyone except the Parisian courtesan Lady Amber, and the woman had guessed most of it. Violet had trained herself so well not to speak of it that she couldn't think in words, only in images, sounds, impressions of pain.

Daniel caressed her shoulder. "Let me start. How old were you?"

"Sixteen."

"Oh, love." Daniel brushed his lips to her hair. "Just a child."

"Girls marry at sixteen."

"Don't justify it. Tell me. Who was he?"

"Jacobi." The word slipped out before she could stop it. She hadn't meant to say it, because it wasn't true, but then again, it was.

"Jacobi," Daniel said, steel in his voice. "And who is he?"

"He didn't . . ." Violet swallowed, tasting the whiskey bitter in her throat. "It wasn't him. Jacobi taught me everything I know. I met him in Paris, when my mother was first starting to understand her clairvoyance. He recognized that I had a gift for figuring out what people wanted . . . what they needed. I was ten. He taught me all the tricks, how to give them a show, an experience they'd never forget. I wanted . . . I pretended . . . that he was my father."

"And he took advantage of that?"

Violet chanced a glance up at him. Daniel's eyes held a

hardness she'd not seen in him before. His ancestors, she thought dimly, had been brutal barbarians, killing each other in bloodbaths for pieces of rocky land in the Scottish Highlands. Violet had done research on Daniel and the Mackenzies—they went back for centuries, to a man called Old Dan, who'd been granted the Scottish dukedom in the fourteenth century.

That Daniel had likely carried a heavy claymore and been given the dukedom based on how many other men he'd cut to bits. Violet looked into Daniel's eyes and saw that Highland barbarian looking out at her.

"No," Violet said. "That is . . ." The red-bearded man had been nothing like Jacobi. Jacobi had dark hair, brown eyes that could be kind, and pale white fingers that shook if he didn't drink enough wine.

"Then who? Give me a name."

"I never knew his name. Jacobi owed him money, a great deal of money, which he couldn't pay. So when the man came to collect, and threatened Jacobi . . ." Violet swallowed, her throat tight.

"Jacobi gave him you instead." Daniel's words were flat.

Miserable, Violet nodded.

Daniel made no move, not even drawing a sharp breath. His eyes in the growing firelight were dark golden—hard, harsh, glittering. "Tell me what happened," he said.

"I couldn't believe what Jacobi had said. I thought it must be a mistake, that I misunderstood." The words came now, loosened in the same way floodwaters loosened debris. "Jacobi left the room. He looked sad and angry, but he left." The man with the red beard and eyes blue like faded sky had picked Violet up from the stool and shoved her against the wall. His breath had smelled like brandy. "He was strong, so strong. I tried to fight. I tried and tried. But he held me against the wall, and he . . . he . . . I was only a girl. It hurt so much."

The hurried, wooden monotone that spoke the words didn't match the horror Violet the sixteen-year-old had felt. It didn't convey her screams, her pleas for mercy, the hot pain that ripped through her when her innocence had been wrenched away.

She'd limped home, torn and hurting, blood staining her skirt. Violet had locked herself in her bedchamber alone, claiming she had a fever. Violet's mother, with her constant fear of illness, had stayed well away.

"I thought I was going to die," Violet said. "I remember being surprised when I lived."

Daniel's arm tightened around her shoulders. When Violet looked up at him again, she was stunned to see his eyes moist.

"What happened to Jacobi?" Daniel asked, his voice steady. "Is he still alive?"

"I don't think so. He's never tried to find me, in any case, and I've kept an ear out—to make sure he doesn't spring upon me. After all this time . . . I believe he's dead."

"Ye left him? Good for you."

"No." Violet swallowed, the next part coming slowly. "I forgave him."

"Lass . . ."

She shook her head. "I was only sixteen. There was no one strong in my life—not my mother, and I had no father. Jacobi came to find me. He was filled with self-loathing. He begged for my understanding. He said the red-bearded man would have killed him had he not paid. I believed him. The man was mean and cold and carried a knife in his boot. I had tried to reach the knife when he . . . But I never could." Jacobi had been so ashamed, filled with the need to make it up to Violet. And she'd let him.

Daniel said nothing, only sat, his body warming hers as the fire slowly heated the room. This hideaway, with him, was safe, but Violet knew how easily safety could be destroyed.

When Daniel spoke again, his voice was quiet. "I know why you forgave him. You wanted everything to go back to the way it was before, didn't you?"

He sounded as though he understood perfectly, as though he'd experienced the same need himself.

"I did," she said. "But it never could be the same, could it?"

"No. It never can be."

Violet gave a mirthless laugh. "I forgave him," she said. "I stayed with him. That is, until he tried it the second time."

"Dear God."

"Jacobi gambled too much. He was forever in debt. When he tried to use me to pay again, not six months later, I had enough of my wits about me to run. I was fast, and the man he owed was too rotund and slothful to catch me. I took my mother and Mary out of our rooms that very afternoon, and we left Paris. I never saw Jacobi again."

Daniel took her hand. He squeezed it between his, the strength of him immeasurable. "Lass, I am so sorry."

Violet let out her breath. "Nothing to be done."

Daniel released her, anger in his eyes. "Don't sound so bloody resigned. What he did was monstrous. You trusted Jacobi, and he hurt you, in a way no father should hurt a daughter. In a way no man should hurt *any* woman."

"But he wasn't really my father." Violet's heart bit with old pain. "That was my childhood fancy. Doesn't mean he returned the sentiment."

"Don't try to make this not his fault. It is nothing *but* his fault. I will find him so I can break his neck."

"I truly believe he's dead. I want him to be. I never want to see him again."

Daniel remained in silent fury, and Violet leaned her head back on the windowpane, spent. The shutters were closed behind the window, keeping out the night and the wind, but the panes were cold.

Dredging up the tale had hurt so much, like tearing scabs from closed wounds to let them bleed afresh. It had been twelve years since the red-bearded man had touched Violet, less than that since she'd run from Jacobi. And still the pain was there.

Childish confusion had receded as adult understanding had come, but the anger, shock, and horror hadn't died. Jacobi and his red-bearded creditor had killed young Violet that afternoon, making her disappear forever.

"So that's why you hit me so hard in London," Daniel said. "I put you in mind of the bloke, which scared you senseless, and you struck out."

"Yes. I didn't . . ."

Daniel's hand clamped down on hers. "Don't tell me you didn't mean to. You did mean to, every bit of it. I scared you, and you tried to defend yourself. Only natural. But I'm not sorry I tried to kiss you. *That* I'm going to do again, and again. And I'm used to women trying to kill me, so no worries there."

The cynical look in his eyes broke through Violet's haze of pain. She remembered what he'd said when he'd walked her home from the theatre—she remembered every word of every conversation they'd ever had.

Everyone who hears my name knows my mother tried to off me with a knife when I was a tiny babe, before my dad threw me out of the way and stopped her.

"I'm sorry," Violet said. "About your mother, I mean."

Daniel shrugged. "I was a wee babe. Don't even remember."

"But it hurts you."

Daniel let go of her hand, pushed himself from the window seat, and walked halfway across the cluttered room. "Are you asking for a look at my haunted childhood, since I made you tell me about yours?"

Violet started to say no, but she knew that was exactly what she wanted. She'd shown her shivering vulnerability, and she wanted to see his. "Yes."

"You drive a hard bargain." Daniel turned to face her, crossing his arms over the shirt she'd ripped open. The shirt was open to his waist now, his brown chest exposed, the tattoo bared, his kilt sagging on his hips. He was delectable, but the folded arms shut her out, shut everyone out.

"Ye want me to tell you how I felt when I found out about my mum trying to kill me. Well, do ye know *how* I found out? My dad didn't tell me. No. He never talked about it, though he was in the room that day, wrestling her down to take away the knife. I found out by whispers among the servants that my da killed my mum, and then the same whispers among the lads at school. And me not knowing what was the truth. The only person who knew for certain how my mother died was Dad, and he never told a soul, until he met up with Ainsley and gave her the tale." Daniel balled his fists. "He wouldn't even share it with his own son."

"I shouldn't make you talk about it," Violet said. But she wanted to know. She couldn't lie to herself about that.

"Yes, you should. I don't blame Dad anymore. He was buried in his own troubles. My mum hurt him something awful, believe me. But knowing that the one person who is supposed to cherish you—your mother—hated you so much she wanted to kill you is a blow to a boy."

"Your father cares for you," Violet said. "So does your stepmother. I saw that in them tonight."

"Oh, aye, they're caring folk, they are. But it took me a long time to decide to give my trust to anyone, and maybe I haven't done that yet. My dad did his best raising me, but he was busy chasing women, you see. Beautiful, expensive courtesans or beautiful, expensive married women—ladies he never had to let fully into his life." His gaze went remote. "Most of them didn't want to have anything to do with me—why should they? But some of them liked children, were hungry for kids of their own, poor lasses. They brought me little presents and played games with me, put up with my little-boy chatter. I'd start hoping my dad would marry one of the nice ones, so I'd have a mum like the other chaps at school. But as soon as I'd start thinking she'd stay, the lady would disappear. Dismissed by my dad, never to be seen again. When I was very small, I figured that meant the lady decided she hated me after all. Like my own mother had. As I grew older, I realized that my father simply didn't want the woman around anymore. I got angry at him. Whenever I started to care for one of his women, he'd take her away from me. I said so to my dad, and that I'd never forgive him for it. He wasn't impressed. Finally, I ceased bothering to care."

Daniel was a grown man now, hard-muscled, tall, formidable, with that hint of Old Dan Mackenzie in him. But Violet saw, behind that, a flash of the angry and confused little boy who'd learned to hide his hurt behind anger.

"Your father married again, though," Violet said.

"Oh, aye. By the time he met Ainsley, I was old enough to understand that here was a woman who could make the poor old sod happy." Daniel chuckled, the hurt little boy falling away. "To push Dad at her, I pretended I was in love with Ainsley myself. I told him I wanted to take her as my mistress. Trying to make him jealous, and me all of sixteen." He laughed again, this time in true mirth. "Dad saw right through me, the wise old man. He finally let Ainsley land him, thank God. Took a weight off me mind, that did."

Violet smiled in spite of the tightness in her chest. "A happy ending."

"Aye, some people get them."

What about us? Will you have a happy ending, Daniel Mackenzie? Will I?

He looked at her with eyes that held heat. Violet wanted him— yes, she did—but she felt open and naked, quivering and exposed. She clasped her hands together. "What do we do now?"

"I don't know, love. You've had a world of hurting, haven't you? And so have I, and there's no easy way for either of us to trust another person."

He had a way of putting things plainly. Violet wanted to trust, but the old darkness reached out and swatted any threat of softening away. Every single person in Violet's life had betrayed her, except Mary and her mother. And Celine was so wrapped up in herself, her health, and the spirit world, that some days she barely noticed she had a daughter at all.

Daniel turned abruptly and made for the door. Violet's heart beat swiftly as he slid a bolt across the top of it and turned again to face her.

"Well, there's a couple of things we could do. We could go our separate ways, make a clean break, and get the hurting over with right away. Let it bleed, let it heal, never see each other again. Easy enough to do."

Violet's heart squeezed with an ache and an emptiness she'd never felt before. "We could," she said hollowly.

"But you don't want to, do you?" Daniel came to stand in front of her again, feet planted apart, arms folded over his open shirt. "I see it in your face. You want to try, to fight, and find out what happens."

"But I don't know how." Violet tightened her fingers. "I don't know how to fight, not like this. It isn't lifting tables, or releasing ectoplasm . . ."

"It isn't fooling people, no." Daniel's eyes were still. "It's truth. It's life."

"I don't know anything about life. I only know how to run."

Daniel reached his tanned and callused hands out to her. "Then grab hold of me and hang on. We're both scared about where this will end up, and when the hurting will come. If the hurting comes, it will be bad, I already know that. But hang on to me, and we'll find out together, all right?"

Chapter 17

Daniel kept his hands out. He waited for Violet to rise and push past him, to run from him back to her boardinghouse, or all the way out of Marseille.

His chest hurt with pain for her. If Jacobi was still alive, he wouldn't be for long. He'd taken Violet, an amazing and precious woman, and destroyed her, not only in the eyes of the world, but inside herself. It was as though Jacobi had snatched up an exquisite and priceless marble by Michelangelo and smashed it to powder—worse, because Violet was a living, breathing woman. Alive, and in pain.

Daniel would find not only Jacobi but the man who'd touched her and make him pay for every moment Violet had hurt. For every pain, every tear, every breath of panic.

Violet looked up at Daniel for a long time, her blue eyes still but thoughts racing behind them. Her loose braid fell across the black canvas bodice, the breasts it hugged rising with her breath.

Finally she lifted her hands, fingers visibly trembling, and placed them in his.

Daniel closed his fingers over hers, feeling the cold of her skin, her fear. He pulled her to her feet. Violet's hair was mussed, her eyes large, her dark face powder half brushed off to reveal patches of white skin.

Daniel tugged her against him and closed his arms around her. He felt her trembling turn to all-out shaking as Violet clutched at the back of his shirt.

Ideas for avenging her spun through Daniel's thoughts, but he wouldn't frighten Violet with them. There was a time for slaying dragons, and a time for holding on to someone and making the terror go away.

Violet's fear, it seemed, wouldn't let her simply hold on. She jerked his shirttails out from the back of his kilt and again pulled at his waistband.

Daniel's heart was beating as rapidly as hers, and he was hard for her—aching—but he caught her wrists and pulled her away from him. "I think I said this before. Let me savor you."

"I can't." Violet spoke breathily. "I need to burn through the fear. I want it done, before I know it's happening . . ."

She shook out of his grip and yanked once more at the kilt's waistband. The pin that held the kilt in place broke open, and the plaid sagged from Daniel's hips.

As Daniel grabbed for the slipping kilt, Violet was shoving open his shirt, pushing it from his shoulders. She moved like a frightened animal, desperate and trembling.

"*No*, lass."

"But you want me." Violet sounded confused. She stroked down the front of the kilt, finding his hard cock and sending up a spike of madness. "You want me."

"Aye, that I do." Daniel had to drop the kilt to seize her wrists. Violet fought, but Daniel was stronger. "I'm burning for you, lass. Have been for some time. But this isn't what you need."

"Yes, it is. It is."

"No." Daniel pulled her with him to the long, scrolled French sofa, currently covered with drawings. He shoved these to the floor and seated Violet on the couch. He'd missed one paper, and it crinkled under her skirts.

Daniel knelt in front of her, still keeping his hands around her wrists. She stared at him in frantic bewilderment.

"We'll not be rushing through this," he said. "No finishing before you realize what happened. No getting it over with." Daniel brought her closed fists to his lips and kissed each in turn. "What you need is to learn slow goodness. How to enjoy each and every moment of it, how to embrace it to your heart and taste it. And I'm just the man to teach you."

He didn't give her any time to think or react. Daniel kept hold of her hands as he moved up from his knees and sat next to her on the sofa. His loosened kilt spread across her colorful peasant skirts.

Daniel lifted one of her hands, opened it, kissed her palm, and placed her hand on his bared chest. Violet's eyes widened a little as she contacted his skin, and he saw fear flash.

"Do what you like," he said. "Touch. Feel. Scratch. Whatever you want. But slowly."

Violet's lower lip shook once before she pressed her mouth into a firm line. She let her hand rest, still, on his chest a moment, then she curled her fingers a little bit, points on his skin. The tip of her middle finger just brushed his nipple.

Would he be able to sit still for this? Daniel's heart beat hard, his skin dampening in the warming room.

Violet swallowed as she drew her finger across his tight areola. Fire trailed from her touch, but Daniel held himself back from reaching for her.

He watched Violet's fear start to lessen as she focused on his chest. Daniel never seemed to be able to keep his skin covered when he worked on his engines out of doors or helped his father with the horses. Every summer his skin turned a rich red brown and took its time fading over the winter. Now his chest, back, and arms were a light bronze, and the tattoo, which he'd gotten in London from a man from the Japans, was dark against his skin.

Wisps of Violet's hair tickled him as she leaned closer, but Daniel held himself back. This was already killing him, but she needed to learn not to be afraid of him.

Violet's breath brushed his areola, which tightened even more. Daniel's cock tightened in direct response.

Now she was almost nuzzling him, breathing in, as though getting herself used to his scent. Daniel couldn't stop the little grunt in his throat.

Violet raised her head, cheeks flushed. "Don't."

"Don't what? Enjoy a beautiful woman examining me?"

"I don't know." Her puzzled look was endearing.

"Let me put this another way," Daniel said. "When we were in that inn, far away from everywhere, ye weren't afraid of me." He remembered her response when he'd slid his hand inside her nightgown, when he'd begun to seduce her with slow kisses. "You kissed me back. You weren't running away then."

"It was different. Not real, somehow."

It had been plenty real. Daniel remembered every second of it. "Well then, if it's easier for you, this doesn't have to be real either."

She frowned. "But it is. Too real."

"But it's the same, isn't it? We're hidden away while the city teems around us. No one here but you and me."

Violet shook her head. "This is very real. But I want it to be real." She looked up at him, hope and fear mixed in her eyes. "Can it ever be?"

"It can. Oh yes. Come here a minute." Daniel snaked his arm around her and very gently pulled her to him, until her head was resting on his shoulder. "Let's just sit here, shall we? And take what comes?"

This was definitely going to kill him. Never, ever had Daniel contented himself with merely sitting still with a woman, however beautiful. But his ladies, usually older than he—he couldn't bring himself to be with courtesans who were barely more than girls—rarely wanted to sit still. They wanted Daniel and didn't hide it.

Violet was like an untamed colt, one that had been mistreated, who looked out at the world in frightened uncertainty. Daniel didn't want to break her, as trainers sometimes did with the young horses. He needed to gentle her, to earn her trust.

Her head was warm on his shoulder, and Daniel felt Violet start to relax. If he had to spend another night snuggled down in a cozy nest with her, only sleeping, so be it. Daniel might have to lock himself in his private bath when he returned to his hotel, but he would accept that.

"I don't understand desire," Violet said softly.

Daniel leaned to catch the words, unsure he'd heard correctly. "What's to understand? Desire comes naturally. The most natural thing in the world."

"Is it?" Violet settled herself more comfortably on his shoulder, her hand stealing to his bare chest. "I watch others seek passion—so many girls want me, as a fortune-teller, to promise them true love; men ask me if their true loves will have them. It can lead to much pain too—women ask me to tell them whether their husbands are betraying them, and they're so hurt inside. It's awful. I wonder that anyone wants to seek another's bed at all."

"Mmm. That's right cynical of you, sweetheart."

"It's just that I've seen so much pain. All because of what people call desire."

Daniel knew that some cock-brained men had no interest in what their ladies felt—either physically or emotionally. They believed a woman was for a man's use, nothing more. Courtesans told Daniel they liked him because he talked to them. To *them*, as people, not as bodies paid to behave the way he wanted.

Violet wasn't only a body, though Jacobi and this other man had forced her to be just that. They'd taught her that desire meant pain and fear. Her own needs had to have grown as she blossomed from girl to woman, but those needs would have been mixed with terror and shame. Daniel had met other women who'd been forced. They either grew cynical and decided that being used by men was their lot, or they shattered completely.

Violet had done neither, but her struggle to go on had been a hard one. Still was, if Daniel was any judge.

He caressed Violet's shoulder, trying to choose words that wouldn't upset her. "I know a few reasons why we give in to passion, my sweet. First, it's scientific. If you've read Mr. Darwin, he claimed we all live to make as many copies of ourselves as we can, knowing we'll have to leave this earth someday. If we didn't make those copies, there soon wouldn't be many of us left, would there?"

Violet smiled a little, in spite of her anxiousness. "He was talking about animals. Not people."

"Many people I know act like animals—you'd be amazed." Daniel brought up his other arm to enclose her in a circle of warmth, but he didn't hold her tightly. No trapping her. "*I'll* tell you that we seek passion because it can be a wonderful thing. The intimacy of it. You'll never be as close to another human being in any other way." He kissed the top of her head, liking that she didn't fight being surrounded by his arms. "Besides, it just feels good."

"To men, perhaps," Violet said, perfectly serious. "Women don't feel what men do."

Daniel blinked in surprise. He turned his head and looked down at her. Violet looked back at him serenely, entirely believing every word she'd said.

"My sweet Violet, I'll lay you ten to one odds you're wrong about that."

The answering sparkle in Violet's eyes made Daniel's body go incandescent. Her assurance was returning, the dark terror she'd been reliving starting to ease.

"Oh?" Violet said. "How much would you be willing to put up?"

"Let's say a shilling. I wouldn't want to beggar you."

"Done." Violet held out her hand. Daniel took it, his smile turning wicked. Violet looked away again, confident she could never lose this bet. Poor woman.

"Anyway, how would you prove it?" she asked. "You only have a woman's word for it, and I must tell you, Mr. Mackenzie, that women can be notorious liars, especially when they want something."

"Telling me pretty tales so I'll give them money? Aye, you're not wrong about that. But I'm going to prove it. Here and now."

Violet glanced up in alarm. "What do you mean here and now? You said . . . I thought . . ."

"I said I wouldn't rush you. And I won't." Daniel touched her cheek. "But I never promised I wouldn't make you feel astonishingly good."

Her eyes flickered with fear again. "Daniel, I don't . . . I'm not ready."

Daniel's need to erase her fear surged. He drew her into a hug, touching his lips to her temple. "I won't enter you, love. Not tonight, if you don't want it. I promise." Daniel always kept his promises, no matter how difficult they might be.

Violet looked confused. "Then how will you prove it? You can't by simply putting the thought into my head. I won't believe you."

Daniel couldn't stop his laughter. "Violet. Lass." He let his voice go low, coaxing. "You are good at knowing what people want to hear from those on the other side. You are an expert at giving them a show that amazes them. Well, this is *my* area of expertise. You give yourself into my hands, and I guarantee you'll be handing over your shilling so fast the room will spin."

"You are very sure of yourself, Daniel Mackenzie."

"Because *this* I know how to do. Tonight you'll feel no pain and no fear. Only good things. Better than good. All right?"

Violet's assurance vanished. She obviously had no idea what Daniel meant to do, and that was very sad.

"Remember when we were up in the balloon?" Daniel asked. "Sailing across the land, going where the wind took us?"

Violet's smile returned, her eyes softening in remembered delight. "Yes. That was wonderful."

"It will be like that."

She didn't believe him. "How can that be? I've never felt anything like it before." Violet looked hopeful. "Will you take me ballooning again sometime?"

"Of course I will. I told you, we'll go up in Scotland. Beautiful, and the winds are unpredictable. Very exciting. But for now . . ." Daniel eased Violet back against the scrolled end of the sofa. "You must let me try to win the wager."

Violet wet her lips, the nervous movement stroking moisture across her mouth. "What do I have to do?"

"That's the beauty of it. You don't have to do anything." Daniel positioned himself so he sat on the edge of the sofa, with Violet lying back against the cushions. "I'll take good care of you."

Violet nodded, the gesture stiff.

"But you talk to me," Daniel went on. "If you want to know why I'm doing what I'm doing, or you get scared, you tell me. Promise?"

"Promise." The word was barely a breath.

"All right then." Daniel let his voice go soft. "Off we go."

Chapter 18

Violet had no idea what Daniel meant to do. All kinds of scenarios flashed through her head, every one of them frightening.

Against her fear came the gentleness in his voice when he said, *I'll take good care of you.*

Violet trembled, but she waited.

Daniel unlaced her boots and drew them, one at a time, from her feet. Violet flexed her toes in her thick stockings, her feet cramped from the night's sitting and the walk from the carriage.

Daniel's hands were strong. He cradled both feet, drawing his thumbs around her instep, massaging the tension there.

It felt good, yes, but a foot rub was a long way from the so-intimate act they'd been speaking of. Even Mary rubbed Violet's feet sometimes.

But then, a massage from Daniel was a great deal different from one from Mary. Mary was briskly competent. Daniel, on the other hand, gave Violet a slow smile, which turned mundane foot rubbing into something bordering the erotic.

Daniel lifted one stockinged foot as he moved his thumbs

over the arch of it. Then he leaned down and carefully bit her toes.

Violet gasped and tried to jerk her foot away. "What if my stockings were dirty?"

Daniel captured her again. "The efficient Violet? Put on soiled stockings? I don't think so. But if it worries you . . ."

He slid his hands up her leg until his fingers caught on the tie of her plain garter. Violet remembered how Daniel had checked her for breaks or hurts when they'd crash-landed the balloon. The frisson of delight as his fingers had touched her calves had unnerved her then, and it unnerved her now.

Daniel's hands were firm and sure, and he made short work of the garter. Her stocking loosened, and Daniel slid it down and off her leg.

He slid off her other stocking in the same way then moved Violet's bare feet back to his lap, beginning another massage.

"You have lovely toes." But Daniel was looking into her eyes, his smile so sinful Violet wasn't certain whether to squirm or laugh.

He lifted one foot, cradling her heel in his hand. He kissed the tips of her toes then the ball of her foot. The tickling tingle became a burn of pleasure.

Daniel slid his hot touch up her bare leg, her skirt and petticoat rising as he went. Her loose lawn drawers moved upward under Daniel's skilled touch, until his thumbs brushed the soft skin on her inner thighs.

Violet had never realized how sensitive she was there. When Violet washed herself, her thighs were as neutral to her as the inside of her arms or the space between her shoulder blades.

When Daniel touched her, her perception changed. His fingers did a sweet dance, streaks of heat, a feeling Violet couldn't define. She found herself clutching the back of the sofa, her fingers sinking into its soft fabric.

Daniel's fingers stopped, and Violet swallowed disappointment.

"Ye all right, love?"

"Yes." Violet could barely say the words. "I'm . . . fine."

"Good. Because these come off next." Daniel tugged at the buttons of her drawers.

Her eyes widened. "No . . . I mean, I don't think I can."

"But I must win my wager." Daniel's eyes were dark in the firelight, his smile soft. "A gentleman never backs out of a wager. He pays his debt of honor. Or collects his debt, as the case may be."

"You're not making any sense," Violet stammered.

"That's because I'm dying for you, and my thoughts are a bit incoherent."

Daniel didn't look as though he were dying. His fingers were steady as he unbuttoned her drawers, his gaze holding Violet's.

Swiftly and competently, Daniel slid the drawers down over her hips. In no time at all, Violet found herself sitting bare bottomed on the sofa, her skirt hiked up over her knees.

She automatically grabbed her skirt and petticoats to pull them down again. Daniel caught her hands, kissed them, then set them to either side of her while he pushed her skirts all the way up to bare her thighs.

Now the panic started to come. Violet clutched his hands. "Daniel."

The red-bearded man had done this—pushed up her skirts, though he'd ripped open her drawers instead of politely unbuttoning them. Violet had thought the cloth tearing from her had hurt, but she'd been unprepared for the searing pain that followed.

"Violet," Daniel said, his voice cutting through the fog. "You're not there. You're here. With me. On the sofa in my somewhat untidy flat. And I've got you, sweetheart."

Yes. She was here. With Daniel. Far from the trivia of her daily life, the endless need to keep busy, busy, so she could forget.

"Keep me here," Violet pleaded.

"I will. I promise you."

Daniel gently extricated himself from her grip, smoothed his hand over the top of her knee, and kissed it. "I want you to do something for me. Imagine something very"—he kissed her other knee—"sensual. The most sensual thing you can think of. One that pleases *you*, not one you think would please me. Keep it locked inside yourself. You don't have to tell me what it is if you don't want to."

Sensual. Violet strove to calm her breathing as she thought. The most sensual image she could call to mind was . . . Daniel.

Daniel lying on the floor of an empty bedroom, his hands behind his head as he laughed up at her. Daniel sitting up, cross-legged, his eyes narrowing as he closed his lips around a black cigarette.

Daniel's hand on Violet's waist, daring her to take the cigarette and put her lips where his had been . . . He'd watched her with eyes the color of dark whiskey, as he watched her now.

Violet snapped back to the present. She realized Daniel had moved his thumbs to her bare opening, drawing them along the slickness there.

Violet went still, breath catching. Daniel stroked lightly, barely touching her, but the contact was there. The watery sensation of it made her dizzy.

"Sensual," Daniel repeated. "Close your eyes. Hold on to those thoughts. No others."

Easy to say. No one had ever touched her there except the red-bearded man long ago, and he hadn't exactly touched her. Pried, forced her apart, hurt her. Nothing like Daniel caressing her as though he cherished her.

Violet couldn't stop her trembling, but she closed her eyes again. She forced her mind back to Daniel in the bedroom, his smile when she showed him she wasn't afraid to take the cigarette, his look of satisfaction when he leaned down and tasted the smoke on her lips.

Her thoughts switched to waking up next to Daniel in the inn, the warm scent of him in the bed with her. How he'd slid his hand so carefully inside her nightdress to tenderly cup her breast. He'd moved over her, giving her the deep, intimate kiss before the innkeeper's wife had come in with breakfast.

Violet's imagination took it further. In her fantasy, they stayed in the bed together, no innkeeper's wife interrupting. Violet would close her arms around Daniel, running her hands down his body, bare beneath his nightshirt. She'd find the warmth of his backside, lift the nightshirt to touch him.

Dimly, in the present, Violet felt Daniel's fingers stroking her, touching her. Then another warmth, his breath on her thighs.

Violet's eyes sprang open. Daniel held Violet's skirts out of his way as he kissed her left thigh, his unshaved whiskers brushing her skin. He touched her opening again then lifted his hand away and replaced it with his mouth.

Violet sucked in a sharp breath. What . . . ? She went stiff, tight, uncertain.

Daniel parted her legs, but carefully, kind hands on Violet's thighs. He kissed her, breath as hot as she was, and then his tongue . . .

A groan escaped her lips. Daniel licked her, kissed her again. He chuckled. "Close your eyes, sweet. Lie back. Think about whatever you were thinking. You were obviously enjoying it."

Violet stared down at him a moment longer. She'd never dreamed a man would think of doing *this*, but her education in such matters was lacking. After what had happened to her, she'd shut herself off from all interest in what men did to women.

Daniel was rapidly taking away her blinders.

Violet leaned back on the arm of the sofa, forcing her body to soften. What Daniel did didn't hurt, didn't frighten her. It was more . . .

She had no idea. The feeling amazed her. All Violet knew was that when she closed her eyes again, Daniel said, "That's my good lass," and leaned to her.

He flicked his tongue over her opening, first rapidly, then slowly. He licked, nipped, tasted, then slid his tongue inside her.

Violet tried to go back to her fantasies, but all she could picture was herself and Daniel in the big bed at the inn, both of them damp with warmth and sleep. In her vision, he slid down her body, pushed up her nightdress, parted her legs, and did exactly what he did to her now.

Daniel licked inside her once more then put his whole mouth over her point of fire. Violet wanted to wrench herself from the feeling, and at the same time to press Daniel harder down upon her.

She thought he'd have to stop—surely he'd stop—but Daniel never did. He went on licking, nipping, suckling, teasing, licking again. His hands on her legs kept her open for him, and the rough of his whiskers touched her most intimate places.

Dark shivers replaced Violet's trembling. He had to *stop*, but Daniel went on. There was no pain, no hurting, no forcing, just the tender pressure of Daniel's mouth, the sweet wildness of his tongue.

Violet's skin dampened as heat flowed through her, loosening every limb and yet tightening her at the same time. She was aware of her blood pounding, every beat of her heart sending the goodness of Daniel through her.

Her fantasy—the sweet, beautiful fantasy of being in Daniel's bed, his wife, *his*—dissolved. Violet clutched at the vision, not wanting it to go. But Violet's body fought for attention. Wild waves of feeling poured over her, and all thoughts vanished.

She'd never felt anything like this before. Her gladness on seeing Daniel standing before her in the theatre, alive and whole, had been something like it. The joy of flying in the balloon, rushing on the wind, was more like it. Just as Daniel had said it would be. He'd known.

Violet had no idea what was happening to her. One of the waves swept her up, higher, higher, her body one point of astonishing feeling. Everything coalesced and centered on one point of aching heat, and on Daniel.

She was drowning. Dying. She must be. "Help me! Daniel, please help me!" Violet dragged in a breath, which ended in a sob. "Please!"

Another wave of pure joy hit her, and more words came out, but she had no idea what she said. Violet heard one last *help me!* and then tears came.

She was sobbing, her face wet, something inside her shattering and breaking open.

Daniel rose from her, triumph in his eyes, but his arms went around her, and he pulled her close. Daniel kissed her hair, soothing, holding her, warming her and keeping Violet safe from all harm.

Daniel held Violet as she shook like a terrified kitten. She was weeping, tears wetting his open shirt and bare skin. Daniel hoped to God he hadn't just broken her.

As he stroked her hair, Daniel finished loosening it from its braid, and let the warm weight of it flow over his hands. It felt beautiful, as he'd known it would.

Daniel had sensed the moment Violet had relaxed into what he did. Her body, which had been stiff and resisting, had taken over, knowing what to do.

But now Violet continued crying, weeping as though she couldn't stop.

"You all right, love?"

Violet looked up at him, her eyes streaming. "Yes. I'm sorry."

"Don't be sorry. Tell me those are tears of joy. I won my wager, didn't I?"

She wiped her eyes, her sobs easing. "I think so."

"You *think* so? Lady, you crush me." Daniel fished in his discarded coat for a handkerchief and wiped the tears from her cheeks. "Will you tell me what you were thinking about? Ye don't have to, ye know. Don't worry, I'm only curious."

"The inn," Violet said, her voice very quiet. "With you."

He could like this. "Which part? Me stuffing all that breakfast into my mouth? Simple French country fare can be the best in the world."

"In the bed." Violet blushed, looking down. Violet, shy. This was new. "As we were. Except you were doing . . . what you just did."

Heat filled Daniel's blood. "I wanted to stay there all day long, you and me getting to know each other. Damn that we ever had to leave."

"We could go back." Her voice held hope.

Daniel pulled her closer. "'Tis not a bad idea. Perhaps we could make the journey tomorrow."

Violet shook her head, regret in her eyes. "My mother and I have a performance tomorrow."

"The day after, then. I'll come steal you away again. Though we'll have to go by train all the way—I don't think Monsieur Dupuis will let me near another balloon anytime soon."

"Can we truly? You're not lying to please me?"

"Of course not." Daniel put on his best shocked voice, learned from the pile of nannies the Mackenzies employed. "I'd give up everything to whisk you away again, this time to repose at our leisure. I'm sure the innkeeper and his wife would be pleased to see Mr. and Mrs. Mackenzie back again."

Violet's eyes flickered, but she snuggled her head into his shoulder. "What will we do there?"

"All kinds of things, my Violet. Anything you want. Maybe I'll show you just how many different ways a man can make a woman feel pleasure."

"You would want to do that? I mean, I thought that men only sought . . ." Violet trailed off, as though unsure how to finish.

"Their own pleasure?" Daniel asked. "You've lived among Sassenachs too long. If a Scotsman tried to use a woman only for his pleasure, he'd get clouted about the head. Come to think of it, you clout pretty well yourself."

"I said I was—"

Daniel pressed his fingers to her lips. "I was teasing. Not one more word about it." He was glad to see, though, a sparkle of spiritedness return to her eyes. "I pushed you too fast and assumed you were hungry for the touch of Daniel Mackenzie. Never thought you'd try to kill me so hard, but I know now I frightened you."

She nodded. "You did. I didn't know what I was doing."

"Are you still frightened of me? It's all right if you are. I'm a terrifying man."

Violet's smile came. "Absolutely horrifying."

"Good." Daniel nuzzled her hair. "Because I'd like to keep on kissing you. This place has finally warmed, and I'm not ready for the city streets yet. Now, admit it, that was pleasure you were feeling, wasn't it? Deep down, belly-clenching, blood-heating pleasure."

She nodded. "I thought I was drowning."

"You're supposed to feel like that. As though your mooring has been ripped away, and you're floundering in the water, not knowing if you'll ever come up again. And not sure you want to."

Violet nodded again, her hair moving on his shoulder. "Yes. Exactly like that."

"You owe me a shilling."

Another sparkle. "So, you were only after money, were you?"

Daniel pressed his hand to his heart, which was pounding. "You love to wound me, don't you? I'm a master of pleasure. I'd give it for the fun of it, and damn the wager. But you're not getting out of it that easily. I intend to collect."

"Oh, do you? You'd rob a poor, defenseless Romany woman?"

Daniel liked how easily she fell into teasing with him. "You're a fraud, Violet . . . whatever your name is."

Violet only smiled again, keeping her secrets secret.

Daniel pulled her closer, sliding his hands around the black canvas bodice, which he itched to unlace. To hell with secrets, her past and his, pain and heartbreak. He had Violet with him tonight, hidden from the world. Here, Violet belonged to Daniel and he to her.

When he kissed her, Violet's lips readily opened to him. They shared the warm, intimate kisses of lovers. Daniel had softened something inside her, broken a small chink in her wall. He'd break down the whole bloody thing if he had to.

Their lips moved together, mouths seeking and giving. Violet's hand on his knee warmed him through the kilt.

When that hand slipped to land on Daniel's aching, hard-as-a-rock cock, his entire world stopped.

Chapter 19

Daniel made himself go completely still. Violet was gazing at him in fear again, her hand frozen in place.

He knew any move might scare her away, undoing all the work they'd done here tonight. No matter how intensely Daniel wanted Violet, he had to leave what happened up to her.

"You do as you like." Daniel smoothed a wisp of tangled hair from her face. "Just as you like."

Violet kept her hand in place, neither exploring him nor pulling away. Indecision and terror chased each other through her eyes, but Daniel remained still. He was an expert on patience—horses needed patience, so did machines. Years with each had taught him much.

Violet kept her focus on his face, trying to read him as she always did. Her brow puckered as once again, she couldn't.

Daniel wanted to tell her she couldn't read him because he was open all the way down. Daniel didn't have secrets—the only time he kept secrets was when truth would hurt someone. Otherwise, the depths of him were the same as his surface. Violet could look all she wanted, but she'd see only Daniel. He had nothing to hide.

Violet's hand tightened around him through the kilt, her eyes stilling as she did so. Daniel swallowed a groan.

"I don't know what to do," she whispered.

"You won't have to do very much for very long."

Her look told him she wasn't sure what Daniel meant. The man who'd stolen her innocence had taken still more— Violet's trust, her curiosity, her ability to simply be with a man. Daniel would make him pay when he found him, and Daniel would find him.

Violet moved her hand again. Daniel groaned and gently took her wrist. "Wait, darlin'." He drew out the pin at his waistband and pulled his kilt the rest of the way off, then settled the plaid over both of them, wrapping them in a blanket of wool.

"Now then. Explore as you like."

Violet's lips parted, but resolution joined the fear in her eyes. Slowly she slid her hand down Daniel's torso, under the plaid.

When her fingertips brushed his cock, she drew a sharp breath and jerked her hand away. But she didn't give up. Violet reached out again, another quick touch, then another, as a person might do when worried an object would give an electric shock. Each touch lasted a little longer than the last, until finally Violet let her fingers rest fully on him.

This had to be the hardest thing Daniel had ever done— keeping himself motionless, letting Violet find the courage to continue on her own. *She* had to do it, or she'd be forever uncertain.

Daniel saw Violet's panic flare again, but she drew a deep breath and mastered it. Hesitantly, she closed her fingers all the way around him.

Daniel let out a faint groan. He stretched his arms across the sofa's back, fists clenched, and closed his eyes.

Violet rested against his shoulder, her fingers moving a little. "When I do this, does it make you feel exactly the way you made *me* feel?"

Daniel swallowed another noise of desperation. "I've not made a scientific study of it, but yes, I think it does."

"Oh."

"*Oh* is a good way of putting it. Vi, you're killing me."

She stilled. "Shall I stop?" The question sounded innocent, but he heard her strength returning behind it.

"No!" Daniel struggled for control. "If you have pity on me, no. Please. Don't make me beg."

Too late, Daniel was already begging. He opened his eyes to find Violet regarding him in fascination. She watched him the same way she had on the balloon when he'd tinkered with the engine.

Now, if they could be doing *this* in the balloon . . .

God, why did he have to think of that? Daniel's imagination put them soaring high above the winter fields. Only this time, his kilt lay on the bottom of the basket, and Violet was smiling at him, her hands full of him. A little later, she'd slip to her knees.

"Oh, Lord." Daniel snaked his hand under the plaid, wrapped it around Violet's, and guided her down him in one stroke. "Like that," he said, voice broken. "Like that, lass."

Violet froze again when Daniel took his hand away, and he prayed he hadn't frightened her. He was about to pass out and fall off the sofa anyway, though, so it really didn't matter if she stopped.

Violet took a breath, laid her head again on Daniel's shoulder, tightened her hand around his hardness, and stroked as he'd shown her.

Daniel shook down to his boots. The sweet friction made everything within him loosen. Her quick slides, clumsy at first, became smoother as Violet gained confidence.

A new world opened for him. Daniel was no stranger to bodily pleasure, but the way Violet had warmed and trapped his heart made for a very different experience.

Desire clamped his body until ordinary sensations were gone. The musty scent of the room, the heat from the fire that made the space close, and the hum of activity on the street far away—all dissipated. Daniel was aware only of Violet, of holding her warmth against him and the beauty of her touch.

His climax came before he was ready. Daniel shoved the startled Violet away, grabbed his handkerchief, clamped it around himself, and lost his seed into it. His hips pumped, wanting to drive into Violet, not his somewhat unsatisfactory hand. But Daniel wouldn't hurt her for the world.

He slung his arm around Violet and pulled her to him. The kiss that followed was frenzied and desperate. Daniel's blood burned, as though some drug raced through his veins. He needed Violet, needed everything about her.

She kissed him back as fiercely. Strong, proud Violet.

By the time Daniel had spent his seed, they were curled together on the narrow confines of the sofa. Violet lay against Daniel, and he stroked her hair, kissing it, their silence saying more than Daniel could shout.

❧

Violet lay against Daniel's side in the warmth and quiet of the room, breathing in peace. She liked that Daniel didn't want to talk. She could bask quietly in his warmth as he ran a slow hand through her hair. Whenever he bent down to kiss her, the kiss was soft but holding the remnants of passion.

I think I'm falling in love with you, Daniel. The words whispered through her. *No, it's too late. I've already fallen.*

Violet needed to soak up this moment, this happiness, to save for forever. She had so few good moments in her life that she stored each as she would a precious jewel.

The peace of Daniel's cluttered room was shattered by a sturdy knock at the door.

Daniel grunted and snatched up the kilt that covered them both. He gently moved Violet's feet aside, then rolled to stand up, wrapping the kilt around him as he moved to the door.

"Bloody neighbors," he said. "Probably coming to borrow something so they can have a look at the lovely lady I've brought home. Don't worry, I'll send them away."

The knock sounded again. "Daniel," came a woman's voice, quiet but determined. "I know you're in there."

Violet's happiness sloughed away like wet sand. She leaned down and plucked her drawers from the floor, standing up to pull them on, her skirts falling to hide her bare legs.

"Perfect," Daniel grumbled. "Not what I need to make my night complete. I hope she didn't bring the shrimp with her."

What that meant, Violet had no idea, but Daniel seemed perfectly sanguine to open the door to one of his mistresses.

His body blocked the doorway as Daniel peered out. "Yes?"

"Do let me in, Danny. It's freezing out here. I know you brought the fortune-teller with you, so if you are both decent, I need to come in. I'm not so easily shocked as all that."

Daniel glanced back at Violet to see that she was dressed—barring her stockings and shoes, which Violet hastily kicked under the sofa. He gave Violet an apologetic look and pulled the door wide, admitting the wind, and the woman.

The lady wasn't a courtesan. Worse. She was his stepmother.

"Hello, dear," Lady Cameron Mackenzie said as Daniel closed the door and leaned back against it. "I'm Ainsley Mackenzie. You're Violet?" Ainsley strode across the room, her hand outstretched. "Your maid is searching frantically for you. She's in the coach."

"Oh . . ." Violet began, but Ainsley broke through.

"I thought it no coincidence Daniel disappeared from the soiree at the same time the comtesse lost track of her fortune-teller. I had to bully the coachman mercilessly until he confessed he brought you both here." Her smile shone out. "I adore a good fortune-teller. Have you got the true gift, or is it just for fun?"

Ainsley held Violet's hand firmly, looking straight at her. Violet's quick assessment—which she couldn't stop herself making—showed her a woman confident and content, but one who hadn't always been so. Ainsley had a darkness in her eyes that spoke of loss. She also carried worry that she would lose again. The fear was buried deep, but present.

"Where's Gavina?" Daniel asked warily.

"At the hotel, sleeping—in theory. More likely, she is ruthlessly questioning Cameron about the evening and everything we did at the comtesse's. I knew Gavina would want to tear into your work here if I brought her. Not to mention ask repeatedly why you are here alone with Miss Violet, and why Violet's hair is down and her shoes off."

Violet self-consciously pulled her bare feet under her skirts. "You say Mary is looking for me?"

"Yes, quite desperately. I wouldn't have interrupted for the world, but she seemed terribly worried. Which is how I guessed you weren't a courtesan, in spite of Daniel spiriting you away for an assignation. A courtesan's maid would discreetly stay away, no matter what the situation. I hope I don't offend you, my dear."

"Stepmama . . ." Daniel began.

"Never mind, Danny. Dress yourself, Violet, and I'll take you to the coach. I'll wait for you in here if you don't mind. It's much warmer."

Ainsley, wife of a duke's brother and former lady-in-waiting to Queen Victoria, plopped herself on the window seat and took an absorbing interest in one of Daniel's drawings.

Daniel fetched Violet's stockings and shoes from under the sofa, then sat down next to her, warming her as she pulled on stockings and garters. Daniel had to help relace her boots— Violet's fingers were shaking so much she couldn't do them up herself.

Most of Daniel's shirt buttons had gone flying when Violet had torn into him, so he had to make do with securely buttoning his waistcoat and arranging his frock coat to cover himself. Ainsley stood up when they were ready, setting aside the line drawing she'd been studying.

Violet glanced at the drawing as Lady Cameron put it down. Neat lines showed a cross section of some machine, with labels, letters, and numbers. Violet was pretty sure part of the machine had wings.

"What are you building here?" Violet asked in curiosity.

"Just jotting down ideas." Daniel fetched his greatcoat and wrapped it around Violet.

Ainsley smiled. "Our Danny's a bit of a genius, but I'm afraid no one but Ian really understands what he comes up with."

"I've told you, it's all perfectly simple, Stepmama."

"*If* you're an engineer. Which I am not. Shall we go?"

Daniel slid his arm around Violet as they walked back down the stairs and moved swiftly through the wind and passages to the main street. Daniel betrayed no shame that he'd been caught by his stepmother dallying with Violet. He walked along without comment and handed both ladies into the coach as though he'd been escorting them to a respectable night out at the opera.

Mary waited inside the carriage, her eyes round. She wouldn't say why she'd been chasing after Violet—in fact she said nothing at all.

Daniel took the seat next to his stepmother, and the two of them began a lively conversation as the coach turned for the main streets. Daniel talked with Lady Cameron in a relaxed manner, teasing her as much as she teased him.

Violet thought of the story he'd told her of the lonely little boy who'd hoped that one of the women his father brought home might stay and be his mother. Daniel might not have found a mother, but he'd discovered a comrade in Ainsley, a lady he obviously respected and admired. And loved. Lady Cameron had filled the space in Daniel that had been empty. The pair had a warm, strong relationship that Violet envied.

The coach stopped at Violet's boardinghouse all too soon. Daniel jumped down and handed out first Mary, then Violet. Mary thanked Daniel politely then ran ahead into the house, opened the door, and waited for Violet.

Violet's time with Daniel was over. She unwrapped the greatcoat he'd lent her and handed it to him, feeling herself lose part of him as she did so.

Daniel gave her a smile that spoke of the sensuality of the evening and touched her cheek. Violet clutched the warmth of it to herself like a cloak.

"Don't kiss her in front of her respectable boardinghouse, for heaven's sake," Lady Cameron said from the coach. "You'll ruin the girl."

Daniel's eyes filled with laughter. He stuck out his hand, shook Violet's, and executed a bow. "Until tomorrow, my lady."

Violet didn't want to let him go. Daniel had opened a new world for her tonight, and she wasn't ready to leave it.

Daniel released her hand, and she realized she'd been clinging to it. "Go on, now," he said in a gentle voice.

Violet swallowed, managed a "Good night," and turned to follow Mary into the house.

She tried to linger in the doorway so she could watch

Daniel swing into the coach and roll off into the night, but Mary closed the door behind Violet, cutting off her view.

"I never knew he was so rich," Mary said. She started up the stairs, and Violet ascended slowly behind her. "Looks like he's taken with you, miss. If you keep him on a string, you'll be the making of us all."

Keep him on a string. After the beautiful night Violet had just lived, the phrase sounded vulgar and coarse.

"There's no question of me keeping him on a string." Violet had to let Mary unlock and open the door to their rooms, because she knew she'd never manage keys tonight. "When we leave Marseille, I'll likely never see him again." And that would leave a large hole in her heart.

"Then best you get as much money and as many jewels as you can from him now," Mary said, ever practical. "And don't trust the jewels to a bank. A gentleman can always make a bank give them back to him."

Mary's expression was ingenuous. She saw no objection at all to Violet becoming Daniel's mistress—a very sensible solution for women in need of money, to her mind.

But Mary's words continued to tarnish the brightness of the night. "Mr. Mackenzie won't be giving me any jewels," she said.

Even as Violet spoke the words, she envisioned herself sitting at a dressing table with Daniel coming behind her, smiling his wicked smile, diamonds in his hands. He'd lay the necklace across her bosom, fasten the clasp with gentle fingers, and lean down and press a kiss to her neck.

Violet craved it. Not the jewels, but the intimacy of it. Daniel choosing a gift with Violet in mind and warming her as he gave it to her.

"Miss?"

Violet jumped, finding herself back in their faded sitting room. She crossed to the window, but a glance outside showed her that Daniel and his coach had already gone. "I'm sorry, Mary. Now, *why* were you searching for me so desperately?"

Mary looked worried. "It's your mum. She's had one of her premonitions."

"Oh dear." Violet's euphoria faded. Her mother often had dire visions of their future, which, unfortunately, sometimes came true. "Is she all right? Have you put her to bed?"

"I did, but she went on something awful. Begged me to find you, said she wouldn't settle until you were safe back here. It was a bad one tonight. She foresaw all kinds of dire horrors, especially for you. Fire, smoke, and death, all mixed up. She's very afraid, miss."

"I see." Violet sighed. She patted Mary's shoulder, gave her the pouch of tips she'd earned from her fortune-teller's bowl, squared her shoulders, and walked into her mother's bedroom.

Chapter 20

Ainsley wanted to stop at a restaurant.

"They won't let us in this late," Daniel said.

"Nonsense. There's the little one next to the cabaret—they serve people far into the night. Besides, they have the most marvelous torte you must try. Cake smooth as butter, with raspberry jam between the first two layers and luscious chocolate glaze dripping down the sides."

Daniel looked at her with fondness. Ainsley had been a friend from the moment he'd met her. "You do love your cake, Stepmama."

"So do you, Stepson. I remember when we made our way down the boulevards of Paris, trying cake at every patisserie in the city. Drove your father wild."

Daniel grinned, remembering Cameron growling like a bear as Daniel and Ainsley dragged him all over Paris for *cake*. Cameron had been falling in love with Ainsley at the time, though the man had done everything to avoid admitting it. Pushing those two together had been one of Daniel's most onerous but enjoyable tasks.

The torte, as Ainsley promised, was excellent. She spent

the first half of the dessert in silent enjoyment of the confection. The little café was dim, the clientele noisy, but Daniel and Ainsley had procured a private table at the front window and were left relatively alone.

Ainsley finally laid down her fork, drank a dollop of wine, and put her elbows on the small table.

"Now, Daniel, tell me everything about this Violet."

Daniel forked up another mouthful of jam-smeared torte. "This is a change. You usually beg me *not* to mention anything to do with my women. You wish me to remain the innocent sixteen-year-old who ran away from school and was your coconspirator. I have to remind you, I wasn't so innocent at sixteen. I'd already had two mistresses and plenty of briefer affairs."

"Of course I don't want to know about *that*. I'm asking you about Violet. Why do I ask? Because you look at her in a different way than you do the others. Don't tell me you don't. I want the entire story."

Daniel set down his fork, which was a crime, because the torte was like bites of heaven. "No story. Her services as a medium were offered to me to pay a gambling debt. Then she tried to kill me, then I chased her to Marseille, then I took her ballooning and nearly killed *her*. So we're even."

It was difficult to keep from laughing at the expression on Ainsley's face, but Daniel did it. Going back to shoveling in more torte helped.

"You see?" Ainsley said after a stunned pause. "I knew there was a story. Who is she? She's very lovely, even under that theatrical powder. Not a Romany at all, I take it. She's from London or I'm a Dutchman."

"You're still plenty Scottish," Daniel said. "South London, though I believe Vi had a French father. So she says. Or else she's truly a Russian siren hiding in France to escape persecution—the impossibly beautiful Princess Ivanova, with her friend, the Countess Melikova, who can speak to anyone on the other side." He said the last in dramatic tones.

Ainsley's fork stopped halfway to her mouth. "*That's* who she is? I've seen the bills about town. Their show is even recommended by the hotel. Oh, we *must* see it."

"I have seen it. It's complete and absolute flummery. They're very good at it."

"Better and better. I'll tell Cam. We'll all go. I can't wait."

"They have a performance tomorrow," Daniel said. "Or, tonight, rather. I think it's getting on for the wee small hours."

Ainsley ate another thoughtful bite. "What you haven't told me is whether you plan to make an honest woman of her."

Daniel scraped the last bit of chocolate from his plate then pushed the plate and fork aside. "Why this sudden rush to shove me down the aisle? Are you that eager to make an honest man of *me*?"

"I want to see you happy, is all. You flit about the world from country to country, car race to balloon race to horse race, city to city, woman to woman. As though you're seeking something, but don't know what."

"Enjoying myself. Sowing wild oats. Learning. I'll set the next land-speed record for motorcars this year, see if I don't."

"With Violet by your side?"

Ainsley always did know what Daniel hid in his heart. Daniel the boy had fumed when his father had caught him at his many pranks or hauled him home every time he ran away, though Daniel realized now he'd *wanted* to be caught at those things. As much as Cameron raged, at least his father was paying Daniel some attention.

When Ainsley, a slip of a young woman with fair hair and lovely gray eyes, had come into the lives of Daniel and Cameron, she'd discerned Daniel's vices with a canny shrewdness. She'd known about his gambling, the dubious connections he'd cultivated, his affairs, his decadent friends. Daniel had given up much of this and settled down once Ainsley became his stepmother, to please her more than out of any fear she'd tell Cameron.

Now Ainsley peered at him with her knowing look, telling him his own secrets.

Of course Daniel planned to win the motorcar races with Violet by his side. No other woman Daniel had met had shown such interest in his projects and ambitions. Violet had looked at Daniel's sketches and drawings and understood right away what he was trying to do, and even more importantly, why he wanted to.

"She's fearless," Daniel said. "Bless her."

"So what will it be? Marriage? Or a torrid affair? And once you ruin her, what will you do?"

Daniel curled his hands as he held on to his patience. "You make me sound like a seducer in a melodrama."

"You're a Mackenzie," Ainsley said. "And your father's son. As Mac likes to say, Mackenzies break what they touch. Remember that."

She had a point. Daniel shrugged. "It's up to her. Violet can have it as she likes."

Ainsley leaned forward, lowering her voice. "Daniel, it's never up to us. Us ladies, I mean. Gentlemen do as they please, and women have to fight for every scrap. She's been hurt before. I saw that in her. I for one don't mind if she's a stage actress or a fortune-teller, or whatever she is, as long as she makes you happy. I don't think she's after your wealth. I've met predatory women before—good heavens, your father was surrounded by them. Violet doesn't have the look, at least not when she looks at you. As I said, I saw what was in her eyes."

Daniel waited until she'd run down. "Finished?"

Ainsley contemplated her empty plate. "Yes, I think so."

"I'll tell you a secret then. I believe the one who'll end up with the hurting this time is me."

Ainsley looked up at him, her eyes softening in sympathy. "That bad, is it?"

"Getting there," Daniel said. He let Ainsley close her hand over his and squeeze it. "Definitely getting there."

"Poor Daniel. Well, you know you will have my help. At any time, for any reason. I owe you—you know what for— and I love you, Danny-boy." Ainsley gave his hand another squeeze and released him. "Now, shall we try another cake? Or perhaps you could take me to the cabaret so I can watch the cancan."

"Cake," Daniel said quickly. "Dad would thrash me good if I took you to the cabaret to look at naked women."

"Don't be silly. I like the dancing. I can't imagine how they're able to kick their legs so high. And anyway, it's not sordid. They wear drawers."

"In some cabarets, especially this late, they don't always."

"Oh." Ainsley looked thoughtful. "Yes. I can see where that would be a bit racy. Especially with the kicking."

"Cake," Daniel said firmly, and he waved the waiter over before Ainsley could argue any more.

~~~

Violet floated. She suspected the heat of the collected bodies in the theatre, smoke from the incense she'd wafted about, and lack of sleep caused some of it.

The rest was remembered joy. Violet walked about the stage in numb oblivion, going through the motions of their performance, speaking entire sentences before she knew she'd said anything. She was grateful for her costume with the veil, which would hide the glazed look in her eyes and the idiotic euphoria on her face.

Celine had kept them all awake until six this morning with her hysteria over her visions. Smoke, fire, grave danger. They needed to leave Marseille at once.

Or perhaps not. The trouble with Celine's visions was they were maddeningly vague. Celine wasn't certain where the disaster would take place. If they fled Marseille, their fate might await them in Cannes, Monte Carlo, Italy, or on a boat back to England.

Most of Celine's premonitions didn't come true, but every so often, one did—frequently enough to make Celine terrified of them. Privately Violet believed her mother in possession of a vivid imagination she didn't bother to control. Disaster, large or small, came into everyone's life at some time. It was inevitable. The world was a dangerous place, no matter how one tried to cushion oneself against it.

On the other hand, it didn't hurt to be careful. Violet assured Celine she would check that the boardinghouse and the theatre were as safe as possible. She and Mary finally got Celine to sleep, with the help of a little laudanum. Celine was much calmer when she woke, and they made their way to the theatre, which seemed solid enough.

The house was full tonight. Celine came into her own when she performed, and the night wound on without incident.

And Violet floated. Daniel had awakened something inside

her she wanted to examine. It was new, wonderful, and somewhat bewildering.

He'd promised to take her to the inn again. Daniel might remember, or he might not. It didn't matter. Violet would have memories to savor, regardless.

Halfway through the show, she saw Daniel slide into the back row, gallantly assisting his stepmother to a seat. Violet stilled, her attention instantly pulled to him.

Perhaps *this* was the disaster her mother foretold—Violet falling deeply, irrevocably in love with Daniel. The heartbreak of it would bring her oceans of pain.

Daniel waited until Ainsley had seated herself, he flashing his grin at the men and women in seats next to them. No doubt charming them all to pieces. Daniel's father hadn't come, she noted. Possibly staying behind to look after his young daughter. An unusual sort of man if so.

Once Daniel sat down, he sent a smile and a nod at the stage. Straight at Violet.

Sweet moments. Forever seared into her heart.

"Violet," her mother hissed behind her. "Ask the young man about his mother."

Young man? Daniel?

No, Celine meant the man who stood in the fourth row, worry on his face, waiting for Violet to allow him to speak to Celine. Violet couldn't remember a thing the man had just said.

"Forgive me." Violet turned back to him, pitching her voice low, soothing. "You want to know about your mother?"

The performance went on. At its end, when Celine drooped, Violet emerged in front of the curtain. "I thank you all. The countess must rest now."

She didn't do the dramatics of pretending someone called to her from backstage—some of the audience had returned from the previous performance, and Violet didn't like to repeat. No one must believe this a staged show. It had to be natural, spontaneous, every time.

Violet glanced across the house to see Daniel on his feet, applauding heartily. His stepmother stood next to him, also applauding and looking delighted. Ainsley was a foot or so shorter than Daniel, which emphasized Daniel's height. Daniel shot an approving smile straight at her.

Much as she wanted to stay out front gazing at Daniel, Violet knew she couldn't. She swept the audience a graceful gesture—a princess would never bow to commoners—and retreated backstage.

Even in her daze, Violet remembered to secure the take. She got her mother and Mary away out the stage door with the money, and returned to the dressing room alone to change to her plain shirtwaist and skirt.

The last time she'd left this theatre, Daniel had been waiting for her. Violet's heart beat faster as she made her way out. He might not be there tonight, since he'd come with his stepmother, but Violet couldn't stop her anticipation.

She stepped out the back door, preparing to close and lock it.

A strong hand landed on her shoulder. Daniel's gaze was all for Violet as he pushed her gently back inside. Once they were in the hallway, his arms went around her, and his mouth came down on hers.

He kissed her for a long time, slowly, no frenzy tonight. But the kiss held heat and stole every bit of Violet's breath.

Daniel eased away and touched her lower lip. "Ready?"

Violet swallowed. "Ready for what?" To take her to the country inn? This late? Or back to his wonderfully cluttered flat where he'd begun to awaken her? "Where is your stepmother?"

"Returning virtuously to the hotel to her husband and child. You and I, on the other hand, are off to enjoy ourselves. Thoroughly."

Violet tried a smile. "Another balloon ride?"

Daniel's answering smile was hot. "Maybe. Then again, who knows what I'll do?"

Violet's mouth went dry. "I have to lock up. Everyone's gone."

Daniel was looking her up and down. "You are lovely, as usual, but we'll be needing something a little more formal if I'm taking you out."

"Are you taking me out?"

"I am. What about that beautiful gown you were wearing onstage? Still have it with you?"

"It's in my valise. But I don't want anyone seeing me in it as Violet."

"Of course. You're right. But this is a theatre. Do you keep other costumes here? Ones you haven't worn yet?"

"I don't but . . ." Violet swallowed, his excitement catching. "There is a costume room."

"Let's have a look then." Daniel gestured for her to lead the way.

The next hour was filled with laughter. Daniel lit all the lamps in the costume room, and they went through the wardrobes. Most of the costumes were for fanciful dramas, comedies, or operettas, plus some very skimpy things Violet assumed were for the fairies in *A Midsummer Night's Dream*.

Daniel pulled out a confection of a gown called a robe à l'anglaise, from the eighteenth century, all puffs and lace, a narrow bodice, the wide skirt to be held out with panniers. "Very Marie Antoinette," Daniel said, holding it up. "You'd look beautiful in it."

"I'd look ridiculous on the avenues of Marseille in it," Violet said. "Oh, look at this one."

She lifted out a gown that had been made for a more modern play. The skirt was a dark blue satin, and the velvet bodice, cut low across the bosom, was beaded with shimmering onyx and stones that glittered like diamonds. Violet knew they weren't real diamonds, theatres being notoriously short of cash, but the illusion was perfect.

The bodice had small puffed sleeves made to be worn off the shoulder. The gown left the arms very bare, intended to be worn with gloves. Plenty of those in the cupboards.

"Put that on," Daniel said. "And we'll go to the fanciest restaurant in town."

Violet gathered the satin and beaded velvet to her bosom. "*Steal* the gown? The theatre manager would go spare. And make me pay for it. *If* he didn't cancel our contract. Both probably."

Daniel came to her, took the gown, and held it up against her. "I want to take you out. You can't go in a prim shirtwaist.

I want you to rival the fanciest women in Marseille, respectable or otherwise. Wear the dress, or we don't go."

Violet strove to keep a teasing note in her voice, though the heat of Daniel through the dress made her thoughts incoherent. "Will we go elsewhere if I keep to my prim shirtwaist?"

"No. Dress. Now. Don't worry. We'll bring it back."

His eyes held his usual glint of mischief, but also something deeper that she couldn't decipher.

Violet knew she should go sedately back to her boardinghouse, count the take, settle her mother, and look through the requests for private consultations. She should not steal a gown from the theatre's costume room and go out on the town on Daniel's arm like a common courtesan.

But Daniel had made clear he didn't want to spend his evening with a young woman in sensible clothing. If Violet refused him and went home, like the good, respectable daughter she worked hard to be, she'd spend her evening as she usually did, alone, tired, looking after everyone but herself.

Being the good girl could be so very lonely.

Violet turned away with the dress and went resolutely behind the changing screen. She threw off her skirt and shirtwaist, putting on the costume over her corset and underthings.

"I need a lady's maid to do up the back," she said, holding the bodice around herself as she emerged.

"At your service." Daniel turned Violet around and expertly fastened every button up the bodice. He did it swiftly and competently, which told Violet he was used to helping women dress.

Violet remembered the beautiful courtesans she'd seen him with and swallowed a sudden burn of jealousy. *Don't think of it*, she told herself. *I'm with Daniel tonight.*

She found gloves, but Daniel wouldn't let her wear her own shoes. Lace-up boots didn't go with the shimmer of the satin gown, he said.

They searched until they found a pair of high-heeled slippers that fit Violet. Violet suspected they went with the Marie Antoinette gown, but it didn't matter. They were silver satin, fit, and looked perfect. A velvet cloak to keep her warm completed the ensemble.

Daniel helped Violet bundle her own clothes into her valise, took the key from her to lock the theatre door, then walked her down the alley to the waiting carriage at the end.

The vehicle was another sumptuous conveyance, with lacquered inlay and soft cushions. The driver greeted Daniel with friendly courtesy.

Daniel took Violet to the most fashionable restaurant in town, a giant dining room with a soaring ceiling punctuated with multitiered golden chandeliers. Smart waiters in black glided about the room, crowded at this hour. Violet's gown received many admiring glances, the onyx beading shimmering as she moved.

Daniel ordered a feast. He gave Violet champagne, bubbly and sweet, delicate salads, roasted squab in a smooth sauce, tiny fish in an aspic. Elegant food for elegant people.

After the meal, Daniel ordered up hothouse strawberries, which were served alongside a bowl of sweet cream. Daniel plucked up a strawberry, dipped it into the cream, and tilted his head back to bring the confection to his mouth. He closed his lips over the strawberry, tongue coming out to lick the cream.

Suggestive, sinful. He swallowed the strawberry, looked over at Violet, and laughed.

"You look shocked." Daniel dipped another strawberry into the cream. "Don't you know I'm a wicked man? Here, have one."

He held the strawberry out to Violet, its peak plump with soft cream. Violet leaned forward and closed her mouth around it. Daniel didn't let go, waiting until she'd taken a bite.

Violet flushed as she came up, noting the people around her staring at their wonton display. Some looks were disapproving, but some were indulgent, the latter from couples watching as though remembering their courtship days.

Daniel fed Violet another strawberry. She bit down on the bright berry, contrasted with the smooth cream, the combination delightful.

Feeling bolder, Violet finished her strawberry, picked up another, slid it though the cream, and fed it to Daniel. Daniel closed his eyes as he bit down, cream dotting his lips.

He'd talked about desire—*Deep down, belly-clenching, blood-heating pleasure.* Violet was feeling it now, in the middle of a restaurant, in the middle of a crowd, with she and Daniel doing nothing more than feeding each other strawberries. When they finished the bowl, laughing together, they washed the berries down with more of the heady champagne.

If this is what it is to be bad, I never want to be good again.

Daniel also engaged Violet in conversation. Real conversation, as though they were friends. He told her about some of his travels and asked Violet about hers. Violet and her mother had performed in many cities, mainly on the Continent—France, the Italian states, Bavaria, Prussia, the Netherlands. Daniel, on the other hand, had traveled more extensively—from Russia through the Austrian Empire, to the Ottoman Empire, including Greece, Egypt, and Constantinople, and to other parts of the Middle East.

"I climbed aboard a dhow and sailed away to Smyrna, Acre, Jaffa," he said. "If it had an exotic name, I went. I found the Tigris and Babylon and the heart of the Persian Empire. I learned that such places are much more romantic when read about as a small boy under the covers than when picking scorpions out of my boots, but it didn't stop me."

How wonderful to have the money and leisure to simply go where you wanted. No fetching hot water bottles and soothing away worries, no standing in front of people who had terrible hope in their eyes, waiting to talk with those they could not let go. No chilly boardinghouses and worrying about the rent, no keeping an eye on theatre managers so they didn't cheat you.

But one needed money for freedom. If Violet had the money Daniel did, she'd make sure her mother had a host of servants to look after her, then Violet would run away and see the world. She knew the journey would be that much better if Daniel took it with her.

When they finished the champagne, Daniel took Violet to see a play, a comedy that was ridiculous and a bit risqué. Violet laughed as hard as the rest of the audience as the hero bounced onto the stage holding a golf club so that it appeared to stick out of his trousers. The heroine made requisite quips about his rigid club, both hero and heroine oblivious to the innuendo. Silliness, but the audience, well lubricated with wine, champagne, and brandy, found it hilarious.

Next, a cabaret. Violet watched the dancers in fascination—she loved dancing of any kind—while Daniel sat back in their little private booth, his feet up, a black cigarette dangling from his fingers. The show had more than dancing ladies—there were acrobats, men and women dancing together, and two men who told jokes, very funny indeed. Violet laughed and clapped and drank more champagne. During the last act, which was more dancing, Violet leaned back next to Daniel and shared a cigarette with him.

Daniel watched her take a pull, then he removed the cigarette from her mouth, leaned to her, and bit her lower lip. Violet tried to complete the kiss, but he sat back again, a half smile on his face, and resumed the cigarette.

Violet shivered, her body as hot as it had ever been.

So this was wickedness. Everyone who'd seen that exchange must suppose Violet was Daniel's mistress, or his courtesan for the night. Violet supposed she was. And she could feel no shame.

Or fear. Daniel was making it no secret he wanted to be her lover. The dressing up, the restaurant, the conversation, the cabaret acts, and the champagne were all to relax her. Daniel leaning to take her lip between his teeth had been the most natural thing in the world. Violet felt no panic, only a frisson of pleasure.

She closed her hand around Daniel's. He sent her a sideways look, eyes warm. He lifted her gloved hand to his lips and kissed it. His gaze was all for *her*, not the nearly naked women on the stage.

The final curtain went down. "Time to go," Daniel said.

He led her out ahead of the crowd, signaled to his hired coachman, and handed her into their conveyance.

"Where to now?" Violet leaned against the cushions and closed her eyes, her sleepless night and the laughter tonight making her pliant and warm.

"Hotel."

She opened her eyes in surprise. "With your father, stepmother, and sister?" Not that she wouldn't mind meeting them all. She liked Daniel's stepmother, whom Violet thought she could be friends with. Perhaps. She'd never had a woman friend before, so she wasn't sure how one went about it. "Isn't it a bit late for a visit?"

"Not that hotel. This afternoon I took rooms in another. I'd rather take you there than back to my dusty flat, with my work strewn about. I'm sorry about that, but last night I didn't have another choice."

"I liked seeing your work." Violet found his ideas fascinating. "How many rooms did you hire in this city?"

"A few. I often do that. Never know when I might feel like sleeping somewhere different. Or lying low for a few days."

Violet reflected again how wealth allowed a man to do anything he wanted.

The hotel was small but elegant, and what Violet supposed was meant by discreet. The doorman and footmen didn't blink when Daniel handed out Violet and led her inside.

Daniel had a suite, of course, on the first floor, up a long flight of carpeted stairs. A parlor paneled in light polished wood with periwinkle blue and cream upholstery fronted a bedroom, entered through double doors.

Violet looked into the bedroom as Daniel closed the door to the suite. The bed was wide, a carved four-poster bedstead hung with velvet curtains. It looked comfortable, a nest for the rich. Perhaps she'd find out how comfortable it was tonight.

The thought made her throat close, the dratted panic welling up just when she wanted it to go away forever. That was the trouble—the panic could rise at unexpected times, catching Violet unguarded. Her fear of the fear was almost as bad as the panic itself.

She found Daniel's hands on her waist, he turning her away from the doorway. "We'll stay out here, if you like." His look said he'd seen Violet stiffen, seen the relaxation start to drain away. "But someday, I'll show you that a bed is a fine place, and not just for sleeping."

Her stiffness started to ease with Daniel's arms around her. Violet thought of the kiss in the hall at the theatre, which had been intense but brought no panic.

She nodded, and Daniel kissed the tip of her nose. "Good," he said.

Daniel left the bedroom doors open but led her back to the sofas in the sitting room. These weren't the stiff horsehair sofas found in so many boardinghouses Violet had inhabited. They were long and elegant, with plush cushions, made for comfort. A tea table stood between them, waiting to serve.

"I can order up another feast," Daniel said. "Or more champagne."

Violet put her hand to her belly, the beads cool on her fingers. "Goodness, I think I've eaten my fill. And if I drink more champagne, I might fall asleep. Or become very silly."

"Champagne is supposed to make you silly. It's a silly drink. Whiskey has much more body. You'll like the Mackenzie malt. Rich, deep, a nice mouthful." Daniel traced her cheek. "Tell you what, love, I'll order up pudding—or as they call it here, dessert. More strawberries." Again his eyes held both a mischievous gleam and watchfulness.

Violet nodded. "I think I'd like that."

Daniel winked, turned away, rang for a footman, and walked outside the room to meet him and give the order.

In a short time, another footman wheeled in a cart with a carafe of clear water and goblets, a bowl of cut strawberries, and another silver bowl kept warm over a tiny flame. Daniel handed the man a tip—Violet caught a glimpse of a large wad of banknotes—and the footman withdrew.

"I hope that isn't cream," Violet said, sitting down to dish out the strawberries. "Over a flame like that, it will be curdled."

"Better." Daniel sat down next to her. "Something the French excel at, leaving us poor Scots in the dust. The entire British Isles, in fact." He lifted the silver dish's cover. "Chocolate."

Chapter 21

Daniel enjoyed watching Violet's apprehensive look dissolve. He watched her become the real Violet—not the persona on the stage, or the harried drudge to her mother, or the woman broken by her past. She was simply Violet, who was interested in his machines, laughed at inane farces, and was unfolding in her first experience of desire.

The elegant dress brought out the blue of her eyes and the rich darkness of her hair. Violet should always be dressed in beautiful frocks and have nothing more to worry about than what opera she'd watch or how many kisses she'd let her lover steal. Her beauty should have been the stuff of legend, not hidden away in hired houses or behind costumes.

Daniel poured out the water. He took a sip as did Violet, enjoying the clean taste after the overly sweet champagne.

"Like this." Daniel speared a cut strawberry with one of the tiny forks on the tray, dipped the strawberry into the bowl of glistening, warm chocolate, and lifted the result to Violet's lips.

Violet leaned forward and tentatively bit down on the berry, then she closed her eyes in rapture. "Oh," she said after she'd swallowed. "Oh my."

"I don't know how the French and the Swiss can make chocolate that's smooth as silk and tasty enough to drown in, but I won't worry," Daniel said. "I'll just eat it and be happy."

Violet licked a drop of chocolate from her lower lip. "I've never been able to afford chocolate like this. It's heavenly."

"Aye, who wants a heaven with streets paved in gold? I'd rather have rivers of chocolate. And whiskey. An even better combination. Coupled with the taste of a good cigar."

"You're decadent."

"I've taught myself about the finer things. Uncle Mac taught me plenty too. He's quite the hedonist."

Violet looked interested, as she always did when Daniel talked about his family. "Are your other uncles hedonists too?"

"Not so much hedonists as intensely focused. Dad's focus is horses. Ian—mathematics, Beth, and his children—not in that order. With Hart it's—well, making the world jump to do whatever he wants it to. Uncle Hart was very much the sensualist, though, in his younger days. Had his own private house with women to cater to his every pleasure. I do mean every pleasure. Now that he's with Eleanor, he's given up the house, but he hasn't stopped being a sensualist. At least, in deep privacy, with Eleanor—which he thinks is so secret. The way she blushes, though, I know their time together becomes plenty interesting."

Violet looked surprised. "But he's a duke."

Daniel laughed. "And they should all be stuffed shirts? Uncle Hart is a master of pleasure. He could be the ultimate hedonist if he chose. I tried to get him to tell me some of his secrets, but he sent me off, so I had to learn them myself."

He speared another strawberry, dipped it in chocolate, and let the chocolate run in a ribbon back into the bowl.

Violet's gaze went to the dripping chocolate, her lips parting as Daniel lifted the fork to her. The room was already warm, and Violet leaning forward in pursuit of the strawberry made Daniel break into a sweat. *God help me.*

Violet closed her mouth around the strawberry, her eyes drifting shut. She finished the strawberry, a drop of chocolate falling to her chin. "I'll get chocolate all over this frock if I continue."

She reached for a napkin, but Daniel leaned forward and licked her chin clean. "I can think of a way to remedy that." He let his smile grow as hedonistic as Mac's ever did. "Take off the gown."

Violet started. Her gloved hand went to the décolletage, over which her plump bosom swelled.

For a moment, Daniel thought she would refuse—and well she should—then she breathed a laugh. "Perhaps I had too much champagne, but I think it a good idea."

Daniel hid his relief. "I think so too. For me as much as for you."

Without giving her time to change her mind, Daniel shrugged off his frock coat, then his waistcoat. With the room so heated by the large coal stove, it was a relief to take off the outer layers.

"I'll need help with the buttons again," Violet said, her look shy.

No trouble. Daniel's breathing was unsteady as Violet turned and presented her back to him. Daniel slid next to her on the sofa and undid the buttons, one by one.

Her bare back came into view above the corset. Daniel ran his hand across her skin. Soft, smooth. He kissed it.

Violet had stripped off the gloves, and now pushed down the front of the gown as she stood up. With great care, she slid out of the skirt and bodice and laid the gown on the other sofa, along with the gloves.

She sat down again in her corset and petticoats, her shoulders and arms bare, and looked at Daniel. "You might get your shirt dirty as well."

"Aye." Daniel unfastened his collar and the shirt, pulling them off, then got out of his undershirt as well. He liked the way Violet's gaze flicked to his chest then to the tattoo on his arm.

Violet's look was still shy, but she forked up a strawberry, covered it in chocolate, and offered it to Daniel. Daniel licked the thread of chocolate that spilled down from it, then drew the berry into his mouth. He smiled at Violet as he chewed, tasting sweet, bright strawberry and smooth, rich chocolate.

"My turn." Daniel prepared another strawberry, but he held

it away as Violet reached for it with her mouth. He let the chocolate snake across her collarbone before he tucked the strawberry between her lips.

As she feasted on the strawberry, Daniel leaned down and licked her collarbone clean.

Chocolate and Violet. A wonderful combination. He felt the swallow in her throat, and kissed it.

When he looked up at her, she was smiling, her eyes relaxed. She'd plucked up another strawberry with her fork while he'd savored her, and now she loaded it with chocolate. She held the fork over Daniel and let chocolate swirl deliberately over his bare shoulders.

The chocolate was warm and tickled. "Oh yes?" Daniel asked when Violet sat back and ate the strawberry herself. "And what are you going to do about that?" He pointed at the wavy line of chocolate.

Violet hesitated a moment, not looking at him, then she very slowly leaned to him. She stilled for a long time, her breath brushing his skin, before she completed the move and touched her tongue to the chocolate.

Daniel smothered a groan. He let his hand come up to the back of her neck, his body tightening as Violet licked across his shoulder.

With any other woman, Daniel would end the playing at once, lay her down on the carpet, get rid of the rest of their clothes, and consummate what they'd started.

But no other woman was Violet. The story she'd told him last night had made Daniel furious but also made him understand how fragile she was. He didn't want to frighten her away, destroying what little trust he'd already gained from her. But proceeding slowly was fine. If it took Daniel the rest of his life to seduce her, so be it.

Violet raised her head, chocolate on her mouth. Daniel kissed it off, slowly imbibing the sweet chocolate from her plump, warm lips.

"My turn," he said.

Daniel took his time drawing a curlicue design across her chest, giving her a slow smile as he let the chocolate dip between her breasts. He fed Violet the strawberry before he gently lowered her to the sofa and started savoring her.

Violet's hand came up to land on his shoulder, fingers tight. Then her fingers relaxed, as though she'd thought to stop him then determined to enjoy what he did. Daniel slowly kissed her breast, sucking a little to rid it of chocolate, leaving a tiny mark behind, *his* mark.

Beautiful, sweet Violet. He'd never met anyone like her. He was falling in love with her, and he didn't even know her last name.

Daniel raised his head and kissed her mouth. He tasted the strawberries on her tongue, the dark tang of chocolate. The kiss was unhurried, exploring.

Violet was sensuality itself, in her white linen corset against the blue of the sofa, her breasts rising over the corset, her hair coming down, her blue eyes dark in the dimly lit room.

"*She walks in beauty, like the night,*" Daniel said.

"We're not walking, we're lying on the sofa." Violet's smile spoke of a night of drinking champagne. "And we are being very naughty."

"Oh, are we?" Daniel traced her lips, which bore a faint ring of chocolate. "I think we could be even naughtier."

"So do I."

Violet's smile was inviting, but Daniel saw the flicker of fear return to her eyes. She'd built a wall to keep her panic at bay, and he saw the worry in her that the wall would crumble at the slightest touch.

"Violet." Daniel rested his crossed arms on her breasts. "When you're not afraid of me—truly not afraid—you tell me. All right?"

Violet drew a sharp breath, but she nodded.

Daniel touched her cheek. "Remember what I told you? You need slow goodness, not to rush. You and me, we have all the time in the world."

He saw her skeptical little frown and pressed his finger to her lips, stilling her answer. "Even if you don't believe me, *I* believe me," he said. "You and I will tear apart this town. In the meantime . . ." Daniel sat up again and reached for the bowl of chocolate. "I plan to get you very messy." He took the spoon from the bowl and let a huge dollop of chocolate fall on her chest.

Violet squealed, then laughed. She put her hand into the bowl, scooped up chocolate onto her fingers, and smeared it across his pectorals.

Daniel's eyes widened. "Och, if that's the way you want to play it . . ." He grabbed the chocolate bowl, discarded the spoon, and started smearing chocolate on her with his hands.

They tumbled from the couch the short distance to the rug, then they were touching, licking the chocolate from each other's bodies. Daniel reached up and brought the chocolate down to them. He swept it across her lips then kissed her again, slowly, sweetly. Chocolate and Violet all mixed up.

She looked surprised when he put the chocolate right on her tongue, then softened as Daniel took it from her in a long kiss. He suckled her tongue, and Violet wrapped her arms around him to kiss him back. Violet was laughing and beautiful, and Daniel determined to slide his mouth over every bit of her exposed skin.

They continued to play until the chocolate was gone, and the night of champagne and sleeplessness began to catch up to Violet. In the early morning, Daniel carried her to the bedroom, she limp in his arms and showing no protest. He laid her on his bed, covered her up, and came down next to her, prepared to enjoy another hour of sleep with this wonderful woman.

~~~~~

Violet woke to sunshine and to Daniel sprawled next to her, his bare chest and arms stained with chocolate.

She smiled as he drew a breath in a long, soft snore. Another night of touching, kissing, enjoying, and Violet had not felt any fear.

But it was morning now, and her mother would be waking, wondering where Violet was. Violet needed to go home, to again become the dutiful daughter, the one who decided how they would all hold together.

As though he knew she watched him, Daniel cracked open

his eyes. He looked at her a moment then he groaned and rubbed his forehead. "Damned champagne. Pure whiskey doesn't leave me with this head."

"Wait. Don't sit up."

Violet scooted to the head of the bed, knelt back, and rested Daniel's head on her knees. She began massaging his temples in a light, circular motion.

"Mmm," he rumbled. "That's nice."

Daniel was nice, with the covers around his waist, his chest touched with chocolate. His short hair was sleek under her fingertips, warm with sleep.

"I do this for my mother," Violet said. "She's susceptible to headaches and says I make them go away."

"I see why." Daniel hummed again.

"I have to go home." Violet couldn't keep the note of sorrow out of her voice.

Daniel tangled his fingers through one of her hands and brought it to his lips. "One day, love, you won't have to. You'll send the world to hell and stay with me." He kissed her fingers again, slow, sensual. "That will be a fine day."

Yes, it would be. But for now, Violet had her mother, her obligations, and the wretched reality of life.

Daniel rubbed the back of her hand with his thumb. "I'll see you again soon. Later today, in fact. I'll arrange everything."

He must mean going back to the country inn. Violet knew that if she went there with Daniel, she'd surrender to him.

But first, she'd tell him everything, every dark detail about herself—what had happened afterward with Jacobi, the other reasons Jacobi had convinced her to stay, and why she'd found the courage to finally flee him. Daniel might loathe her and turn her away, but he deserved to know.

What she'd experienced with Daniel so far had been playful and lovely. Daniel, a wealthy and pleasure-seeking man, might want nothing more than play. In that case, nothing mattered. He made the rules of the game, not Violet.

But she could not move forward until she told him. It mattered to her.

If Daniel still wanted her after that, she'd surrender her body, never mind her fears. But she'd let it be his choice.

Violet leaned down and kissed him. The kiss turned long, passionate, filled with need.

Daniel was the one who broke away. He threaded his fingers through her hair and gave her a look that was so tender her heart ached. "Go do what you need to, Vi. And wait for me to come."

She nodded. It took a while for both of them to leave the bed; more touching and kissing slowing them. Violet dressed with Daniel's assistance, but the lump in her throat was so hard she couldn't swallow the coffee the hotel staff had left outside the suite's door.

*

"Violet, darling, where on earth have you been?" Celine put another two lumps of sugar into her tea and stirred it noisily as Violet slipped into the sitting room at the boardinghouse. "I have two people wanting private séances today, and we must be ready." Celine's tone softened as she looked Violet over. "Where did you get that lovely dress? You look very fetching in it, my dear."

Violet looked down at herself, aware that she still wore the borrowed costume and slippers. She'd have to sneak them back into the theatre sometime today. But she'd been loath to stuff the beaded dress into her valise at the hotel and resume the shirtwaist and skirt. Daniel had picked out this ensemble, and she wanted to wrap the wonderful evening around her as long as she could.

Violet poured herself the strong tea the boardinghouse provided and took a sip. It was disagreeable, especially after the excellent food she'd tasted last night, not to mention the chocolate. But the champagne had rather given her a headache.

Mary answered a soft knock on the door. One of the boardinghouse's maids put her head around it.

"Mademoiselle, a man has come to see you," the maid said to Violet. "I put him in the parlor downstairs. He is waiting there."

Daniel? Violet thought excitedly. *So soon?* But when Daniel decided to do something, Violet had noted, he did not wait to do it. She'd have to explain that her mother had appointments today and would need Violet after all, but Daniel would no doubt have contingencies for that.

Violet thanked the maid and said she'd be down at once. She went to her room to smooth her hair and wash the remnants of chocolate from her face before she descended to the ground floor. Drawing a long breath, she opened the door of the parlor.

And found herself looking at Monsieur Lanier, the banker who'd hired them a couple of nights ago. With him stood two men in the uniforms of the French police.

Violet halted, frozen.

"Yes, that is the one," Monsieur Lanier said. "Told me she was a princess from Russia. Then she and her friend tried to rob me."

The policemen looked stern. "Mademoiselle, we will have to take you for questioning," one said.

Violet stared at them for another stunned moment, then she turned and ran.

It wasn't panic that made her run, or a sense of guilt. The agreement was that if the police in whatever town they were in came after them, Violet, the swiftest runner, would lead them on a merry chase. This would give Mary time to gather what she could and take Celine to safety. Violet would meet up with them later at the designated rendezvous.

Violet picked up her skirts and ran down the street, the old-fashioned high-heeled slippers clicking on the cobbles. The police came right behind her, swift on their feet.

The boardinghouse maid really should have mentioned the visitor's name and that he'd brought the police, Violet thought in irritation. Probably the policemen had told her not to. The landlady, who didn't much like them, must have agreed. Blast and bother.

Violet had no money with her, but she knew how to be resourceful. She'd slip away from the policemen and find some way to get herself to the meeting point.

This meant she'd have to leave Daniel behind. Violet had never regretted departing any town, even the lovely ones, but now her heart swelled with pain. She didn't dare send Daniel word, even a good-bye. She and her mother must disappear again.

The beautiful time she'd had with Daniel, her awakening, was over.

He'd searched for Violet the last time she'd vanished. Would he this time? Or would Daniel have lost interest in chasing her?

She knew where his family lived in London. She'd made it her business to know. Violet could write to him and explain, sending the letter to Ainsley. *After* she got her mother to safety. Daniel might not answer, might not look for her, might not even bother to read the letter. But she had to try.

Violet swerved into a narrow, arched passage between houses, trying to be light on her feet in the foul-smelling muck. She'd gone halfway along it before she realized the policemen were no longer following her. The entrance to the passage remained empty, the only sound the echo of her shoes and her labored breathing.

Violet let her satin skirts drop, never mind the muck. Damn it. If the policemen had given up on Violet so soon, they'd gone back to find Violet's mother.

Celine couldn't be arrested. She'd take ill if she went to jail, unable to bear the cold, the foul airs. She was too delicate for such things. And Mary—Mary had been arrested for stealing clothes once upon a time in London, released only because the magistrate said he didn't have enough evidence for a trial. Mary had stolen to feed herself and her child, who had died all the same of some pestilence that had raged through the poorer parts of London.

Mary was much more resilient than Celine, but if the police discovered her past arrest, they might ship her back to London. A magistrate might not be so lenient for a second offense, and who knew what influence Monsieur Lanier, a rich and respectable banker, would have.

Violet jogged back through the passage to the morning streets. Those on early errands stared at her in her beaded velvet and satin as she ran past. She reached the boardinghouse again, yanked open the door, and dashed inside and up the stairs.

The police were clustered, with Monsieur Lanier and the landlady, at the door to their private rooms. The landlady's keys clinked as she prepared to unlock the door.

Violet rushed forward. "No!"

The landlady, ignoring her, unlocked and threw open the door.

The sitting room was empty. Celine and Mary were gone, the breakfast things scattered, the tea cooling, the remnants of an omelet congealing.

Violet exhaled in relief. Mary had gotten Celine away. Her mother would be safe.

Violet, on the other hand, was seized, her hands shoved together in front of her, iron cuffs clapped around her wrists.

The cold of the cuffs stirred Violet's panic. Pushed aside for too long, it rose like a monster—*Trapped, trapped, can't run.*

The panic made her fight. She kicked and bit, screams escaping her mouth before she could stop them. Her terror was complete when she felt a hand go down the front of her bodice—she was certain the two policemen and Monsieur Lanier were about to share her between them. And no one would help her.

The policeman jerked his hand from her bodice. "Nothing. She didn't hide the money there."

Violet, her breath ragged, managed a glare at them all. "My solicitor will have something to say about this." She tried for imperious tones, but her voice came out weak and scratchy.

"You see? She's not Russian at all," Monsieur Lanier said. "A pure fraud. Probably from the gutters of Paris."

He wasn't far from wrong. Violet lifted her head, pressed her mouth shut, fought down her panic, and didn't struggle anymore. As the police marched her down the stairs, the two spinster sisters and other tenants popped out of doorways to watch as Violet was taken into custody.

The policemen took Violet to a barred police van. A crowd had gathered around it, the populace eager to see who was being rounded up this morning. A few men laughed as one of the policemen shoved Violet into the cart and slammed the door. The driver clucked to the horses, and Violet was taken down the streets of Marseille to the nearest jail at a slow walk.

Chapter 22

At least they didn't put Violet into a cell. *Small blessings.* She rested her shackled hands on the wooden table in the tiny room they'd brought her to. They'd given her a sip or two of coffee then left her to stew for several hours. Her panic had receded, leaving her exhausted and worried.

Violet looked up as a man in a plain suit walked inside, laid a stack of papers he'd been carrying on the table, and sat down opposite her. The man didn't look at her but started leafing through the papers.

"Now then," he said in smooth French, but with a hint of Marseille dialect. He spread two of the sheets in front of him. "You are Princess Ivanova . . . with no surname." He looked up at Violet and gave her a sardonic smile. "Or should I call you Your Highness?"

"It makes little difference what you call me," Violet said in freezing tones. "Monsieur . . . ?"

"Bellec. I am a detective."

"I see." Violet could think of a number of haughty responses—*I am certain your mother is very proud*—but she decided it was best to play this quiet, cold, and superior.

"I'll give you that you use Princess Ivanova as your stage name," Bellec said. "But I need your real one. The landlady thinks it's Perrault, but that's not true, is it?"

"Why have you arrested me?" *Upstart*, Violet's tone said. "I have done nothing wrong."

"If you'd done nothing wrong, why did you run from the policemen?"

Violet maintained her frigid pose. "They frightened me. In Russia policemen often harassed me and the countess. We were not loved there. I feared these policemen were the same."

He chuckled. "You play the part well, Mademoiselle. Or is it Madame? And where are you from in Russia? Saint Petersburg? Moscow? Easy for me to telegraph to the police there and find out, you know."

Violet bathed him in silent scorn. She could only hope that her time here, keeping this detective guessing, would give her mother and Mary a chance to get out of the city. The agreement was that if they were forced to separate and run, they would meet at a certain hotel in Lucerne, and from there decide what to do. Celine should have enough for the train with her, and so should Mary. Only Violet had empty pockets, since she'd foolishly left her money in her room in her eagerness to rush to the parlor.

If Violet could get away from the police, perhaps she could find Daniel and beg for his help. Or she could hide in his little apartment until she could leave Marseille. The apartment was old, the lock on the door likely easy to pick.

"I demand to know why I was brought here," she said, keeping up her part.

"Because you're a fraud, Mademoiselle," Detective Bellec said in an easy manner. "At least, that is what you are accused of. You went to the home of Monsieur Lanier to give him a show and took his money. Then, when he didn't give you enough, you tried to steal it. Interestingly, he is more upset about your fraud. Monsieur Lanier said you employed a number of tricks—spirit knocking, moving the table, making the walls glow . . ."

"And how does he say I did these things?"

"Oh, there are ways. Phosphor-luminescent paint. Devices

to make knocking noises—things like blocks of wood strapped to the knees. Tables moving with levers under the wrists. If I searched your pockets, would I find any of these things?"

"Certainly not." Mary would have packed away the accoutrements and taken them with her. Violet's valise, even if found and searched, would contain none of those things. More small blessings.

"The thing is, Mademoiselle, you've been accused, and we have to investigate. If we find nothing, well then." He shrugged as if to say *not my problem*. "But I will warn you that Monsieur Lanier is poised to sue you and the Countess, um . . . Melikova . . . if you somehow wriggle away from the police."

"Detective Bellec, I do not wriggle."

"Maybe not, but . . ." Bellec leaned forward, his smile and nonchalant manner gone. "I dislike frauds, Mademoiselle. They prey on the gullible and take their money, same as a thief. Worse, because you coerce your mark to hand over the money willingly. You make people think you can talk to those dead and gone; you get inside their heads and play them for fools. A fraud is the worst kind of criminal, Mademoiselle. Even murderers are more straightforward."

Violet stared at him, a chill in her heart, because she agreed with every word he said. She was a fraud, and she did take money from the gullible.

But she and her mother had to survive, and Celine truly believed in her abilities. The only fraud at heart was Violet.

Jacobi had shown Violet how to make a living using her mother's eccentricities, and once she'd started, Violet hadn't been able to stop. She was in a trap, no way out. She and her mother had no other means to live on, no place to go.

The detective rose and gathered his papers. "I'll let you sit here awhile longer and think about all those fools you took money from. Money meant to feed their families, pay their rents, keep their children warm. Meanwhile, I will investigate. And if I find good proof of your fraud, you will go to court, and I will do my best to see that you pay to the full extent of the law."

Bellec turned his back and walked out, no longer affable, his coldness sharp.

Violet, left alone, leaned her head back and tried to stop the tears that threatened to pour from her eyes. Bellec wasn't going to let her go. Mary would have done her best to take the damning evidence away with her, but if she missed something, or she and Celine were caught . . .

The future looked bleak. But the most frightening thing about going to prison was that Violet wasn't sure she wouldn't welcome it. At last, she'd be able to stop.

An hour later Detective Bellec returned, a uniformed policeman behind him. Bellec was in a bad temper.

"Your pimps are here," Bellec snarled, his face dull red. "That's what I assume they are. Two foreign men, filthy rich, demanding you be released into their protection. What is the law, when money can buy freedom for criminals?"

The uniformed policeman unlocked Violet's cuffs as she blinked at him in shock. *Two* men? Was one Daniel? But how would Daniel have known to find her here?

"They are commanded to take you out of the country and not let you return," Bellec continued. "May they have the joy of you."

Violet still didn't answer. Anything she said would be useless, as would bowing her head in shame. She got to her feet in silence, gave the detective a cold glare, and followed the policeman from the room.

The uniformed man led her down a dingy hall, up dingy stairs, and out into an equally dingy foyer.

Violet's knees nearly gave way when she saw Daniel, in kilt, tailored greatcoat, and tall hat, looking every inch a wealthy aristo. With him was a bigger man, dressed in similar fashion—Lord Cameron, Daniel's father. Lord Cameron's face was harder than Daniel's, and he bore a deep scar on his cheek—where his first wife had slashed him with a knife, the stories said.

If the floor would open up and let Violet sink into it, she'd go willingly. Daniel, bailing her out of jail, with his *father*. Heaven help her.

"Hello, Princess," Daniel said, sotto voce, as he closed his hand around her wrist. "Your carriage awaits. So does your mum. This is my dad. Shall we go?"

Daniel balled his fists on the carriage seat, trying to stifle his rage. His anger had begun when he'd seen Violet's mother and maid come flying down the street from the boardinghouse as though the hounds of hell were after them.

Daniel had been on his way to see Violet again, ready to sweep her away for another adventure in the country. He'd taken time to bathe, breakfast, and dress, then he'd run to her like an eager swain.

Violet's maid had been carrying two overflowing valises, Violet's mother hobbling behind the maid, sobbing. Daniel had ordered the carriage to stop. He'd stepped down himself, taken the valises and tossed them into the carriage, then helped the two terrified women inside.

His rage had increased when he heard Mary's half-coherent story that the police had come to arrest them. Mary and Violet's mother had fled, leaving Violet behind.

Daniel had ordered the two to remain in the coach while he sprinted alone to the boardinghouse. He'd found no sign of Violet when he arrived, but a crowd had gathered in the usually quiet street. One of the loiterers had told him that a young lady staying in the boardinghouse had been taken away in a police van. Probably a thief, possibly a lady of the evening.

Red fury had filmed Daniel's vision. His father had a famous temper, and Daniel had inherited it. Daniel had spent his life trying to conquer it, preferring to win over the world with honeyed words, but sometimes the temper won.

He had to enlist Cameron's help to bully their way into the Marseille police station and extricate Violet. The detective in charge, a man called Bellec, had wanted to make an example of her. He hated frauds, he said.

Bellec also hated foreigners coming to tell him his job, especially rich and titled ones. Bellec's ancestors had no doubt herded scores of aristocrats to the guillotine.

Bellec and his superiors agreed to give up Violet only if Lord Cameron gave them his word to take her and her entourage out of the country. If Bellec saw Violet again, he said, he would make sure she went to prison.

Daniel hated the defeated look Violet wore when the uniformed policeman brought her out to the foyer. She held her head high, even then, glaring defiantly at everyone in her path.

But she looked at Cameron in worry, and the first question she asked when Daniel got her into the coach was, "Where is my mother? Is she all right? Is Mary with her?"

The shiftless mother had left her own daughter to the police, and Violet's worry was for *her*.

Daniel still didn't trust himself to speak. His father answered for him, his rumbling voice filling the coach. "Your mother is waiting at the railway station. With my wife and daughter."

Violet blinked. "With Lady Cameron?"

"You're leaving town," Daniel said, unable to keep silent any longer. "And we're coming with you."

Violet's eyes widened. "Coming with us? No, that's not necessary . . ."

"It is entirely necessary," Daniel said. "A condition of them releasing you, in fact. We're going to Berkshire, and you and your mother are coming with us."

"But . . . Daniel, no. You can't leave. Your experiments . . . Your papers and drawings in your flat . . ."

Daniel wasn't in the mood to worry about trivial things. "Simon stayed behind to box everything up and send it on. It's more important to get you out of town."

"I'm . . ." Violet wet her lips, looking from Cameron to Daniel. "I'm grateful. Thank you. How did you know where to find me?"

"Dad knows people," Daniel growled. "But what the devil happened? And why was your mother hurrying off to save her own flesh, and your maid pushing her on, leaving *you* to take the blow?"

Violet shook her head. "Mary was right. Mother would never survive being arrested. If I had gotten away, we would have met elsewhere."

"So you were the sacrificial lamb, were you?" Daniel asked. "What was your idea—divert their attention so your mum could get away?"

"Of course it was. My mother isn't strong."

"She seemed plenty fit sprinting down the street, leaving you in the dust. A mother *protects* her children, Vi. She doesn't throw them to the wolves."

Violet looked bewildered. "She didn't. She doesn't."

"Then what the bloody hell do you call that? She took my help fast enough. As soon as your Mary convinced your mum she could trust me, your mum was in the coach without fear, urging me to get her away to the train. Leaving you to take the consequences."

"It's what we do," Violet said, sounding patient, damn her. "If something happens, we scatter and meet in an appointed place. My mother was only following the plan."

"When I told her you'd gone to jail, she was still ready to fly." Daniel drew a breath to say more, but Cameron broke in.

"Leave it alone, Son."

Daniel didn't want to leave it alone, but he made himself close his mouth. He knew Cameron understood Daniel's rage at a mother who would leave her child behind in danger. Daniel could pretend indifference about what his mother had done to him, but it had left scars.

Daniel balled his fists again and sat back in his seat. He wanted to strike out in disgust, but there was nothing to hit.

"Daniel's not wrong," Cameron said to Violet. "You don't leave people you love to rot for you."

Violet's brows came down. "I'm sorry, gentlemen, but neither of you have any idea what you're talking about. We do what we have to do. It's survival. Until you've had to live on your wits on the streets, please do not lecture me on how I or my mother should behave."

Daniel was too angry to answer. Cameron pulled out a cigar and lit it. He leaned back, filling the coach with fragrant smoke. "I like her," he said to Daniel, then continued to smoke in silence.

"I will pay for my railway ticket," Violet said, her voice stiff. "All our tickets. If I am required to leave the country, we can part ways in Paris, and my mother and I will travel on someplace else, Bavaria perhaps. We'll be all right then."

"No," Daniel said. "Mr. Bellec made it clear we are to

make sure you remove yourself from France. The only way to do that is to watch over you all the way to England. So you'll be coming with us to Berkshire, Vi, whether you like it or not. And I'm not letting you out of my sight until we get there."

Berkshire. Daniel had to be mad. Violet's stomach fluttered. She was still unbalanced by her arrest and confinement, not to mention Daniel's abrupt rescue. Daniel was furious with her and with her mother, but he seemed to think nothing of cutting short his stay in Marseille to herd Violet out of it.

All too soon, Violet found herself boarding a train car, a private one hired by Lord Cameron. He'd taken the entire car, which had a little parlor and dining area in front and four tiny bedrooms in the back. It even had a bathroom.

Cameron and Daniel oversaw the loading of what little luggage they'd managed to bring. Ainsley's servants and Mary settled their charges then left for the compartments Cameron had purchased for them. Mary looked startled that she'd have a compartment to herself, all without having to pay her own ticket.

Cameron took over one of the small dining tables in the private car and started leafing through racing newspapers in both English and French. A little girl with red gold hair placed a large plush horse on the table, climbed confidently into Cameron's lap, and looked interestedly at the newspapers with him. Cameron absently hooked an arm around the girl's waist and pressed a soft kiss to her hair.

Daniel didn't speak to Violet at all. Ainsley, on one of the sofas, reached out a hand to her. "Come and sit with me, Violet, dear. You've had quite an ordeal."

Celine had already taken a soft armchair by one of the windows, looking completely at home in the elegance. She fanned herself and let out a breath as the train jerked forward. "Yes, quite frightening. Poor Violet. Was it very awful?"

"A bit," Violet said, sitting down next to Ainsley.

"I could not have stood a jail cell," Celine said. "The aura would have been too much for me."

"They didn't put me in a cell, Mama. Just a room with a chair and table."

Her mother looked relieved and disappointed at the same time. Violet knew Celine would have loved to hear horror stories about rats and squalid jail cells.

Ainsley's look held sympathy. "Don't worry, we will fill you both up with hot tea and plenty of cake. And then put you to bed. It's early, but you must be tired."

As the train gained speed, Marseille falling behind, several waiters wheeled in a cart loaded with food. Violet's stomach rumbled as they set out breads and meats, cheese, tea, cakes, and—heaven—coffee.

Violet ate the cakes Ainsley shoved at her and gulped coffee. By the time her head ceased spinning and her stomach calmed down, they were well into the countryside.

Violet set down her coffee cup. "I am very grateful to you for helping us," she said to Ainsley. "You are all impossibly kind. I intend to pay you back for the tickets."

"Nonsense," Ainsley said. "But we will speak of it later."

Ainsley bent a glance at Daniel, who was seated at another table drinking coffee, his back to them. Violet knew Ainsley and Cameron had helped her for Daniel's sake, no other reason.

She also knew Daniel was quite angry, and rightly so. Violet had many things to tell him, and he might be even angrier afterward. But she wouldn't shy from it.

Ainsley sent Violet a shrewd look. She rose briskly, going to Celine. "Now, then, Madame, you are drooping and need to sleep. You too, Gavina. Come along. No, sweetheart, do not bother to argue."

Gavina, who was seven, had started to protest, then caught the look in her mother's eye and snapped her mouth shut. A child who had learned at a young age when not to argue.

Ainsley held out both hands, one for Violet's mother and one for Gavina. She marched them through the door of the rocking car that led to the bedrooms. Cameron, in silence, pushed aside his tea leavings, rose, put a folded paper under his arm, and strolled casually out the front door of the car, heading for the main part of the train.

Leaving Violet alone with Daniel. Daniel went on drinking coffee, his silence heavy.

Violet rose from the sofa, picked up her empty cup, and went quietly to his table. She sat down opposite him and poured out another stream of coffee into her cup. Daniel watched her, not pretending to ignore her, but he still didn't offer to speak.

"You saved me today, Daniel," Violet said. "I know I can never repay you for it, but you saved my life. Monsieur Bellec was not going to let me go."

Daniel had lifted his cup to drink but now he clattered it back to his saucer. "Damn it, Violet, stop talking about repayment. I don't want any kind of payment from you."

"I know you don't. But you deserve to know some things about me." Violet set down her coffee and twined her fingers together on the tabletop. If she clasped her hands hard enough, maybe they wouldn't tremble.

Daniel waited, saying nothing.

"I was born Violet Devereaux. My father was a Frenchman, as I've told you. His family emigrated to England before he was born. We lived in South London—you guessed right about that—in a poor but respectable neighborhood. My mother learned when I was about eight that she had clairvoyance, or so she thought. She started out giving séances for friends then was hired by others to do them. She decided to go to Paris when she'd saved enough in fees to try our luck there. That's where I met Jacobi, who taught me about how to give a memorable stage performance and sell more tickets. I've taken many names since then, all to sell tickets and keep us out of trouble." Violet took a breath. "The name Violet Devereaux is the real one. But my married name is Violet Ferrand."

Chapter 23

"Married name." Daniel sat still, the words meaningless to his stunned brain. He felt the same as when she'd crashed the vase into his head.

"Yes." It was a whisper, filled with shame and a little bit of defiance.

Daniel was on his feet, his realization returning. *Married?*

"Yes." Violet said again.

Daniel walked to the door that led out of the car then swung around and strode back, his temper rising with every step.

All the Mackenzies had berserker rage within them, inherited from generations of men fed up with people trying to kill them and steal their land. Daniel's grandfather had used the rage to terrorize his family. Uncle Hart had used it to terrorize England. Uncle Ian's anger had turned around and terrorized himself. Daniel felt the rage beat through his veins now—at Violet, at himself, at whoever had made her like this.

"Bloody hell, woman!" His Highland Scots erased every bit of English elocution ever drilled into him. "When were ye planning to tell me? Or were ye at all? If you'd gotten away from the police by yourself, I'd have never seen you again, would I? You would have run, just like ye did in London, just like ye've done time and again in the past, haven't ye? Not bothering to tell Daniel, that poor blithering idiot, that ye'd gone!"

Violet's face was stark white. "I *was* going to tell you. About both things. I promise. I planned to tell you all about the marriage at the inn if you took me there today. But the police arrived . . ."

"*If? If* I took you to the inn?" Daniel slammed his hand to the table, making the coffee cups dance. "Did ye think I had no intention of doing that? Even though I'd said so? Did ye think I was playing with you?" His anger rose. "So you said, aye, ye'd like to go back to that cozy inn with me, looking happy about it, but all the time ye thought I was *lying*?"

"I didn't think you lied," Violet said, her words heating. "I thought you meant it at the time. But you might have forgotten or changed your mind. How was I to know?"

"Why the devil would I change my mind?"

Violet's own temper sparked in her eyes. "Because you're an aristocrat! You can afford to ride across France in a private train car and hang up a costly balloon in a tree and shrug about it. You can do anything you want, Daniel Mackenzie. Why should you bother telling the truth to me?"

"Well, you haven't bothered much telling it to me!" He put his fists on the table. "But I've *never* lied to you, Vi. I've been nothing but honest. That's my trouble, ye see. I'm painfully honest. I don't like secrets, so I don't keep them." He straightened. "But let's come back around to you being married. Where is the lucky fellow? Does he know you gad about the world and seduce hapless young men? Am I just another mark? You knew all about me and my family the minute I walked into your dining room in London. Did you look at me and decide I was ripe for the plucking?"

Violet flinched at his words, but Daniel didn't feel like being kind. She'd played him, the same way she'd played Mortimer and all the other young men around the table that night. And Daniel, dazed by her beauty, had tumbled right on his ass.

Violet's lips were bloodless. "You mean the moment I met you, was I supposed to hold out my hand and tell you my life story? How could I know my life story would even matter to you?"

"Would *matter* to me? Everything about you matters to me, Vi. What if I were fool enough to get on my knees and propose to you? Would you have mentioned the marriage then?"

"I told you—I planned to tell you tonight at the inn." Violet's eyes were filled with fury, but also tears. "I *am* telling you tonight. It took me a long time to gather the courage to say the words—I know you'll probably toss me to the wind once you know everything, but I want to tell you. I'm trying to."

"Don't throw this back at me, love. I've been square with you from the moment I met you. And you've returned half-truths, lies, and evasion. Hell, you even dumped me in a cart when you couldn't wake me up."

Violet jumped to her feet, the cups clattering again as she jarred the table. "And *I* didn't ask you to follow me across Europe, or to spring upon me in the theatre in the middle of my performance. I thought you'd want to stay far, far away from me."

"A simple *You know, Daniel, I'm married* might have convinced me to."

"I doubt it." Violet's eyes sparkled blue. "You take whatever you want, damn all who get in your way. You want to test your theory about flying, so you take my wind machine, you take your friend's balloon, you fly it into a tree—but it's all right, you'll buy him a new one. We're stuck in a storm, but it's all right, you'll charm the innkeepers into giving us the best room in their house. And a woman you want to bed is caught by the police, but no matter—you'll get your father to call in favors and take her out. *Why?*" Violet balled her fists. "Why not leave me alone? If I've lied to you and evaded you, why the devil don't you just *leave me alone?*"

Her words rang against the *clackity-clack* of the train as they sped into the heart of France. Violet looked so empty, so starved, that Daniel almost relented. But his temper wouldn't let him.

"Why the devil should I leave you alone?" he shouted back. "You seem to like my company. You've had the power to send me away anytime—why didn't you use it?"

"Power? I don't have any power over you at all! You do as you bloody well please, no matter who doesn't like it. Me, your friends, country innkeepers, your glittering courtesans . . ."

Violet broke off, snapping her mouth shut, as though she hadn't meant to say the last.

"What glittering courtesans?" Daniel made a show of looking around the empty room. "I don't see any glittering courtesans. Maybe they're hiding under one of the sofas?"

"I *saw* you," Violet said, her voice hard. "The night we got back from the country. You were with gentlemen friends outside a restaurant, and lady friends too. They were quite beautiful. They were covered with diamonds, which is why I call them glittering. Please, do not pretend you are anything but a wealthy aristo who has any sort of woman he wants—respectable and not-so-respectable—happily going from one to the other."

Daniel's confusion cleared. "Do you mean you saw me outside the bistro? My obnoxious friend Richard provided the female company that night. The glittering ladies went home with Richard and his cronies, and I went to my hotel to be interrogated by my precious little sister. I'd just been with *you*, Vi. I wasn't interested in them."

Violet stared at him as though he'd lost his mind. Daniel supposed the fashionable world would think it odd that, plied with the most expensive and willing ladies in Marseille, Daniel would ignore them for a struggling confidence trickster with beautiful blue eyes. But that was because they hadn't met Violet.

"We'll be discussing this lack of trust in me," Daniel said. "Thoroughly. But I noticed ye've neatly turned the tables back to me being a complete bastard instead of talking about what we started out to. Tell me about this marriage. Every detail. Who is he?"

Violet's bosom rose in the beaded gown, the costume she'd not yet had a chance to remove. "I married Jacobi. To save my reputation, he said."

"Jacobi." Daniel's hatred for the man spun higher.

Violet wet her lips. "It is one reason I forgave him. I thought, at the time, he'd been as much of a victim as me. He made me a married woman, in name only, to protect me." She stopped, and fresh pain filled her eyes. "And because I was pregnant."

Dear God. Daniel's rage drained swiftly away. Violet watched him with trepidation, waiting for him to turn her away as she feared. Daniel knew, realistically, that with any other man her fears might not be unfounded. He'd just have to convince her he wasn't any other man.

"Was the father the man who took you as . . . payment?" The word tasted sour in Daniel's mouth.

"Yes."

She said it so calmly, but Violet wasn't calm. Her hands trembled, and she couldn't look directly at Daniel.

"Where is the child?" Daniel asked in a quiet voice.

Violet was silent for a long time, and when she raised her head, Daniel knew. Pain bored into his heart as though someone had stabbed him. "I never had the child. I miscarried."

"Violet . . ."

Violet held up her hand, fingers stiffly spread. "No. Wait. I want to finish. I was onstage with my mother when it happened. She had no idea about any of this." Violet smiled a little, that heartbreaking smile that made Daniel want to kill every person who'd ever hurt her. "I was too young and ignorant to understand what was wrong with me. A lady in the audience, a courtesan called Lady Amber, saw what was happening. She came backstage, took me away to her house, and got a doctor—a real doctor, a good one—to help me. The doctor saved me, but couldn't save the child."

Violet trailed off. The train's wheels clacked into the silence, the train rushing along at a great speed toward Paris.

"I'm sorry, Violet," Daniel said, not moving. "I'm so, so sorry."

"Perhaps it was for the best." Violet got the words out, but her voice broke.

"No, not for the best. It's never for the best. You tell yourself that so you can bear the hurting. My stepmum, she lost a babe that came from an unscrupulous man, but it grieved her all the same."

Violet's tears dropped to her cheeks. Daniel came to her, gently seated her on the sofa where she'd sat with Ainsley, and sat down with her.

"Tell me the rest, love."

Violet looked up at him, her eyes wet. "There is no rest. Jacobi was kind to me, trying to make amends. But when he was in debt again, when he offered me again, as I told you, I packed our things and took my mother and Mary out of Paris. I never wanted to live through that again. I haven't seen Jacobi from that day to this."

Daniel let silence fall between them for a time. Her hurting was real, no more lies. "Was it a legal marriage?" he asked after a time. "You were very young. Are you certain?"

She nodded. "There was a priest, our names in the register, a license, witnesses. I'm fairly certain it was all legal. Whether Jacobi is alive or dead now, as I said, I have no idea. I might be a widow. I don't know."

"Have you never tried to find him? Obtain a divorce, or annulment?"

Violet shook her head. "I never wanted to see him again. I did keep an ear out for mention of him, but I never heard anything. And he never tried to find me." Her shoulders slumped. "It didn't matter to me. I had no intention of marrying anyone else, so the fact that I'd married wasn't important."

Not important. Daniel had to stand up again. If he strangled Jacobi, not only would it feel good to his restless hands, he would set Violet free.

Daniel turned back to her. "It's important to me, love. I'll hunt down Jacobi, and if he's still alive, I'll shake an annulment out of him. If you haven't seen him in years, the marriage might be null anyway. Abandonment or disappearance can dissolve it. Or Jacobi might have ended it so he could marry someone else."

"He could have. I never had the opportunity or the money to bother with it. As I say, I wanted nothing to do with him. Ever."

Daniel nodded. "Yes, you ran away. You're good at that—

running. How was it the police caught you this morning? I'd have thought you light on your feet."

"I told you, I wanted them to catch me. My mother needed to get away."

Daniel's anger surged again. He went swiftly back to the sofa, leaned down, and planted his fists on either side of her. "You mean you sacrificed yourself for her, just as you sacrificed yourself for Jacobi, just as you sacrificed any chance at a normal marriage because he convinced you to. You sacrifice, and you run, and Violet, *you have got to stop*."

"How can I?" Violet's eyes held defeat. "What else is there?"

The defeat pierced Daniel to the heart. "I'm going to show you what else. I said so before—not that you believed me. Ye think me the frivolous Mr. Mackenzie, the flirt, the ne'er-do-well. Hell, I can barely *say* ne'er-do-well. But unfortunately for you, I've seen the true Violet. I've watched you leave your sacrificing, drudging flimflammery behind you and open yourself to the world. I've seen you spread your arms and scream out loud as the wind carried you. And I'm going to see that again. I plan to drag you out of yourself, sweetheart, whether you like it or not."

"And then what? Crash me to the ground again? It's what gentlemen do to ladies when they're finished with them."

"And I so love the way you try to turn me into a villain every time. Makes me angry, that does. But if I say I'm going to show you everything in life you missed, I mean it. I'm not Jacobi, or a man who thinks it just to use a girl's innocence as payment. And I'm not the marks you play upon to fleece. I don't care about your parlor tricks, or your phosphor-luminescent paint, or your fake talking boards. I'm going to show you real life. Real joy. Whether you like it or not, whether you believe it or not. No, don't agree or disagree right now. It doesn't matter."

"It doesn't matter what I think?" Violet's pride was back.

"No, it doesn't." Daniel straightened up, feeling his smile return. "It only matters what *I* think right now. You've put yourself into my hands, love, and I'm going to show you the world. The way you're supposed to see it." He reached down and pulled her to her feet. "But right now, you're going to sleep. Because when we reach our destination, no more rest for you. And no more looking after everyone. I'm going to look after you now, and that's all there is to that."

Violet came against him, the onyx on the bodice sharp under his hands. She looked up at him, a storm in her eyes, her body rigid.

Daniel kissed her. Violet's lips shook, but she kissed him back, her mouth softening a little under his. Daniel cupped the back of her neck and let the kiss become thorough.

When he drew back, Violet looked up at him with eyes filled with despair but also desire. She'd hurt so much, lost so much. Daniel wanted her with an intensity that nearly crushed him. When they finally came together, the world would shake apart.

But for now, they were in his father's private train car, with his stepmother and baby sister in the bedrooms in the back, not to mention Violet's mother. His father would soon stroll back from the smoking car or wherever he'd been to join Ainsley. He didn't like to be without her for long.

And Violet truly needed to rest. She was drooping, exhausted, too pale. Daniel kissed her lips again, then made her walk with him into the back to an empty bedroom. He kissed her good night at the doorway, Violet's eyes still full of fear and longing.

Violet shut the door herself, cutting off temptation from either of them. Daniel exited the car and made his way to the platform on the back. There he smoked cigarettes until the frigid winter wind calmed him enough to let him go back inside.

~~~

They changed trains in Paris early the next morning, without pausing to sample the pleasures of the city. The new Tour Eiffel dominated the skyline with its steel girders crisscrossed like lace against the morning sky.

Violet hadn't been to Paris except to change trains since the tower had been built. She gazed at the tower with longing, wanting to go to its very top. Maybe someday. She felt a momentary frisson of delight when she realized that in the balloon she'd ascended even higher.

For now, Violet was happy to move on from Paris, though England was not necessarily where she wanted to go. But they would be staying in Berkshire, Daniel said, a long way from London and her problems there.

Daniel had told her she had to stop running away, but he couldn't imagine the sorts of things Violet had run from. Daniel had always had a secure life, a caring family.

Daniel's early life might have been lonely, but watching Lord Cameron with him, Violet could see the man loved Daniel with everything he had in him. Even if Cameron hadn't known what to do with the energetic Daniel as a boy, he'd never entirely deserted him. That Daniel had been energetic, Violet had no doubt.

Daniel was still energetic. He helped his father direct everything as they changed trains to move on to Calais, and made certain Mary and his parents' servants were comfortable in their compartments. He helped look after Gavina, taking his little sister around the train when the journey grew dull, keeping her busy. And the whole while, he talked; with his father about sport; with his sister, interesting things they saw out the windows; with his stepmother, music, plays, fashion, and interestingly, cake.

Ainsley had lent Violet some clothes so she could remove her stolen costume and pack it away. What Mary had managed to carry off was mostly their stage accoutrements and a change of clothing for Celine, but nothing for Violet.

Ainsley seemed to think nothing of lending Violet a walking dress and two or three day dresses—for the time being, she said. They would of course go shopping for Violet when they reached England.

Ainsley's kindness was without artifice, tinged with friendly understanding, and easy to take. Another new sensation for Violet.

Daniel never said a word to Violet about their argument. He didn't keep his distance from her, but he didn't try to be private with her either. Daniel included her and Celine in all the conversations, talking easily but neutrally as the train ran on into Calais, where they'd spend the night. He was cheerful at the restaurant where they took a meal, bade Violet a polite good night at their hotel, and retreated to a lounge with his father.

Not until they were on the boat crossing the tossing Channel the next day did Daniel seek out Violet alone.

Violet hung on to the rail in the bow of the ferry, looking forward, the rumbling of the boat's huge engine somehow soothing. Celine, who hated boats, had stayed in their cabin with Mary. On her way above, Violet had glimpsed Lord Cameron, his wife, his daughter, and Daniel in the parlor for first-class passengers. Instead of stopping to join them, she'd come out here to be alone with her thoughts. The cold wind kept most passengers below, so Violet had the deck to herself.

She watched, mesmerized, as the gray water tossed white foam under the bow. The sea was ever changing, yet always there, tons of water somehow adhering fast to the planet. The bow wave surged and broke, surged and broke, but never stopped the boat, which kept plunging onward.

Warmth came behind her. Daniel brought his arms around either side of her to rest his gloved hands on the rail. "I couldn't stay away from you," he said, his breath in her ear. "Seeing you out here with your face to the wind, the courage of you, looking straight ahead into whatever comes."

"It isn't courage," Violet said. "The smoke from the engines is too thick in the stern."

"Don't ruin the image, love. And I'm not wrong. You aren't staring backward—smoke and all—at the retreating shore of France. You're watching England rush at you, your home, come what may."

Daniel brushed his lips to her cheek, sweet heat. Violet didn't dare turn her head, didn't dare kiss him back. Because once she took hold of Daniel, she'd never want to let him go.

"What is Berkshire like?" she asked.

"It's a fine place, as far as England goes. Scotland is, of course, much better. But in Berkshire there's enough flat to train the horses, plus it's not far to take them to Newmarket and Ascot when it's time. And there are miles of roads, which I need for my motorcar. Spring is beautiful there—little flowers poking up in the green, lambs in the fields, the aristos rushing to London for the Season, leaving the countryside blissfully quiet. Perfect."

Violet had lived so much in cities, with cobblestones beneath her boots, that she'd never experienced a country spring. In the cities, spring happened only in gardens. If those gardens were open to the public, Violet saw the spring. If not, she kept to gray streets and gray skies. "I look forward to seeing it."

Daniel pressed his cheek to hers. "I'm looking forward to showing it to you. London first, though. For a few days."

Violet jerked. "London? I thought we were only changing trains there and going on."

"Ainsley said at breakfast that we needed to stop, and she's right. If we go racing through without pausing to pass the time of day with my Aunt Isabella, our life won't be worth living. She's queen of the London Season, she is. Uncle Mac takes it all in his stride, jollies her along. He's good at turning people up sweet, Isabella likes to say."

"I thought that was you." Violet strove not to smile.

"Cheeky lass. I learned it from a master. We'll have to pay a call, which means Isabella will snare us into attending one of her soirees, which means you'll be wanting to shop for a frock. I know ladies."

"I can't stay in London, Daniel. And I can't go to a soiree. We ran off owing Mortimer back rent. We'll be arrested as soon as we're seen."

"You're afraid of *Mortimer*? Don't be daft. I took care of Mortimer—ye owe him nothing. I bought the house, as a matter of fact. You're welcome to stay in it if you like. It has all the hidey-holes already for your gadgets. Madame and Mademoiselle Bastien can be back in business."

Violet turned around fully to stare at him. "What do you mean, you took care of Mortimer? And you bought the *house*?"

Daniel shrugged. "Property is a good investment, so they say, and I wanted Mortimer to leave you the devil alone. He's a bloody hypocrite, you know. He owed half the bookmakers and moneylenders in London, not to mention me. Probably still does. No one should gamble who doesn't have a head for it."

Violet's mouth went dry. Daniel was telling her that instead of going to the police after Violet had assaulted him, he'd decided to buy a house from Mortimer, pay her debts, and look for Violet himself. "You're a madman."

"Not really. Mortimer's an ass, and you're a beautiful woman with more bravery and spirit than he ever will have. He wanted to use you to pay off his debt, and I'm sick to death of people doing that. Never again."

Daniel's determination was palpable, as though he were erecting a wall of it between Violet and the world. Comforting, and a little terrifying. Violet didn't know how to respond. No one had ever tried to protect her before.

"I was surprised you didn't want to stop in Paris," she said. "To find Jacobi."

"To run up and down the streets of a huge city looking for one man? By myself? Not likely. I have agents to do that for me while I sit comfortably in Berkshire. Or maybe not comfortably. Dad expects me to work, not lounge about, and I have plenty to do."

Violet wondered what *she* would do, and what Daniel would expect her to do. And did that frighten her? Or excite her?

Daniel closed his arms all the way around her, pulling her into warmth. His lips touched her cheek, then her ear, her hair. Though her thick coat and his kept them apart, Violet felt the beating of his heart, the heat of his body, Daniel's strength. In the swirling vortex of her life, Daniel was becoming the only solid pillar.

In London, Violet's uncertainty began to return. She'd supposed she and her mother would arrange some kind of rent with Daniel and move into Mortimer's former house—although with all that had happened there, Violet would prefer to find a boardinghouse.

Ainsley, on the other hand, assumed they'd stay with the Duke of Kilmorgan.

Violet wanted to jump out of the coach carrying them to the heart of Mayfair and run back to the train station. Ainsley continued explaining as the carriage rolled along, seeing nothing amiss. The duke had a very large house on Grosvenor Square, which had room for everyone for a few days. Of course the guests would stay there.

Celine thought it a fine idea. "A duke," she said, her eyes alight. "Just imagine, Violet, how very grand. And how kind. I'll do a reading for him, and the duchess. Gratis, of course."

"Mama, you will do nothing of the sort," Violet said hastily.

"Nonsense. Even dukes like to know the news from the other side. And a duke's house on Grosvenor Square sounds ever so comfortable."

Violet sent Daniel an appealing look. He had taken the seat next to Ainsley, across from Violet and Celine. Cameron and Gavina had taken a second conveyance, Lord Cameron declaring they'd be fools to all try to fit into one coach. Mary had been given a seat next to the coachman on the first carriage, Cameron and Ainsley's servants piling onto the second.

Daniel seemed to understand Violet's dismay. "Ainsley," he said. "You know Uncle Hart is a frightening thing to spring upon a guest, especially after a long journey. Ian and Beth's home is very comfortable and much less intimidating. Better for Violet. Mac and Isabella are always full up, and they're not exactly restful either. If Dad would keep a regular house in London, life would be more convenient, but there it is."

Ainsley's brow puckered. "But Ian . . ."

She looked worried. "I'll speak to Beth," Daniel said reassuringly. "All will be well." He turned back to Violet. "Ian and Beth have three rather noisy children, though, Vi. Do you mind?"

If the children were anything like Gavina, who'd included Violet in every one of her rather entertaining conversations, Violet wouldn't mind at all. "I like children," she said.

Celine hesitated. "I'm not certain . . . My nerves . . . And a duke is so very civilized."

"Then it's settled," Daniel broke in. "Violet will bed down at Ian and Beth's, while her mum goes to Uncle Hart's."

Celine's eyes widened. "Me, stay without Violet? I've never done without Violet before."

Ainsley leaned forward and patted Celine's knee. "No

need to worry. The duke has plenty of servants to do every little thing for you. There's even a servant who will ring a bell to summon another servant if you wish. You'll feel like a queen."

"Well." Celine looked less fearful. "I suppose I can try. Violet will be nearby, will she?"

"Not far," Ainsley said. "Good. This will resolve things nicely."

Daniel tipped Violet a wink. They were conspiring—Daniel and his stepmother. About what, Violet wasn't certain, but Daniel looked triumphant.

Chapter 24

"Ye anxious to rest and sleep?" Daniel asked Violet when they rolled away from the ducal mansion, where the remainder of the party had disembarked.

The tall house on Grosvenor Square had poured servants in black and white who'd descended on the first coach, then the second. The air had been full of voices—greetings, questions, orders.

The duke's servants hadn't behaved as Violet assumed they would. They were neither cowed nor fearful, scurrying or resentful. They welcomed Lord and Lady Cameron with energy, and one of the footmen swung Gavina up onto his shoulders. A maid came down the stairs leading a small boy by the hand. Ainsley exclaimed in joy and swept him up, never minding that his little boots were dirty.

Stuart, Violet surmised, Daniel's half-brother. Cameron took his son from Ainsley after Stuart had finished kissing his mother, and swung him high.

When Daniel stepped down, Stuart sang out to him, and Daniel paused to take his hand and give him a loud kiss on the forehead. The footmen then surrounded Daniel, talking excitedly, asking him questions about the balloon crash in France, about what he'd do now.

Of the frightening duke, there was no sign. He and the duchess were out taking tea with a cabinet minister and his wife, the majordomo reported, and their young lordships were riding in the park with their riding master. They'd all be home soon.

A horde of maids surrounded Celine with a solicitation that pleased her. Violet had been a bit apprehensive about leaving her mother with strangers, but the servants were giving her every deference. Ainsley and Cameron would be staying here too. Celine liked Ainsley, and Mary agreed to remain to look after her instead of going with Violet.

And so Violet drove off alone with Daniel.

Ye anxious to rest and sleep? he'd asked. Not really. Everything was too new, too nerve-racking to let her calm. And now Violet had another household to meet, that of the elusive Lord Ian.

"I'm not tired at all," Violet said.

"Then we'll make a stop first before I get you settled. Bertram," he called up to the coachman. "Just drop us at my house, will you? You can take Violet's things on to Uncle Ian's."

"Yes, sir, Young Master Daniel," Bertram said, and the coach swung around a corner.

"They'll be calling me Young Master Daniel when I'm eighty." Daniel sat back—next to Violet now. "Ah, well, I don't really mind."

Violet had met plenty of families in her travels. Because of her line of work, most of them had been torn by grief—wives losing husbands; mothers, sons; sisters, brothers. She'd also seen families like the Laniers, where one member believed in the spirit world and was tormented for that belief.

She'd rarely seen a family with as much camaraderie and acceptance as the Mackenzies. Violet hadn't met the duke yet, or Lord Cameron's other brothers or wives, but the way Ainsley and Daniel spoke of them made her know there was no envy or hatred between the Mackenzies. She'd seen families filled with jealousy, or bare tolerance of one another, or absolute sorrow. She rarely encountered families comfortable and at peace.

Daniel was lucky, so very lucky. Violet loved her mother, but she wasn't easy friends with her. Violet was more like a lady's companion, taking care of Celine, making decisions for her, living life for Celine's comfort.

Not looking after Celine while they stayed in London, however long that might be, felt strange to Violet. Like an emptiness, a feeling she should be doing something but not quite putting her finger on what.

Daniel's house wasn't far from the duke's. Violet knew London well, and she watched their progress south through darkening Mayfair, down Davies Street to Berkeley Square and around it to Hill Street.

The house the carriage halted in front of was tall like its neighbors, with a gray façade and white corner bricks. The door was black, with no knocker, indicating its owners were not in Town. There were no lights in the windows, no curtains in most of them either.

No servants came out the door to greet Daniel or welcome him home. Daniel climbed down by himself and reached up to hand out Violet. He pulled his valises from the back and told Bertram to drive on to Uncle Ian's then return for them later.

Daniel unlocked the door with a key while the carriage rattled away, and he led Violet into a quiet, dusty interior.

"I promise you, my aunt Beth keeps a better house than this." Daniel dropped his cases at the base of the stairs. A match scratched and flared, and Daniel lit candles that had been left ready on a hall table. "Had the gas turned off while I was gone, because I don't have anyone to keep the place. One day I'll fit it out with a proper staff, add speaking tubes to the kitchen and lifts to carry things up and down the stairs. But I'm never home long enough to put my plans in motion. So I make do."

The house was narrow, two rooms deep on the right side, the left side taken up with the staircase. Violet looked up the dark stairs, black shadows flickering in candlelight.

"I imagined you'd have a dozen people to rush down and take your coat," she said. "And another dozen on hand to give you brandy, cigars, coffee, and stand by to hold things for you because you have only two hands." Violet craned her head to look around again, taking in the sumptuous paneling and cornice molding, the elegant chandelier that adorned the front hall. She let out a sigh. "If I had such a house, I'd live like a princess. Servants to bring me tea and cakes, and hot water for my bath."

Daniel shrugged. "I got used to living rough on my travels. I've traveled with Bedouin tribes and explorers who lived on the edge of savagery. But it taught me to fend for myself. Took me a while after I returned to remember to ask servants to do anything at all. My dad's cook was forever running me out of her kitchen."

Violet wanted to laugh. "Good heavens. A man who cooks for himself?"

"Don't make fun of me, sweetheart. I make a mean omelet and chips."

"I'm not making fun. I'm envious. How wonderful to go where you please, live how you please." Violet turned in a circle, taking in the enormous hall. "Did you see the temple at Karnak?"

"Yes. You'd love it. I also went to Petra, which is astonishing. I'll take you someday."

Violet turned around again, not answering. She longed to travel, to see the world that existed outside cramped parlors of European towns and small theatres smelling of gas. She wanted to fly on Daniel's balloon across a dry desert while camels ran beneath her. She wanted to *know* how colossal was the Colossus, climb the pyramid at Giza, see the tombs in the Valley of Kings.

She'd been constantly told that her lot was to stay home and take care of others, and to be content with that. But Violet was far from content. She felt like a wild bird confined to a cage for another's pleasure.

I'll take you someday, Daniel said offhand. He said everything offhandedly, but he'd made clear when he'd grown angry at her on the train, that he meant every word he said. And expected her to believe him.

Daniel took her hand, squeezed it, and led her down the

hall to the rear door on the ground floor. "I've brought you here to show you my pride and joy," he said.

He opened the door, lit more candles, and stood back to usher her inside.

Candlelight gleamed on a roomful of metal, from what looked like every foundry in England. Tools of every shape and many Violet had never seen before lay scattered across tables along with cast metal parts of all sizes. Carriage wheels leaned against a wall, and long rods were stored in one corner. Tubes, coils of wires, nails, studs, screws, and bolts were everywhere, some neatly tucked into boxes, others strewn haphazardly.

In the middle of the room, mounted on a bed of bricks, was an engine—a large engine, sitting proudly alone. A long shaft ran back from it, attached to axels with no wheels. Parts of the body of the vehicle were welded together over the long drive-shaft, with a stool behind the engine, a tiller and pedals in front of the stool.

Daniel waved at the machine with a proud flourish. "You, Violet, are gazing upon what will be the fastest motorcar in all of Europe. When it's finished."

The most complete part was the engine. Violet walked around the car, taking in the gears and chains, the crankshaft, and various other pieces she couldn't identify. She hadn't seen many motorcars, let alone had the chance to examine the engines, but she'd read about them. She'd once contemplated buying or building a combustion engine to somehow help in their acts, then discarded the idea as too expensive. But she'd grown interested in the machines for their own sake.

"The cylinders are in there?" Violet pointed to a vertical metal container. "This is different from what I've seen."

"Because I wanted more cylinders, more power. So far, Daimler and his partner, Maybach—bloody geniuses with engines—are using two cylinders that meet in a V shape. My cylinders are in a straight line, and because I want this beast to move faster than any other motorcar has so far, I've got four of them. But then there's the weight to consider. Herr Benz has got it right on body design for lightness, but his engines are small and slow. Herr Daimler is better on power, but his cars are getting gigantic. The problem both men have is that they're still thinking about how to make a carriage go without horses. I'm thinking more of a motorcar built for its own sake, the body to fit the engine, not the other way around. I think I've solved the weight issue and streamlined the body all right. The bugger is keeping it cool."

"Won't four cylinders going at once make the car shake apart?" Violet asked, interested. "Or take an enormous amount of fuel?"

"Not necessarily. If I can get a fuel pump efficient enough, I can make it go with the same amount as the smaller engines." Daniel patted the cylinder block. "And if I can make a powerful enough engine, I can build the fastest motorcar in the world."

Violet didn't ask him why he'd want to. She knew. To speed along at a breathless pace, to feel the wind on her face, to laugh at people's astonishment as the motorcar flew on by . . .

"I do have a few problems, though." Daniel rubbed his forehead. "Besides how to keep it cool, I mean. I need to redesign the wheels—a simple rubber strip on carriage wheels won't work at these speeds. I have a man at a rubber factory doing some ideas for me now—I want to use air pressure to create a cushion. Plus I'm not happy with the tiller as a steering mechanism."

"You have another problem," Violet said.

Daniel looked the motorcar over again. "Don't think so. I've thought it through pretty thoroughly, love."

"That problem is—how are you going to get it out of your parlor once it's built?"

The engine was already too wide, the shaft too long, to maneuver the car out the door and down the hallway.

Daniel slanted her an amused look. "I did think of that, my sweet. I'll be taking it apart again, won't I? While you're buying new frocks with my stepmother, I'll pack all this up and have it hauled down to Berkshire. Dad's fixed up one of the large outbuildings for it. Dad has no interest at all in engines, but he indulges me in space to tinker."

Daniel loved this hunk of metal. Violet saw it in the way he looked upon his creation, in the way he laid a tender hand on it. She was excited about it too—she'd always had an unlady-like fascination with motorcars, steam engines, and other machines.

"I'd be interested to see it go when you're finished," she said.

"See it go? Vi, my love, you're going to help me *make* it go. That's why I brought you here today. I need your help to finish the thing. I thought if you saw it, you'd be more eager."

"*My* help?" Violet stared in surprise. "How can I help build a motorcar?"

"Because you understand mechanics. I knew that as soon as I saw your wind machine, and you so proudly said you'd put it together yourself. I could use your knowledge to design the cooling pumps, which won't be much different from your wind machine. Ye have a keen mind, lass. I intend to use it." He grinned at her. "Did you think it was only your body I was after?"

Violet let out a nervous laugh. "I knew you were wooing me for my machines."

"Oh, I'm wooing you for an entirely different reason. The fact that you can build intricate machines is a separate blessing."

Violet imagined any other lady growing offended at his words. Lady Victoria, the debutante who'd clung so tightly to Daniel in Marseille, would have walked off in a huff. Violet only wanted to laugh.

Daniel came around the engine to her, his arm stealing around her waist. "Say you'll help me, Vi. I want this done for the time trials in Paris, and I want you by my side when we win them."

Violet could never think properly when Daniel was close to her. He was warm in the cold of this shut-up dusty house, with its treasure in the back parlor. When he was near her, she wanted to do anything for him, be anything for him.

And to kiss him. She rose on her tiptoes, sliding up his body, and kissed his lips. Daniel was still angry with her, she saw that under his teasing, but she couldn't stay away from him.

Daniel's mouth was stiff, his whiskers rough under her lips. He returned the pressure but without his usual heat.

Violet kissed him again. Daniel made a surrendering noise in his throat, and this time, his answering kiss was fierce. He crushed her up to him, his broad hand forming to her backside.

Violet slid her hands up his back, wishing the thick greatcoat and the clothes beneath were gone. Touching his skin in the hotel in Marseille had been heady, licking sweet chocolate from it had been heaven itself. What they'd done in his small apartment, with his papers crinkling under her on the sofa, had sent her to madness.

She wanted the fire of his mouth on her opening again, the touch that had spiraled her to joy. That madness had held no pain, only the sensation of soaring free.

I need you with me every moment, Daniel Mackenzie. And it terrifies me.

Violet never heard the footstep through the roaring in her ears, but she became aware of a *presence* in the room. She broke the kiss and stepped back.

Daniel looked at Violet in puzzlement, brows drawn, his attention all for her. Then he lifted his head and saw the man in a greatcoat standing next to the motorcar, running a gloved finger over the cylinder block.

"Uncle Ian."

Daniel's words were a greeting, but the man didn't turn around.

Daniel didn't seem bothered by the abrupt appearance of his uncle. Ian didn't look at Daniel but continued gazing at the motorcar and its configuration of gears as though he saw and understood every nuance.

"Well?" Daniel asked. "Have I got it?"

Ian turned his head slowly, finally looking straight at Daniel. He had golden eyes, lighter than Daniel's, and as penetrating as a hawk's. "Yes," he said.

Chapter 25

Daniel went to Ian and clapped him on the shoulder then quickly removed his hand as though worried how his uncle would react to his touch. "Thank you."

Violet wasn't sure what the exchange meant, but Daniel was beaming. "Violet, come and meet my uncle Ian. The most maddening man in the world."

Violet didn't understand that either, but she stepped forward and held out her hand. "Pleased to meet you, my lord."

Lord Ian Mackenzie was tall, like the other Mackenzies she'd met, and broad of shoulder, with dark red hair. But he was different from the others as well. While he shared the restless energy she'd seen in Daniel and Cameron, Ian channeled his into a focus that was more intense even than Daniel's.

Ian remained motionless for a moment or two, then he clasped Violet's hand as though he had to remember the correct response to the gesture. Ian's grip was plenty strong, though, no hesitation or shyness.

He withdrew his hand with the same slow deliberation and remained standing in front of Violet. Ian's gaze met hers fleetingly, then moved past, but Violet knew she was still the subject of his attention.

There was a stillness about him Violet hadn't seen in Daniel, a calm he'd found, but she sensed it had come only after a long struggle. Ian was not a man who would be effusive, she decided, but not because he had nothing to say. Violet saw behind the amber eyes thoughts from the fleeting to the most profound, chasing one after the other.

"She was worth finding, don't you think?" Daniel asked Ian. "I am forever in your debt."

Ian again met Violet's gaze very briefly then turned back to the motorcar. "Worth finding," Ian said. "But easy to find."

Daniel rolled his eyes. "Easy, he says. All I had to go on was a false name and that you vanished from Mortimer's house in the middle of the night. Oh, certainly. I should have found you in a trice."

Ian's answering words came out in a monotone, each one the same speed and emphasis. "Names are not important. You asked me to look for one middle-aged woman, one young woman, and one maidservant. Five such parties purchased tickets on trains from London on that night. Two went west to Somerset and Dorset and to middle-class homes and families. One went north to Leeds—a cook, a lady's maid, and a maidservant to work in a house. Two parties went to the Continent. One went north. They spoke Dutch and the mother and daughter were leading members of their church. The final set went to Marseille. A few days after they arrived, advertisements for the Countess Melikova and Princess Ivanova went up in the streets. You told me they worked as mediums, and Countess Melikova was billed as a clairvoyant. Simple."

Violet listened to his speech, eyes widening. "Good heavens, how did you know where all those people went and that they bought tickets, and so forth? And that they spoke Dutch?"

"Telegrams," Ian said.

"Add to that the fact that Uncle Ian knows everyone in Great Britain and half of France," Daniel said. "The one thing he stated in all that was the most interesting bit: *Names are not important.* Ian looked for the people, not the names. Names, as you know, are so easily changed."

Violet's face warmed. "So I have heard."

Daniel shot her a grin. "This means you'll never be safe from me, Vi. No matter how far or fast you run, I'll find you. I will tear apart the world looking for you. I guarantee that."

The intensity of his look made Violet shiver. He meant it.

Ian had lost interest in them. He gave the motorcar one last look, then he walked out of the room to the hall. "Beth is waiting," he said over his shoulder.

"And that is that," Daniel said. He held out his arm to Violet. "Time to go, love. Welcome to my crazy family."

They stayed in London three days. During that time, Daniel watched Violet relax, little by little, into the bosom of the Mackenzie family.

His choice of having her stay with Ian and Beth had been wise. Violet would have remained quiet and withdrawn against the power of Hart, and even against the exuberance of Isabella and Mac. Violet's mother withstood Hart, Daniel saw, because she was so absorbed in her own world that she didn't notice him. The way Hart's stern power bounced off Celine was a delight to watch.

Beth, of all the Mackenzie ladies, had grown up a pauper, in the rougher areas of London, which gave her something in common with Violet. They'd both struggled to survive and had suffered cruelty. Daniel caught Violet and Beth once or twice in deep, serious conversation, which broke off when Daniel entered the room. And then they'd look mysterious— or worse, laugh.

Daniel used the time in London to run errands and get his motorcar taken apart and packed into crates. Simon, who'd arrived a day after Daniel with the rest of the baggage, kept a watchful eye on things. Once Daniel was certain his engine was safely away to Berkshire, to be met by Cameron's trusted man, Angelo, Daniel turned his attention to his most important errand.

He visited Mr. Sutton in his Park Lane home, this time sending word ahead for an appointment. When he arrived, the thin, spare Mr. Sutton saw him in the same quietly luxurious study that Daniel had been ushered to before.

Daniel had decided after debating with himself not to use Ian's skills for this matter. The way could grow dangerous, and Ian wouldn't bother to hide what he was doing. Ian could take care of himself, but Beth would never forgive Daniel for putting Ian in any kind of danger.

Sutton waited for Daniel to seat himself before he began, without preliminary. "I see in your eyes again that what you want me to do is about a woman. I believe I made clear that I have no interest in domestic troubles."

"The man I want found is a criminal," Daniel said. He accepted brandy from Sutton's butler and sipped it, reflecting that it was some of the best he'd tasted. "A Frenchman by the name of Jacobi Ferrand. He might be dead; he might not. I don't know."

"Then go to the police. In France, preferably."

"The crime was a long time ago. And yes, it involved a woman. I mean to make him pay for what he did."

Sutton heaved a little sigh, which barely moved his body. His eyes, on the other hand, were ice cold. "Revenge is a waste of time, Mr. Mackenzie. Trust me. Be knight-errant to your woman another way."

"I intend to pay you handsomely for the information."

"No doubt. But it's a fool's game. I want no part of it."

Daniel sat back and took another sip of brandy. "I'll have to convince you, then. She isn't just any woman. She's different."

"So every man has said since time immemorial."

"Yes, that's true. I've met plenty of women, Mr. Sutton. From a young age, I have had mistresses whose beauty and skills would astound you. Skills they taught to a young man, because I was ever so rich. I also got to know them—courtesans are living, breathing women, you might be surprised to learn. With dreams and ambitions, some longing for a better life, one in which they won't have to rely on wealthy men's sons for survival. I became quite good friends with some of the ladies and am still. And then I met Violet."

Mr. Sutton was listening but striving to look uninterested. "Another courtesan?"

"She's neither one thing nor the other. Which is why I say she's different. She's not from the upper-class families whose mothers throw their daughters at me with alarming ruthless-ness. She's not a courtesan, selling her body and skills in exchange for diamonds and riches. She's not a street girl from the gutter, selling her body to survive. She's not a middle-class daughter, striving to live spotlessly and not shame her parents. Violet faces the world on her own terms, making a living the best she can with the skills she has. And every-where, everyone has tried to stop her. They've used her body to pay their debts. They've used her cleverness to bring them clients. They've used her skills at understanding people to make them money. Everyone in her entire life has used her in every capacity she has, and yet, she still stands tall and faces the world. They've beaten her down at every turn, and still she rises. This is a woman of indomitable spirit. And I want to set her free."

Sutton watched him in silence a moment. "A nice speech, Mr. Mackenzie. You mean you want this woman for yourself."

"Aye, I do. And I intend to persuade her as hard as I can to stay with me. But first, I need to find this Jacobi and get her free of him—if she is indeed still bound to him. He might be dead. He might have annulled the marriage and remarried. The vengeance part of it, I'll deal with on my own. I only need you to find him and discover whether his marriage to Violet is legal."

"And if it is?" Sutton looked more interested now.

"Then I go in with my barrage of solicitors and make it un-legal. Annulment, divorce, whatever it takes. I have plenty of money at my disposal and have many friends in the legal profession in both France and Britain. I don't anticipate a problem."

"You have the optimism of the young," Sutton said. "Any-thing you want, you reach out and take."

"It's a besetting sin of the family. Uncle Hart had his own personal brothel at my age, where he trained ladies in the art of exquisite pleasure. *He* trained *them*, not the other way around, the pompous bastard. Dad had his own racing stable, Uncle Mac was already a celebrated artist with a scandalous marriage. I'm a bit late in the proceedings for a Mackenzie."

"Yes, the famous Mackenzies. I never let my name near the

scandal sheets, Mr. Mackenzie. I don't like people knowing my business. If I find this Jacobi Ferrand, for a little more money, I can make sure you never know what happened to him. No scandal sheets. His name will never be mentioned. But your woman will be free for you to marry or whatever you intend to do with her."

"I intend to take her ballooning over Scotland. But never mind assassinating him. Just find the man, and I'll do the rest."

Sutton gave Daniel a nod. "If you make a mess, or it gets into the newspapers, it will have nothing to do with me. Understand?"

Daniel took one last sip of brandy and rose. He stuck his hand out to Sutton over the desk. "I understand perfectly. News will reach me in Berkshire for the next few weeks, and then Paris at the Grande Hotel. I hope to hear from you before then."

Sutton closed Daniel's hand in a strong grip. "I'm sure the journey will be profitable all the way around. Give Mr. Simon my regards."

Daniel nodded as he released Sutton's hand, finally seeing a glimmer of respect in Sutton's eyes. Daniel thanked him again, and departed to put other things in motion.

~~~~~

The brief stay in London was marred by only one incident, but that incident told Daniel that Violet was not as calm as she appeared.

It started innocently enough when the entire family gathered to take tea at Hart's. The collective children were there, ten of them, from Mac's adopted daughter, Aimee, who was going on twelve, to wee Lord Malcolm Ian Mackenzie, Hart's youngest, at the tender age of three.

The children returned to the house with collective nannies, breathless from romping in the park of Grosvenor Square. They all liked Violet, so they mobbed her, Gavina claiming precedence to sit on her lap. Celine looked on indulgently, happy with the children as long as they stayed across the room from her.

Daniel watched Violet's face soften as she listened to the clamor, lifting Ian's daughter Megan onto her other knee. She looked around at them all, amazingly making sense of the mixed-up stories.

At one point, she asked into the chaos, "Where is Aimee?"

"Still in the park," Eileen, Mac's other daughter, announced. "She was playing with her hoop and didn't want to leave. Not even for tea." Her tone said, *Can you imagine?*

Violet stilled, her face draining of color. "You left her out there alone?"

She set the two small girls on their feet, rose swiftly, and made for the parlor door. Without stopping to ask for her coat, she rushed through the hall and the foyer, opening the heavy front door herself.

"Vi," Daniel was after her. "Where are you going?"

Violet turned as she stopped at the edge of the busy street, too many carriages preventing an easy crossing to the park. "Aimee can't be left alone. She's only twelve, Daniel. She can't be alone." Violet's breath came too quickly, the panic in her eyes sharp.

Mac had come out after them, Eileen holding his hand. Eileen looked worriedly up at Violet. "It's all right, Violet. We're in a safe place. The park is only for the people who live here. And their guests."

Violet shook her head, her words tumbling out. "Predators are everywhere. A young girl isn't safe. We have to find her."

Daniel grabbed Violet as she was about to dart into the path of a large landau. "We will, love. Don't you worry."

"She's not wrong." Mac, who was usually the most ready of the Mackenzies with a smile and a joke, looked grim. "She shouldn't have stayed behind. But Aimee's fearless."

Mac stepped out into the same traffic, but he held up his hands, and people stopped. Daniel sent a protesting Eileen back into the house, caught Violet's hand, and led her across after Mac.

Violet's pupils were wide, her breathing hoarse as they made it to the inner part of the square and the park there. The gate was open, two nannies with their unruly charges having walked out and let it swing behind them.

Mac strode into the park, scanning the flat green and its walkways for Aimee.

A red-haired girl ran toward them, her blue skirts flapping, strong legs in high-laced boots moving rapidly. She pushed a hoop ahead of her with a stick, her face set in determined focus. Several boys about Aimee's age, also pushing hoops, ran madly to keep up with her.

Aimee crossed a path and nearly ran into her father. She pulled up short, eyes shining, smile wide. Her hoop rolled on without her and fell flat into the grass. The other boys stopped, expressions disgruntled, their hoops rolling away.

"I won!" Aimee flung her arms around Mac. "Did you see me, Papa? I'm faster than any of them."

"I did see, sweetheart." Mac hugged her back and ruffled her hair. "You're astonishing."

Aimee danced happily out of her father's embrace. "Did you see, Violet?" She stopped. "Violet, what's wrong?"

Violet leaned on Daniel's side, her hand to her chest. Daniel led her to the nearest bench and sat her on it. Aimee, concerned, came to sit beside her.

"It's all right, Violet." Aimee patted her hand. "You'll feel better in a moment."

"She was worried about you, pet," Daniel said. "And she's right. You shouldn't have stayed out here alone."

Aimee looked at him in confusion, and at Mac, who clearly agreed.

Innocence. Aimee had no idea what could happen to a twelve-year-old girl in this giant city—anywhere, in fact. Aimee had never known the horror of what Violet had experienced, and Daniel and all the Mackenzies would make certain she never did.

Aimee, still confused, patted Violet's hand again. Violet looked at Daniel, tears in her eyes, but her breathing had slowed.

"Come on, love," Mac said, holding his hand out to Aimee. "Let's go home and make ourselves sick on too many cakes for tea."

Aimee stood up readily. She ran and fetched her hoop then returned to Mac, took his hand, and walked out of the park beside her adoptive father, a spring in her step again.

Daniel took Aimee's place on the bench and folded his hands around Violet's. "All right now, lass?"

"I'm sorry." Violet drew a long breath. "I grow angry at my mother for her hysterics, and here I am, having them myself."

"For good reason. I don't want Aimee to ever feel anything but safe, which means we should have been more diligent watching her. And Mac will be, you can be certain."

Violet shook her head. "I'm never going to be free of this, am I?"

"The panicking? You are. Because you're with me now, and I'm going to keep you absolutely safe."

Violet looked skeptical, not because she thought Daniel was lying, he understood, but because no one had ever protected her before.

But none of that mattered. Daniel would protect her, he vowed, from this day to forever. Whether Violet believed him or not.

~

Celine, at the last possible minute, refused to go to Berkshire. The country frightened her. It was too big, too wet, too terrifying. She liked cities with modern houses, parlor stoves, and good plumbing. In short, Violet thought in irritation, she'd found a cushy billet with the duke and didn't want to leave it. But Celine also expected Violet to stay with her. She couldn't do without her Violet.

Before Violet could argue, beg, or resign herself to being her mother's drudge again, she learned exactly how determined the Mackenzie family could be.

Violet was going with Daniel and the family to Berkshire, and that was that. If Celine wanted to stay in London, she could remain at the duke's house as long as she pleased. Eleanor and Hart were staying in London for a time, as were Isabella and Mac, the two couples having social obligations they couldn't yet leave. Ainsley and Cameron, Beth and Ian, the children of all four families, and Daniel and Violet, on the other hand, were going to Berkshire, come what may.

When this was explained to Violet's mother, firmly, by Eleanor, Celine turned surprisingly obedient. Of course Violet should have time with her friends in the country, Celine said. Mary, who also had a horror of the country, would remain with her to look after things. And Celine could cultivate the duchess's friends as new clients. She'd again become the most sought-after medium in fashionable London.

Violet had her misgivings about that, but Eleanor, the duchess, with her lovely blue eyes and wide smile, took over.

"Indeed, my friends will love her," Eleanor said. "Madame Celine is quite a wonderful medium. She's called forth my great-great-grandmother Finella, and we even reached the legendary Malcolm Mackenzie, the only member of the Mackenzie family to survive the Forty-Five—that was the Scottish uprising under Bonnie Prince Charlie, Violet. His Highland Scots was so thick that the little spirit guide—what's her name—Adelaide—could barely understand him. Hart says it's all nonsense, but he had quite an interesting chat with old Malcolm, asked him for advice about the estate and the distillery and other things. Malcolm said he was flattered we'd named our youngest son after him. We all had a lovely time."

Eleanor related this with a mischievous twinkle in her eyes, and Violet felt better. If anyone could keep Celine in check, it would be the Duchess of Kilmorgan.

Violet enjoyed the short train journey to Berkshire, in which she was again surrounded by children.

Gavina had long since decided that Violet was one of the family. Danny would marry her, and they would have babies, and Gavina could help look after them.

"Only until I grow up," Gavina said confidently to Violet as she sat next to her in the train compartment. "Then I'm going to be a jockey."

"Girls can't be jockeys," Jamie said in his resigned, I'm-older-than-you-and-know-better manner.

Jamie, as the oldest Mackenzie son, had the awe of the others. Never mind that five-year-old Lord Hart Alec Mackenzie was the actual heir to the dukedom. Alec didn't seem at all conscious that he was the social superior of his cousins. Jamie, Ian's son, had the rule of them. From what Violet observed while staying with Ian and Beth, Jamie had inherited his father's intelligence as well as his mother's spirit.

"Dad says I can be the best rider he's ever trained," Gavina returned hotly. "Angelo says so too, and Dad's jockeys aren't too proud to give me advice. You see if I'm not a jockey, Jamie Mackenzie."

"All right, Gavina," Ainsley said. "You have made your declaration. Now be polite. We have a guest."

"Violet isn't a guest, Mummy," Gavina scoffed. "She's going to marry Danny."

Fortunately, Daniel was in a different compartment with Ian and Cameron and couldn't see Violet blush.

"The Mackenzie men can rather bowl you over," Beth said gently to Violet as Ainsley continued to quiet the argument. "Daniel is no different from his uncles. You believe your life is plodding along, and suddenly you are places you never thought you'd be."

"Gracious, yes," Ainsley said, turning back to the adult conversation. "But make certain it's your choice, Violet, and make sure Danny knows it. The Mackenzies can be very . . . persuasive."

Violet was aware that the children had stopped arguing and were listening as hard as they could.

"They can be," Violet said. "And you are right about finding myself in places I never thought I'd go. For instance, I've never been to Berkshire."

Ainsley and Beth, and what children were in the compartment with them, laughed, and the moment eased.

The journey to the middle of Berkshire itself wasn't long, but sorting themselves into coaches and carts to reach the house once they arrived at the Hungerford train station took much time. All the children wanted to go with Violet, but there wasn't room, and compromises had to be made.

Finally Cameron dictated who would go where, in a manner that brooked no argument. Violet went off with Beth and Ian, their children, and their two dogs to a house that was old, huge, and rambling.

In spite of its size, the house had a homey feel, much like

Beth and Ian's London house did. Each family had its own suite in upstairs rooms—Ian walked straight up to theirs, barely giving a nod to the staff who came out to greet them.

Violet found she'd been given two rooms to herself, a little sitting room and a bedroom next to it with a wide, canopied bed. The windows of both overlooked a slope of ground down to the canal at the base of a meadow. The air was soft, the hills gentle, trees lining fields tinged with green. All was beauty, quiet, peace.

Violet wanted to embrace that peace to her and never let it go. To this point, her life had stretched before her, bleak and predictable, a straight road, gray and empty. Now the path was obscured with uncertainty. Violet knew that when she broke through this obscuring thicket, she might find the road straight and empty again. And the thought terrified her.

But the next week was the happiest of Violet's life. Every morning after breakfast, she accompanied Daniel to the shed to work on the motorcar.

Daniel had no intention of having Violet simply watch him work—he expected her advice and opinions, and her help. Their hands together held bolts and sockets, rods and gaskets, or smeared grease on bearings. Violet got filthy and tired, but then Daniel would look up at her, give her his searing smile, hook an arm around her, and pull her close for a kiss.

The casual intimacy drove her wild. Daniel did nothing more than kiss her, though those kisses were full of promise and wickedness.

She and Daniel didn't spend all their time in the shed, however. Daniel worked plenty with his father with the horses, as he was a partner in his father's training business. Violet was also drawn into Ainsley's and Beth's activities, and those of the children.

When Violet said innocently at supper one night that she'd never been on a horse, a ripple of horror went around the table. The Mackenzie brood, as usual, ate supper with the adults, though the littlest ones had already been put to bed.

"You've never been on a *horse*?" Eileen, Isabella's daughter, asked. She wrinkled up her face. "How can someone never have been on a horse?"

"Not everyone's uncle runs a racing stable," Ainsley said, admonishing. "Different people have different lives, Eileen."

Eileen stared in frank astonishment. That a person could live without horses apparently had never occurred to her.

"That's all right, Eileen," Violet said quickly. "I've always lived in cities, you see. And I travel quite a lot. I've never had the opportunity to learn to ride. We always go in coaches or trains."

"Easily remedied," Daniel said. "Tomorrow after breakfast, we'll get you up on a horse. Ian and Dad had to teach Beth to ride, once upon a time."

"Yes, and they terrified the life out of me," Beth said. "But I grew fond of dear Emmie. She's still in the pastures at Kilmorgan, in her twenties I believe. A fine old horse."

"Violet will need someone placid like Emmie," Daniel said. "How about Medusa?"

Violet started. "I don't think I want to climb aboard a horse called Medusa."

"She was named that because she gets her mane in a perilous state," Aimee explained. "No matter how much grooming. It's like snakes around her head. She looks so funny."

"But she's a sweetheart," Daniel said.

"Nah," Jamie said. "I think Violet needs someone like Bessie. A little spirited, but her gaits are smooth and easy to sit. She has a lot of heart, that horse."

An argument ensued, up and down the table, about what horse would be just right for Violet. They all participated, except, Violet noted, Ian.

Ian only ate and watched his family. He loved to watch his family, Violet had noticed. Any tension drained from Ian whenever he looked at his wife or children. His face would soften, his mouth quirked into a little smile, and his eyes warmed.

Ian had at first been wary of Violet staying with them in London, until he'd discovered that Violet could tell him everything about any person she saw passing by the window. They made it into a game, Violet and Ian watching passers-by then each relating what they'd seen and comparing notes. Ian was good at it, finding far more nuances about the person than Violet.

Ian was not as good reading a person's emotional state, however. Violet trumped him there. But Ian could remember every article of clothing and how each was arranged, what the person was carrying, and conclude from all this where they'd come from and where they were going. Ian won every match without triumph or gloating—he just did it.

Now as he watched his family and listened to the children argue, he was as calm and relaxed as Violet had ever seen him. Here, in this place, Ian Mackenzie had found happiness.

In the morning, the entire family turned out to see Violet and her first riding lesson, including all the dogs. The Mackenzies were surrounded by dogs at all times, she'd learned, even in the town houses of London. One called Old Ben, she'd been told—the duke's dog—had sadly passed a few years ago, but two more dogs, Venus and Mars, both springer spaniels, had joined the family since then.

All six now wandered among the children, the younger dogs taking interest in the proceedings, the older ones seeking out warm places to lie down. Angelo, the Romany man who was in charge of Cameron's stables, led out a horse Violet supposed wasn't any larger than any other horse. The mare's legs were long and her back broad, and her mane was snaking out of its row of little braids.

The horse was saddled with a man's saddle, not a prim sidesaddle. Violet had dressed in a riding habit and hat Ainsley had lent her. The habit's skirt was narrow, not made for riding astride.

When Daniel came out of the stables wearing tight-fitting breeches and boots—no kilt in sight—Violet stared in surprise.

"Am I riding or are you?" she asked.

"Both of us, love. Medusa's big enough to hold two."

"I believed I was to have a lesson." Violet didn't really care about whatever arrangement they'd made, because the sight of Daniel's thighs outlined by the close-fitting breeches had made all thought cease.

"Your first ride shouldn't scare you off it," Daniel said. "You and me will have a nice, pleasant saunter, and you'll get used to feeling a horse under you. Tomorrow, we fit you up with a saddle and show you how to sit."

Angelo boosted Daniel onto the horse's back. Daniel looked very English in his black coat and tall hat, his feet in polished boots resting quietly in the stirrups.

Angelo caught Violet around the waist and lifted her onto the horse in front of Daniel. Violet was seated on the pommel, sidesaddle, Daniel's arms coming around her to take up the reins. His body cut the wind, which was still knifelike with winter.

The family waved them off. The horse, in spite of her fearsome Gorgon name, moved placidly along the path that led from the stable yard down to the canal. One of the newer dogs, Mars, followed, ignoring Daniel's admonishment that he remain behind.

Violet looked down past her boots and the horse's formidable shoulder to the grasses passing far below. "We're an awfully long way from the ground."

Daniel chuckled behind her. "This from a woman who ascended more than a thousand feet in a balloon."

"That was different. A balloon isn't a live animal. How can she hold us?"

"By weighing fifteen hundred pounds and being mighty strong. We're nothing to her. Give her a pat. She likes that."

Violet reached down and tentatively stroked the mare's neck under her mane. Medusa was warm, her coat shaggy with winter growth. She shook her head a little and walked faster.

"She likes you," Daniel said. "Again."

Violet patted her. "Nice horse. Nice Medusa."

Medusa's head bobbed, and she made a low noise in her throat.

"See that?" Daniel transferred the reins to one hand and closed his other arm about Violet's waist. "We'll make you a horsewoman yet."

Daniel turned them onto the towpath that ran alongside the canal. Even in the cold, canal boats moved west, large horses pulling the barges. A few barges were steam driven, but most still had horses.

This was the Kennet and Avon Canal, Ainsley had told her, which nearly a hundred years ago had carried tons of goods from the Thames at Maidenhead to the Avon. Trains had made the slow canal boats a less desirable method of transporting cargo, but boats still ran.

Daniel said cheerful hellos to the men leading the barge horses, tipping his hat as he rode past.

"Now then, Young Master Mackenzie," one called. "How does your father do?" Mars ran among them, seeking pats from bargemen's children, before he loped after Daniel and Violet again.

The boats dropped behind. Daniel rode across a bridge over one of the canal's locks and south, winding into more remote country. Hedgerows separated fields, and the roads between the hedges dipped, shutting out everything but green walls and sky.

Daniel navigated Medusa along a meadow path until they reached a little copse under the ledge of a hill. The copse cut the wind, which had prevented them speaking much since they'd left the canal.

"The other reason I wanted to ride out here with you was to be alone with you," Daniel said. "I love my family, but every time ye turn about, there's another one tugging at your sleeve."

"I like it," Violet said. The way the Mackenzies included her in everything had unclenched something inside her she hadn't realized was tight.

"Aye, but there's no privacy."

Daniel slid his feet from the stirrups, but he made no move to dismount. Medusa stretched her neck toward the nearest tree, tearing off a clump of foliage between large teeth. Mars trotted off to investigate something in the brush.

"I thought ye might not want them all listening in when I told you a few things," Daniel said. "I had some telegrams this morning, answers to inquiries I'd made."

Violet froze in the act of patting Medusa again and turned to look at him. Daniel's eyes were quiet, all teasing gone. "What inquiries?" Violet asked sharply.

"About Jacobi." Daniel paused. "I found him, Vi. He's still alive, and in Paris."

Chapter 26

Daniel watched Violet stiffen, the contented light vanishing from her eyes. "What do you mean, you found him?"

"Should say I *more or less* found him. I thought we'd discover he'd died, as you'd supposed, but he's in Paris . . . somewhere. Pinning him down is tricky, because he's slippery, but we'll get him. I also had inquiries made about the marriage." Daniel gentled his voice. "It was legal, Vi. Still is. He hasn't ended it."

Violet's chest rose. "No?"

"But I have solicitors on it, to see how we can get you free."

Violet closed her eyes briefly, fighting something inside her. When she opened her eyes again, her face was pale under the brim of her fetching black hat.

"Jacobi is Catholic," she said. "He might not agree to divorce or even annulment under any circumstance. Perhaps I should leave it alone. I'd rather let him think me dead or too far away to bother about."

"Ye need to be free of him," Daniel said sternly. "I thought you'd want to be."

"I do." Her eyes flickered with fear and remembered pain.

"But if there's a battle . . . I'm not strong enough for a battle just now. I've only found my breath in the last few days."

"Violet . . ." Daniel caught her around the waist, gently sliding her down from the horse. "Let's talk on the ground."

Violet landed with a light thump, and Daniel swung down after her. Medusa wandered away in search of grass, but Daniel knew she wouldn't go far. She was placid, she liked her warm stall in the barn with her friends, and she'd not run off.

"I don't want to see Jacobi," Violet said in a hard voice. "Never again."

Daniel took off his hat and dropped it to a dry patch on the ground, letting the breeze ruffle his short hair. "You might not have to see him at all. But I'm going to get you free of him. I won't stop until I do."

Violet started to walk a step, but her knees buckled. Daniel caught her and turned her to him.

"You're so strong, love." He found the pins of her hat, loosened them, and pulled the hat off to join his on the ground. "You can face this."

Violet lifted her head. Her eyes were dry, piercing. "If I see him, I don't know what I'll do. I've tried to understand, tried to reason why he would do what he did to me, but I find no reason. I loved and admired Jacobi—I'd have done anything for him—and in return he destroyed my life. He's still destroying it."

He was, damn the man. "Jacobi was a selfish bastard who used you to get himself out of a tight spot, and that's the end of it. He decided he didn't need to face the consequences when he could shove a girl in front of him to face them for him. I've met men like Jacobi before, almost got killed because of one. He doesn't deserve your understanding."

Violet's brows drew together. "What happened to you? How did you almost get killed?"

"It's another tale of my harrowing adventures. I was meant to take the blame for a murder a man I thought was a close friend did. When the victim's friends and brothers came for him, my friend was nowhere in sight, but there I was—he'd told them I'd done it. Lucky for me, I had a good knife and was fast on my feet. I got out of the town, out of the country, out of that part of the world."

"Dear God, Daniel."

Her eyes were wide with concern. Daniel shook his head. "It was a long time ago. I learned, didn't I?"

Violet drew a breath. "I'm glad you're all right. I would have lost you before I'd even met you."

The worry in her eyes touched him. Violet was starting to care for him, and that warmed Daniel better than the hottest fire.

"But I'm here, lass. I was meant to escape, because now I'm here with you."

"And Jacobi's going to take it away from me." Her bleak look returned. "I've finally found a chance at happiness, however brief, and he won't let me have it."

"'Twill not be brief." Daniel gathered Violet against him. "I promise you that. I'm a selfish bastard too."

Violet closed her hands around the lapels of Daniel's coat. "You say I'm brave, but I'm not at all. I don't want to lose what little I've found."

"*Little?* Trying to flatter me, are you?" Daniel pressed a kiss to the tip of her cold nose. "I told you I'd show you life, and I will. Taking the motorcar to the time trials is my excuse to go back to France. You'll come with me. Not to skulk in a dull hotel while I hunt down your soon-to-be-former husband. We'll work on testing the motorcar by day, and at night I will show you what it's like to be the lady of Daniel Mackenzie. I'm going to woo you so hard you'll run to shove my solicitors down Jacobi's throat."

A sparkle of her usual spirit returned to Violet's eyes. Daniel was glad of it—he hated to see her so broken. "I will, will I?" she asked.

"You will, love. The motorcar will be finished in a few days, and then it's off to Paris and the races."

Violet's hands tightened on his coat. "I don't know. I thought I'd have more time to think about this."

Daniel gentled his voice. "I know you did. But trust me, it's best to face something head on, smash it, and move on with your life. Lingering and wondering, waiting and worrying . . . that kills you."

Violet looked up at him. "Did that happen to you?"

"I was a boy who thought he was to blame for his mother's death. It ate at me—I kept wondering what I'd done to make her want to kill me. I resented my father for not telling me sooner exactly how she'd died. I realize now I should have had it out with him and been finished with it. I didn't understand that Dad had been hurting all those years same as me, and blaming himself. We wasted a lot of time."

Violet nodded, not answering. She didn't have to speak. She understood.

The wind slid in with its icy fingers. In the cold, Violet was a thing of warmth, softness to his hardness. Daniel held her closer, parting her lips in a kiss.

She tasted of the winter and the wind that pushed them. At the same time, Violet relaxed under Daniel's hands, she leaning into him as though seeking refuge from the chill.

When Daniel eased back from the kiss, he saw the fear still in her eyes. Violet's instinct to run was sharp. Running had been how she'd survived, but Daniel knew she'd only survive now if she stopped running.

He traced her cheek. "I'll be with you, love. Every step of the way."

Violet shivered. "I'm so afraid of going back. I never want to go back."

"It's not going back. Right now you're stuck in a mire. This will be you fighting your way out and going on. Facing down Jacobi is moving forward, not back."

Violet swallowed. The animal-like panic in her eyes flashed out then receded as she sought to suppress it. "You make me out to be stronger than I truly am."

"You are stronger than you think." Daniel cupped his hands around her elbows. "And don't worry, sweet. I'll be right beside you to make sure you don't fall."

Violet's eyes softened, and Daniel bent down to kiss her again.

Mars chose that moment to rush them, bending himself around Violet's legs and running into Daniel's. Daniel's knees gave, and Violet laughed.

"Bloody dog," Daniel growled.

"It's cold," Violet said. "He wants us to keep moving."

"Yes, all right, let me round up the dratted horse. Don't laugh so hard. If she's run for the barn, we have a long walk ahead of us."

But Medusa hadn't strayed. Daniel got himself into the saddle, then helped Violet climb up in front of him. She expressed surprise when Daniel didn't turn at once for the house, but he continued the lesson, riding onward, holding Violet fast and not letting her fall.

The remaining days before their departure to Paris passed too quickly. Violet lay in her bed the last night in Berkshire, too warm under the covers in the overheated room.

Her sleeplessness came from fear, not discomfort, the old panic sharpening itself inside her. All very well for Daniel to say it was best to face Jacobi and her fears, that Violet would be strong when the time came.

She saw no reason why Daniel and his lawyers couldn't take care of everything without her. She might have to sign papers of some sort, but she could do that in an office in London, couldn't she?

But Daniel was immovable. Violet was going with him to Paris. She'd look upon Jacobi and spit at him, then they'd go win Daniel's race.

Violet shuddered. If she saw Jacobi again, she wasn't certain what she'd do. She might go into one of her panics. She might run from him while he laughed. Or worse, she might feel sorry for him and forgive him again. Jacobi had played upon her the same way she played upon her mother's audiences. He might play upon her still.

But Daniel wouldn't let any of this happen, would he? He'd be there, making certain all went well. He wanted her to face Jacobi as Violet the woman, not the terrified girl.

I'll be with you, love. Every step of the way.

And then what? What would Daniel want from Violet after that? To be his lover? His wife?

Violet doubted the Duke of Kilmorgan, Hart Mackenzie, with his eagle eyes and penetrating stare, would allow Daniel to marry a lower-middle-class trickster from Southwark.

Daniel was in line to inherit the dukedom, albeit after Hart's two sons and Cameron, but tragic things could happen to entire families—illnesses, accidents. Daniel could be duke before he knew what happened. The Mackenzies might accept Violet if she would only ever be simple Mrs. Daniel Mackenzie, but perhaps not if there was a chance she'd become Duchess of Kilmorgan.

Violet rolled over and kicked off the covers again. The house was silent, the children having at last been herded to bed. Knowing that Violet and Daniel were to leave tomorrow, the little ones hadn't wanted to settle down.

Violet would miss them.

She sat up, reached for matches, and lit the candle in the old-fashioned chamber stick on her bed table. Tomorrow, she was leaving the shelter of this house for the world again, and the world was a dangerous place.

It's best to face something head on, smash it, and move on with your life, Daniel had said the day he'd first taken her out on Medusa. *Lingering and wondering, waiting and worrying . . . that kills you.*

He was right, and not just about Violet facing her past. She needed to face her present too.

Violet thrust her feet into slippers, opened the door of her room, and ventured into the corridor. She nearly tripped over Venus, who panted up at her, tail thumping.

"Shh." Violet put her finger to her lips, then reached down, her long braid falling over her shoulder, and patted the dog. Venus yawned noisily and got up to follow Violet.

The house had two long wings. The wide upstairs hall ran from one wing into the staircase hall, down a half flight of stairs, and up another half flight to the other wing of the house. Violet had been put in the guest wing, opposite the one that contained Daniel's room. She knew exactly which was Daniel's room, though, because she'd made it her business to know.

Silently Violet picked her way across the dark landing, her single candle lighting the way. She'd come to learn that one of the boards creaked in the middle of the landing—she avoided it.

Venus followed, her nails clicking when they left rugs for

bare floor. Outside Daniel's door, Venus sat down on her haunches and looked at Violet expectantly, tail moving.

"I need to go in alone," Violet whispered. She might be ridiculous explaining things to a dog, but she felt the need to. Venus looked up at her in seeming understanding.

Violet opened the door and slipped inside the room. Venus gave a resigned sigh and lay down in the hall as Violet shut the door.

Daniel's chamber was large and dark, the fire burning in the grate not as high as the fire in Violet's room. The flickering light showed a large, low-post bed against one wall, with a lump of blankets on it. From the lump came a very distinctive snore.

Violet had to smile, though her lips were stiff with fear. She crept forward, stepping carefully so as not to trip on a corner of the carpet, or a discarded boot, or perhaps another dog . . . She put to use her experience moving through the dark at her mother's séances to glide noiselessly to the bed.

Violet raised her candle. She had a moment of watery fear, worrying she'd gotten the room wrong, then the candlelight fell on Daniel's face.

He'd pushed the covers half off him and lay with his chest exposed. He'd been wearing a nightshirt, but sometime in the night had dragged it off and tossed it to the floor. The rest of the covers were mounded over his legs, dipping across his hips.

Daniel's face was rough with new beard, his hair sticking up on the pillow. His eyes were closed, lips parted, and again came the snore.

Violet stood gazing down on him, unable to move. Daniel was a beautiful man, carved flesh and bone, well muscled from his athletic and frenzied pace of life. Violet couldn't compare him to a god because he was so wonderfully human. Daniel was of the earth, and Violet was glad of it.

Wax dropped from the candle to splash on the sheet. Violet quickly blew out the candle, set it on the bedside table, and reached down to shake Daniel's shoulder.

A grunt came from Daniel's lips, but he didn't wake. Violet shook him again. She tried to say his name, but no sound would come from her mouth.

A hot hand suddenly closed around her wrist. Daniel grunted again as he peeled open his eyes, the amber glint of them catching in the firelight.

The grunt dissolved into *Mmm*. "What a nice dream." Daniel gave Violet a slow smile, his grip not loosening. "It stays even when I wake up."

"D—" The word stuck fast in Violet's throat.

Daniel's fingers softened on her, and he tucked his other hand behind his head. "Are you walking in your sleep? Or am I still dreaming?"

Violet swallowed. Her mouth was still too dry, and she coughed. Daniel didn't rush her. His hold turned to a caress, fingertips brushing the inside of her wrist.

Violet forced out the words in a hurried rush. "Daniel, I want to be your lover."

"I didn't think ye'd run in here in the dead of night to discuss your accounts." Daniel's brows drew down. "Ye didn't, did ye?"

"Don't tease." She could barely breathe.

Daniel caressed her again, his touch burning. "I can't help myself. I'm a wicked man." In spite of his glib words, a guarded light lingered in his eyes.

"I'm wicked too," Violet said. "I want this. I'm afraid, but I want this with you." *In case I never have another chance.* "I want to be your lover. Entirely."

Another caress as Daniel's chest rose sharply. "Are ye sure?"

"Very sure." Violet knew she should do something seductive—sit on the bed, touch him, flirt with him— anything but stand there like a frozen statue. "Please, Daniel. Before I can't."

Daniel studied her a moment longer, his fingers moving gently on her wrist. "If I were a stronger man, I'd send you away. Virtuously. For your own good. And mine." Daniel released her, reached up, closed his hand around the lace of her nightgown, and pulled her down to him. "But I'm not."

Chapter 27

Firelight kissed Daniel's body as he pulled Violet close. He did it gently, not forcing, his grip light. Violet knew she could get away if she wanted to, but she didn't want to. Not this time.

Daniel tugged her down until she lay on him, the barrier of covers between them, propped up on her hands so she didn't come down on his bare chest. He let go of the nightgown to loosen its buttons—one, two, three, four, five. Daniel kept his gaze on Violet's face as he loosened the placket enough for him to brush his hand inside.

Warm, rough-skinned fingers lifted the weight of her breast. Violet remained frozen, her hands on the mattress shaking with her weight. Daniel drew his hand over her breast, fingers closing over her nipple, which was already tight.

Daniel withdrew from the nightdress. Violet wanted to grab his hand and put it back inside, but she stopped herself. She wasn't certain what she should do, how to proceed. Daniel had been so tender with her in Marseille, but they'd never completed the act. She didn't know what was expected, or whether Daniel would simply pin her down and have her. Perhaps that was the usual method.

"I don't know what to do," she said rigidly. "You have to tell me."

Daniel's smile beamed in the darkness. "I'll do better than that, sweet."

He reached up with both hands, unbuttoned the last of the nightgown, and pushed it from her shoulders. Cool air, only a little heated from the fire, touched her skin.

"I won't rush you," Daniel said. "We have all night."

The nightgown's sleeves bunched at Violet's wrists, and her breasts hung free, unfettered. She'd never been bare in front of a man before. The red-bearded man hadn't undressed her—he'd simply shoved up her skirts and ripped her drawers out of his way.

This is different, she told her terrified self. *This is Daniel. This is what it is to be a man's lover, not his payment.*

Daniel slid both hands to her bare waist, caressing. He drew his touch up to her breasts again, both hands cupping her now. Violet took a sharp breath, but she made herself still, to *feel*.

What she felt was the heat of Daniel's fingers, his strength as he lifted her breasts in his hands, his gentleness as he caressed them. Her back wanted to arch, to press her breasts into the cups of his palms. Violet resisted, not knowing what he wanted.

"Love." Daniel lifted one hand to her face. "It's all right. No one will come in."

"I still don't know what to do." She couldn't find the words to explain. Violet, who knew all about people and how to read every one of their emotions, had no experience here.

Another caress to her cheek. "This goes both ways, remember? If you're feeling hungry, you feel hungry. *I'm* hungry for *you*."

"I don't know how to. I don't know what to do . . ."

"No rules for this in your world, are there?" Daniel's smile was lazy. "I'll tell you a secret. There is no guidebook. No rules. It's giving pleasure and getting it in return. Some lovers out there like to dictate every move, but not me. I'm all for enjoyin' it and ourselves. Nothing we do in this bed tonight is wrong."

Violet tried to still the shaking inside her. Her fear was deep, going back to a precise moment that had shaped the direction of her life. She'd changed in one instant from trusting girl to broken woman, no in-between.

Daniel wanted her to find the in-between, to live every second of the life she'd lost. And still Violet didn't know what to do.

"In Marseille, you let me touch you," she said.

"Yes." Daniel's voice was a pleasing rumble. "I remember."

"Let me do that again. I wasn't afraid then. Or less afraid anyway."

Daniel slid his hands to her wrists, taking them out of the sleeves that still confined her. Her nightdress fell gently across her lower back. "I think I'll be able to stand that, lass." He made a show of letting go of Violet, stretching his arms, tucking his hands beneath his head. "Touch all you want, wherever you want. Move the quilts and pillows when you need to. Let nothing get in your way."

Daniel watched her from half-closed eyes, firelight brushing gold to his unshaved whiskers. Perspiration gleamed on his throat, the hollow of it a shadowed dip between the hard spread of his collarbone.

Firelight also burnished the wiry curls on Daniel's chest. His abdomen was flat, speaking of his active life. The indent of his navel was visible above the covers, but the blankets that snaked across his hips cut off her view of anything lower.

Violet placed both hands on his chest. Daniel wasn't a statue; he wasn't a god. He was warm, living flesh, with a beating heart and a slow smile.

Violet closed her eyes and enjoyed the sensation of his aliveness, his *being*. That she was allowed to touch this beautiful man made her slightly dizzy.

She opened her eyes again to find Daniel still watching her, wondering what she would do. The fact that he didn't know gave Violet confidence. He was expecting nothing. He only waited.

Violet spread her fingers, the hair on Daniel's chest wiry but soft. She watched a curl twine around one of her fingertips and smiled.

"Do you know how beautiful you are when you smile, lass?" Daniel said softly. "It's like being touched by sunshine."

Violet didn't know how to respond. Daniel's smile could warm her to her toes, make her day brighter, but she was embarrassed to gush.

She spread her hands across his chest, finding his flat nipples, which were drawn to points as tight as hers. Not lingering, Violet moved to the hardness of his abdomen and dipped one finger into his navel.

Daniel laughed. His hands came up, then he stopped himself and forced them back to the pillow. "I said there'd be no rules, but I might have to beg you to not tickle me."

"You're ticklish?" Violet asked in surprise.

"Exceedingly so. Especially on my belly."

"Oh." Violet lifted her hand away. Then she gave him a mischievous look and danced her fingers across his abdomen.

Daniel snorted with laughter and caught her wrists. "Little devil."

Violet struggled with him, the playfulness relaxing her a bit. He was strong, though, telling her he could do as he pleased with her if he chose.

But he didn't choose. Violet easily slid her hands from his grip. "Peace."

Daniel waited, not trusting her, then finally he rested his arms back up alongside his pillow. "You're dangerous, woman."

Their tussle had shifted the covers down his legs. Violet stilled as she saw his cock resting against his lower abdomen, hard and waiting for her.

Violet had touched him before, had felt him come undone under her hand. But Violet had not yet looked at Daniel's full length, at the firm ridge of it, the sign of what their playfulness was leading to.

A rush of panic came at her. Violet closed her eyes as she silently beat it back.

She'd been afraid for so long, and she did not want to let fear ruin this moment. Daniel was giving her a gift—himself—without hurrying her. He was being as patient with her as she'd seen him be with his father's horses, as he coaxed the most timid to trust his touch.

Daniel knew how to watch, wait, encourage, and pull the best out of the horse. He could do the same with the children, and even his engines. He was a remarkable man.

Violet's panic rose like a wave of blackness, cutting off her breath and her vision. She fought it silently, too afraid even to move.

Daniel's touch broke through it. Violet pried open her eyes. Daniel lay without speaking, his fingers brushing her wrist, the softest touch. He knew what she feared, what she fought, and he didn't grow impatient, or angry. Daniel waited, the small touch on her hand guiding her back down from the dizzy heights of terror.

Holes of light poked through the dark wave, which started to recede. Violet drew in a cleansing breath, her heart beating too rapidly.

She realized she still wore her slippers, backless mules that weighed on her feet. She slid off the slippers and let them drop to the floor, then quickly pulled her nightgown all the way off.

Daniel didn't stop his gaze roving down her body, though he remained motionless, his hands again resting on either side of his pillow. "I must be the strongest man in the world. Have to be, to lie here while you're like that." His gaze flicked down her again. "You are the most beautiful thing I've ever seen, do you know that?"

Violet didn't stop to enjoy his praise. Fear stirred inside her again, and she needed to conquer it.

Daniel was beautiful. And sensual. When he'd made her feel so heavenly in his little apartment in Marseille, he'd instructed her to think sensual thoughts. Violet had brought up the memory of Daniel sharing the cigarette with her in London, and lying with her in the bed in the country inn.

The picture before her now was even more sensual. Daniel Mackenzie stretched upon the bed, quilts kicked to its foot. His hands were raised, out of the way, while his half-closed eyes showed his need.

Violet, who thought she'd never desire a man in her life,

wanted this one. Not only was Daniel beautiful, but he was caring. He'd proved himself honorable many more times—without trying—than Jacobi ever had. But with Jacobi, Violet had been a child looking for a father, not realizing that adults were fallible and could be cruel and even evil.

Violet was a woman now, wanting the man who wanted her.

Daniel did nothing as Violet slowly and carefully climbed over him. She rested her hands on his wrists, as though reassuring herself that by pressing him back into the mattress, he couldn't grab her, force her, do as he pleased.

Violet spent a moment looking at him lying under her, then she leaned to him and kissed his lips. Daniel let her keep holding him down, raising his head a little to meet the kiss.

They played that way for some time, kissing and tasting. When Violet lifted her head, knowing what would come next, edges of the panic threatened to return. "I still don't know what to do."

Daniel gave a little shrug. "There's not much to it. That hard thing you're feeling against your thigh goes right inside you. That's it, really."

Violet wet her lips. "I knew *that*."

"Well, then." Daniel's smile returned. "We're a step forward. How about we see what happens?"

But he didn't move. Daniel was letting Violet make the decision, letting her guide how far they took this. Daniel obviously wanted her—he was hard and ready, the pulse in his wrists beating swiftly under her clenching fingers.

Violet drew a long breath. Holding it, she eased herself down toward the blunt hardness that waited for her. Her breasts touched his chest as she slid back, and new fear touched her heart.

"It's all right," Daniel said. "I'm here with you."

Tears welled in Violet's eyes. Still holding Daniel's wrists, Violet slid her hips back and froze when his tip touched her opening.

"Take it slow." Daniel's gaze was intense. "I'm not going anywhere."

Slow goodness, he'd said. He'd proved to her that women

could feel pleasure, that passion wasn't entirely on the man's side. She'd been surprised, but he'd been right.

Violet made herself inch back. Daniel made a faint sound in his throat as she slid a little bit onto him. Then she felt him, penetrating her, entering a place where she'd only ever felt pain.

Another wave of panic lifted Violet and threatened to cast her into the wall. She'd hurt when she impacted, maybe shatter.

But no, when he'd put his mouth to her opening, it hadn't hurt. It had been beautiful. So beautiful that Violet had dissolved into powerful delight.

Daniel's voice worked through her terror. "I'll do this with you, Vi. We'll do it together."

Violet nodded. She could barely see him now. Before Violet could stop herself, she thrust her hips back, moving all the way onto him.

A long way. She was tight, but slick, and he went deep. A spark as sharp as lightning streaked through Violet, her skin heating as though she'd plunged into fire.

"*Daniel.*"

"I'm here, love."

"Don't let me fall," she begged.

"Never. I never would."

For some reason Violet knew if she let go of his wrists, she'd fall indeed, down into a black well of nothing. She'd never get free. She needed to hang on to Daniel, to not let him go.

Daniel gave her a slow smile, his eyes golden embers in the firelight. Violet kissed him, and then she couldn't stop kissing him. Exciting, fierce kisses, nothing slow about them.

At the same time, Violet waited for the grating pain, the intense hurt that had robbed her of everything she was. It didn't come. There was only Daniel inside her, his mouth on hers, his body moving as his hips began to work.

The sudden friction broke something open inside her. Violet threw back her head, wanting to scream. She bent back down, tears streaming from her eyes, and kissed Daniel. He lifted his hips again, thrusting.

A little faster, a little harder. Perspiration gleamed on his skin. Violet's tears kept falling—she couldn't make them stop.

This was a new beginning, Violet reborn, phoenix-like, in the fires of passion. The feelings inside her were novel and raw, burning her from the inside out.

Daniel rose a little on his elbows, continuing his thrusts. Violet couldn't make herself let go of him, but Daniel didn't seem to mind. His eyes half closed as he watched her, their gleam of gold like summer sunshine.

His lips parted as he pushed upward into her, thrusting hard, loving her. It was a moment of terrible beauty, Violet loosening and letting go, fear and ecstasy coalescing.

She heard herself cry his name. The silent, sleeping house might awake, and Violet didn't care. She kissed Daniel again, her tears dropping to his lips, then she whispered his name instead.

Daniel's eyes opened all the way. "Violet," he said clearly. "Oh, Christ."

He said it like a prayer, and then his eyes lost focus and a groan escaped his lips.

Daniel at last moved his wrists out of Violet's grip, proving he could have at any time. He caught her against him, his hands hard on her back, pulling her down to him.

Not imprisoning her. Loving her.

The last of Violet's tears trickled away as the ecstasy Daniel had introduced her to struck. She felt nothing but Daniel inside her, his arms around her, his breath on her face, his lips on hers.

Madness. Beautiful madness, where nothing mattered, and all was heat and wild freedom. Daniel opened the prison door for her, and Violet ran for the light.

～

Daniel caressed Violet's bare back as she lay limply on top of him, he still inside her.

His world had just changed. No dream could ever be as good as waking up to see Violet, the most beautiful woman in the world, standing over him, haloed by the firelight. An angel, one who looked down at him with dusky blue eyes and declared she wanted to be his lover.

Daniel knew what it had cost her to come to him. She'd barely been able to move or to speak, and yet she'd come.

He ran his hand through the silken weight of her hair. Violet holding him down had seemed to give her some comfort, as though reassuring herself that she could have control.

Daniel hadn't minded. Violet pinning him in place while she'd lowered herself onto him had been the most erotic thing he'd ever experienced. Maybe one night he'd suggest she tie him down—Daniel tethered to the headboard, unable to stop Violet doing anything she wanted to him.

He let out a little groan of pleasure, and Violet raised her head.

"I thought you'd fallen asleep," she said.

"No, just basking." Daniel threaded his fingers through her hair. "Don't want to sleep and miss this."

"I ought to have known you weren't asleep. You snore something awful."

"Huh. The dogs don't seem to mind."

Violet's smile was shy. "I don't mind either."

"Then my greatest dream has come true. A lovely woman who wants to share my bed doesn't care if I snore."

"I didn't say *that*." Her laughter shook him.

Daniel brushed her hair back, studying the dark blue of her eyes as her laughter wound down. Her warm breasts were fine cushions against his chest. "You all right, love?"

Violet knew what he meant. "I think so."

"But you aren't sure."

"Not really. I'm still scared. But better."

"Good." Daniel moved his hand to the back of her neck to pull her to him.

Violet resisted. "I ought to go."

"No, you ought to stay." His pull turned to a caress. "And we should do that again."

"If I stay too long, someone might catch me sneaking back to my room . . ."

"And they'll think it about bloody time." Daniel touched

the end of her nose. "My very scandalous family isn't easily shocked."

Violet looked uncertain. Daniel kept caressing, and eventually, she came down to him, her body relaxing into his. "Let's not go to Paris. I like it better here."

"Not go to Paris? Don't be daft. I need to show off my motorcar and win that race. You know it's an amazing machine. Thanks to your help."

"You know what I mean. You keep telling me I'm strong, Daniel, but I'm not. I'm afraid. I don't know what seeing Jacobi again will do to me."

Daniel ran his hands up her arms. "I know what *not* seeing him will do to you. You'll never be shut of him in your mind if you don't face him again."

Plus Daniel wanted to ask Jacobi a few things. He'd pry out of him the name of the red-bearded man and pay said man a visit.

For that, Daniel would go alone. He wasn't sure what would happen to Violet if she encountered her actual attacker, plus he didn't want Violet to see what Daniel would do to him.

"My reason tells me you are right," Violet said. The dim light and fear chiseled her face into sharpness. "But I'm having difficulty convincing myself."

Daniel traced her cheek. "Vi, I keep telling you that you're one of the strongest women I know. I'm going to teach you to believe it." He traced her cheek. "*And* I'll teach you to drive the motorcar."

Violet's eyes widened. "Me? Drive your precious motorcar?"

"Why not? You understand how it works, and you've helped me put most of it together. Think how green with envy the other lads will be, when I sail in with the fastest motor ever made with the most beautiful woman in the world at the tiller."

"You're very convinced no one else has come up with a design like yours."

"Very convinced." Daniel also knew he'd turned Violet's focus from her fears again. "I'm going to win this year. With you by my side."

Her eyes took on a tinge of excitement, she also forcing her thoughts from horrors of the past. "Do you really think we'll win?"

"I do." Daniel slid one hand behind her and tugged her back down to him. "But not, I'm thinking, right this moment."

This moment was not for the future, it was for finishing the best night of his life. Later they'd face what they needed to face, do what needed to be done. Now was the time to pull Violet close and continue what they'd begun.

Violet softened as she came to him, and Daniel proceeded to savor her all over again.

The house was still dark, the clocks striking five, when Violet crept back to her bedchamber. Daniel had seemed to think it perfectly fine if she were caught in his bed when the servants came in to stir up the fire and open the curtains, but Violet told him firmly that she would go. His kiss good night was long and lingering, but finally, he let her depart.

Violet had resumed her slippers and lit her candle again, not at all surprised to find Venus still lying outside Daniel's door. The dog snorted as she came awake, climbed to her feet, and yawned. She readily followed Violet down the short flight of stairs to the main landing and up again to the other wing. The house looked exactly the same as when Violet had moved through it a few hours ago, but Violet had profoundly changed.

An icy draft blew up the stairs when Violet was halfway up, as though someone had opened the front door below. The wind extinguished her candle and swirled her nightdress around her ankles.

Violet stopped, freezing in place. Perhaps whoever it was wouldn't see her and would walk on through the house, leaving Violet alone in the darkness.

Venus, on the other hand, stared down the stairs and wagged her tail, her body wriggling in joy. A heavy tread sounded on the stairs. Violet didn't move, but she sensed the person come toward her, closer and closer. Before he reached

her, Violet realized with some dismay, that he was Daniel's
uncle, Hart Mackenzie, the Duke of Kilmorgan.

What's more, he'd seen her. The duke stopped next to her
and peered sternly down at her through the gloom. "Are you
lost, Miss Devereaux?"

Chapter 28

Hart's golden eyes were shadowed in the dark but still pinned her fast.

"No. I was just . . ." Violet gestured with her flameless candle. "The privy."

"There's a water closet at the end of the guest wing. In the opposite direction."

"Ah. It's a large house . . ."

Hart laid his hand on her shoulder, turned her, and marched her the rest of the way up the half flight of stairs to her wing. He led her straight to her bedroom and opened the door. How he knew which was hers when this was the first she'd seen of him here, Violet had no idea.

Hart walked her all the way inside. He took the chamber stick from her hand and matches from his pocket and lit the candle.

Violet's fears came pouring back. Hart was a duke, one of the most powerful in Britain. He could do anything he liked. Violet was clad only in her nightgown, not even a dressing gown to cover her, and it must be fairly obvious what she'd been doing.

Hart set down the chamber stick. The candle flame wavered in the draft from the open door, which he didn't close.

The draft also brought a scent to Violet that she recognized from being with Daniel. That, paired with Hart's mussed hair and his lack of greatcoat though he'd been outside, drew her conclusion.

Her heart burned. Did the duchess know he'd been dallying with a woman? The anger at him for betraying his remarkable wife made Violet's head come up.

"Was there something you wanted, Your Grace?" she asked in icy tones.

"You were with my nephew."

"Perhaps."

"No perhaps about it. You're his lover."

Violet gave him a haughty look, perfected from her performances. "Daniel is a grown man, and I am a grown woman."

Hart looked Violet straight in the eye. Ian did that when he had something important to say. Hart did it to unnerve people and keep them unnerved. "I know all about you, Miss Devereaux. Your father was the last son of a poor French family who were excellent at getting something for nothing. Thieves and confidence men, every single one of them, and you with your séances and table turnings are carrying on the tradition. I'm going to ask you bluntly, what are your designs on Daniel?"

Violet's heart hurt again. "No designs at all. I'm helping with his motorcar, and that will be the end of it. No doubt I will remain in France while Daniel returns here. My mother will join me there. I thank you for looking after her while she resides in London. I take it she is still there?"

Hart ignored the question. "You plan to end your association with my very wealthy nephew? Who recently came into all the money in trust for him?"

Violet kept her head high. "I am not interested in Daniel's money, regardless of what you think."

The duke's gaze roved her, but not in lechery. He was assessing her the same way she assessed him.

"I know Daniel is trying to get you out of an unwanted

marriage," he said. "I don't mind him doing so. A woman shouldn't be trapped. But after that, you walk away."

Violet's anger caught in her throat. "I intend to. Daniel owes me nothing."

"No," Hart said in a hard voice. "He doesn't."

Violet knew Daniel could send her away whenever he wished. She'd always understood that. Whatever control he'd let her have in the bed tonight was illusion. If Daniel wanted Violet to stay with him, that would be his choice. But Violet leaving could be hers.

Now that Hart stood before her and told her to go, however, Violet knew what the pain of it would be. Daniel called her strong, but she knew she wasn't strong enough to leave Daniel behind for his own good.

"You might ask Daniel what he wants," Violet said, voice losing its steadiness.

"Daniel is young, he's wealthy, he's generous. Any woman would like to get her claws into him."

Violet remembered young Lady Victoria, who'd clung to Daniel's arm while she all but demanded Violet predict that Daniel would marry her. Lady Victoria had slavered over Daniel's wealth, powerful family, and handsomeness, and hadn't cared one whit for the man himself.

That Hart could equate Violet with the steely little debutante hurt. "I've told you I'd go. But it's Daniel's choice too, isn't it?"

"He's from a family that makes notoriously bad choices. Including me. I've made hellaciously awful ones. If I can save Danny from them, I will. I'm sure you need money, Miss Devereaux. Name a sum and go. A clean break. That's best."

"You insult me."

"I'm realistic, and so are you."

"I don't want your money." Violet stopped. The desperate voice inside her told her to reach out and take what he offered. When her association with Daniel was over, she'd need money. She'd concluded that Daniel was right that she should face Jacobi and finish with him, and then the rest of her life was hers. But life was hard.

"You do want it," Hart said. "I won't name a sum. I'll simply give it to you—*after* you've walked away from Daniel."

"A bargain you could easily forget." Violet met Hart's gaze with a pride to rival his. "I'll make a different bargain. You let the decision for me to leave be mine and Daniel's, on our terms. In return I won't let on to your wife that you were with a woman tonight. Or maybe I will, if you don't leave me in peace. The duchess is a kind soul, and she doesn't deserve to be betrayed by one such as you."

To Violet's surprise, the duke took on a look of pure astonishment. "With a woman . . . ?"

"I'm not a fool, Your Grace." Violet assessed him again. "You were outside, in the grass, with a woman, drinking brandy—to keep warm no doubt. I do hope you won't catch cold."

Hart stared at her, his shock palpable. "Miss Devereaux, you are laboring—"

"Leave her be, Hart."

The voice that rumbled through the open door to Violet's room didn't come from Daniel. It came from Ian Mackenzie.

Ian walked into the room, his gaze going not to the two people standing in the middle of it, but to the flame of the candle on the dresser.

"Goodness," Violet said shakily. "Does no one in this house stay in bed?"

Hart turned to face his brother. Hart was still angry, Violet could see, but when he looked at Ian, his face softened. There was love there, a powerful love that Violet had rarely seen.

"Well?" Hart said, his voice rough with impatience.

Instead of answering Hart, Ian moved his gaze from the candle flame and fixed it on Violet, or at least on Violet's shoulder. She saw him start to look back at the candle once or twice but then firm his resolve not to turn his head.

"When you are in Paris, you must look after Daniel," Ian said to Violet.

Violet blinked. "Me look after *him*?"

"Danny is like me," Ian said, ignoring her response. "He will go after what he wants and let nothing stand in his way.

But I have learned to be careful. Daniel, though, will do anything, even sacrifice himself, to win."

Ian's gaze didn't move from Violet's shoulder. One of his
hands was curled to a fist, the other half clenched. Ian too was
fully dressed, but no scent of outdoors came from him. He'd
been on his way out, not on his way in.

"You're not just talking about Daniel's motorcar race, are
you?" Violet asked.

Ian didn't change expression, but he switched his gaze
fully to Violet's eyes. "Don't let him."

Hart broke in. "Ian . . ."

Hart might have been a dust mote for all Ian paid attention
to him. "Don't let him," he said to Violet.

The intensity of Ian's gaze was unnerving. Violet wondered how he could exude more power with that look than
Hart could with all his harsh commands.

"I won't," Violet said to Ian.

"Promise me."

"Yes, I promise."

Ian looked at Violet for a few more heartbeats, then he
broke the gaze, studied the candle flame for a count of three,
then made to leave the room. He turned halfway back when he
reached the doorway.

"Hart was not with another woman," he said to Violet. "He
was with Eleanor. They like to meet in unusual places and try
unusual things." A look of amusement, a flicker only, passed
through Ian's eyes. "Beds are more comfortable."

Hart, the great Duke of Kilmorgan, flushed dark red. "Yes,
thank you, Ian."

Ian shared another amused look with Violet, turned for the
door, utterly ignored his brother, and walked out of the room.

Hart watched him go, again with the look of intense affection. "Ian has difficulty *not* saying exactly what he feels," he
said.

"So do you," Violet countered.

"Touché. But Ian's not wrong about one thing—Daniel is
reckless, and he's headstrong. I don't want to have to tell Cameron that Danny crashed his motorcar at this time trial of his

or bled to death in a knife fight with your husband. You seem to be a very careful young woman. If you insist on staying with Daniel, you had better take care of him. If something happens to him, I will hold you to blame."

Violet let out her breath in a huff. "I've just promised Ian I'd look out for him. But I don't know why either of you believe I can control every move he makes. Daniel does as he pleases."

"Do your best. If you want to prove you are good for Daniel, then make sure he comes to no harm."

Violet had not lost her fear of the duke, but overbearing men always put her back up. "Is that a threat, Your Grace?"

"It's a fact. Good night." The duke gave her a proper bow and at last departed, closing the door behind him.

He left Violet in a jumble of feelings—anger, outrage, wonder.

The fact that both Ian and Hart had stopped by to explain to her that Daniel needed looking after betrayed their worry about him. Cameron never said a word, but Violet had seen the same concern in him too. In Mac as well, as careless as he pretended to be.

Daniel was a beloved son, the Mackenzie men were telling her. And Violet needed to make certain he came to no harm.

Violet wasn't sure she could. She couldn't imagine that she had any power over Daniel, that he needed her the way she'd come to need him.

Even while she stood in the middle of her bedroom, worrying about what the duke and Ian had told her, the physical memory of joining with Daniel lingered. She still felt the absolute joy of lying in Daniel's arms while he made her feel like the most cherished woman in the world.

Her life had changed tonight. She knew that the Violet going forward would be nothing like the Violet she was leaving behind.

~

"Here we go," Daniel said to Violet. He leaned over the door to the driver's seat where Violet sat waiting, taking a moment to gaze upon his creation as well as the delectable woman inside it.

The motorcar, in all its glory, sat on a long, straight, empty farm road outside Paris, ready for a test run and Violet's first time driving it. The body, painted a sunny yellow, was long, low, and narrow, the wheels with their pneumatic rubber casings riding high around the chassis.

The gear chains and driveshaft were secure beneath the car, protected from breakage by a welded metal casing. At the very front of the car was the pump he and Violet had come up with, based on Violet's wind machine, to cool the monster engine. A high-backed bench stretched across the inside for driver and passenger, the padded, tooled leather giving the machine a touch of luxury. Beautiful Violet sitting upright on the seat made the whole thing perfect.

Daniel rubbed his ungloved hands together, breath fogging in the crisp winter air. This moment had been a long time coming.

"We put the gear in neutral," Daniel said, reaching over the door to move the stick. "This little lever here makes the ignition ready to go, and this one keeps it from sparking too soon. Then we ease in on the throttle to give it some fuel—like that. Pull out the choke and hold on to it—cuts off air to the fuel mix, better for starting. Right? Now, don't move."

Daniel lifted the hand crank from the space behind the seats, into which Simon had also packed a large picnic basket and some blankets. Daniel moved to the front of the car and inserted the crank into the starting hole.

Remembering to keep his thumb cupped with his fingers—he'd seen men break their wrists starting engines like this—he pulled up hard on the crank. The engine coughed once, tried to catch, then died. Daniel cranked again. "A little more throttle!" he called. Violet nodded and reached for the lever.

On the fifth try, the engine roared to life.

Daniel snatched away the now loose crank, tossed it into the back, and returned to Violet's side.

"More spark, that's it. And ease off on the choke. Excellent. Listen to that!"

The engine was loud, a constant sound, but at the same time it purred like a big cat. Daniel grinned as he wiped grease from his hands. The beast was alive.

He'd tested the motorcar in Berkshire a few times with Simon, but he'd not let Violet into the vehicle, as much as Violet had protested, until he made certain it was safe. He and Simon had put the brakes and gears through intense workings, Daniel fine-tuning and fiddling until everything was perfect. He'd spent the last few days, since their arrival in Paris, testing everything again. This morning, he'd announced that it was time for Violet to have her driving lesson. They'd brought the car out here via horse-drawn van, then Simon had helped unload it and left them to it.

Daniel climbed into the passenger seat, liking that the car was narrow enough that he and Violet had to sit close, arms and shoulders touching. "Ease back the clutch," he said to her. "Slide it into gear, give it some throttle . . . and off we go."

The car jerked then moved forward in fits and starts as Violet strove to figure out the correct balance between clutch and throttle.

Daniel sat patiently beside her, remembering how hard he'd worked to master the art when he'd driven his first motorcar. That had been at Gottlieb Daimler's factory, where he'd ended up ordering a car for himself. He'd gone from there to Mannheim to buy one of Benz's creations as well.

He'd had both motorcars shipped to his London house, drove them about a little, to the delight of his friends and neighbors, and then stripped them down.

The motorcar he'd built for today held none of the parts of the others, because that would be cheating. Daniel had learned everything he could by studying those cars, plus what others were doing in Britain, France, and America, then he built his from the ground up, based on his own ideas.

The car jerked along a while longer, then suddenly they were rolling forward, gliding smoothly. Violet's concentrated scowl turned to a big smile. "It's going!"

"Of course it is. You're making it go. Now, how about the next gear?"

Violet struggled to maneuver the lever into position as well as work the clutch and hold the tiller steady. "Maybe you should have made this a two-person machine," she said loudly over the engine. "Like a boat. One person to hold the tiller and the other to row."

Daniel let out a laugh. "Nay, driving alone is pure freedom. No horses, no coachmen, no grooms, no waiting on anyone else. Just you and the wind and the machine rumbling under you."

"Until you run out of fuel," Violet said. "Then you go nowhere."

"You're a pessimist, love. Don't throw cold water."

"I'm practical. How can I flee the police if the car won't run? With a horse, I can just gallop away."

"Until the horse drops dead. Let's try the brakes now."

Violet pumped the foot brake and the motorcar slowed. Daniel showed her how to gear down and brake some more, then pull the hand brake at the end. The car rolled more slowly until it stopped altogether.

Violet swung to Daniel, her eyes shining, smile wide. "I did it! I drove it."

She looked so happy like this, free of everything but the excitement of what she was doing. Daniel wanted to kiss her, but he held himself back. Let her enjoy the moment.

"Aye, that you did," Daniel said. "And ye did it well, just as I knew you would. Now, want to see how fast it will go?"

The look in her blue eyes said she did. "What do I do?"

"First we ready ourselves." Daniel reached into the back again and pulled out the other things he'd had Simon pack. He handed a bundle to Violet.

She stared at it. "You really want me to wear these?"

Daniel pulled a leather helmet over his head and settled goggles on his eyes. Gloves went on next. "If ye don't want bugs in your hair and dust in your eyes, yes."

Violet watched him then laughed. "You look like a fly." Her gaze dipped to his plaid-covered lap, and Daniel tightened. "A Scottish fly."

"Enough making fun of me, woman. Put it on."

Violet didn't look like a fly in her gear. She looked adorable.

They hadn't lain together since the night in Berkshire. Daniel had spent all the nights since reliving every moment of what they'd done. Every heated, erotic moment.

But Daniel had no intention of ruining what they'd begun by pushing her too hard. To that end, they had separate bed-chambers in the Grande Hotel, filled their days working on the motorcar, and filled their nights showing Violet the splendors of Paris.

Daniel had Violet get the car moving forward again and guided her to the first gear, then to second. When they were moving along at a smooth pace, it was time for the top gear. "Ease in more on the throttle. More . . . more . . . *yes.*"

The motorcar sped up, then sped up some more. Violet fought the tiller—Daniel really needed to find a more efficient steering mechanism. The wheels skidded on the mud of the farm road, but Violet moved the tiller from side to side, naturally finding her way out of the spin.

The car kept moving. Fast and faster. Fields stark with winter rushed by on either side of them.

Violet flashed Daniel a triumphant look, then she laughed. Wind buffeted them, freezing and bracing.

"It's like flying!" Violet shouted, and let out a whoop.

Violet embracing the world. A beautiful sight.

The road curved sharply to the right. Violet's eyes widened as the bend zoomed up fast. Daniel had his hands with hers on the tiller as they pulled it around the bend, the wheels slipping and sliding under them.

The car went into a spin. Daniel was thrown back into his seat, but Violet set her face and hung on to the tiller, her tongue pushed between her teeth. She wrestled with the car, pulling and pushing the brakes and gears until the car came out of its wild skidding and moved in a straight line again.

Daniel thought she'd gear down and stop the car, but Violet gave him a look of wild glee and pushed the motorcar to go even faster. She leaned forward, the joy on her face wonderful to behold.

They were moving fast, faster than Daniel had thought the car would go. The best speed anyone in Europe or America was reaching at the moment was about fifteen to twenty miles per hour. Daniel and Violet had left twenty far behind. Forty was more like it. Or fifty.

Violet let out a wild noise. Every bit of fear in her was gone. She was free. And Daniel loved her.

Desire, liking, admiration, exasperation—all had rolled together to form purest, warmest love. He knew he needed this woman in his life. Always.

Violet threw back her head and laughed. Daniel laughed with her, and she looked over at him, a hot smile on her face.

The next bend made them stop laughing. Violet screamed, pumped the brakes, and worked the tiller. They hit a deep patch of mud, and the motorcar spun freely across the narrow road.

The back end of the car went all the way around, and kept going. Daniel saw the furrowed field coming at them before he grabbed Violet and dragged her down, throwing himself over her.

The back end of the car went up a bank, and the front end swung across loose dirt in a sickening wave. The rear wheels stuck fast, the engine stalled, coughed, and then died. The front wheels at last ceased their wild spinning and went still. A crow cawed as it sailed by them, and then all was silence.

Chapter 29

"Vi." Daniel wrenched himself up, not liking how still Violet lay beneath him.

Violet blinked and stirred, and Daniel's heart banged with relief. Her goggles were half off, and she pulled them from her face as Daniel hauled her up.

The car's back end was mired in a furrow of rich black earth, the front end lifted a little off the ground. They were well and truly stuck.

Violet looked around, then her smile flashed. She let out another whoop and threw her arms around Daniel. "We were going so fast!"

Daniel grinned. "Not anymore."

Violet didn't appear to care. She pulled Daniel against her and tried to kiss him, but she banged into his goggles, and she laughed.

Daniel pulled off his goggles and dropped them behind the seat. He closed his arms around her, and their mouths met in a wild frenzy. Daniel was shaking, but not with cold.

The motorcar was a cramped space. But not so cramped Daniel couldn't lay Violet down across the seat and keep kissing her. Her leather cap came off, her hair wild, and she kissed Daniel back with fervor.

Daniel reached down and slid Violet's skirts upward. He expected her to break into panic, to push him away when he tugged at her drawers, his hardness heavy on her.

She didn't. Violet kissed him, ran her hands up his back, pulled off his leather helmet to let it fall outside the car. She let him skim off her drawers, the lawn fluttering like a white flag.

In very little time, he was inside her, connected to her, as he'd been dreaming of for days. Violet's eyes widened as he thrust, and again Daniel waited for her to dissolve into panic. But Violet lifted herself to him and pulled him close in frantic need.

It was awkward, rushed, crazy, freezing wind pouring over them. But the elation of the wild ride, the watery terror of the crash, the need they'd awakened in each other mixed and combusted.

Violet clung to Daniel as they rocked, he thrusting madly into her. The scent of newly turned earth, the scorched smell of the engine, and the scent of Violet and desire heightened the wild feeling of loving her.

Moments later, Violet's face softened with the beautiful pleasure he'd taught her to enjoy. Daniel kept going, feeling himself start to release far, far too soon.

"Love. Love." He scraped back her hair, his lips heavy on hers. He shuddered, burying himself as far as he could in her warmth, softness, scent.

"Love," Daniel said one more time, his heart in the word. Violet touched his face as they both found the height of release, kissing, clutching, holding.

Daniel shuddered again as he wound down, their kisses softening into heat and languid joy. The frigid wind rushed around them, but the look in Violet's eyes warmed him like a midsummer sun.

A farmer with a draft horse had to drag them out of the mud. How embarrassing. Violet stood by, her clothing restored, while Daniel chatted amiably with the farmer, drawing a smile from the dour-faced man. Charming the world as usual.

The car wouldn't start again—mud in the fuel pump, Daniel said, and the driveshaft might be bent. The farmer had to pull them all the way back to where Simon waited with the cart to take the motorcar into Paris.

"Aye, well," Daniel said, shrugging away the damage with his usual aplomb. "If I miss the Paris trial, I can have it fixed up for Nice. This sweetheart will do well on the hill-climb, I'm thinking."

"I couldn't stop it," Violet said. She wondered in the next moment whether she meant the car or her grab at Daniel that had led to them making love.

That coupling had been rapid and raw. It should have frightened Violet into one of her attacks of hysterics, but it hadn't.

Perhaps the amazing freedom of the speed she'd found, the crazed fear of the spin and crash, and Daniel's body hard on top of hers had let loose a wildness inside her, pushing away fear.

The feeling of the car responding for her and her body connecting with it had been almost as heady as connecting with Daniel. She couldn't stop her smiles at Daniel as they sat in the motorcar, now rolling behind the sturdy draft horse. Daniel's dark amber eyes were warm as he smiled back. Violet wanted to wrap the day around her and keep it forever.

But that night Daniel said they needed to continue their hunt for Jacobi.

Daniel and whatever contacts he had in Paris hadn't found Jacobi yet. Violet couldn't be unhappy about that, because Jacobi could be dangerous—or at least, he had dangerous friends. Violet hadn't quite understood that when she was younger, but looking back, she realized that Jacobi had known some rough men. Jacobi had gambled hard, but he and his friends had also fleeced plenty of people. She'd thought him amazingly clever until she'd understood better.

She also knew that Jacobi had an animal's instincts and knew how to protect himself. If Daniel hadn't found him yet, it meant Jacobi knew someone was looking for him and had gone to ground.

Daniel's idea for flushing him out was simple—he let it be

whispered in the right circles that Miss Violet Devereaux was now Mrs. Daniel Mackenzie. Jacobi would hear of this and perhaps seek them out. If not, Daniel had other ideas he'd try.

To back up the ruse, for the past few nights, and again tonight, Daniel had Violet dress in rich finery, then he took her out on the town.

I told you I'd show you life, and I will.

The life Daniel showed her was one Violet had only had glimpses of. Even their outing in Marseille paled in comparison. Now Violet put up her hair and bared her shoulders and walked among the wealthy and fashionable.

During her weeks in England, the four Mackenzie women had collaborated to covertly produce a full wardrobe for Violet. In London Violet had consented to be fitted for a few dresses with Beth's modiste, which Violet had insisted on paying for. Ainsley had looked triumphant when she'd said that they'd used the measurements to have the modiste make Violet many more clothes—evening gowns, walking dresses, morning gowns, and sturdy, warm dresses for when they worked on the car.

Violet's protests went unheeded. Isabella, Beth, and Eleanor joined in to persuade Violet to accept the clothes, and she had to give in gracefully. As much as Violet had to work to swallow her pride, she admitted that the ladies truly had been kind. She'd someday find a way to give them kindness in return.

The result of the Mackenzie ladies' planning was stunning. When Violet walked down the staircase of the Grande Hotel that evening, heads turned, gentlemen and ladies alike staring at her in admiration.

The gown she'd chosen was close-fitting, hugging her breasts and waist, the neckline lower than any she'd ever worn. Violet's shoulders were bare—the gown had no sleeves at all—and only thin, diamond-studded straps held the bodice in place.

The fabric was silk, in a deep, iridescent blue that changed hue as Violet moved. Long satin gloves covered her arms up over her elbows, and small diamonds, Daniel's latest gift, glinted in her hair.

A maid came after Violet with a fur wrap that would protect her from the cold, but the ensemble was meant to bare as much of Violet as tastefully possible. She was a graceful statue, come to life.

Daniel met her at the bottom of the stairs. He was resplendent in black coat and pristine white dress shirt, but he wore the formal kilt of the Mackenzies. For evening, instead of boots he wore leg-hugging socks and low shoes. Though his kilt drew stares from all, Violet noticed the ladies appreciating his muscular legs as well.

Daniel held out his arm, and Violet slipped her hand through its crook. The maid draped the furs over Violet, and Daniel led her out.

They'd done this for three nights running, the staff of the hotel always scurrying to serve them. Daniel Mackenzie was a wealthy Scotsman, from a prominent family. The lady? She was an enigma, but it didn't matter because she was Daniel Mackenzie's wife.

Daniel led Violet along the carpet stretching from hotel doorway to the low-slung carriage that waited for Monsieur and Madame to step inside.

The coach was the most luxurious money could hire. The inside was polished wood trimmed with the curving floral designs of the new art styles. Kerosene lights lit the inside, velvet curtains shut out the night and the hoi polloi, and coal boxes warmed their feet.

Daniel sat next to Violet on the cushioned seat, no false preservation of propriety. He slid his arm across the back of the seat, behind her, enclosing Violet in his warmth.

"How long?" Violet asked nervously.

"I imagine he'll emerge soon," Daniel said. "And then you'll be free." He patted her silk-clad knee. "You're good at playing roles. This one is no different."

"It *is* different. This is real."

"I won't argue with you." Daniel stretched out his long legs, which brushed hers through her thin skirt. "But you're doing brilliantly."

He leaned back and proceeded to enjoy the ride. Daniel enjoyed everything he did, from grubbing over his car in tattered clothes, to smoking with the foundry workers where he'd taken the car to be repaired, to rubbing elbows with Paris's elite.

They went to Restaurant Drouant first. Daniel took a table in the most visible part of the restaurant and was as relaxed here as he was when they ate privately in their hotel parlor. He spoke in a friendly way with the waiters, who were happy to bring him the best from the kitchen and the wine cellar.

Violet watched Daniel as he flashed his smile, as warmth lit his eyes, none of it false. He was a generous man, and that generosity came from his heart. Daniel truly didn't give a damn what others thought of him. He gave because he liked people, and not to gain praise or prestige.

I love him for it. I love him for everything he is.

At the moment Violet lived in a bubble of astonishing happiness. What would come after Paris, after finding Jacobi, she didn't know. The future stretched out, unknown and frightening.

After dining, Daniel took her to the Moulin Rouge, to be seen, and then to secret casinos—he seemed to know many of those. In the carriage before they arrived at the first casino, Daniel took a velvet pouch from his pocket, removed an eye-widening diamond bracelet, and clasped it around Violet's wrist.

Her jaw sagged. "Daniel . . . You can't . . ."

Daniel tipped her face to his and gave her a rough kiss on her lips. "No, my sweet. You're supposed to gush and coo and tell me how wonderful I am. That's why gentlemen give baubles to beautiful ladies."

Violet had to laugh. "No, it isn't."

"Aye, you're right. We do it so they'll rush to bed with us in hopes of getting more diamonds."

"I'm sorry you've known so many mercenary women." Violet touched the bracelet, marveling that this amazing man wanted to be with her. "They don't deserve you."

He shrugged. "I learned young not to engage my heart."

"So did I."

They regarded each other without speaking for a moment. The lonely boy Daniel had been shone out briefly, hidden again when he leaned to give her another kiss, this one slower, savoring.

The carriage pulled to a halt, much to Violet's disappointment. "More excitement," Daniel said, moving to the door. "The night is young . . . No, wait—it's mostly over. But no matter."

"You exhaust me," Violet said.

"You're loving every second of it."

Violet smiled, his energy contagious. "I am."

It was heady to be so carefree and unworried, to do whatever she wished. Daniel didn't insist on dictating where they'd go or what they'd do. He knew everyplace and everyone in town, so he presented Violet with a variety of choices, and they both chose what they thought they'd like best.

The casual friendliness of it warmed her. She and Daniel talked easily, sharing opinions, agreeing or disagreeing, putting their heads together to discuss things and laugh about them. They moved from ultra-extravagant operas to risqué cabaret shows without a blink. They drank champagne, brandy, and thick red wine. At the illegal casinos tucked away in covert houses, Daniel put stacks of money on roulette, hazard, and cards, losing without a qualm, but mostly he won.

"My uncle Ian taught me how to figure odds," Daniel said. "He's never, ever wrong, which can get frustrating. Never, for instance, engage him in billiards. You'll lose before you even approach the table. But I learned much from him as a youth, and now I've added my own experience."

Daniel had a mathematical mind that rivaled his uncle's. He could figure a string of numbers without writing a thing down, look at an equation then use it to make a piece of machinery work better, and calculate gambling odds on the fly. Daniel often praised his uncles and father for their cleverness, but Daniel had obviously inherited their nimbleness of mind.

Violet enjoyed being one of the glittering ladies who sat with their gentlemen while they played cards. Tonight Violet saw that two ladies at their table were subtly signaling what their gentlemen had in their hands to a third man who was quietly doing very well off them. Violet kept her indignation in check and tried not to smile when Daniel won most of the hands anyway.

Their ongoing subterfuge paid off at the end of the night. As Daniel and Violet emerged into the cold dawn from the last casino, a man in a long coat and battered hat stepped in front of Daniel and blocked their way.

"You're to come with me," he said. "Or face the consequences."

Several other men stepped out of the shadows. Violet didn't recognize them, but she recognized the type—hired bone-breakers.

Simon, who'd been quietly following them all night, materialized a little way up the street. Daniel made the little signal that told him to keep back.

"Dramatic," Daniel said. "But about bloody time. Shall we?"

Chapter 30

Violet's heart wouldn't slow. All the way from the sixth arrondissement to the eighteenth, she tried to take long breaths, to quiet the banging in her chest that was making her sick. Daniel, blast him, only leaned back in the seat, watching out the window as they went. He had Violet's hand in his, though, not letting go.

Jacobi's henchmen rode with the coach, though Daniel hadn't allowed them inside. No one was to threaten Violet, touch her, or even come near her. If any did that, all agreements were off.

They went to an area of Montmartre Violet had not frequented before. The narrow house they stopped before was respectable looking enough, the street clean, the houses quiet.

They went through a front door and into a cold staircase hall lit with kerosene lamps. Up a flight of stairs and into a room in the back of the house, which was warm and well furnished.

Violet's legs were shaking so much as they climbed the stairs that she feared she'd fall. Daniel slid his arm around her waist, lending his strength.

But Violet drew away from him and made herself walk on her own into the room, to face the man who'd risen from a chair in front of a paper-strewn table. Her mentor, and her husband, Jacobi Ferrand.

Violet's first thought upon seeing him was that he wasn't the old man she'd assumed he'd be. But, she supposed, when she'd been ten years old, a man in his thirties would already have seemed old to her. Now he was only about fifty or so, and while his hair had gray in it, he was far from decrepit.

Jacobi had never been tall, and Daniel topped him by a foot. His shoulders were slightly stooped, which made him look smaller, but his brown eyes under thick brows were keen and sharp. Violet had known those eyes to be full of interest in her and pride when she learned her lessons well.

They'd also filled with horrified guilt when he'd comforted her after the red-bearded man had gone. The guilt had still been there when he'd married her in the little church near his house, handing money to the priest and the few witnesses he'd pulled off the street.

Jacobi looked Daniel over. Violet saw Jacobi trying to read him as Violet had when she'd first met him, frowning when he found it difficult.

Jacobi's gaze went from Daniel to Violet, taking in her costly gown, the furs around her shoulders, the diamonds in her hair, and especially the wide band of diamonds on her gloved wrist. He hid his brief flash of avarice under a wide, warm smile and stretched out his arms.

"Violet. My little flower. I could scarcely believe it when I heard you had returned to Paris, married, no less. My child, all grown up. Have you no hug for your Jacobi?"

Violet took a step back. "No, I'm afraid I haven't."

Jacobi lowered his arms, looking hurt. "I know. I know. I was bad to you. But that was a long time ago, when I was a foolish, foolish man. I didn't understand what I was doing."

"Mmph, so you say," Daniel said. He kept to French. "But why don't we come to the reason you summoned us here, eh? Which was not for a fond reunion. Tell me your terms."

"Terms?" Violet blinked.

"Of the arrangement," Daniel said. "Jacobi is blackmailing me. Didn't I say?"

~⁓~

Daniel's pride in Violet swelled. She'd had every right to refuse to walk in here, to beg to remain in the carriage, to not accompany Daniel into the house.

Instead she stood straight and gazed at Jacobi with the coldness of a queen. Good. Daniel wanted the man who'd ruined her to understand that Violet couldn't be broken.

"*He* is blackmailing *you*?" she asked in imperious tones.

"Could you expect otherwise?" Daniel asked her.

"He married you under false pretenses, my dear," Jacobi said. "*Our* marriage is still legal. I am not dead, as you can see, nor did I seek an annulment. You are still Madame Jacobi Ferrand; therefore, you can't be Madame Daniel Mackenzie. I am, however, willing to keep quiet about our marriage for a reasonable fee from Mr. Mackenzie."

Daniel shot him an amused look. "Or, you can cooperate with my solicitor and annul the marriage, and I'll leave you in peace."

Jacobi looked Daniel up and down one more time, again trying to assess him and again failing. The failing bothered him.

"Violet belongs to me," Jacobi said.

"I belong to no one," Violet said, outrage in her voice. "Least of all to you."

Jacobi turned from Daniel and gave his full attention to Violet. "You are my *wife*. There are laws. I did bad things in the past to you, I know that, and believe me, I am sorry. I have always been sorry. But I was young and stupid, my little Violet. I owed money to a very bad man, lost it to him in his own gambling den. I was afraid, so afraid. And now—God has given me the chance to earn your forgiveness."

He was good, Daniel decided. Jacobi spoke with true remorse, a catch in his voice, shame in his eyes. He'd mastered the technique.

"Is my forgiveness that important to you?" Violet asked him.

Jacobi lowered his eyes. "All these years, Violet, I've been haunted by my failure to you. I've wanted to make it up to you for so long. Of course your forgiveness is important. The most important thing in the world."

Tears glistened on Violet's lashes, but she held herself rigid. "Then I'll never give it to you."

Jacobi looked up, confused. "But . . ." He drew a breath. "Dear God, my Violet, when did you become so hard?" He flicked a glance at Daniel. "Did *he* teach you?"

"No, *you* did." Violet moved to Jacobi, one slow step at a time. "You taught me everything I know. How to read people. How to manipulate them. How to know when the game is blown and it's time to run. You taught me all that. And then you betrayed me. But it shouldn't have come as such a surprise to me. Looking back, I see that you kept me beside you all those years as collateral, knowing that if you couldn't pay your debts one day, you'd still have me, a young and unstained girl, as a bargaining chip. I didn't understand this at the time, but some gentlemen will pay a fortune for a girl like that. You befriending me, teaching me—it was the same as someone investing in stocks and bonds." Violet reached Jacobi and stopped. "So, look me in the eye and tell me you didn't think of that the day you first saw me amazing children in the park with my card tricks."

Jacobi looked straight at her. "I didn't."

"You're a liar," Violet said clearly. "You taught me how to do that too."

Jacobi lost his hurt look. "And you were so very good at it. Did you lie to him too? He's a very rich man from a very rich family. You must be fleecing him for all he's worth."

Daniel said nothing. He folded his arms across his chest and let Violet speak. "I told him all about you," she said. "Everything you did. Everything *I* did."

Jacobi nodded. "I taught you that too. Honesty is often the best way to take in a mark."

"I told him what happened because I respect him," Violet said. "I had no way of knowing whether he'd turn away from me in disgust, but he deserved to know."

"I'm glad you did," Jacobi said. "It made him look for me,

which brought you back to me. Where you belong." His voice softened to real affection, and he reached up to touch Violet's cheek. "My little flower."

Violet slapped him, the sound of the blow ringing. Jacobi's eyes widened, and he pressed his hand to his face.

"Good for you, love," Daniel said.

Violet leaned to Jacobi, her eyes hot, voice sharp. "I do *not* belong to you. I never did. I was afraid to come here tonight, because I was afraid I'd panic when I saw you. I was even afraid I might forgive you, because you'd tell me your remorse, and I'd feel horrible if I didn't relent. I didn't want either of those things to happen, so I didn't want to see you. But he made me come." Violet didn't look at Daniel, didn't point at him. "Because Daniel knew I *needed* to see you. I needed to see that you're a pathetic, weak, friendless soul. That you're base enough to lock a sixteen-year-old girl into a room with a man and walk away, knowing that man was going to rape her. Oh, you don't like the word?" Violet leaned closer to Jacobi, who cringed away.

"He *raped* me, Jacobi. Yanked up my skirts, tore down my drawers, and entered me. It hurt—it hurt like nothing had ever hurt me before or has ever since. I vomited when it was over, and I dragged myself home, limping and bleeding. I couldn't sleep for days, couldn't eat, panicked at every noise in the night, and at the sound of every man's voice. And you had the gall to *apologize*, to make me forgive you, to offer to marry me, because *you* couldn't stand feeling remorseful. It would have been easier if you'd thrown me out and had done. But no, you kept me near, not letting me forget, making me believe *I* would be a bad person if I didn't understand. You were still manipulating me, still playing me." Violet stopped, her hands clenched, her eyes sparkling with rage. Daniel watched her force herself to stay calm. "Well, I never will forgive you. Never. You will have to live with your remorse and without me. I want the annulment or divorce, whatever it has to be."

Jacobi still held his red cheek as he stared at her. Daniel saw Jacobi realize he'd misjudged Violet. He'd always believed her weak and easily won. The fool.

Jacobi pointed at Daniel, who'd leaned against the edge of the table, settling in to watch Violet carve him up. "Your marriage to Mackenzie is not legal. You can hate me forever, but by law, you are bound to me."

"Well, I am here to become *un*bound to you," Violet snapped. "Then I will rush to bind myself in truth to Daniel, because he is a hundred times the man you are. A thousand. He knows me better than anyone else in the world, and I'm not afraid to trust him with that knowledge. He is generous, greathearted, understanding, kind—everything you are not. And I love him for it."

Daniel's heart thumped in thick, hard beats. He balled his fists, not wanting to disturb the tableau of Violet glaring at her old mentor, her back straight and eyes steely. She was beautiful.

"Do you mean that, sweet?" he asked.

Violet's eyelids flickered, but she drew a strengthening breath. "I do mean it. I love you, Daniel."

"Then the world is a beautiful place." Daniel unfolded his arms and left the table to put a heavy hand on Jacobi's shoulder. "You lose, Monsieur. I have brought a sheaf of papers with me, which will start the process of annulment. By the way, two of the men I have following me for protection are not pugilists, but solicitors, to see that everything is done nice and legal. One of them is French, an expert in French civil law, and one English, also well versed. The Englishman, however, is also very good at boxing and not above threatening to break fingers to get clients to sign things." Daniel had borrowed that gentleman from Mr. Sutton, who believed in combining the might of paperwork with the might of fists. Daniel put his other hand on Violet's shoulder, this touch much more gentle. "You might want to go, Vi. This could get messy."

"No." Violet was so rigid she might shatter. "Not until I'm finished with him."

Daniel released Jacobi to face Violet. "You are finished with him, love. I just saw you dismiss him from your life and from your heart. Now leave the mopping up to me."

Violet swallowed, still shaking. He saw anger, triumph,

and outrage in her eyes, the hard emotions swirling. Daniel
touched her cheek. "Do you trust me?"

Violet hesitated for a time, then she shot a glare at Jacobi
and gave Daniel a nod. "Very well."

"Good girl." Daniel pressed a kiss to her lips. "Simon will
take care of you, and I'll be along soon."

Violet didn't bow her head. She let Daniel walk her to the
door, new strength in her.

She'd faced down her past and a man who'd betrayed her,
and had realized finally that the betrayal was not her fault.
Jacobi was weak, and Violet was strong. She could turn from
him now and walk into her future.

"Oh, and Violet," Daniel said as she started out the door.
He sent her the warmest smile he had, putting his whole heart
into it. "I love you too."

Violet's answering look held a joy so fierce it made Daniel's heart sing. Violet gave Daniel a brief kiss on the lips, full
of fire and promise, and then she was gone.

Daniel knew the moment the door closed again that everything changed. Jacobi dropped his defeated pose and stood up
straighter, which made him look taller and more robust. The
air became charged, the real confrontation about to begin.

Jacobi met Daniel's gaze. "You're a fool, Mackenzie. I'll
never give her up."

"I think you will," Daniel said calmly.

The two solicitors had entered the room as Violet exited,
the French solicitor carrying the satchel of legal papers Daniel
had asked him to draw up. Daniel took the stack of papers
from him and thumped them to the table. "Come here and
sign these," Daniel said to Jacobi, "and I might not relieve my
temper on you."

"Threats of violence. How English."

"I'm Scots. We're not violent without good reason, but
when we are . . . watch out."

Jacobi stood his ground. "If I don't sign, what then? You'll
make her your mistress? Or go to jail for bigamy?"

Daniel shrugged and pulled out the chair in front of the table. "If you don't sign, I will find another way. Solicitors are clever, and I know many." Daniel strengthened his grip on the chair, gesturing Jacobi to it. "Or I could simply shoot you. That would end Violet's marriage to you quickly."

Jacobi's face lost some color. "You'd do that?"

"I don't like you, Monsieur Ferrand. Who knows what I'll do?"

Jacobi looked from Daniel to the solicitors, who waited quietly as they'd been instructed. Jacobi lifted his head. "I won't sign. You were a fool to come here, Mackenzie. Did you think I wouldn't be ready for you?"

"No," Daniel let go of the chair and tightened the glove over his right hand. "Of course you'd prepare for my visit. That's why it took you so long to contact me."

He advanced on Jacobi. Jacobi watched, uncertain, as Daniel stopped in front of him, still adjusting the glove.

"I had a mixed upbringing," Daniel said. "My father didn't pay as much attention to me as I wanted, but he did teach me good things. How to ride horses, how to take care of them, how not to suffer fools. My uncles had a big part in raising me too. From Uncle Mac, I learned how to appreciate a beautiful woman and how to make her the center of my world. Uncle Ian taught me about aiming for what I want and letting nothing—no person, no thought, no fear—stop me. He also taught me how to outthink opponents without letting on that they're being outthought." Daniel smiled a little. Ian had never come straight out and said any of this; Daniel had learned it from years of observing the man. "From Uncle Hart, I learned about ruthlessness. Hart also taught me about cultivating people to have on my side. Money isn't enough. You need friends, people who believe in you. Loyal ones, so when you need them, they're right behind you."

"You Scots like to hear yourselves talk."

"At least you're no longer calling me English. Now, from my dear aunties and my stepmother I learned about love. *Real* love, not just using people to make yourself feel good. Which is how I know that you can bleat on about Violet being your girl, but you never loved her. You taught her things and were proud when she parroted you. You had no idea what handing her over to that man to pay your debts would do to her. I think that in your muzzy little brain, you thought she owed it to you, that she'd be happy to let another use her to help you."

Jacobi's face hardened. "She was . . . ungrateful."

"I'm glad you said that. You've just made things so much easier. But I want to tell you about a few more people who raised me, while we have a moment. My dad and uncles have valets who are amazing. Trust the Mackenzies to pick up odd strays to work for them instead of going the usual route. Angelo, my dad's man, can do anything with horses. He taught me all about gentleness and how to make a beast trust me. Hart's man, Wilfred, once was an embezzler. He taught me all kinds of tricks about how paperwork and ledgers can be manipulated, and how to spot when someone is trying to do it to me. Uncle Hart liked him so much he made him his secretary, to make sure others weren't trying to cheat him. Uncle Ian's valet is a pickpocket, and trust me, I made him teach me everything he knew."

Daniel held up the knife he'd just plucked from Jacobi's coat pocket, and Jacobi's eyes widened. "He taught you to be a criminal?" Jacobi asked with a sneer.

"Not a criminal. I never steal from the innocent, like you do. Let me tell you about one more man, my Uncle Mac's valet, Bellamy. Know what he taught me?" Daniel tossed the knife into his left hand and balled up his right. He grinned. "Pugilism."

He gave Jacobi a swift, tight, and very satisfying punch to the face. The man's head rocked back, and blood streamed from his nose.

"Your mistake," Jacobi said. "You're paying for that."

Daniel knew he would pay. Jacobi would never have let Daniel in here to find him alone. Jacobi had prepared, as he'd stated.

Four men came through the door to the next room, four more from the hall. Bad odds, but nothing Daniel hadn't faced before. Simon would have gotten Violet well away by now, which was the point of Daniel standing and talking at Jacobi for so long.

As his borrowed pugilist engaged Jacobi's men, Daniel grabbed Jacobi and hauled him down to the table, shoving his face to the wood. "Give me the name of the man you let touch Violet. Now."

Jacobi gasped, then he laughed a little, blood puddling on the tabletop. "I don't remember."

Another thump of his head, and Jacobi grunted. "I think you do," Daniel said in a hard voice. "Want me to jog your memory again?"

"He's no one you can best. Trust me."

"You don't know my friends. I don't mean the ones I brought tonight." Daniel slammed Jacobi's head into the table once more. "*A name.*"

Jacobi groaned and whispered it. Daniel didn't recognize it, but he knew plenty of people who likely would.

Two men hauled Daniel off Jacobi, and Jacobi sat upright, catching his breath and wiping blood from his face.

Daniel was ready to fight. He wrested himself free, then dove in, yelling. He blocked a blow, and punched, his fist connecting with a gut. An upward cut to another, then a third man grabbed him from behind. Daniel elbowed the man as he spun loose then threw a punch upward to the man's jaw. Daniel still had the knife clenched in his left hand, ready.

This wasn't stage fighting, where each opponent waited politely for the hero to be free to engage him. The men came at Daniel at once, four on him. Daniel fought off four pairs of fists, feet, knees, elbows, he making practiced jabs with his knife before a chance bang to his wrist made him drop it.

No matter. He'd finished making speeches to Jacobi, but if Daniel had gone on, he could have explained that he'd learned all kinds of fighting in addition to what Bellamy had taught him. Daniel had learned much in the backstreets of Paris and Rome, as well as in Greece and the dark cold of Russia. He'd learned fast knife fighting in Morocco and Alexandria. The London man from the Japans, who'd given him the tattoo, had shown him some even more interesting hand-to-hand fighting—Daniel had never been able to best him.

He enjoyed putting all the fighting techniques to use. He might take a beating tonight, but Daniel would hold his own all the way. Violet would be safe, and Daniel would get her free of Jacobi no matter what he had to do.

After that? Well . . . Daniel had plenty to concentrate on here first.

The men Jacobi had hired were quite skilled. The odds were four to one, since the French solicitor wasn't a fighter at all. The poor man had already surrendered, sitting on a wooden chair and shielding his head with his arms. That left Daniel and Sutton's solicitor to fight against eight.

And Jacobi? He'd disappeared.

No, there he was, the bastard, slipping away into the hall. Going for reinforcements? Or just running for safety?

Daniel tried to fight his way toward him. But as good a fighter as Daniel was, trying to beat his way out from under four trained men wasn't easy.

As Daniel took more blows—to his head, his gut, his chest—he swore he heard voices he recognized. Not the pugilists Mr. Sutton had lent him, who were, with Simon, protecting Violet on her way back to the hotel, but the voices of men he'd known all his life.

Couldn't be. His head must have gotten pounded too hard.

Daniel kept punching, kicking, elbowing, grabbing, tripping. He had one of the men down, groaning, evening the odds a bit.

Over the shouts and sounds of furniture crashing he thought he heard Mac Mackenzie say, "This looks like a good game. Save any for me, Danny?"

Daniel couldn't afford to take his attention from the three men he was fighting, but the room seemed to suddenly fill up with Scotsmen. Loud voices, grating laughter, kilts.

Cameron Mackenzie, towering over everyone, grabbed one man fighting Daniel by the neck and punched his face. The man grunted then crumpled.

Daniel shook his head, his ears ringing. What the devil?

With Mac was Bellamy. The big man with the scarred faced never smiled much, but he was smiling now as he dragged a man off the other fighter and started hitting him. A third Mackenzie, Ian, stood in the doorway, surveying the fight. Probably calculating the odds.

"Ian!" Daniel yelled. Blood came out of his mouth. "Get Jacobi. Hold him."

Ian took a step back out of the room and vanished. Mac was laughing, swinging his fists. "And Hart says Paris isn't fun anymore."

"What the bloody hell are you doing here?" Daniel shouted.

"Helping you," Cameron answered. "Don't be ungrateful, Son."

No more conversation. Fighting needed to be done. Even now that Daniel's insane father and uncle and Bellamy were here to even things up, there was still a long way to go.

Daniel looked longingly at the door through which Jacobi had run. Had Ian caught him?

"Go!" Mac yelled at him, pushing Daniel to the door. "Cam and Bellamy and I have got this." Mac laughed as he turned around and fended off a blow. "Like old times, Cam."

Daniel made for the table where he'd left the stack of legal papers and found them gone. Damn Jacobi.

Daniel pushed his way out of the room and found the hall empty. So was the staircase and the room next door. He looked up the staircase and down. Which way?

He chose down. Jacobi might think he could still catch Violet outside. He wouldn't, though. Simon had his instructions.

When Daniel reached the ground floor, Ian appeared at the end of the hall. Without a word, Ian seized Daniel by the shoulder and steered him through a door and down another flight of stairs. Silently they went through another door together at the bottom and into a kitchen.

A fireplace was stoked high at the end of the room, sending out soothing warmth. Jacobi crouched on the hearth, thrusting papers into the fire.

Idiot. Daniel could just have another copy drawn up. But that would take time, and Jacobi could find somewhere else to hide or try to send more men to put Daniel out of the way.

Daniel gave Ian a nod. Both men charged Jacobi at the same time. Jacobi saw them and got to his feet in alarm, scattering papers. Then he picked up a pistol that had been hidden under the papers, aimed it, and fired it at Daniel.

Daniel felt the bullet go into his chest. He ran two more

steps, then his legs didn't work, and he fell heavily to his knees. Ian was shouting, running at Jacobi, who shot again. Ian went down—hit or taking cover, Daniel couldn't tell.

Daniel fell forward, onto his face, his cheek meeting the flagstone floor, and everything stopped.

Chapter 31

Violet heard the gunshot and was out of the carriage before Simon could stop her.

Violet had refused all Simon's pleas that she return to the hotel to wait for Daniel, because one thing Violet had learned about Jacobi was that he was a snake. Whatever Daniel thought Jacobi had planned, Jacobi would have put ten more contingencies into place. So she'd stayed, no matter how hard Simon had talked.

She'd been astonished to see three Mackenzie men and Bellamy arrive in another coach and go into the house, Mac pausing to flash her his big grin and tell her they'd come for the rescue. Simon had stopped Violet rushing in behind them, but when she heard the shot, she couldn't remain inside the coach.

Violet landed hard on the ground in her soft slippers, catching up the small train of the elegant dress. Simon tried to herd her back into the carriage, but Violet would have none of it. She ran for the front door.

When the second shot came, her heart lurched. The sound had come from, of all places, *below* her. Violet realized she stood near stairs that led down to the scullery, and the shot had come from behind the small windows there.

"Simon, this way!" she called, even as she ran down the flight of dirty, coal-stained stairs to the bottom.

Simon hurried down and pushed past her, reaching the kitchen door first. He turned the handle, and the door opened readily, not locked or bolted. Simon was surprised to find it unlocked, but Violet wasn't. Jacobi always left himself many easy exits from a building.

Violet ran through a squalid scullery into a kitchen, and stopped.

Daniel lay facedown on the flagstone floor, a pool of blood spreading from under him. Ian Mackenzie had a hand over his own arm, crimson under his fingers. Rage lit Ian's eyes, but he turned from Jacobi when he saw Violet in the doorway.

"No!" Ian shouted at her. "Go!"

Violet couldn't move. Daniel lay motionless, his head turned on the floor, bruises and blood nearly black on his paper-white face. He wasn't breathing. A dark, damp mark spotted the back of his jacket, the sign of a bullet. Jacobi stood by the fireplace, his face starkly pale, a mixture of horror and triumph in his eyes. He held a pistol.

Everything froze in place. Ian had shoved himself between Daniel and Jacobi's gun, and Simon was in front of Violet, protecting her.

Violet scarcely noticed. All she saw was Daniel on the floor, and nothing else in the world mattered.

Images poured through her head. Daniel sticking out his hand in greeting in the overcrowded dining room in London, smiling because he knew Violet was a fraud. Daniel had teased her from the beginning, pushing the planchette on the talking board so it spelled a rude word, finding the rigging that worked her effects, knocking out ghostly messages in Morse code—*You are lovely, do you know, lass?* He'd seen right through Violet, and he'd laughed at her.

She saw again Daniel daring her to take smoke from his cigarette, using the excuse to kiss her. Then Daniel standing in front of the stage in Marseille, laughing again, when she'd believed him dead. Indestructible.

He'd given Violet a taste of true freedom when he'd taken her up in the balloon, letting her leave the littleness of her day-to-day life behind. And he'd kissed her.

Slow goodness. Daniel had freed Violet from her prison little by little, teaching her to trust, showing her how to let go of pain and seek pleasure. And teaching her that letting go was not wrong.

Oh, and Violet. I love you too.

He'd said it offhandedly, but what Violet had seen in his eyes had been real. He'd meant it.

Violet had finally found a man who loved her for herself, for what she was. Something precious and incredibly rare, and Jacobi was taking it all away from her.

Violet had been alone before, but Daniel had changed everything. Before meeting him, she had been resigned to walk along her chosen road, alone, that road bleak and unending.

But now Violet knew differently. She'd tasted the magic.

Without Daniel, she would be rudderless. Empty. Alone in the dark.

She'd be the sixteen-year-old girl at the moment her innocence had shattered. From that instant, until she'd met Daniel, Violet had been existing. Walking, eating, sleeping, but not alive.

Daniel Mackenzie had smiled at her, and her world had changed. Violet had dragged in her first breath of life.

And now Jacobi had taken happiness and love away from her—again.

Violet heard the scream well in her throat, the desperate *No!* Then she was running forward, breaking away from Simon.

Jacobi's pistol discharged again, and Violet felt a sharp pain in her thigh. But she couldn't stop. She reached Jacobi and clawed at his face.

Jacobi lifted his arms to defend himself. Violet's hand landed on the pistol. The steel was hot, the stench of gunpowder harsh. She closed her hand around the gun, black and heavy, and tried to rip it away from Jacobi.

Jacobi struggled with her for it. The barrel now pointed at

Violet's heart, which was already so shattered she'd never feel
a bullet go into it.

Ian grabbed Jacobi, and Simon got his hands around Violet. The pistol turned, Violet still struggling to take it away
from Jacobi.

When it went off again, the sound deafened her. Violet
stumbled back from Jacobi in wild fear, but she now held the
pistol.

Jacobi looked at Violet in vast confusion, blood bubbling
on his lips. He said, "My flower . . ." Then life left his eyes,
and he fell forward onto her, sliding down the front of Violet's
beautiful dress.

Violet dropped the pistol. Simon grabbed it from the floor,
but Violet hardly noticed. She took staggering steps to Daniel's lifeless body and fell to her knees beside him.

She gathered Daniel up and rocked him, his blood warm
against her. No tears could pour from her eyes—they were
dry and aching. Her entire body hurt, and nothing would ever
be right again.

"Daniel, I love you," she said. The words tumbled out,
faster and faster. "Don't leave me. Please, Daniel. You are my
life. *I love you.* Don't leave me."

Daniel's blood was all over her, mixing with her own from
where she'd been shot and Jacobi's on the silk bodice. Violet's
wound brought pain, but nothing like what burned through
her heart.

She realized the rest of Daniel's family had come down to
the kitchen—Mac, Daniel's father, Bellamy. Cameron dropped
to the floor beside Violet, his eyes holding stark grief.

"Danny." Cameron's gravelly voice broke, the tears Violet
wanted to cry wetting his face. He stroked Daniel's hair.
"My boy."

Ian was there. He leaned past Cameron and tried to lift
Daniel. Violet held Daniel fast, not wanting to break any contact with him.

Cameron snarled. "Ian, leave him."

"Simon knows," Ian said. With amazing strength, he took
Daniel straight out of Violet's arms, and laid his limp body on
the floor.

Violet's tears came then. She curled up into a ball and pressed her hands over her face. Cameron's arm came around her, and he wept with her without shame. Whatever Daniel might think about his father, Cameron loved Daniel with a powerful love, one that matched Violet's own.

Simon was bending over Daniel, *hitting* him. Simon's fingers stained red, and he was slamming his closed fist to Daniel's chest, over and over.

Violet cried out. Simon kept pounding. Daniel grunted, his eyes flew open, and he gasped, then coughed.

"Damnation," he said, voice so weak it was barely audible. "The papers. Someone get the bloody papers."

"Don't matter," Simon answered, breathless and still on his knees. "I think your lady is a widow now."

Violet staggered up. Cameron was on his feet with her, his arms around her. They went down again beside Daniel, Simon moving for them. Daniel's face was ashen, his breathing labored. He was alive, but barely.

Daniel looked up at Violet in dismay. "What are you still doing here?" His voice rasped. "Simon, you're sacked."

"Shut up, Daniel," Violet said. "I love you. Do you hear me? *I love you.* I'm going to keep telling you that, every day if I have to, all right?"

Daniel could barely move his mouth to smile, but the look in his eyes was enough. "Fine by me."

Cameron stroked Daniel's hair, his tears still falling. "Be quiet, Danny," he said. "Just rest now."

"I still want to know what you're doing here." Daniel could barely speak as he glared at his father, but he kept talking. Bloody stubborn man. "But later." He closed his fingers weakly around Violet's. "Stay with me, Vi, all right? Now and always."

Violet's tears came again, but they were cleansing. She nodded. "Now and always."

Daniel squeezed her hand, then his fingers loosened, too weak. "Good. Love you, sweet Violet. Damn, but I love you."

Violet lifted his hand to her chest, holding it tight. "Stop talking now. You need a surgeon."

"Mmm." Daniel's eyes slid closed, but his fingers remained firmly around hers. "That's my Violet. Ever practical."

Daniel woke again, flat on his back in his Parisian hotel room, hurting all over. But it wasn't so bad, because Violet lay next to him, clad in a thick dressing gown, her hair in a long braid. She was asleep, her lashes dark against her face, her breathing soft and even.

Images and sensations swirled back at him—Jacobi, the fight, pain, Violet's voice as she told him she loved him.

She was beautiful when she slept. And when she was awake. When she was naked and when she was clothed—but especially when she was naked.

Daniel lifted his hand—after a moment of trying to remember how that worked—and smoothed Violet's hair.

Her eyes flew open, and she half sat up. "Daniel."

"That's me." Daniel put his hand to his head. "I think. What the devil happened? Did we get the papers back from Jacobi? The solicitors keep copies, but I need him to sign . . ."

Violet's fingers on his lips stopped his flow of words. "Jacobi is dead. Buried already. The papers are no longer necessary."

Daniel stared. "Dead and buried? Dear God, how long have I been asleep?"

He vaguely remembered Simon's voice saying that Violet was now a widow, but everything after the gunshot was a bit fuzzy. Except Violet's repeated declaration that she loved him. *That* he remembered.

"The surgeon sewed you up a week ago. Your father found the best in Paris and dragged him to you. The best nurses too."

"Kind of him." Daniel remembered his surprise at hearing Mac's voice, seeing Ian and Cameron in Jacobi's house. "What is Dad even doing here? And my uncles? Was there a spontaneous gathering of Scotsmen in Paris?"

Violet's sudden smile was like June sunshine. "My mother had one of her visions."

Daniel rubbed his forehead, which was aching. "You mean she saw me fighting eight men at a small house in Montmartre?"

"She saw both of us fighting for our lives. She said it was a confusion of fighting, gunshots, blood, you falling dead. She grew so alarmed she demanded to be taken to Paris to make sure we were all right. Your aunt Eleanor decided it was best she come."

Daniel hurt too much to laugh. "You win, love. I'll never cast doubt on your mother's gift again. And I suppose my entire family, who can't keep themselves to themselves, had to traipse after her?"

"Ainsley offered to come with my mother alone, but your father wouldn't let her go without him. Then Ian insisted on coming too, and Beth refused to remain behind if he did. Mac and Isabella grew worried enough to abandon their soirees and come over with them. Everyone is here, except the duke and duchess, who stayed behind to watch over the children."

"All right, so they came to Paris." Daniel tried to sort his thoughts. "But how did they know exactly where to find us, if your mother's vision wasn't precise?"

"One of the pugilists you borrowed from Mr. Sutton returned to the hotel to make sure Jacobi hadn't sent men to waylay us here. He found your family waiting in your rooms and told them where you'd gone. The ladies stayed put—after a great deal of argument, I hear—and your uncles and father came." Violet paused. "Your father has been very upset. He cares a great deal about you."

"Dad?" Daniel nodded quietly. "Aye, I know. He's awkward about showing it, but I know." Cameron had always been gruff, and slow to show affection, but Daniel had always known love was there, even in the frustrating times.

"He wasn't awkward when we thought you were dead," Violet said. "He cried."

"Poor man. And then I lived."

"Don't make fun. He thought he'd lost you. So did I." Violet's voice broke, her eyes filling with tears.

Daniel touched her cheek. "I told you before, love, I'm resilient. I stayed alive so I could be with you."

"You had a fever, a terrible fever. The surgeon thought you wouldn't survive. I was so afraid."

"Don't fret, my sweet. I'm very good at recovering." Daniel

caressed her cheek again, thumb brushing away tears. "You know, if Jacobi is dead, you truly are free now."

"Yes."

"And yet, you're still here."

Violet's lips curved into her smile. "Yes."

"I'll see if I can't make ye stay, Mrs. Mackenzie."

"I'm not . . ."

"Not yet. But you will be."

Violet bit her lip, the light in her eyes dying. "Daniel, I killed him. I had the gun in my hands, and I turned it around and fired it at him." She closed her eyes for a moment. "Mac told the police that Ian and Simon struggled with Jacobi for the gun after he shot me, and the gun went off. Simon corroborated, and Ian . . . just said nothing."

"That's Ian. Has trouble lying, so he shuts up." Daniel scowled. "Wait. *Shot you?*"

Violet moved aside a fold of her dressing gown to show a thick bandage around her thigh. "The surgeon said it was clean and did little damage. It just needs to knit. Same with Ian's arm."

Daniel's anger surged, which made his head pound. "Bloody hell, woman. Ye were supposed to go with Simon back to the hotel. Not run in after me to get yourself shot."

Her blue eyes sparkled. "If I hadn't stayed, Simon wouldn't have been there to save your life."

"But if you had died, love, I wouldn't have wanted to live."

Violet stilled. Daniel caressed her face again, his heart pounding and making him sick. If he'd lost her . . .

He cupped his hand around the back of her neck, pulled her down to him, and kissed her. The kiss grew long, warming, seeking.

"I almost lost you," Violet whispered. "Don't ever do that to me again."

"Never." Daniel kissed her softly again. "Marry me, Violet Devereaux."

Violet caught her breath. "Marry . . . ?"

Daniel attempted a shrug, flinched from the wash of pain the movement brought, and stilled until it receded. "We've been pretending to be man and wife. Why not make it real?"

Her look turned cautious. "I'm not the sort of woman a man like you marries. It would be a misalliance."

Daniel stopped smiling. "Listen to me, love. The Mackenzies are aristocrats only because one of our ancestors saved the life of a king in 1300 and something. The king was grateful, so he called that Mackenzie a duke. Queen Vicki decided she'd show how much she loved the Scots by making my grandfather duke in the English peerage about fifty years ago. But we're Scottish, not English, and we're not obsessed with titles. The great Hart Mackenzie, Duke of Kilmorgan, isn't even clan leader. Oh no, Hart bends his knee and pledges fealty to The Mackenzie at every clan gathering, and he's not ashamed to do it. My family would be far happier if I married you, an intelligent woman with the fortitude to stand up to me, than if I married someone like Lady Victoria Whatsit, a wisp of a girl who only wants a rich husband. They'd have to have dinner with her, you see, and your conversation is so much more interesting."

Violet was laughing. "Daniel."

"Therefore, you should marry me, Violet. It's the only reasonable solution."

"I'm older than you."

"I prefer it that way. I grew up fast, and I have no patience with girls fresh out of the schoolroom."

"And I'm a fraud. You knew that the moment you met me. I've been so many different people."

"And now you'll be Violet Mackenzie." He touched the tip of her nose. "I know exactly who you are. And so do you."

"Yes."

Daniel's heart beat faster. "Yes, you know who you are?"

"Yes, I'll marry you." Violet's smile broke through, the look in her eyes telling him all he needed to know.

"Vi." Daniel closed his eyes. The emotions pouring through him made his body ache like hell, but the pain was a small price to pay. He opened his eyes again. "Vi, you're . . ." Daniel gave up and pulled her down to him. "Don't ever go," he said, voice harsh. "Without you, my life would be . . . just going through the motions."

Words died as Daniel held her. Violet rested her forehead

against his, her tears falling to his cheeks. "I can't go back to being without you," she said. "I can't."

"Then we won't ever be apart." Daniel slid his hand beneath her hair. "We won't ever."

"I love you, Daniel Mackenzie."

"I love you Violet . . . Whoever you might be today."

"Mackenzie," she said, and her smile filled his world. "I will always be Violet Mackenzie."

"The best name I've ever heard," Daniel said, and lost himself in her kiss.

Chapter 32

The next several months were a whirlwind. Daniel recovered, then recruited Simon to help him finish the last task he wanted to accomplish before he left France.

Daniel fairly quickly ran the red-bearded man to earth. Jacobi had given him the name Edmund Collard, who, it turned out, owned several bistros and gambling establishments in Paris. Collard also loaned money to gentlemen at high rates of return—usually to use at his roulette tables—then threatened dire fates if the men couldn't pay him back.

Daniel had spent his convalescence learning much about Collard's day-to-day routines, and he entered one of Collard's bistros one night when he knew the man would be there.

Collard sat at a private table in a corner, a few gentlemen with him. His finely tailored suit, well-made gloves, and neatly trimmed beard and side whiskers made him look like any other respectable Parisian businessman. He held a thick cigar in one hand, a glass of tawny port in the other as he spoke to the gentlemen at his table.

Collard appeared to be perfectly ordinary, with the exception of his eyes, which were like cold steel.

Daniel saw those eyes turn to him as he walked to Collard's table. Collard took in Daniel's expensive suit and gold-headed walking stick with the air of one who could calculate worth in the space of a moment. Daniel looked like a wealthy Briton come to Paris to spend his money, which was exactly how Daniel wanted to appear.

As Collard assessed him, Daniel reached the table and leaned to him. "A word in private, if you please, Monsieur."

Collard looked him over again. Daniel had set this up carefully, making certain Collard learned that a young, wealthy Scotsman who liked to gamble sought to borrow money from him. The young man had gotten himself into a bit of a bother, went the rumors Daniel had made sure circulated. He would put himself completely into Collard's hands.

Collard nodded, unhurriedly laid aside his cigar, excused himself to his friends, and led Daniel through a door in the back of the restaurant. On the other side was a room full of ladies and gentlemen gathered around five roulette wheels. The clacking of the wheels, the heat of the bodies, the scent of smoke and perfume, and the groans or laughter of the players filled the space.

Daniel followed Collard through another door and into an office, where Collard offered Daniel a brandy and poured it himself. Daniel accepted the brandy, took a sip, then dashed the rest of the liquid into Collard's face.

Collard blinked a moment in surprise, then dangerous rage flared in his eyes. He reached for a bell on his desk, but Daniel brought the walking stick down on Collard's wrist. Collard struggled, but Daniel held his wrist firmly.

"I've come on behalf of a friend," Daniel said, amazed his voice was so steady. "You knew her as Violette."

Collard's face remained blank. He'd never heard of her.

This was the man whose face Violet had seen as she'd lost her innocence, as well as any sense of comfort in the world. Because of him, Violet had faced pain, terror, and humiliation, followed by years of fear, confusion, and shame. Collard and Jacobi between them had robbed her of a normal marriage, a family, and any idea that life could be punctuated with moments of happiness.

And Collard couldn't remember her name, if he'd even bothered to learn it.

Collard had ruined Violet in all ways, and Daniel wasn't about to let him get away with that. And who knew how many other young women he'd destroyed before or since? Or would destroy in the days to come?

"I'm not going to tell you about her," Daniel said. "Who she is and what she's like. Because you don't deserve to know. I'm not going to share one single second of her with you. I'll just say that though you did your best to destroy her, she wouldn't stay destroyed. Because she's far stronger than you, far better than you can ever hope to be. And the fact that you don't even know what a monster you are means I'm ending this conversation right now."

Daniel let up on his walking stick but drew it back and swung it at Collard's head. Collard raised his hands, snatching the stick as it came down, jerked it from Daniel's grip, and tossed it aside.

Daniel didn't mind. Before Collard could recover, Daniel was on him, his fists coming down on Collard's face again and again. The man fought back, and Daniel struggled with him, his still-healing torso aching.

Daniel's ancestors had been warriors. Old Malcolm Mackenzie had survived Culloden by cutting his way out of a pack of Englishmen who'd just slaughtered his four brothers and his father. Then he'd turned around, killed his family's killers, and gone on a rampage of revenge.

Only a few generations stood between Daniel and Old Malcolm, who hadn't been old at the time. Malcolm had been twenty-five when he'd cut his way to freedom, the same age Daniel was now. Tonight Malcolm lived again in Daniel, and Daniel's bloodlust responded. Revenge was something Scotsmen knew all about.

Daniel had little memory of what he did in that room. He only saw the bearded man's face, which quickly grew red with blood, and Collard's eyes, which lost their anger and filled with fear and desperation. Daniel heard Collard begging for mercy. But Violet had asked for mercy too, and Collard hadn't given it to her.

People did come; the fight wasn't silent. Hands tried to pull Daniel back—French police, he saw dimly—but Daniel's madness had taken over.

Ian felt this way, a part of Daniel realized. This same black rage had risen within the younger Ian when he couldn't make himself understood—when Ian hadn't understood himself what he was feeling. The rage had come out in violence, the only thing that could assuage it.

Even stronger hands pulled at Daniel now. Daniel thought he recognized Hart Mackenzie, but when his vision cleared a little, he realized the man was Lloyd Fellows, Hart's half-brother and a Scotland Yard detective.

Daniel shook off Fellows and kept fighting. Collard had curled into a ball, whimpering and bloody. Daniel was bloody himself, his beautiful new jacket a mess, and he didn't give a fuck.

"Daniel." Fellows shook him. "You've got to *stop*."

Daniel swung to him, feeling blood on his face, madness in his heart. "Why? He didn't stop for Violet."

Fellows's hands clamped down on Daniel's shoulders, and he spoke loudly and carefully. "You have to leave, Daniel. If you stay, I might have to arrest you for murder. Go. I have this."

Daniel looked up at the uncle who'd lived the first part of his life enraged at the Mackenzies for robbing him of what he thought was his. The anger was gone from Fellows now, replaced by contentment, especially now that he'd married. But he too possessed the steely rage of the Mackenzies. The blood of Old Malcolm ran in his veins as well.

"I need to do this," Daniel said, out of breath.

"You *have* done it. He'll not last much longer. But you have to let me finish it."

"Why?" This was personal.

"Because I'm a policeman," Fellows said, his feral smile worthy of any Mackenzie. "I have friends in the Sûreté. This man is running an illegal gambling house, and I'll wager he'll resist his arrest."

Daniel still didn't want to go. His blood was hot, and his temper wasn't mitigated.

But the logical part of Daniel knew Fellows was right. If Daniel killed the man, as low a life as he was, Daniel would be arrested and tried for murder. Fellows, on the other hand, a detective chief inspector of Scotland Yard, with many friends and connections in the Sûreté, would be lauded for bringing down a criminal.

Daniel nodded, still struggling to breathe. He ached all over, though his berserker madness barely let him acknowledge it.

"Don't let him get away," Daniel said.

"No," Fellows answered. "You can trust me."

Daniel nodded again. Even more than his uncles, even more than his father, Fellows understood. He'd battled the dark for a long time.

Daniel looked down at Collard. The man's face and head were bleeding freely, his hands swollen and broken. He looked up at Daniel in dire fear, which made Daniel feel slightly better.

Collard then threw Fellows a look of hope and calculation, which made Daniel laugh. The man had no idea what Fellows was capable of.

Laughing hurt, though, so Daniel only gave his uncle a salute and made his way out of the room. One of the policemen guided him to a back door that led out into the night.

Simon, waiting in the little lane behind the building, got Daniel into a coach. Daniel was a mess, and he was pretty sure he'd opened up the gunshot wound again, but he didn't care.

He didn't want to go to Violet like this, so he went to his father instead. Violet wasn't at the hotel in any case, it turned out—she'd gone out with Ainsley and Daniel's aunts for shopping and supper.

Cameron came down and helped Simon and the doorman get Daniel up the back stairs to Cameron's suite.

Daniel, spent, collapsed onto a sofa. "I did it," he said as Cameron shoved a full glass of whiskey into his hands. "I avenged her."

"I know you did, Son," Cameron said, and the pride in Cameron's eyes was all Daniel needed.

The wedding of Daniel Mackenzie and Violet Devereaux took place in May at Kilmorgan Castle. No longer a castle, Kilmorgan was a giant of a Georgian-style house, stretching itself across a green expanse before a backdrop of distant mountains. The wedding was conducted in the ballroom. The entire house streamed with white ribbons, lily of the valley, pink and white roses, and blue forget-me-nots. Violet's gown had a close-fitting creamy silk bodice beaded with mother-of-pearl and a smattering of real diamonds, and sleeves of fine lace. A silk skirt, decorated with more lace, flowed gracefully from her waist. She wore a veil, sheer gauze suspended from a crown of roses and forget-me-nots. The entire ensemble was stunning—Violet gazed at herself in the mirror after the Mackenzie ladies and daughters dressed her and scarcely recognized herself.

So many things had happened between her finding Daniel shot in the kitchen in Montmartre and Violet standing at the end of the crowded ballroom, guests turning expectantly as she walked in on Cameron's arm.

They'd won the uphill race at Nice in Daniel's newly repaired motorcar, Violet driving it to victory. They'd returned to Berkshire, where Cameron and Daniel threw themselves into training the horses, and Violet became swept up in that as well. She traveled with the family to the opening race in Newmarket and realized that this was the first of many times she'd come here with the Mackenzies. This was part of Daniel's life, and now she was part of it too.

Then they'd gone to Kilmorgan, where Violet had stood a full minute after she stepped out of the carriage to stare at the vast house in shock. She'd learned quickly, though, that the large place warmed when filled with the entire family, ten children, and six dogs.

Daniel would not talk about how he'd injured himself again in Paris, why his hands were a skinned mess and his chest had to be restitched. Only once did Daniel mention where he'd gone to get into such a state, and that was on the train after Nice and the hill race.

"This chap with the red beard," he'd mentioned casually as

he and Violet sat alone in a first-class compartment. "You'll never have to worry about him again. I hear he's dead."

"Dead." Everything around Violet seemed to stop, despite the train rushing onward.

Daniel leaned back in the seat, as casual as ever, a glass of his favorite whiskey in his hand. "Apparently he ran illegal roulette rooms in Paris. His other crimes included usury and extortion, plus involvement in a few murders of gentlemen who couldn't pay him back. He got himself killed while resisting arrest, I heard. I had this from my uncle Fellows, who was there."

Daniel was lying to her. Blatantly and glibly. He was aware Violet knew he was lying, and he didn't care.

The red-bearded man was gone. No matter how it had happened, the result was the same.

Violet wasn't certain what she felt—relief, triumph? Nothing. Or maybe something. But she was numb.

It was over. Daniel had made certain of it, whatever he'd done. For her.

Violet kissed him softly, lifted his glass of whiskey and took a sip herself, then snuggled down onto his shoulder.

Now Violet stood in the decorated ballroom, her hand on Cameron Mackenzie's arm. The tall Cameron would lead her down the aisle to Daniel.

Ian Mackenzie waited next to Daniel, having agreed to be his groomsman. While they'd still been in Paris, waiting for Daniel to heal, Ian had pulled Violet aside. "You kept him safe," he said. "Thank you."

"Safe?" Violet shook her head. "I got him shot. I did everything *but* keep him safe."

"He lived because of you. He did everything for you." Ian paused, glancing away as though gathering his thoughts before looking directly at Violet, his golden eyes like a flash of sunlight. "He needs someone to live for. Not just inventions."

Violet tried a smile. "His inventions are very important to him."

Ian's expression didn't change. "Family is more important. Now you are his family."

And that was the end of the discussion.

The guests in the ballroom turned as Violet walked past

them. They were all members of the family, or close friends and neighbors. No one else, Daniel had said severely. This was to be a private occasion, no showing off to the world.

For the private occasion, the ballroom was packed. Most of the guests were Mackenzies, the room filled with blue and green plaid. Some were McBrides, Ainsley's brothers—the four of them and their families at the front of the room. Celine was there with Ainsley, looking ready to dissolve into tears.

Daniel had given the house in London he'd bought from Mortimer to Celine, who had been gushingly grateful. Celine planned to keep sitting the séances, she said, with Mary's help. Her timely vision of Daniel needing help had made her more eager than ever to share her gift.

Bagpipes sang Violet down the aisle. Mackenzie clan members watched her come—tall men with hair every shade of red from darkest auburn to bright carrot. The Mackenzie, the clan chief, a straight and tall man with white hair, made Violet a bow as she walked by.

But when Daniel smiled at Violet as she stopped beside him, nothing else mattered. The warmth of Daniel, the gleam in his eyes, was the only thing Violet needed. He'd saved her life.

The bishop began. The ceremony wound its way along, and Violet made the correct responses, barely hearing herself. Only the words of the vows mattered—Violet plighting her troth to Daniel, he promising to care for her until the end.

Then she was wed. Daniel lifted the veil from Violet's face and kissed her.

The crowd behind them let out whoops and screams. Pipes played, children shrieked, and shouts and laughter rang out.

The festivities began. There was the wedding feast, laid out across several rooms. Then dancing and flowing whiskey, the party lasting through the afternoon and on into the night.

Violet laid aside her veil and joined in the Scottish dances that Ainsley and Eleanor had taught her. Violet loved dancing alongside Daniel, holding hands with him, or threading through the other dancers in the line. The pipes, fiddles, and drums were energizing, the room filled with joy. At one point,

Daniel was coaxed into doing a sword dance, which he performed with athletic grace. Then Jamie Mackenzie performed it, showing the same grace and skill, to the delight of all, and Ian's pride.

"He's a good lad," Ian said to Violet, squeezing her hand hard. "My son. He's *happy*." The last was said with even more pride.

The Mackenzie children stayed awake long past their bedtimes, until they dropped off one by one. Gavina and Stuart begged to be allowed to have Violet and Daniel carry them up to bed, and Violet happily concurred. Violet too was wearying, though she was pleasantly tired, not exhausted.

"'Tis not really for us," Daniel said, as he climbed to the nursery beside Violet. Stuart was already asleep on his shoulder, his golden red hair tousled, though Gavina resolutely kept her eyes open. "The wedding of a clan member reassures the others of the continuation of the clan. At least that's the excuse for all the drinking and dancing." Daniel winked. "And other things, as the night goes on. My family is not prudish."

Violet laid Gavina in her bed in the large nursery, while Daniel tended to Stuart. Violet leaned down and kissed Gavina good night.

"Night, Violet," Gavina said happily. "Since you're married now, you and Danny can have lots of babies. Hurry, please." She delivered her demand, then closed her eyes and drifted to sleep.

"My sister knows her mind," Daniel said. He put a gentle hand on Stuart's back, the fondness in his eyes plain to see. Daniel leaned down and kissed his brother's forehead, then he took Violet's hand and led her out of the room.

The hallway outside the nursery was deserted. Daniel leaned Violet against a wall by a large window and curved over her. "I know my own mind too. 'Tis a family trait. I'm dying for ye, Mrs. Mackenzie."

His kiss took Violet's breath away. Daniel had her pressed to the wall, his strength pinning her, the wooden paneling hard against her back.

The feeling of the wall behind her and a strong man before

her stirred the fringes of Violet's old panic. But Violet forced herself to the present. This was *Daniel*, leaning into her lovingly, his mouth coaxing, tender.

She and her husband kissing in the hall was *now*, her life. Daniel had taught her that a man wanting a woman could touch her gently, could draw from her the greatest pleasure she could feel.

Daniel kissed Violet until she knew nothing but him, this heat, his mouth, the caress of his lips. His hands warmed her, arms coming around her to pull her from the wall and into him. The panic floated away into the darkness.

Daniel stopped to kiss Violet several times as he led her down the stairs and to the large bedroom in the Cameron family wing. Locking the door behind them, Daniel pushed Violet step by step toward the bed, unbuttoning her clothes as they went. Violet, laughing, unbuttoned his.

Halfway across the rug, Violet was out of her bodice, Daniel, his coat and waistcoat. At the dressing table, Daniel's collar and shirt came off as did Violet's corset, lovingly unlaced by Daniel's strong hands. At the chaise at the foot of the bed, it was Daniel's socks and shoes and Violet's petticoats.

When they reached the bed, Daniel lifted Violet into his arms, wrapping her legs around his waist. He kissed her as he held her, hands firm on her back, then he laid her on the mattress and divested her of drawers and ruffled camisole. Off came his kilt then, landing in a pool of plaid on the floor.

Daniel, unclothed. Lamplight touched his bronzed skin, tanned from the sun, except where his kilt would shield him—there he was Scottish fair.

Violet loved looking at him. His arms were corded with muscle, his chest broad, the inked design of the dragon cutting across his forearm.

He looked her over in return, and Violet flushed with excitement. Daniel's scrutiny of her bare body wasn't debasement. This was intimacy, love, need.

Daniel gazed at her with slow desire, his eyes the color of whiskey in the darkness. He moved his gaze from her legs to the join of her thighs, up over her waist to the rise of her breasts. He lingered there for a time before his gaze rested on her face, the love in his eyes intoxicating.

Daniel climbed onto the bed, but instead of coming over her, he stretched out beside Violet, running his hand across her belly. His cock lay hot against Violet's side, but Daniel didn't hurry. As much as she knew he wanted her, Daniel was taking his time.

Slow goodness. Violet held her breath, uncertain she could wait for slow goodness tonight.

Daniel's hand dipped between her legs, drawing from her a moan of delight. He kissed her, his mouth opening hers, while he let his fingers dance. Heat spiraled Violet upward, erasing all thought, all worries, everything but Daniel and the feeling of him touching her.

Violet caught his shoulders in her strong grip, pulling him to her. "Now," she said hurriedly. "Please. Now."

Daniel smiled, his wickedness returning. "My pleasure, love."

His smile died as he moved over her. With one thrust, Daniel was inside her, and Violet rose over the top, any lingering terror chased away by a darker wildness.

Violet let herself be carried by the wave, Daniel there to hold her. He let her fly free, but at the same time he grounded her, keeping her safe.

"I love you!" Violet shouted it, no longer fearing the words. She was his, and he hers. Together. For now. For always.

"I love you, Vi, my sweetest Violet." Daniel's words came fast, breathy, his body rocking against hers. The joining was fierce, Daniel bracing himself as he thrust into her again and again.

They perspired in the warm room, the fires stoked high so the bridal couple would not grow cold. Violet ran her hands over Daniel's body, welcoming him, loving him inside her. Daniel's eyes widened as his end came, the sparkling depths holding the love of ages.

Violet gathered that to her as she gathered Daniel into her arms. They fell together to the bed, spent. In love. Trusting. Daniel would never hurt her.

The beauty of that streaked through her, and told Violet she was home at last.

"Ready, love?" Daniel watched Violet as she grabbed hold of the balloon's basket, her eyes lighting with anticipation. "All right then." Daniel called down to the men who held the massive bubble of the balloon as it strained for freedom. "Let her go!"

The men released ropes, sandbags dropped away, and the balloon rose. The cool Scottish air grew colder, the wind from the mountains and the sea beyond it catching them.

Daniel put his arm around his wife as they went higher and higher. The small farms became square patches in the rugged country of the Highlands, and tree-covered hills spread before them. Far away was the misty gray blue of the northern sea.

Violet took in every bit of it, the delight on her face beautiful.

"As promised," Daniel said. "Ballooning over northern Scotland. Nothing else comes close to being more stunning."

Violet's expression was one of delight and sheer joy. No more fear, no more dread.

"You like it?" Daniel asked her, knowing the answer.

"It's marvelous." Violet turned away from him, tipping the basket, but she laughed and caught the ropes to steady herself. "You're right. It's the most beautiful thing in the world."

"Next to you," Daniel said, meaning it.

Violet laughed again as she spun around. The Highlands floated quietly beneath them, the balloon rising ever higher.

"How do you feel?" he asked her.

"Free." Violet flashed a smile that made Daniel's life worth living. "Effortless. In love with you." Another smile, this one warm and serious. "I saved this up to tell you now—we're going to have a baby."

Daniel stopped. The wind sighed around them, the roar of the modified wind machine breaking the silence.

Then a wave of pure happiness hit him, a new kind of happiness, one Daniel had never known before. "Are we?"

"Yes." Violet touched his hand. "Thank you."

A child. A wee one. First it would be an adorable baby, then a child like Stuart and Gavina, then a lad or lass to grow into a tall young man or woman, the pride of the family.

Daniel threw his head back, looked at the heavens, and let out a whoop that should be heard all the way to the Orkneys. He caught Violet around the waist and pulled her close.

"Anytime, love." He laughed. "Anytime."

Violet laughed with him. Daniel slid his arms around her as Violet gazed at the land flowing below them and stretched out her arms to embrace the world.

And she soared.

A child. A wee one. First it would be an adorable baby, then a child like Stuart and Gavina, then a lad or lass to grow into a tall young man or woman, the pride of the family.

Daniel threw his head back, looked at the heavens, and let out a whoop that should be heard all the way to the Orkneys. He caught Violet around the waist and pulled her close.

"Anytime, love." He laughed. "Anytime."

Violet laughed with him. Daniel slid his arms around her as Violet gazed at the land flowing below them and stretched out her arms to embrace the world.

And she soared.